INDOCTRINATION
Crime, Corruption and the Journey to Promise

Craig A. Banks

INDOCTRINATION
Crime, Corruption, and the Journey to Promise

ISBN: 979-8-218-41110-7

DEDICATION

To my wife Deborah the love of my life

And to my children

Sharell, Christopher, and Akila whose conversations bring me joy.

Craig A. Banks

PREFACE

This book has all the makings of a spectacular read. Romance, **murder, action, mystery, drama, and betrayal.**

This book is both fiction and non-fiction.

Indoctrination is a fascinating book of fact combined with fiction about a successful Black man who was sabotaged by the corrupt legal system in Indianapolis, Indiana. The state was controlled by a powerful organization called the *Indoctrination of Black Men* whose purpose was to stymie the advancement of African Americans. The establishment's origin was rooted in England by King George lll. Although the United States got their independence from England in 1776, the thirteen colonies agreed to pay homage to the throne by allowing it to legally own a percentage of all Black people born in America indefinitely, as a truce ratified in Paris. The negros became mini corporate entities under England's law concerning corporations. The profits from that endeavor made England and the United States, the richest countries in the world.

The corporate entity, Taleeb Anderson, stood before Lady Justice. She wore a blindfold that covered her eyes to prove to the world that justice was blind. The Lady used a scale that she had stolen from the Egyptian Goddess Maat, to measure Taleeb's guilt or innocence. It was at that moment Taleeb knew; the Lady was a tyrant as she passed down a sentence that was unjustifiable.

Craig A. Banks

CONTENTS

INTRODUCTION

The reason I called the book Indoctrination was because of my college professor. He was dying of cancer and wanted to leave and indelible impression on the minds of students before he passed away. While I was attending his lecture trying to get my doctorate degree, the professor gave the class research assignments on the most renowned individuals that we learned about in our undergraduate and graduate programs.

By using scholarly sources authorized by the university, I investigated Taylor & Herzberg's Theories of Motivation. Both these men influenced how we conduct business management today. I used twenty sources for my research paper. Three of my sources supported the Herzberg & Taylor's theory and 17 sources did not. It was exceedingly difficult to find any professional in the business management field who supported Herzberg & Taylor's theory. The three men that supported those theories express their support over a hundred years ago.

After our research was completed and up for debate, the class concluded that every theory that we learned about in our undergraduate and graduate program was debunked. The philosophies that I thought were fascinating became adolescently ridiculous. Our professor did a great job showing us that we were indoctrinated with information that was not true. From that moment forward, I began researching my own core beliefs and discovered that I had been programed to serve corporate America.

This book encapsulates overcoming adversity. I have excelled in my endeavors by solving problematic issues. For example, I raised my youngest of three children with a felony on my record. Finding employment as a felon was taxing, therefore I started my own business. While working for myself, I received three college degrees as a single parent despite the overwhelming obstacles surrounding me.

I hope this book will inspire young men and women to make sound choices and do everything they can to stay out of the legal system. It only takes one bad decision to alter your path to success.

INDOCTRINATION: Crime, Corruption, and the Journey to Promise

CAUGHT UP

Ⅰt all started in the winter of 2002 when Taleeb went to the City County Building to pay property taxes on a house that he lived in and a duplex he rented out to his tenants. Taleeb hated going downtown because it was hard to find parking and it was too busy. Of course, he couldn't locate an empty parking meter, therefore he had to pay $6.00 to park in the garage. "Damn, I'm only going to be here for 45 minutes", thought Taleeb. Taleeb was a practical person and paying $6.00 for parking a car less than an hour was impractical. Figures automatically started calculating in Taleeb's mind. He became agitated at the final cost he was paying for each minute of parking.

To make matters worse, it was cold and windy outside. The wind seemed like it had a mind of its own. When Taleeb opened his car door, the wind tried to tear it off the hinges. Profanity escaped Taleeb's lips with every curse word he could think of. He had to use a little muscle to close the car door and suddenly the wind shifted and helped him slam the door extra hard. Taleeb knew at that moment he was going to have a bad day. Apparently, he wasn't the only one having an unpleasant day as he watched the wind grab a man's hat off his head and throw it down in the middle of Washington street. It was as if the invisible force wanted to teach the man a lesson for wearing the fancy hat while it was in a bad mood. Even though the wind was unseen, it showed its presence everywhere. It even had time to play a cruel game with the hatless fellow. Every time the gentleman got close enough to pick up his hat, the gust would whisk it away again. It flipped and spun the hat in every direction. Before the airstream moved on to other victims, it finally whirled the hat high in the sky until it disappeared out of the man's sight.

Taleeb loathed wintry weather and to add to his disgust, he had to walk a couple of blocks to get to his destination. He had better things to do than watch a man chase a hat, but it was amusing he had to admit. The comic show continued as Taleeb watched people walk super-fast with the aid of a metaphysical force that lunged them forward, while others walked in slow motion as they walked against the vortex. Taleeb was in a hurry and would rather be pushed forward by the wind but instead he was going against it.

Once inside the City County Building (CCB), the security guard asked him to take off his belt, coat and empty his pockets. Taleeb put the contents in a plastic tray and placed them on the conveyor belt along with his leather trench coat. The conveyor belt moved the objects through a scanner to be checked for weapons. Then Taleeb walked through a sensory device to get scanned. Low and behold, the device beeped, and the security guard made him pull up his pants legs to his ankle. Everything checked out and Taleeb was able to take care of his business. A year ago, people didn't have to go through the hassle of getting into the building. Anybody could walk into the CCB without ID and there were no security guards present. All that changed under President Bush's administration because of September 11, 2001 attacks.

The media explained how poorly skilled pilots from a technically inferior country flew into the airspace of the most powerful nation on earth without being detected. The United States trained those Afghanistan pilots how to fly American planes. After the men were trained, those same pilots committed suicide by crashing those American planes into the United States' most sacred iconic buildings. The irony behind the attacks sounded confusing. Afghanistan was the culprit of the disaster but the US waged war against Iraq who had nothing to do with the planes flying into the buildings. It was simply unbelievable.

After Taleeb completed his errands, he exited the building. Taleeb was in a hurry to get to his car, but he slowed down when he saw a nice-looking dark-skinned woman sitting at a table inside the Food Court across the street from the CCB. She looked like she was waiting for someone because she kept looking around. Taleeb quickly went inside the eatery to get out of the cold and to watch the woman. He ordered a cup of coffee and kept his eye on the pretty lady to see if someone would sit at her table. Twenty minutes passed and no one showed up. Taleeb assumed she was waiting on one of her girlfriends and was conveniently late. Taleeb grew impatient and hoped his theory was correct. He approached her table, introduced himself, and asked her, "Are you expecting someone?"

"My girlfriend was supposed to meet me here 40 minutes ago, but she got held up in traffic. "Oh, by the way, my name is Jasmine."

"It's a pleasure to meet you, Jasmine. My name is Taleeb."

"Have a seat Mr. Taleeb." Jasmine was about 5'9" inches tall and medium built. Her sandy brown hair danced around her shoulders every time she moved her head. Taleeb looked into her pretty brown eyes and could see that she was unhappy. There was something dark and mysterious about Jasmine, but Taleeb thought his mind was playing tricks on him.

Jasmine detested light-skinned Black men because she thought they were conceited. She dated two of them in the past and they were constantly admiring themselves in the mirror. She didn't care for dark-skinned men who thought they were cute either. She wanted a real man that would cherish her and not himself.

After studying Taleeb's physique, Jasmine guessed he was around 6' 2" and weighed around 195 lbs. or 200 lbs. After he took off his London Fog coat and placed it over the back of the chair, she could tell he was an athlete. She liked the way his muscles rippled in his tailor-

3

fit suit. Jasmine marveled over his hair texture. Taleeb had long curly hair at the top front of his head. On the sides and back of his head, the wavy hair slowly faded away at the ends. Taleeb had a part chiseled on the left side of his head and he wore black diamond earrings in each ear. Taleeb's beard was cut low, giving the hair on his face a shadow look.

It was refreshing, thought Jasmine, that Taleeb's fingernails were clean because men with dirt under their nails were nasty. Taleeb's deep baritone voice was like a symphony to her ears. She couldn't take her eyes off his pearly white teeth between those butter pecan lips. His skin was flawless, and she felt embarrassed because she wanted to have sex with him. She looked at his big hands and feet and lost track of their conversation. She couldn't understand why she wanted to have sex with this stranger. Jasmine got angry at herself and with Taleeb.

"I bet this man has women all over Indiana", she thought, "and I'm not going to be his next one-night stand." In fact, she wasn't going to date a man that looked better than her, plus his hue was too light. Jasmine had rules and guidelines that she followed when dealing with men. She didn't date married men; she didn't have sex on the first date, and she didn't date light-skinned men. But today her feelings were all over the place and she had to get a hold of herself.

Taleeb lightly called Jasmine's name to get her attention. She seemed to be lost in a world of her own. Jasmine went from her constitution of dating men to daydreaming about the way her name rolled off Taleeb's tongue while they were making love. Taleeb called her name again and Jasmine snapped out of the secret place and said, "Oh, I'm sorry I was worried about my friend, she should have been here by now."

"That's what makes you a good friend because you are worried." Jasmine smiled and asked, "Are you in a relationship?"

"I'm not married", said Taleeb.

"Ok, but do you have a girlfriend?"

"Not really."

"Not really!" said Jasmine, "either you do, or you don't. It's a simple yes or no question."

"I go out on dates from time to time, but I don't have a significant other." Jasmine didn't believe him because his answer was evasive. There was no way on God's green earth that this man was single. Nevertheless, Jasmine found Taleeb to be an interesting person and she wanted to get to know him better.

"Do you have any children, Taleeb?"

"Yes, I have a 12-year-old daughter and a 11year-old son."

"How old are you, Mr. Taleeb?"

"I am 30 years old, and my last name is Anderson."

"Where do you work?"

"I am a Real Estate Broker on the east side of town, and I work for myself." Jasmine continued to bombard Taleeb with questions, and he slowed the interrogation down by asking Jasmine the same questions she asked him. They had a great deal in common, Jasmine had a daughter the same age as his little girl. Their favorite food was seafood, and they were both successful. Jasmine also had a respectable position at the United Postal Service, as a supervisor.

After they exchanged phone numbers, Taleeb stood up from the table and told Jasmine it was a pleasure meeting her. "Could I take you out to eat at a nice restaurant this weekend, he asked?"

"Of course." She could not help herself, but as soon as he stood up, she stared at the contour print in his pants where she shouldn't have been looking. She was ashamed of herself, but Jasmine's eyes wouldn't obey her. In her mind, she kept saying don't look, don't look and her eyes quickly darted to the spot anyway. "I have to get some of that", she thought. Jasmine hoped Taleeb didn't see her eyes veer below his waist.

Jasmine saw her friend coming into the eatery. She stood up and waved her hand high in the air so that Jena could see where she was sitting. They ate in the Food Court all the time at their favorite table near the window. But she wanted Taleeb to see her thick curves that got the attention of so many men. Taleeb viewed the goods and thought, this woman is strapped all the way around.

He tried to leave before Jasmine's friend came to the table because he had a lot of business to take care of and he didn't want to take a chance of meeting someone he may have slept with in the past. Jasmine could sense Taleeb was suddenly in a hurry, but she wanted him to meet her friend. "This will only take a second, I promise." Jasmine's friend came to their table and said in a loud ghetto voice, "Hey girl I'm so sorry I'm late again, but the traffic was jacked up." Before Jasmine could introduce the two, Jena asked, "How are you doing handsome?"

"Jena this is Taleeb and Taleeb this is Jena."

Taleeb said, "I'm pleased to meet you."

"You don't know how pleased I am to meet you with your fine ass." Jasmine squeezed Jena's hand hard, "Ouch! what the hell is wrong with you? That hurt?"

Taleeb grinned showing the dimples in his cheeks and pearly white teeth. "It was nice meeting both of you. I'll call you later Jasmine and he waved at them as he left."

"Who is he going to call later? "He couldn't be talking about you because you don't date dudes like that."

"Where do you know him from?" Jena began asking Jasmine a barrage of questions. "Where does he work? Did you get his number? You couldn't be interested in him, he ain't even your type, and he is light-skinned. Give his number to me girl, I'll let him down really easy for you."

Jasmine said, "Stop, slow down you're looking at my future husband" Jena's jaws dropped open, and eyes got bigger than fifty cent pieces. She almost dropped her purse. The look on Jena's face made Jasmine laugh so hard tears came out of her eyes.

Later that night, Jasmine couldn't stop thinking about Taleeb and hoped he would call soon. It had been three days and she hadn't heard from him. She was tempted to call him, but she felt the man should make the first move. It was sad that Jasmine couldn't talk to her mother, Veronica, about such matters, she thought. Jasmine felt her mom couldn't tell her anything about a man because Veronica picked her men out of a trash can. Jasmine resented Veronica for failing to protect her from being mistreated by Veronica's boyfriend, Harold. Jasmine knew that something horrific happened to her when she was young and that's what contributed to her nervous breakdown and the large gaps in her memory.

Most of Veronica's problems arose because she was an alcoholic and that's why she settled for low-lifes. It was obvious that Harold was the most pathetic of them all. His drug addiction made him steal things around the house to support his habit. He even stole their toaster, iron and the two TVs. He had the audacity to say he didn't do it and Veronica let him get away with it. Finally, three years after the abusive relationship, Veronica had enough and put him out of the house. Two months later, Harold died behind a dumpster in an alley downtown.

Jasmine's father was a 6' 3" Carmel-colored man who often stood in the center of the alley behind their house staring wide-eyed looking at nothing. He was a massive built man without an inch of body fat. Everybody knew Sam was crazy and the neighbors wouldn't drive near the back of Veronica's house while Sam stood there in a trance. Sam was diagnosed with schizophrenia and he took medicine for hearing voices and hallucinations. There were whispers amongst his family members that his mother molested him when he was a boy.

Jasmine talked to Patty, her psychiatrist, about Taleeb. She needed the advice of a professional and friend. Patty was a middle-aged pale white woman with short grey hair who looked 20 years older than her age. Jasmine liked Patty because she was wise and didn't sugarcoat her diagnoses or recommendations. Patty told Jasmine that it wasn't in her best interest to be in a relationship right now.

Patty knew that Jasmine had suppressed memories of her childhood, but Patty couldn't get a breakthrough with Jasmine. Jasmine's problem was that she didn't want to remember her past. Also, Jasmine had a family history of mental illness on the dad's side.

The last five men that were involved in a relationship with Jasmine were incarcerated for rape, assault, and/or battery. One man who had an affair with Jasmine was reported missing. Patty believed Jasmine was dangerous because she was reliving the past she claimed not to remember. Patty believed Jasmine's father had molested her when she was a child and Patty was worried about Taleeb because his physical stature fit the profile of Jasmine's dad.

It was a long day and Taleeb spent most of his time thinking about Jasmine, and he called her when he got home after work. Jasmine looked at the caller ID and her heart felt like it was going to jump out of her chest.

"Hello," she said.

"Hey Jasmine, this is Taleeb, how are you?"

"I'm fine, how is your day going?"

"It's been great, I closed a million-dollar real estate deal yesterday."

"Are you serious?"

"I'm dead serious. Would like you to go out to dinner with me tonight and celebrate?"

"Sure, what time?"

"What about 6:00 pm?"

"Ok 6:00 pm sounds fine, what should I wear?"

Taleeb told her to dress casually. "Would you like to eat at a seafood restaurant?" asked Taleeb. Jasmine said "Yes."

"Have you ever been to Oceanaire?"

"No, I haven't."

"I think you will like it. I'll pick you up at 6:00 pm."

"Ok great, I'll be waiting for you."

The night was young, and Taleeb was in a good mood. He put on a black sweater, black jeans and black dress boots that zipped on both sides. He trimmed his beard and greased his hair. After Taleeb left the house, he stopped to get gas on his way to pick up Jasmine. An older Black woman buying a soda at the gas station marveled over Taleeb's hair style. She told Taleeb that her father used to wear his hair cut like that back in the day. She said the hairdo was called the Rooster. Taleeb was surprised at what the woman said because he created the hair style. He never saw another person with it. Taleeb wanted a haircut nobody else had. Taleeb realized that it was impossible to create a style that wasn't already worn by somebody else.

When Jasmine was promoted to an executive supervisor at United Postal Service, she bought a home in Carmel, Indiana. It was a ritzy area on the northwest side of town. She purchased the house five years ago and was thankful for her accomplishments. Jasmine took her job seriously, but she frequently needed time off from work for medical reasons.

Taleeb pulled up to the house in his black Cadillac Escalade. Before he got out of the vehicle, he checked out his appearance in the mirror to make sure everything was as it should be. When he finished, he got out of the vehicle, walked up to the door, and rang the doorbell. Jasmine's heart fluttered when she heard the doorbell. She had a security camera on her porch and could see Taleeb on the monitor. Jasmine went to the door and invited him inside the house. As soon as Taleeb walked in, Jasmine introduced him to her 12-year-old daughter who looked exactly like her mom. Taleeb asked, "Where is the babysitter?"

"Mia doesn't need a sitter, she's a very responsible child." Taleeb was apprehensive about leaving the girl home alone because his daughter wasn't responsible at all. There were too many children missing these days and he wanted to cancel the date. "Hey Jasmine, I would feel better if we could get someone to watch Mia while we are gone."

Jasmine angrily looked at Mia and slapped the girl hard across the face and told her, "I saw what you did." Mia stood there at attention and didn't cry. Mia seemed callous to the abuse because she stood there emotionless looking straight ahead.

Taleeb asked, "Why did you hit her like that? She didn't do

anything!" he protested.

Jasmine told Taleeb, "Stay in your lane and mind your own business."

Taleeb could have sworn Jasmine's face and eyes had changed. Suddenly, everything about her was different. She seemed to have taken on a different persona. Her voice and mannerisms changed. Taleeb was bewildered and couldn't believe what he was witnessing. He had never feared a woman until now and was convinced he was a magnet for lunatics. He looked at his phone and pretended like someone had just texted him. Taleeb found the words to tell Jasmine that he had an emergency phone call that he needed to take care of and would call her later, as he hurriedly walked back out the door.

Taleeb was worried about Mia but he didn't know what to do about it. He refused to deal with another woman with psychological issues. Later that night, Taleeb tried to put the obscene encounter of Jasmine and Mia out of his mind.

Meanwhile, Jena left 20 messages on Jasmine's voice mail. Jena was really worried about her friend, so she grabbed the car keys off the kitchen table and drove over to Jasmine's house. Jena rang the doorbell five times. Jasmine did not answer her phone, but she looked at Jena on her monitor. She heard Jena outside the door saying, "Jasmine I know you're in there, I'm worried about you girl. Come on and answer this door." Jasmine ignored Jena because she was on a mission to find out where Taleeb lived. She got on a website called *Spook.com*. From that site, she found out all the different phone numbers he used to have. The website also listed five places where Taleeb could have lived but the addresses were hidden. She had to pay the site to get more information. Jasmine gladly paid the fees to find out which location was accurate from the list that was given. Jasmine believed that he lived at the Geist, Indiana location. He looked the part. It was one the most expensive places to live in the state of Indiana.

The address that *Spook.com* listed was incorrect because she went to the Geist home and knocked on the door and a white man answered. She asked him, "Is Taleeb home?"

"I'm sorry, no one lives here by that name."

"Wow that's strange, maybe I wrote the wrong information down."

"Have you seen a tall handsome Black man that drives a Black Cadillac Escalade in the area?" The white man was suspicious and asked her why she was looking for the man?

"Oh, he's an old friend of mine and I wanted to surprise him, but if I call him to get his address it wouldn't be a surprise." The man stood in the doorway looking at the woman's beautiful smile and said, "I'm sorry, I can't help you and closed the door in her face."

Jasmine spent the entire day watching the houses that she thought Taleeb lived in. The homes were the size of mansions off the lake. She didn't know if the river was part of Fall Creek or not because she was unfamiliar with the east side. The large mass of water could be manmade, she thought. It was obvious the people that lived in the area had money. She had to keep her mind on the task at hand. "How many Black men drove a black Cadillac Escalade in that area", she thought?

Jasmine packed a light lunch to eat but she hadn't eaten in days. She sat in her car watching the neighbors as she waited. The neighbors were health conscious; some people were walking fast while others jogged. It seemed like everybody parked their car inside their garages. She wished her community had done the same thing because it made the neighborhood look pristine.

Jasmine nodded off to sleep and when she woke up, she saw a black vehicle entering the garage, but it happened so fast she couldn't tell if it was a truck or SUV. The four-car garage made the dwelling look huge. It was a gorgeous brick home that looked newly built.

She drove near the house where she suspected Taleeb lived. It must have been 7,000 square feet but the only cars she saw coming and going were a Corvette and Jaguar. But Jasmine knew it was a black vehicle inside. Jasmine tried to look through the windows of the garage, but they were tinted black. "Who does that?", she thought. Jasmine was about to give up and hire a private detective until God answered her prayers. Before she walked away from the garage, a light came on inside displaying a mini auto collection. She could barely see the vehicles, but Jasmine saw a black Cadillac Escalade, "Bingo, I got you babe."

Jasmine had lost 15 pounds and her clothes didn't cling to her body anymore. She wasn't eating regularly, and she ran out of medicine. She was going to wait until the time was right and go over to Taleeb's house. Jasmine was going to wear her long fur coat and surprise him with her naked body inside. The average man couldn't resist Jasmine's hour glass body and Taleeb wouldn't be any different.

Being naked every day sitting in her BMW waiting on Taleeb to get home was getting frustrating. Jasmine had to take a chance. When she saw the black Cadillac pull into the garage at 10:00 p.m. on Wednesday, she made her move. She looked through his windows to see if anyone else was in the house.

The coast was clear, and she rang the doorbell. Taleeb opened the door without looking or asking who it was. He thought it was Kevin, his neighbor next door. When he saw Jasmine standing there, he said, "How did you know where I lived?"

Jasmine pulled open her fur coat in the freezing weather. Taleeb was reluctant to invite her in the house, but he didn't want the neighbors to see a naked woman on his porch. He told Jasmine to come in and he immediately closed her coat. Jasmine took her coat off and threw it on the floor. Taleeb's instincts were telling him to get her out of the house but the bulge in his pants overruled his thoughts.

Jasmine said, "Taleeb please give me one more chance to prove I can be a good woman to you, I'll let you do anything you want to do to me."

Taleeb was under the influence of alcohol and wasn't in his right mind. The alcohol showed him a mental picture of all the sexual positions he wanted to perform. But something didn't feel right, and he knew he was going to make a big mistake.

Taleeb was into the breakup stage with one of his girlfriends, and he figured, what the hell. He needed a release after working all day at the real estate agency that he owned for five years. Taleeb had a weakness for pretty women with big butts.

Jasmine looked much thinner from the last time he saw her, thought Taleeb, but seductive. He didn't expect any company and he drank more than usual. Taleeb was feeling aroused, and his senses were dulled. Jasmine got on her knees in front of Taleeb and unzipped his pants. Taleeb wanted to go to the bathroom and pee, but everything was happening too fast. Jasmine began performing for Taleeb like she was auditioning for a porno movie.

Typically, Jasmine didn't indulge in satisfying her man in that way. She preferred having it done to her, but reciprocating the act never happened. She heard Taleeb moan. Jasmine thought, "I got your ass now Mr. Anderson." Jasmine grabbed Taleeb's hand and put it on top of her head; Taleeb grabbed her hair and held on while she worked her magic. Jasmine was surprised that she was getting excited. She knew Taleeb was trying to make it last because he was clinching his jaws and holding his breath. Taleeb wanted to cherish the moment as long as possible. He couldn't hold it longer and yelled out, "Oh my goodness." His legs got weak, and he dropped to the floor. Suddenly,

Jasmine followed suit. Soon after her release, she collapsed next to Taleeb. Jasmine hoped she gained a spot in Taleeb's life while they laid on the floor exhausted.

After they rested a minute, Taleeb took Jasmine on a tour of the house before finally showing her the bedroom. Jasmine thought she had a big bedroom, until she saw his bedroom. It had a fireplace and living room furniture in it. It was breathtaking and Jasmine was impressed.

Taleeb was building up his stamina as he showed her sculptures and how he acquired them. He wanted to have sex with Jasmine the traditional way, him on top and her on the bottom. But first, he went to the mini bar that he had built in his bedroom. He asked Jasmine if she wanted anything to drink or eat and she declined. Taleeb made her a glass of Moscato wine anyway. He gave her the wine and told her she would like it. Jasmine took a couple of sips against her psychiatrist warning, "This is good, she said."

While Taleeb was changing into his robe, Jasmine was enjoying the view, "I want some more of that" said Jasmine pointing to Taleeb's shaft. His body was chiseled by a craftsman, and it was made for Jasmine. Suddenly she started having flashbacks of her father entering her bedroom at night. Taleeb kissed Jasmine on the cheek and told her he would be back in a minute. He called Shonna his babysitter and told her he was sorry, but an emergency had caught him off guard. Shonna was upset with Taleeb because he always had issues picking up Aaliyah on time and she was getting tired of it. "Taleeb its 11:00 o'clock, man. When are you going to get here?"

"I'll be there at 1:00 a.m. and it will never happen again." She had heard all that crap before. Shonna didn't believe Taleeb had an emergency. She knew he must have met another woman because he always had different women in one of his vehicles when he picked up his daughter and they all looked like hookers. If Taleeb wasn't paying

Shonna $500 a week, she would have cut ties with him a long time ago. "Ok, Taleeb, be here at 1:00 o'clock and please don't be late." Shonna was sick of watching Aaliyah because she was a spoiled brat and too old to be in day care.

Taleeb got full custody of Aaliyah when she was 3-years old. Her mother Rianna was the Valedictorian in high school, and everyone was shocked when she got hooked on crack cocaine. Taleeb felt bad for Rianna, he believed that if he had spent more time with her, she wouldn't have gotten hooked on drugs. Rianna's mother told Taleeb that he needed to get custody of Aaliyah because Rianna was prostituting to get high. Rianna's mom said that she was too old to raise any more kids but there was something special about Taleeb that made her believe that he could do a better job raising Aaliyah than anybody else.

Taleeb couldn't believe how hard Rianna fought over the child because Aaliyah had been living at her grandmother's house since the day she was born. Rianna spent less time with Aaliyah than Taleeb did. Rianna's drug habit was her number one priority, but she would have sold her soul to stop Taleeb from getting custody of Aaliyah. Nevertheless, Taleeb got an attorney who was able to prove to the judge that Rianna was a suicidal drug addict. Taleeb got custody over Aaliyah that same day.

Even though Taleeb won the case, raising a child was the most difficult responsibility he ever encountered. Paying child support was much easier. All he had to do was pay the court ordered fees and see Aaliyah on holidays and birthdays. But when he won full custody, his entire life revolved around Aaliyah.

Taleeb read books and played educational games with Aaliyah. She was a difficult child and hated the word "no". Aaliyah didn't obey anything Taleeb asked her to do. Taleeb's mother and sister helped him raise Aaliyah from afar. They lived in Georgia, but they bought her clothes and gave Taleeb advice on how to raise Aaliyah. Taleeb was a bachelor, and his multiple girlfriends also helped him with Aaliyah. Aaliyah knew the women loved her father, but they had to go through her if they wanted to get with Taleeb. That meant buying Aaliyah things and paying for information. The women paid for knowledge about other females Taleeb was dealing with. Aaliyah always gave them bogus information because she would never betray her father.

After making himself another stiff drink, Taleeb hurriedly ate leftover lobster and salad. He was a pescatarian like his dad. Taleeb lit a joint on his way to the bedroom, the weed was called *Loud* because the aroma was strong, the scent could permeate through a plastic bag. The only way to obscure the skunk smell from permeating through the house and car was to put it into a glass jar.

Taleeb was feeling good and weed enhanced his sexual performance. As soon as he walked into the bedroom, he dropped his robe showing off his naked body and Jasmine started screaming. Taleeb's high evaporated like ice in hot lava. His manhood went limp, and he got nervous. Jasmine said, "Daddy why didn't you try to help me?"

"What are you talking about?" Jasmine was hysterical. Taleeb couldn't comprehend what Jasmine's problem was. As he bent over to pick up his robe, Jasmine hit him on the back of his head with a heavy book on his dresser. Taleeb was temporarily dazed and confused. "What's going on?" Jasmine began throwing every item on his dresser at him and talking gibberish. Taleeb smacked Jasmine in hopes that she would come to her right mind. Jasmine snapped out of it and ran down the stairs and grabbed her coat off the living room floor and rushed out of the house.

Scrambling to put on his clothes, Taleeb ran outside to make sure Jasmine was alright, but she had vanished. Taleeb went back in the house to put on a coat. He was going to knock on Kevin's door to see if he had seen her. But Kevin would ask too many questions and Taleeb didn't have time to explain. He stood inside the house by his front door upset with himself, "I knew I shouldn't have been messing with that crazy woman!"

Before Taleeb could think of what to say, the police were knocking at the door. He opened the door to let them in. Four police were on the scene but only two came inside, the other two went around to his backyard. One officer asked Taleeb if he lived there. And he said yes. "Do you have any ID to prove you live here?"

"Yes, it's upstairs in my bedroom."

"Put your hands behind your back."

"Am I under arrest?" The officer didn't respond.

"Where is your wallet upstairs?"

"It's in my nightstand on the left side of my bed."

The officer asking all the questions went by the name John. One of John's partners ran up the stairs to retrieve the wallet. He quickly came downstairs holding Taleeb's wallet in one hand and Taleeb's driver's license in the other hand.

"So, you like to beat on women, don't you Taleeb Anderson? Is that what turns you on?"

"Sir you have this all wrong, I only hit her because she was hysterical, I was trying to help her."

"Sit your monkey ass down in that chair over there." The short officer was afraid of Taleeb towering over him. It was pathetic that the officer was frightened of a handcuffed man with his hands behind his back. John kicked Taleeb in the chest with such force, Taleeb fell back in the chair. John's partner let the other two officers into the house who were in the backyard.

"Hey guys, the lady this coon beat up is on her way to the hospital." Taleeb couldn't believe Jasmine needed to go to the hospital, he didn't hit her that hard.

John said, "Boy we're going to give you a blanket party without the blanket." His men laughed at the comment. Taleeb thought they were going to beat him to death when they pulled out their batons and hit him on every inch of his body. Five minutes into the beating, Taleeb was unrecognizable. The officers added fuel to the fire and pepper sprayed Taleeb's eyes and face. The spray fused Taleeb's bloody eyelids shut, and his face and arms felt like someone poured alcohol on a thousand small cuts on his upper body. Taleeb believed he was going to die because he was inhaling too much pepper spray and he couldn't catch his breath.

"The big buck is good exercise!" yelled one of the cops. The fun didn't last long because John got carried away with the pepper spray. They had to evacuate the immediate area where Taleeb lay bloody on the floor. The men went outside to get fresh air and were surprised to see a large group of neighbors watching them coming out of the house coughing and gasping for air.

The officers went to the backyard for privacy, but people were watching them behind the house as well. When the pepper spray smell died down, they went back inside and searched the home. They took one of Taleeb's gym bags and put his jewelry, money, and marijuana in it. John put the bag in his trunk and told his partners he would split the merchandise with them later. They began tearing up the place looking for other hidden valuables.

A sheriff's van pulled up. The two sheriffs in the van knew the officers on the scene and they enjoyed themselves at the expense of Taleeb. They shoved Taleeb in the van headfirst. After Taleeb's head hit the side of the van, blood gushed out of it. Taleeb told them he was going to sue them, and three officers jumped in the van and started kicking him. Taleeb was having an out-of-body experience, he envisioned himself as a young boy around 11 years old walking in a beautiful garden. He spread out his arms like a bird and touched the golden daisies as he walked by. The sun was shining bright as the young boy glided through the dense marsh. Suddenly, Taleeb began to panic because he realized he was walking to his death. Taleeb yelled out loud, "No!!! I'm not ready," and he rolled over and kicked an officer in his nuts with all his strength. The cop doubled over. He kicked the other one in the ankle, and the man slipped and fell. Taleeb stood up while another officer was hitting him with a baton. Taleeb head butted him in the nose and blood squirted all over their clothes. Another officer got in the van to help his friends and Taleeb bit a piece of flesh out of his shoulder. They intended to beat Taleeb to death, but they decided to shoot him instead. They couldn't kill Taleeb on the spot because there were too many witnesses. Kevin yelled to the officers that they were being videoed and pointed to the cameras on his home.

Kevin was golf buddies with the chief of police. Kevin wasn't thrilled about a Black man living next door to him, but the barbaric way they treated Taleeb was shameful. Kevin sent chief Turner the video he captured from his home camera.

Normally, Turner wouldn't have answered the phone, but Kevin very seldom called and when he did it was something fun to get into or it involved money. Either way the call was important enough to answer it.

"Did you see it?," asked Kevin excitedly. Turner took the phone away from his ear and looked at it confused.

"See what?"

"The video I sent you,"

"No, I didn't" Turner was embarrassed that he didn't know how to retrieve the video on his phone.

Turner yelled for his secretary. "Martha, can you come in here for a sec?"

"Hold your horses," said Martha walking as fast as her old body would take her. "What do you need Mr. Turner?"

"Show me how to get a video off this phone." Martha wasn't too shabby with technology for an old lady, but what her boss wanted was simple. Mr. Turner was a brute and didn't try to learn anything new. He didn't have to be tech-savvy because his employees made him look brilliant.

After Martha found the video for Mr. Turner, he waved her away for privacy. The video was damaging enough to end his career if he didn't get ahead of the situation. Turner asked Martha to pull up the work roster of police officers working that beat and 911 calls. Turner quickly found out who the officers were in the video. He radioed John who was following the sheriff's van. Turner addressed John by his badge number and told him to stand down, "I repeat stand down."

"Relay that to your fellow officers and bring the man you have in your custody to the proper location now."

"Do you copy?"

"Roger, that sir, we are on our way." There was no doubt who the voice belonged to on the radio because chief Turner spoke with a lisp. John believed he was in trouble and wanted to correct the error before he was found guilty of murder.

The men arrived in the remote field that they often used to bury idiots with bad attitudes. The van stopped at the same area where they dumped the last five bodies months ago. John quickly jumped out of the car to tell the men to abort the mission, but they heard the same thing John heard on the radio. John hoped Taleeb wouldn't die. He told his men to take Taleeb to Wishard Memorial Hospital to be on the safe side.

When they got to the hospital, John asked a nurse who was sitting at the front desk for help. After Karen saw the man in a wheelchair bleeding excessively, she went to get a gurney. Karen asked the two male nurses who were on duty for assistance with the patient. The nurses and officers helped put Taleeb on the gurney. Karen placed Taleeb in full leather restraints. She looked at Taleeb laying on the gurney with blood soaking up the sheets. She wanted to spit on him. John told her that Taleeb was a rapist and she treated him like an animal. Karen didn't clean any of his wounds and she left him in the room for 12 hours without food or water.

Taleeb laid in bed trying not to urinate on himself, but his bladder relaxed, and he lost muscular control. Taleeb soiled his underwear and the sheets he was laying on. It was the most disgusting thing he ever felt, lying in his own urine. He was worried sick about Aaliyah. Who was going to take care of her while he was gone? Taleeb knew Shonna was never going to watch Aaliyah again after this debacle no matter what he paid her. Taleeb couldn't believe he made it out of the van alive. He prayed for the Creator to protect his child. In addition, Taleeb began to speak in a language he didn't know, and he asked God to destroy the police officers, nurses and everyone involved with his humiliation.

He never knew that all his prayers were answered. Years later, three of the officers who Taleeb cursed were fired for tampering with evidence, falsifying records, and murder. John was shot to death by the father of a boy he killed. Wishard Hospital was the busiest medical facility in Indiana, and it closed for business under that name permanently. Karen's baby came into the world stillborn, and her husband left her for another woman. The other nurse died in a car accident. Jasmine ended up homeless and the judge had a heart attack and died. Lastly, Taleeb's attorney was disbarred, and the prosecutor got arrested for bribery and bank fraud.

Taleeb smelled like sex, urine, pepper spray and deodorant that was overpowered by an awful body order. There were fresh faces amongst the police officers and nurses; they must have changed shifts, Taleeb thought. Nobody addressed Taleeb's injuries, and the police didn't want to touch him because he was bloody from head to toe.

John told his men what to do when his shift ended. He needed to get at least four hours of sleep so he could think straight because the situation had gotten serious. John knew chief Turner wanted Taleeb at the City County Building ASAP. Turner made it clear that Taleeb better be alive. However, Taleeb looked like he was at death's doorstep. The officer asked the nurse to help him take Taleeb's clothes off and put a gown on him. He didn't want the Sheriff's van soiled with bodily fluid. The nurse went to get the gown and when she came back the cop uncuffed Taleeb from the bed and took off the leather restraints. The nurse said it would be easier to cut Taleeb's clothes off him and she grabbed the scissors. The cop helped the nurse take off Taleeb's underwear and T-shirt and hoped he didn't get blood and urine on his uniform. After they were done, they helped Taleeb put on a gown. Taleeb couldn't see because nobody washed the pepper spray out of eyes or face. The nurse tied the gown behind Taleeb. The police officers took Taleeb outside in the freezing cold, in a gown, bare footed and put him in a van with other Nubians. The men in the van looked at Taleeb with horror on their faces.

The teenager in the van didn't feel devalued anymore after seeing Taleeb. The young man tried to steal an old woman's purse, but the ancient windbag fought him like there was gold stashed in it. He knew he had hit the lottery because she wouldn't let it go. He punched her in the face, and she fell on the ground. But she held on to the purse tighter and snatched it from the young man. He tried to grab the purse again, but she swung around and socked the teen in the face with it. He didn't believe in hitting women, but his drug habit made him lose respect for himself and he decided to kick the old woman in the leg. She yelled out in agony, but she would let it go. The teenager didn't realize the police had rolled up on him until it was too late, and he was tempted to run anyway. One of them yelled, "Freeze or your black ass is dead!" He froze because the police had a reputation of killing Black men for far less than what he did.

"Put your hands up and turn around slowly, if you so much as sneeze, I'll blow your head off." The boy complied with the officer's demands. Although the boy complied with the officer's demands, the Canine Unit let a German Shepherd loose on the teenager. The dog's teeth were capped with Teflon which could shred through metal. The dog ripped a plug out of the boy's leg the size of a baseball. The young man screamed, "Please get the dog please get your dog," but they let the dog pull another plug out of the boy's arm before they stopped the beast. The German Shepherd wanted more blood and his master had to snatch the animal by its leash struggling to tame the out-of-control dog. Slowly, the animal relaxed but the boy looked like a jigsaw puzzle with a couple of pieces missing. But at least he got treated for his wounds and they gave him a bottle of painkillers. They didn't give this dude anything. The man looked like a blood clot, the boy thought.

The van drove around for hours picking up Black men. The van was packed beyond its capacity, and nobody wanted to get close to Taleeb, but it was unavoidable due to the circumstances. Taleeb was freezing and having difficulty breathing because the heater was broken and there was no ventilation. Taleeb thought about giving up and letting death have its way, but he had kids that needed him. Before Taleeb passed out, the van arrived at the City County Building (CCB). The men in the van rapidly got out of it, anticipating that if they didn't, they would suffocate to death. Taleeb came out of his slumber when he felt people brushing up against him. He tried to move but every part of his body was sore. The sheriff driving the van said, "Come on man, let's go." Sheriff Farley saw the man's condition and wasn't surprised that he was unable to move. The cops beat the stuffing out of him. Farley asked his partner to help him get Taleeb out of the van. Taleeb was sneezing and coughing up blood. Taleeb felt like a sick animal being led to the slaughterhouse.

Farley was angry because Taleeb got blood on his uniform. He told his partner, "Drop his ass right here and let's go." Taleeb fell to the cement floor. The guard at the CCB yelled at Taleeb to get up, but he lay on the floor unconscious. Alex was worried about Taleeb's condition. He told the other guards to process the men that got out of the van. Alex ran to the examination room and got a gurney. Alex was in enough trouble already because an inmate died in his custody two days earlier. When Alex got back, he asked two of his comrades to help him put Taleeb on the gurney. They struggled to get Taleeb on the rolling bed. "Wow", said Alex. "This dude must weigh 300 pounds." The other guards mumbled agreeingly as they used all their strength to get Taleeb on the bed. They rolled Taleeb to the doctor's so-called emergency room.

When they got to there, Dr. Rhinehart asked his nurse, "How is this man still alive?" But the question was rhetorical. Taleeb barely had a pulse, and he lost enough blood to be considered dead. He had three concussions, pneumonia, and internal bleeding. Taleeb had a cut across his eyebrow and the side of his cheek that needed stitches. The doctor didn't have the necessary equipment to treat Taleeb effectively, but he was going to try and save the man's life.

The county jail's medical facility equipment was below the recommended standard to perform the basic procedures and that is why they lost a patient at least twice a month. The CCB's chief of staff fabricated the numbers on how many inmates died from suicides and medical issues because he would lose his job if the correct numbers were exposed.

There was dry blood on every inch of Taleeb's face. It was difficult to see if he needed more stitches or not, but the doctor didn't care because he was tired and needed a stiff drink. Dr. Rhinehart felt like he did his job well enough. He needed the pint of Old Grand Dad that he stashed in his hiding place to stop his hands from trembling. He was an alcoholic who lost his medical license in two malpractice lawsuits. Dr. Rhinehart had been sued multiple times for losing his medical equipment inside the patients' bodies after their surgeries were completed. The county jail was the only place that let him work without a license.

The disgraced doctor instructed his orderlies to move Taleeb to the shower and clean him off. The inmates were upset with the inhumane way Taleeb was being treated. But none of them complained because they had orderly jobs that allowed them to move drugs around the building. The doctor didn't want the inmates to use the patient gurney to move Taleeb because he didn't want it to get damaged in the shower. The gurney was made from a durable plastic material with wheels that popped out when it was lifted. The doctor wanted them to carry Taleeb to the shower and lay him on the floor but when the doctor went in his office, the men rushed Taleeb out on the gurney anyway. It smelled awful in the bathroom because one of the inmates was taking a dump. "Damn!" said the guy on the toilet, "Who did this dude piss off?" The men ignored him and turned on the shower. They left Taleeb on the gurney because he looked too heavy to pick up.

Taleeb was going in and out of consciousness. He was dreaming about walking in the rain, he didn't have a clue where he was going. Maybe he wasn't walking at all, it was more like hovering because his feet were not touching the ground, yet he moved in the direction he wanted to go. There were people everywhere coming and going in the big city. Out of all those people, Taleeb was able to spot his grandmother walking in the opposite direction from him. He said, "Mama is that you?"

"Yes, Puddin it's me." His grandmother died when Taleeb was a teenager. He hugged her tightly and asked her, "Where have you been?" Taleeb was crying uncontrollably. He said, "I miss and love you so much." He didn't want to let her go because he knew he would never see her again.

He called his grandmother mama. When his mother and grandmother were in the same room together, he would put their first name on the mama part, so they wouldn't get confused. He called his grandmother Joan Mama and his mother, Emma Mama. His grandmother spent more time with Taleeb than anyone in his family and he loved her dearly.

Taleeb changed the direction he was hovering and followed his grandmother. They levitated out of the rain into a beautiful sunny garden. "Mama where is this place?"

"Atlantis," she stopped Taleeb from going any further.

"Puddin it's not your time yet, I want you to be strong and go back in the direction you were going." Taleeb began hearing a loud sound, Wonk! Wonk! Wonk! … and it got louder and louder. She said, "Hurry Taleeb before it's too late, you have your whole life ahead of you." He was getting ready to hug her again, but she vanished. The noise was scaring him, it was like a clock running out of time. Taleeb levitated back to the place where he first saw his grandmother.

Taleeb woke up handcuffed to the bed and was terrified. A feminine male nurse told Taleeb, "Calm down you are acting erratic." Taleeb had on a gown and hoped the man hadn't done anything to him. "Where am I?"

"You don't know where you are Mr. Anderson?"

"No," "who is Mr. Anderson."

"Oh shit, let me get the doctor."

Taleeb thought he was being experimented on, something bad had happened to him but he couldn't remember what it was. He may have been kidnapped by bandits, why else would he be bandaged with a tube in his arm. He felt pain everywhere. They stole my body parts, he thought. One eye felt like it was missing, and he could barely see out of the other eye. I betcha they took a kidney, he thought because pain shot down his lower back to his thigh. Taleeb began to panic and tried to break out of the cuffs before they took something else.

"Take it easy champ," said the short pudgy man coming in the door. The doctor was an older white man who was balding at the top of his head. He had an honest face, but Taleeb didn't trust him.

"Who are you?" said Taleeb.

"I am Dr. Rhinehart," said the peculiar cross-eyed man. Dr. Rhinehart asked Taleeb a series of simple questions, but Taleeb found them to be arduous.

"Do you know where you are?" Taleeb looked around and it resembled a hospital in a third world country. Taleeb said, "A hospital."

"What hospital?"

"I have no idea."

"What's today's date?" Taleeb couldn't believe he didn't know what day it was, as a matter of fact he didn't know what month it was either. "Do you know your name?" Taleeb began to panic because he didn't remember much of anything. Suddenly he remembered his name, but he was embarrassed to say it.

"My name is Puddin." The Dr. grinned, showing all his stained yellow teeth. The nurse came back into the room and heard Taleeb say his name. It took all his composure to keep a straight face, but a smirk was beginning to form on the corners of his mouth.

"Did you say your name is Puddin?" asked Rhinehart. Taleeb averted his eyes away from the doctor and looked at the walls.

"Come on Puddin, this information is important."

"What is your last name Puddin?"

"Pie" said Taleeb. And that did it, the nurse fell to the floor with laughter and the doctor chuckled. They hadn't had this much fun in a while. They couldn't believe Taleeb was serious and the embarrassed expression on his beaten-up face made the nurse laughed so hard he thought he was going to die from laughter.

Taleeb went from being embarrassed to furious, they were laughing at the name his beloved grandmother gave him. He began to pray in a whisper, Father these men are my enemies and have desecrated the name given to me. Give me the power to defeat my enemies. A female spiritual voice whispered to him, open your eye. Taleeb opened the closed swollen eye, with both eyes opened, the dizzy feeling Taleeb was experiencing subsided. Heat flowed through his arms to his fingertips. A burning sensation moved from the tips of his toes to the center of his chest. The power within his body was unbearable and he yelled out as he tore the right side of the bed off the brackets. Taleeb stood up holding the side of the steel bed frame in his hand like a weapon. The nurse started screaming and the doctor said, "Mr. Anderson we are sorry."

"Please sir think about what you are doing."

"You're going to destroy your whole life." Taleeb thought about what his grandmother told him, "You have your whole life in front of you" and his anger subsided.

"We are here to help you sir," Dr. Rhinehart started talking as fast as an auctioneer. He almost urinated in his pants. This man is dangerously strong, thought Rhinehart.

"Mr. Anderson, you are in the City County Correction building."

"You were arrested for raping and assaulting your girlfriend."

"Four officers filed assault and battery charges against you as well."

"The police officers were hospitalized and are on a paid leave of absence."

"Your name is Taleeb Anderson," and you have amnesia. Taleeb tried to remember but he knew deep inside himself he was incapable of raping someone.

"I never raped anyone, why would I do something like that?" Taleeb believed himself to be a gentle soul, he would never hurt anybody. But Dr. Rhinehart and the nurse were staring at the bed railing he tore off the hinges. It clung to his arm bound by the cuffs around his wrist, and he got depressed.

Taleeb was stunned and bewildered. Dr. Rhinehart got a mirror and put it in front of Taleeb. It scared him half to death. Taleeb jumped back and said, "What the hell happened to him?"

The doctor said, "Mr. Anderson it is you."

"Sweet Jesus, I'm messed up." Taleeb looked at the image in the mirror and it looked back at him. Taleeb had to admit, the man in the mirror looked like he assaulted and raped multiple people. The nurse would have laughed but he was terrified of the confused man. As Taleeb looked at the injuries on his face, he slowly remembered what happened to him.

Dr. Rhinehart told Taleeb he had been in a coma for two weeks and that he had five stitches in his lower back. Taleeb didn't need to be told where the stitches were on his face. He also had a broken cheek bone resulting in the loss of feeling on the left side of his face. The left side of his mouth and gums were numb.

The puggy doctor didn't waste any time releasing Taleeb from his care. Rehabilitation didn't exist because they didn't have the time, money, space nor the resources. Taleeb was escorted out of the broken down so-called medical facility to the processing center where other men were being processed. The men were taken to a huge shower room. They were uncuffed, sprayed with lice and crab chemicals and hosed down with water. Taleeb was given a flu shot and blue gym shoes without laces. Five minutes later, an orderly gave Taleeb an orange uniform.

Word circulated around the County building like a fine-tuned network. The story about Taleeb was exaggerated, it went something like this: *A UFC fighter from Puerto Rico brutalized and raped a woman. When cops came to her aid, they were badly beaten. While the crazy man was being treated for his injuries in jail, he broke out of his handcuffs and beat the nurse with a steal bar he ripped off the hospital bed.*

The inmates were exceptionally nice to Taleeb. Jail wasn't what he expected. Taleeb imagined prison to be like what he saw on TV, three or four men trying to gang rape someone, but Taleeb was treated like a celebrity.

An elderly inmate walked up to Taleeb and said, "This must be your first time being incarcerated?" Taleeb nodded his head up and down.

"I kinda figured you were a newbie; I can tell by the way you're checking the place out. If you don't mind, I'm going to school you on how things work around here. You're sitting in a gold mine and every thang in this joint has a price tag on it. By the way, my name is Jimmy."

"What's up, Jimmy, my name is Taleeb."

Jimmy gave Taleeb the run down on how money flowed in the CCB.

"The juice they give us here is called soft peter."

"Why is it called soft peter?" "Because it stops us from having erections which slows down the sexual activity in here."

"Hallison's, the pharmaceutical company, was allowed to do experiments on us using soft peter. They discovered their product was effective and the side effects were even better. After drinking the juice for two years, you will become sterile. On another note, Bob Barker from the Price is Right sold the jail outfits that we are wearing to Indiana. Bob has a clothing line for prisoners in every state in America that's how he became a billionaire."

The jail was packed like sardines. Taleeb hated to use the restroom because men were sleeping inches away from the toilet in every direction. His bowels needed relief and as he walked to the toilet, it was like a maze. He had to walk carefully, stepping between and over people. When Taleeb sat on the commode, he tried not to let out a loud fart because it would have been embarrassing. While Taleeb eased the air out quietly into the atmosphere and began letting out the waste. An inmate laying near his toes said, "Put some water on it." Taleeb pondered about what that meant but when he smelled the stinky fumes emanating from the toilet, he realized that it meant flush after each time a load came out to keep the smell down. When Taleeb finished using the toilet, he felt like he had just defecated on people's heads because men were sleeping all around the commode.

Ninety-nine percent of the men incarcerated were Nubians,

including the guards. Taleeb believed that was why the conditions inside the jail were deplorable. Taleeb sat on the jail floor watching roaches behaving in a perplexing manner. The roaches were bigger than normal, and they were carrying food on their backs. They were helping each other with the groceries. They moved in unison looking like a skinny brown snake slithering across the floor. They entered a small crack in the wall. One roach was carrying a potato chip that was 5 times bigger than it was. Taleeb was bored because he was getting excited watching roaches behaving like ants when he should have been focusing on the unsanitary living conditions around him.

Jasmine went to courtroom 17 in the CCB to drop all charges against Taleeb. Two days later, the court prosecutor showed up at her house. When she opened the door, he asked "Is your name Jasmine Crawford?"

"Yes"

"If you drop the charges, we will prosecute you for making false report. You will serve jail time for physically assaulting your boyfriend, Taleeb." The prosecutor wanted to put the fear of God in her. "We are going to have Child Protection Services take your daughter away from you and put her in a foster home. Do you want your child in the system Ms. Crawford?"

"No, I don't," Jasmine began crying, "Please sir don't take my baby from me."

"Alright Ms. Crawford, all you have to do is keep that monster behind bars. Do not miss any of your court dates and fully cooperate with us or you will not see your daughter again until she is a grown woman because you will be locked up."

Taleeb had not eaten much in two weeks because they served baloney sandwiches, chips, cookies, and soft peter for breakfast, lunch, and dinner. Taleeb didn't eat meat because he was a pescatarian. The juice came in a plastic bag with a straw tapped to the side of it. Many of the inmates were extremely intelligent and Taleeb respected their wit. An inmate informed Taleeb that the man who invented the juice in a plastic bag, became a millionaire when he sold his patent to the prison system. Of course, the juice was modified with soft peter.

Taleeb was convinced that the Prison Industrial Complex was a hustle. There were countless corporations that invested in the prison system. The state of Indiana paid their bills from proceeds of the prison system. That Complex used a computerized chart that was interfaced with the stock market to pay for all their employees. The stock market had the prison listed under the assumed name called Black-Out Pharma. The numbers were always moving on the budget chart and the algorithm was set up to take 20 percent of its profits each week to pay their judges, police, prosecutors, and politicians.

One of the most draconian laws the Prison Industrial Complex put forth in Indiana was the mandatory jail time for the distribution of heroin. If a person was convicted of selling heroin, the perpetrator would automatically get a mandatory life sentence. The charge was murder in the first degree. That law was in effect for over 60 years, but Nubians began to move away from heroin as a drug of choice. The law changed because a heroin epidemic hit Indiana like a hurricane and a massive number of white people were addicted to the drug. The New law made the crime a misdemeanor. Not only did they change the law concerning the drug, but they also incorporated a euphemism for heroin and called it an opioid addiction.

White heroin dealers went to jail for short periods of time and if they happened to use the drug they sold, the dealer could get into a rehabilitating program for opioid addiction and not serve jail time. All the municipalities in Indiana banned together and began passing out fresh needles for drug users because Aids were spreading at a rapid pace in their counties. Hospitals and other drug programs gave drug users epinephrine when they were discharged. In case of an emergency, their friends or family members could administer the medicine to save their lives. The Republican Party's main objective was to get support from their Democratic affiliates to release millions of dollars in government funding to rehabilitate drug users on opioids.

After spending one month in lock up, Taleeb was finally going to stand in front of a judge to learn of his release. Ironically, Taleeb was hand cuff to the only two white guys in lock up, out of hundreds of Black men. The reason why they were chained together was because they committed the same type of crime and were going to be seen in courtroom #17 for battery cases.

The white guys went in front of the judge before Taleeb. They were repeat offenders. One man had long blond hair that hung in front of his face. He was about 5 '10 and around 30 years old. The other white guy was the direct opposite. He was short with black matted hair. A female judge was on the bench. She was furious with the two white guys because they had appeared in her courtroom on more than one occasion for physically abusing their girlfriends. Nevertheless, she let them out on their own recognizance the same day. They were released without any fines or punishment. The men had horrible records of abuse. Taleeb was happy to see the white men get a slap on their wrist because he knew the judge was going to let him go too. Taleeb had never been arrested, he owned his own business, and he had custody of his 12-year-old daughter.

Suddenly, when the judge called Taleeb's name, a white man wearing a Walmart suit stood up. Taleeb noticed the man earlier falling asleep in court. It was shocking to know; he was the prosecutor. The bored prosecutor said nothing during the white men's cases but came alive when the judge called Taleeb's name. The prosecutor told the judge all the charges that Taleeb had committed and asserted he was a flight risk. Taleeb's public defender materialized out of thin air and said nothing on Taleeb's behalf. Taleeb was angry because he hired a lawyer that didn't show up to court.

Taleeb believed he had to take matters in his own hands. He told the judge about all his accomplishments and that he had never been arrested. He began to explain why he was not a flight risk. He owned a real estate agency in Indianapolis and had full custody of his child. The judge told Taleeb to shut up and that his public defender would speak on his behalf. The wrinkled-faced public defender told the judge he had nothing to say, and Taleeb was escorted back to lock up, Taleeb said to the public defender, "What's going on? Why didn't you speak up for me!?" The man ignored him and walked away.

Everything Taleeb ever saw on television shows about law and order was inaccurate. For example, police officers reading the Miranda Rights to people that got arrested. In real life police never read those rights. And the famous mantra that the media would always recite, "you are innocent until proven guilty." Wrong, Nubians are guilty until proven innocent and that is why Black folks go to jail first before they go to court. And the crappy phrase, no man is above the law. Most white-collar crimes committed by affluent companies and people never do jail time. The punishment is usually a fine that they can easily pay, and the criminals caught in the scandal may have to step down or away from their position. They will always get another job at a fortune 500 company.

To add salt to the wound, phone calls in lock up were $3.00 a minute in 2002 when Taleeb was arrested. Many people who had loved ones in jail couldn't pay their phone bill due to the financial burden the city of Indianapolis put on families. Most minority families' home phones got disconnected because those phone charges came with taxes and other hidden fees. The price the system charged families for phone service was 275 percent more per minute. Not only was the system pimping the inmates, but they were also scamming their families.

Before Taleeb reached his destination in Marion County lockup, he had to finish getting processed. The jail was overcrowded beyond its regulations and was a fire hazard. There was such an outcry by the public concerning the deplorable conditions of the jail that the CCB authorities allowed reporters in the facility to investigate claims of suicides, poor conditions, and overcrowding. Guards trained for weeks before the reporters arrived on how to maneuver the inmates from huge lock up areas to the gymnasium.

When reporters finally arrived at the CCB, only two inmates were locked up in each cell. Trained guards moved the inmates from their cells and housed them in large open areas with hundreds of bunk beds. There were 25 of those open areas and each location housed 100 men. The guards hid 2,500 inmates. They moved the inmates around gradually before the reporters came to a certain location. By the time reporters came to survey an area, only ten inmates were locked up there. It looked like the CCB didn't have enough inmates to stay in business. The reporters weren't asking the right questions as they walked around blindly. They weren't asking about the condition of the building. Or where was the cafeteria? The reporters were only allowed to see areas that were almost empty. The dubious reporters were satisfied with their findings. After they were gone, the guards moved all the men back to their dilapidated dormitories.

Inside the Fraternal Order of Police (FOP), a group of European government officials controlled the police department. They called themselves, the *Indoctrination of Black Men*. They paid the *Indianapolis Sun Newspaper* one million dollars to spread favorable news about their findings in the CCB. Days later, the *Sun* printed in their paper that the CCB was underpopulated. Their investigation found that the building was well-maintained, and the jail needed funding to keep its doors open. The *Sun* boasted about the facility having the least number of suicides then all the prisons in the United States. The paper concluded its investigation saying they found no wrongdoing at CCB lock-up.

Taleeb had to get another flu shot before he could continue getting processed. He told the woman giving the shots that he already got the flu shot in their medical facility. She told Taleeb that if he didn't get the shot, he would remain in the processing area indefinitely. Taleeb took his second shot because he didn't want to eat baloney sandwiches and chips on a regular basis.

Finally, Taleeb was escorted to the D Block of the CCB lock-up. Once he got to the Block section on the other side of the CCB it was more civilized. They had showers, better food, and more guards.

The entire facility had various functions. It was a temporary jail holdover for people serving a jail sentence of up to one year. Before felons from Indiana State's Prisons could be released into society, they would come to the CCB to be rehabilitated. Furthermore, when a person got convicted of a crime, they would reside temporarily at the CCB before they began their journey to various state prisons in Indiana. Taleeb couldn't believe that all the people who got arrested were lumped together in one place. In Taleeb's opinion, nonviolent transgressors should be separated from violent criminals. But the place wasn't segregated, he was surrounded by criminals ranging from child-molesters to murderers, and it was packed.

Taleeb saw a man talking to an invisible person and it was obvious the guy was unstable. Nevertheless, an inmate thought that the crazy man was talking to him, and he beat the mentally ill man senseless. Taleeb was on the verge of stopping the combative inmate but decided to stay out of other people's business.

A pharmacist who sat behind a thick glass window began to call the names of inmates to come get their medicines. The inmates were getting medicine for all types of issues such as Aids, delusions, hearing voices, and every illness known to mankind. The pharmacist made the inmates take their medicine in front of him, but they didn't care because they needed those pills to function properly.

Taleeb got his first phone-call privilege after being in jail for a month and he called his mother, Emma. As soon as he heard her voice, he asked about Aaliyah. Emma told Taleeb that the Child Protective Services (CPS) took her, and Emma couldn't get Aaliyah back because she told CPS that she was moving to Georgia with her daughter, Venus. CPS wouldn't allow Aaliyah to be taken out of state. Emma wanted to be around the immediate family who had slowly migrated to Atlanta. Taleeb's brother, sister and two nephews already lived in the suburbs of Georgia and now his mother was moving there too. Taleeb asked Emma if she could collect rent from his duplex. Emma began to sob and told Taleeb she was too old to manage his financial affairs.

Taleeb took his frustration out on an innocent bystander. While he was on the phone, Taleeb saw two teenagers playing tag with each other. One of them ran past Taleeb and he took the phone receiver and bashed the teen in the head with it. Taleeb was furious with the phone conversation and the two clowns were running around like five-year-olds in the park. Taleeb was at the breaking point of his sanity.

It just so happened that the guy Taleeb hit in the head was in a gang and his three gang affiliates walked up to Taleeb. One of the guy's asked Taleeb why did he hit his friend. Taleeb guessed he was their leader because he was telling the others what to do. Taleeb was anxious to get the party started and hit the leader in the mouth while he was barking out orders to his boys about how they were going to jump Taleeb. Blood splattered across Taleeb's fist up to his shoulder from the blow. One guy tried to pick Taleeb up, but the boy collapsed under Taleeb's weight and the massive blows Taleeb delivered on the youngsters back. Another gang member was hitting Taleeb in the head while Taleeb continued beating the guy that tried to pick him up.

Taleeb was in such a rage about everything that was happening to him, he felt like he was outside of himself, and it wasn't him fighting those guys at all, but it was someone else. Taleeb didn't care about being hit in the head because in a strange way he believed he deserved it. When Taleeb turned his attention to the guy hitting him in the head, the young man said to him, "It doesn't have to be like this man." But Taleeb wasn't listening and grabbed the guy by the neck with one hand and with the other hand he grabbed the guy's genitalia and picked the guy up over his head and slammed him on the floor.

The guards came and broke it up, they asked Taleeb what happened. But he didn't say anything. Six inmates that were incarcerated in the CCB were killed by gang members two months ago. The guard in charge, Leroy, wanted Taleeb to identify the guys who took part in the altercation. Leroy advised Taleeb that by naming the culprits, the gang members could be separated, thereby protecting the other inmates from assaults. Taleeb's first impulse was to knock Leroy's teeth out of his mouth. But he began to calm down as time passed and his anger subsided. Taleeb just glared into Leroy's eyes with hate and said nothing. The guards knew who the gang members were because snitches were everywhere, but Leroy wanted Taleeb's signature confirming it on paper.

Leroy was a short thin African that was nice compared to the other guards. He got upset with Taleeb's silence and said, "Since you won't cooperate, we are going to put you in the same jail cell with the fellows we think were involved with gang activity." Taleeb thought to himself, with all those cameras in the location of the incident, why were they asking him what happened and who participated in the fight? Taleeb had a eureka moment and realized that the cameras didn't work.

Suicides and murders were happening on a regular basis at the CCB, but it was kept out of the news. Illegal drugs were coming in the building by the truck loads, and nobody knew how the drugs were entering the facility. Taleeb thought, if they really wanted to fix the problem or slow down the madness, their cheap ass could fix and monitor the cameras. The only cameras that were working were the ones on the first floor by the entrance and exit doors. Nothing tragic happened on the first floor. Twenty cameras were fake and the orderlies that move the drugs around the building knew it.

Leroy repeated the threat hoping Taleeb would sign the paperwork. "Okay then, you're going across the street with your friends." Across the street was a madhouse with no rules. The guards thought that the gang had started the fight with Taleeb, and he was defending himself. Leroy wanted to break Taleeb's code of silence and told him, "I'm going to lock all of y'all in a small cell." Leroy didn't know Taleeb was a gladiator and that locking him up with four skinny teenagers would have been their worst nightmare.

A group of disobedient inmates from every section of the jail were headed across the street by going through a tunnel in the basement of the CCB. Twenty men who severely violated the rules at the CCB were chained together walking through a tunnel fifty yards long. Their wrists and ankles were shackled with a long chain that linked them together, Taleeb imagined that they were going to be sold in the Atlantic slave trade. They had to take short strides while walking because the leg irons only extended long enough for choppy steps.

The passageway had poor lighting. The light bulbs were on the upper sides of the wall encased with steel bars. Pipes ran across the sides of the wall in every direction. The tunnel looked outdated and unkept. If a person was claustrophobic, they would have needed to be sedated before entering the narrow hallway underground.

Taleeb was linked to the four guys he fought, and their leader said, "Man, we don't have no beef with you. Most of the guys in here are stool pigeons and would have volunteered information about us without getting anything in return for squealing." He said, "Don't worry we got your back from here on out." Taleeb had no animosity toward them, after all, he had started the fight. Once they got to the designated location, the inmates were divided up into different segments of the anarchistic building. Taleeb didn't know or care where they were going. His life seemed to be spiraling out of control and his once peaceful existence was gone. There were many units in the building housing more than 60 inmates per unit. The units had small eating spaces and large sleeping quarters. And of course, the place was stuffed with inmates. The dorms were lawless and unstructured.

Taleeb was hungry and glad they arrived in time for lunch. The inmates that worked in the kitchen brought the food to the units in trays and put them on the floor in stacks and closed the door behind them. Taleeb couldn't understand why the idiots put the food on the floor and not on the tables. The inmates that were first in line took two trays while others took three. By the time it got to Taleeb there were no more trays left. Taleeb was not in the mood for that. He told everybody in the cell that he was going to walk around the tables and the first person he came to who had more than one tray, he was going to cave their head in.

An older Nubian quickly walked up to Taleeb and gave him one of his food trays. Taleeb thanked him and ate meat for the first time in fifteen years. Taleeb didn't believe humans should eat meat because of the way humans' teeth were made. They were flat as opposed to being sharp like a dog. He also believed that beef was made up of pus and pork had Taenia worms in it. Nevertheless, Taleeb didn't give a damn about defiling his body by eating meat anymore.

Taleeb needed to keep his bulk by eating all his food and stop giving it away. He believed he may need his strength to fight, which seemed inevitable. The older guy continued bringing Taleeb food trays for the duration of his time in the unit. The man serving Taleeb his trays said his name was James and he was incarcerated because some tenants claimed he stole their belongings. James was their maintenance man in the apartment complex and had keys to all the doors in the building. However, James asserted his innocence. Taleeb didn't believe James because there was something sneaky about him.

Some of the lights went out in the cell and inmates began to get into their bed. Taleeb was tired and wanted to lay down. Half the inmates were sleeping on the floor without pillows or blankets because there were not enough beds to accommodate them. The only people that had pillows and cover were the inmates that had beds. Guys were also sleeping on the large lunch table because of overcrowding. The units were only supposed to house 30 inmates per unit but instead the amount was doubled.

A big, strongly built Black man walked up to Taleeb and asked him did he want a bed and Taleeb said he did. The man grabbed the only white boy in the dorm by his neck and slammed him on the floor while he slept. The white boy was in the top bunk and when he hit the ground it sounded like the bones in his head cracked. Nobody said a word, nor did they find the event interesting. They continued sleeping and talking as if nothing had happened. Taleeb was horrified and stunned as he watched the white boy lay unconscious on the floor. The bulky Black man broke out laughing. He laughed so hard that he fell on the bed next to him holding his stomach.

It was in that moment, Taleeb realized that Hell was not a certain place where sinner's souls burned forever. Hell had many places for the soul and the CCB was one those places. Taleeb also concluded that Hell was a state of mind. Though he was depressed beyond words, he saw other Nubians around him having fun. They were laughing, joking, and having a wonderful time harming one another. What was Hell to one man was Heaven to another. The gay guys looked happy as Taleeb watched two grown men sleeping in the same bunk together. The sadistic man could not catch his breath from laughter after possibly killing someone. The guy in the bunk next to Taleeb was in ecstasy while he jerked off in the open unconcerned who saw his hand rapidly moving up and down under his sheet. Taleeb believed that Heaven and Hell were the same place. They were subjective depending on one's perspective.

Taleeb served ten days across the street as a punishment for not telling on the gang. He got sent back to the so-called civilized sector of the jail. However, one positive was that the inmates got to play basketball on the uncivil side. Taleeb didn't want to go back because the inmates on the better part of the CCB didn't get to go outside nor was there any type of window to see the sunlight.

Russell Gates owned the CCB, and he supplied heat, air conditioning and general maintenance of the building but Russell wasn't obligated to provide any type of comfort for the inmates. The city of Indianapolis owned the business dealings inside the building and was responsible for the inmates. Russell's main concern was the outside appearance of the building. However, when the Board of Health or other governmental agencies found issues with the CCB, the city of Indianapolis would blame Russell Gates and he would blame the city. They worked together under the table to nullify any violations they received by playing the blame game as a front to relieve themselves of fines imposed on them.

Taleeb had to get a third flu shot before he was allowed to go back to the place he didn't want to go. He began to get curious about all the flu shots he had gotten and asked one of his fellow inmate's, "What the hell is going on with all the flu shots?" James told Taleeb that Eli Tilley pharmaceutical company had a contract with Marion County lock up. "Each vial was worth a hundred dollars, and they wanted to use as many vials as possible to fulfill the contract."

Taleeb wanted to check out the information James gave him. Taleeb called an acquaintance he knew from college named Brandon who worked at Eli Tilley as a lab technician. Taleeb told Brandon about all the flu shots he had to get at the CCB. Brandon told Taleeb that the inmates were at an elevated risk of catching the flu and the shots were mandatory for safety precautions to slow down the spread of the virus. Brandon said, "You only need one shot for the year. It is a shame the way they are improperly administering our medicine to increase their profits. I'll investigate the matter and get back in touch when I have a better understanding of what was going on. Call me back in a couple of weeks? Please be safe in there Taleeb and I'll be waiting on your call."

"Ok, later," said Taleeb.

When Taleeb's attorney came to visit him, they had to converse between a small rectangular opening in the steel door. Everybody standing around the area on both sides of the door could hear their conversation. Taleeb asked Doug when he was getting out. Doug told Taleeb that he was facing 37 years in prison. Taleeb almost fainted, his lips dried up in a split second, his legs got weak, and he lost his footing. Doug went on to say that Taleeb was facing rape charges, 6 counts of battery, 4 of the batteries were on the police officers, one battery on Jasmine and one on his daughter. He had one count of sex trafficking his daughter along with child neglect, abandonment, and endangerment. All of which were lies except for defending himself from the police. Taleeb lost his voice and could not respond. He looked into his Doug's eyes for help and Doug smiled at Taleeb and walked away. Taleeb no longer felt sad about the white boy that laid unconscious or dead on the floor. But when Taleeb got back to the dormitory, sympathy took its course and Taleeb checked the boy's pulse. The young man was dead. After four days of lying on the floor, the body began to reek of a foul odor. Taleeb wanted to tell the guards what happened, but they would suspect him of wrongdoing considering he was sleeping in the boy's bunk. Taleeb decided to stay silent and wait till he got back to D block.

Taleeb stopped doing everyday tasks like shaving and even talking, He felt like a walking cadaver without a cause. Three weeks had passed since Taleeb saw Doug. Unbeknownst to Taleeb, Doug had quit the case without giving Taleeb an explanation. The judicial system provided Taleeb a public defender who informed Taleeb about Doug. Taleeb didn't care anymore about legal counseling because it was apparent that the entire system was a large hate group set up to destroy black peoples' lives. None of them were intended to work in his best interest. Taleeb could not think of anything else but the way Doug smiled at him.

Eight days later, Taleeb went before the judge. The prosecutor and the public defender made an agreement that if Taleeb pled guilty to a class C-felony battery on Jasmine, they would drop all other charges. Taleeb accepted the guilty plea with open arms, but the plea agreement came with strings attached. Taleeb got sentenced to one year on multiple components and if he couldn't fulfill those demands imposed on him it was considered a violation of a court order and he would be sentenced to six months in jail. The components were to be put on the Global Positioning System (GPS) and work-release. It was all about the bottom line, money.

They threw everything at Taleeb including the kitchen sink to get him to accept a guilty plea. He had a choice to fight against the system or plead his innocence in court, however if he lost, he could have gotten 37 years in prison. It amazed Taleeb how they were going to drop all the other charges if he plead guilty. The system trumped up the charges against Taleeb with lies to force him to take a plea deal. Taleeb was entering the system of institutionalized slavery.

Taleeb pleaded guilty because he needed to get his daughter, Aaliyah out of CPS and try to save his business. One of the most heinous crimes the court system had done to Taleeb was that they left all those erroneous charges on his record - verbatim. Even though those charges were dropped, they still would show up on his criminal record for the rest of his life. The system wanted to make sure Taleeb would be their slave-boy forever.

Emma still had to bond Taleeb out of jail after serving three months, even though he pleaded guilty to get out. She paid the bondsman $3000 and gave Taleeb $200 spending money. Soon after, she moved to Georgia. Taleeb was behind on all his bills, and for the first time in his life he thought of all the illegal things he could do to make money. He never associated with criminals and thought drug dealers were low life's but all that had changed. Taleeb respected the criminals he met in lock up and made a couple of friends while he was there. He didn't want to go back to jail and would do whatever it took to stay out of the joint.

The situation was becoming unbearable because the court ordered Taleeb to pay Jasmine $400 dollars a month restitution for one year. Jasmine was a supervisor at the post office and the money was for her missing work. The court sent Taleeb a copy of Jasmine's hospital bill from Wishard Memorial Hospital for zero dollars. It was a slap in the face, Taleeb thought. It was a fact that Jasmine couldn't have missed any work from her so-called injuries. Taleeb also had to pay $700 a month for one year to work-release housing and $167 a month for the GPS monitoring. $400 a month for child support for his son, and to top it all off, Taleeb had to pay miscellaneous court fees. The police officers that were injured during the altercation with Taleeb were told to drop the charges by their superiors. In return, the officers got a paid leave of absence for one year.

The egregious thing about his sudden financial crises, Taleeb had to start paying all those legal fees in one month or he would be arrested for violating his probation. Furthermore, he had to pay those bills without a job. His probation officer notified the Real Estate licensing Broad of Directors that Taleeb was a convicted felon. The agency revoked Taleeb's license. Detectives went to his place of business and let Taleeb's employees know that Taleeb's license was revoked, and they were shutting down the business. After everyone took their belongings, the detectives went through Taleeb's paperwork to see if they could file additional charges against him. When the detectives finished violating their oath of office, they called a locksmith to change the locks on Taleeb's business.

The system was running like a well-oiled machine making it

impossible for a felon to succeed. Ninety-eight percent of the criminals in Indiana went back to jail within six months of their release because of the insidious financial hardships imposed on them by the system that governed them. The oxymoron to politician's war on crime was they were creating perpetual criminals by forcing people to pay money they didn't have, to stay out of jail. That was why Indianapolis had one of the highest crime rates in the United States. It was a self-inflicted wound masterfully crafted by the *Indoctrination of Black Men* that created the polices that governed the system in Indiana. Ultimately, this government entity took their orders from the most powerful secret society in the world called *Godsmen*.

Taleeb had other sanctions imposed on him by the court to expedite his reentry back to jail. He had to do random drug tests and go to anger management classes. He was ordered not to drive on certain streets near Jasmine's home or her family's homes. He couldn't go to his business because he was being investigated but they wouldn't tell him why. The GPS device they put on his ankle monitored his location. The screen on the device would text him if he was in an inappropriate area and notify the authorities.

Taleeb was not supposed to have a parole officer when he got out of lock-up because technically, he was not considered to have been in a jail. He was supposed to be in a correctional custody facility, but Indiana's antics were nonsensical. Nevertheless, Taleeb had multiple non-parole officers. He had to report to Richard when his GPS beeped. Detectives were assigned to randomly check on him regularly. They were allowed to search his house and if Taleeb was in the presence of anyone with a felony record Taleeb would go to jail. He would also go to jail for any controlled substance in his house or on himself. A weapon found in his possession was an automatic five-year sentence. The detectives weren't needed until Taleeb finished his work-release program and was allowed to go home. Taleeb would have done practically anything to stay out of jail. And the powers controlling the system were doing everything to put him back into lock-up. Their agenda was to keep the recidivism rate high to push the war on crime narrative. The politicians complained about how incarcerating criminals was a financial burden to taxpayers but in reality, it was a gold mine for the prison industrial complex.

Taleeb had to catch the bus to his work-release site, but he didn't know how much the bus cost because he hadn't ridden the bus since he was a teenager. The driver was perturbed that Taleeb asked him about the fare.

The bus driver thought Taleeb was a bum and caught the bus all the time. "You know what the fee is man," said the driver. Taleeb closed his hands into fists and got close to the drivers face and looked him in the eyes, "Then why in the hell am I asking you about the price idiot?" The driver was from the hood and wasn't scared of the angry man, but he realized he picked the man up in front of the Marion County lock up.

"Did you just get out?"

"Yes, I did."

"It's on me man, I've been in your shoes before, your fare is paid."

"Thank you."

"I'm going to the work-release building on Meridian do you know where that is?"

"Yeah, I'll drop you off in front of the building." Taleeb only had ten minutes to get to get there and if he was late the GPS would beep Richard. Taleeb was a nervous wreck. He barely got to the six-story broken-down building on time.

He could see inside through the large glass window. Taleeb

buzzed the doorbell and watched a four-hundred-pound Black female security guard come to the door. She opened it slowly and showed Taleeb where to sign in at. Edda looked up his name on the computer and gave Taleeb the keys to his room and told him where it was. Taleeb passed the cafeteria on his way to the room and noticed it was the hang-out area where guys watched TV and talked. He walked up three flights of stairs to get to his room. When he turned the key and opened the door, he was shocked to see he was sharing the room. There were two bunk beds on each side of the room. The room was too small to accommodate four people but that was something Taleeb was getting used to. Taleeb introduced himself to the only man in the room at that time.

"They call me KP, said the man."

"Where are the other Bunkie's?"

"They're probably downstairs playing cards." Taleeb noticed a sign on the door explaining a $50 late fee charge for rent. Each person in the room had to pay $700 a month in rent. The slum lord was making $2,800 per room. There were thirty tiny rooms in the building that were fully occupied according to the pictogram on the wall. The city of Indianapolis was making $84,000 a month plus another $20,040 a month for the GPS ankle bracelets to track their property while they looked for jobs. These million-dollar operations were inconspicuous facilities spread out in the poorest areas in Indianapolis. Taleeb felt like a prostitute being pimped by the Man. If Taleeb didn't pay his dues, he would be escorted back to lock-up.

Thankfully, Taleeb was able to use the facility's phone for 10 minutes without paying for it. He called CPS and asked them if he could speak to his daughter Aaliyah, but they told him he couldn't speak to her on the phone. They told Taleeb if he signed up for their program called *Higher Steps*, he could see her once a week. They gave Taleeb the address and phone number to *Higher Steps*. He called the number and set up an appointment to see his child.

Four days later, Taleeb told the work-release authorities that he had a job interview at *Higher Steps*. If Taleeb wanted to leave the building without violating his components, it had to be work-related. The people in charge of work-release didn't need to validate Taleeb's story because he had a tracking device on him and if Taleeb wasn't back by 7:00 p.m., he would be on his way to lock-up.

Taleeb loathed catching the bus because it was slow and took hours to get from one location to the next. He had to catch three buses to get to *Higher Steps*. The building was average looking with no advertisement on it but the address in front of the place was large enough not to miss. Taleeb pulled the line on the bus and a bell rang to let the driver know someone wanted to get off at the next stop.

When Taleeb entered the building, he saw other families waiting to see their child or children. Everybody there shared the same commonalities, Taleeb assumed. The nationalities in the area were spread out evenly between the Black people, Europeans, and Mexicans. The people looked poor, and they pretended to be happy in front of their kids but deep down inside they were devastated. The sadness and pain they felt permeated through their smiles making happiness look synthetic.

As Taleeb walked to the front desk, he recognized the thin Black lady that worked there. "Rochelle, is that you?" The lady was looking down at her phone and looked up and saw Taleeb. She came around from the desk and hugged Taleeb. Rochelle was genuinely happy to see him, she hadn't seen Taleeb in two years. He was a sweet man and a good friend of her husband, Ethan. Ethan stayed out all night drinking alcohol with an old grade-school friend who was a prostitute. Not only was Ethan getting free sex from the friend, but he had also been arrested four times for drinking and driving. Ethan was placed on house arrest. Their marriage was hanging on by a thread and

Rochelle was going to cut the string soon. Taleeb went to school with Ethan. They played alley basketball together when they were teenagers. When the men got older, things changed. Ethan got hooked on crack and started stealing things. He stole from his family and from Taleeb. The stuff Ethan stole from Taleeb were insignificant and could easily be replaced. But that didn't break up their friendship. What frustrated Taleeb about Ethan was he had a good wife that stood by his side, while he was at the lowest point of his life. Rochelle was waiting for Ethan to get in some sort of program, but Ethan didn't want help because he was happy being a drunkard and drug addict. He was going to lose Rochelle, but Ethan said she was not going nowhere. Rochelle told Taleeb that Ethan wasn't helping her pay the mortgage and she was going to lose the house. Taleeb gave her money from time to time to help them out with the bills. Their bills were inexpensive, and Taleeb didn't miss the money.

Taleeb had to end his relationship with the couple because he could not watch his friend kill himself anymore. Ethan was as tall as Taleeb, but he only weighed a hundred pounds. Ethan was selling his blood to different blood banks around town. All the blood banks eventually banned Ethan from their businesses. They told Ethan he was too thin for his height, and he was a health risk. Ethan started filling his pants pockets with rocks to make himself heavier and when they drew Ethan's blood, he would pass out and bust his head or injure other parts of his body. Taleeb couldn't stomach seeing his friend like that anymore and cut him out of his life.

"Why are you here," asked Rochelle?

"It is a long story, but they took my daughter."

"Oh, I am so sorry to hear that!" She looked up Taleeb's appointment, grabbed his hand, and said come on. While they were walking, she gave Taleeb her cell phone number and told him she would give him whatever information he needed to get Aaliyah back.

Rochelle introduced Taleeb to the pale female mediator name Carla and told her Taleeb was a good friend of hers and to take good care of him. Rochelle smiled at Taleeb and told him everything was going to be alright. She said, "Call me," and walked away.

Carla left and came back with Aaliyah, and she yelled "Daddy!! Daddy!!, I'm so glad to see you." She hugged him like she was never going to see him again with tears in her eyes.

"What's going on with you?" asked Taleeb.

"They have me staying with this filthy woman with five bad kids. Two of the kids are hers and the other kids are foster children. Daddy, I had to fight her two daughters because one of her daughters stood in front of the bathroom and told me I couldn't use it. I asked her did she want to fight me, and she said yes, and I hit her in the eye. She ran away screaming and came back with her big sister, I tried to explain what happened to her big sister, and her sister pushed me, and I beat her up too daddy just like you taught me. Their mother got mad and made me sleep in the bed with four puppies that had peed, and boo-booed all over the mattress. Look at me Daddy, I have rashes on my skin." Aaliyah looked at her dad and started crying, "What happened to you, you look like somebody tried to kill you. Oh my God what happened to my daddy?"

"It's ok, I'm alright, I'm going to fix all of this."

Carla wrote down everything that was said. Taleeb asked Carla could Aaliyah go to a cleaner and safer place. Carla said she would tell the head counselor about the situation. Carla assured Taleeb that the living arrangements for Aaliyah would improve exponentially.

"Just look at my child, what is that on her skin?"

Carla said, "It looks like eczema."

"But Aaliyah doesn't have eczema."

"Aaliyah may have had eczema all her life, but you wouldn't have known that because her skin probably had an adequate amount of lotion or oiled. But now, her skin is very dry."

Aaliyah looked unclean and worried. Taleeb tried with every fiber in his body not to let the tears drop from his eyes but when he blinked tears rolled down his cheeks. And for the first time in her life, Aaliyah saw her father cry. He was embarrassed and knew that crying would only frighten Aaliyah more than she already was, but the tears slipped from his eyelids anyway. Taleeb asked Carla when Aaliyah was coming back home.

"You have to talk to CPS to get any information regarding Aaliyah's return home." After Taleeb's visit was over, he kissed Aaliyah on the cheek and told her that he loved her.

"I love you too daddy."

Taleeb thought about how he could get Aaliyah out of the system. He left *Higher Steps* with the weight of the world on his shoulders. He had to catch the bus to manage all his affairs. Public transportation in Indianapolis was horrible. Typically, the buses ran every hour unless the rider was downtown or on a major street like Meridian or Washington street.

After Taleeb's tedious ride back to the hell hole he lived in, Taleeb called CPS to find out when he could get his child back. They told Taleeb that he couldn't get her back for six months. He was appalled and told them that it was unfair for them to keep his daughter in the system for half a year. The lady on the phone told Taleeb that six months was the normal course of action for a child removed from their parent. Taleeb thought the policy was excessive and should be reevaluated. He felt like Aaliyah was in jail too, for something he had done. They were both in a system aimed at destroying families, thought

Taleeb. He asked God to help him devise a plan to fix the disaster that was eroding his life.

After seeing Aaliyah, Taleeb thought about his 11-year-old son, Toussaint, who was named after the revolutionary leader of Haiti. Toussaint's mother Yvonne hated Taleeb, but he never knew why. Taleeb did everything he could to be in Toussaint's life, but Yvonne poisoned the boy's mind. Toussaint wouldn't accept any of Taleeb's gifts nor did the boy want to be in the presence of someone his mother despised. Taleeb tried to call Toussaint, but the boy didn't want to speak to him, and Taleeb felt like he was a failure as a parent.

The next day Taleeb told Robert who was one of the people who oversaw the work-release program that he had an interview at the gas station on a 116th Street. Taleeb gave him some of the truth, but he couldn't tell Robert that he was attempting to obtain his car from his house nearby. Robert didn't care if Taleeb went to work or not because if he didn't pay his dues he would go back to jail. It was always a winning situation for the powers that controlled the system because they were going to get paid either way.

It was imperative that Taleeb got his vehicle because he needed to get things done in a brief period allotted to him. Waiting on the bus everyday was not an option because he spent half of his day waiting on transportation. The bus didn't go that far northeast, but he got as far as he could go in that direction. He called a cab to get him the rest of the way there.

When Taleeb got to his house his GPS went off texting him to come to the CCB at once. The message was concerning but he had more pressing issues. All his cars were gone, and his house was ransacked. Taleeb knocked on his neighbor's door and Ronald opened it enthusiastically.

"Hey Taleeb, what's going on, Bud."

"Man, that was awful what they had done to you. I called the chief of police on those officers, and they are under investigation. What can I do to help you?"

"Ron, do you know what happened to my vehicles?"

"The police towed them." Taleeb was shocked because his vehicles were not involved in the altercation with Jasmine.

"Thanks, Ron, for your support, I'll talk to you later."

"The best of luck to you Taleeb."

Taleeb made calls to towing companies that towed vehicles for the police. To Taleeb's amazement, an employee at the Sheriff Auction Center told him that his vehicles were sold in the auction two days ago. Taleeb couldn't understand how brand-new vehicles could be sold to someone else while he was still making payments on them. Even more baffling, Taleeb learned that the auctioneer gave the buyers clear titles on the vehicles. Taleeb didn't know that the sheriff department put a lien on the vehicles for the debt he owed them. They had charged him thousands of dollars for storing the vehicles while Taleeb was incarcerated. Because of the liens placed on the vehicles, the sheriff department was able to get clear titles to the vehicles to satisfy the debt.

"Damn", Taleeb thought, I bet this is happening to Black men all over the United States once they are caught up in the system. The sheriff department in the state of Indiana was more powerful than the IRS. The system was bleeding Taleeb dry, and he was going to do whatever it took to pay those devils in full or else they were going to ride him to hell.

BLOOD MONEY

Taleeb went downtown like his GPS told him to do. Richard came out of his office to see if any violators of his program arrived. Richard was a tall slender dark-skinned man that dressed like he worked on Wall Street. He wore a suit and tie that looked like it was on the cover of a GQ magazine. Taleeb was sitting in the waiting area at the GPS center.

Richard approached Taleeb and said, "There was a deviation in your location, you were not where you were supposed to be."

Taleeb told him the truth, "I tried to get my car form my house because the bus was impeding on my progress to get a job."

Richard told Taleeb, "Go back to work-release and don't let it happen again." Richard didn't care what Taleeb was saying because his job was to put Taleeb back in jail for another six months.

When Taleeb got back to work-release, anxiety gripped him like the Boston Strangler. He saw the paddy wagon pull up to the building and pick up two men that didn't get a job within their one-month period, therefore they were escorted to jail. The program nevertheless would let felons stay in the facility without a job if they paid all their fees on time.

Taleeb's roommates had jobs, but they complain about their GPS going off for no reason. The men were paranoid because they were concerned about losing their jobs. Their devices kept texting them to go outside for tracking purposes. Each roommate repeated the same story. They had to stop everything they were doing at work to stand outside for ten minutes until the device reset itself. They said it would happen four or five times a day at work. Taleeb thought it was strange that all three men who worked at various places had experienced the same issues with their devices.

KP told Taleeb that his girlfriend had got a high paying job in Carmel, Indiana selling time shares. Taleeb's ears perked up like a German Shepherd. Taleeb wrote down the information KP gave him. The downside in the details was he needed a car to get there. The place was in an upscale area on the far northwest side of town 20 miles from Darlene's house.

It was imperative that Taleeb got a vehicle and some more money quick. The money his mother gave him was running out. Taleeb told Edda that he was going to fill out an application at Village Mart convenient store on Washington Street off Rural. Taleeb intentionally failed to tell her that he was going to his duplex to collect rent that was due. In addition to collecting rent, Taleeb was going to get his old Ford pickup truck that he kept in the backyard. Taleeb got anxious because if everything went as planned, he could solve his financial problems for a month.

He was taking a serious chance going to the duplex, but KP told Taleeb, he could go 20 yards away from his destination before the GPS would start beeping. Taleeb was praying his roommate was right because his duplex was about 20 yards away from the Village Mart.

Taleeb was desperate and nervous. His heart sank when he viewed his backyard from the Village Mart. Taleeb did not see his truck in the backyard. He notified his tenants via pay phone that he was going to collect rent. Taleeb walked diligently across the street through people's yards making sure he used as little footage as possible.

It was a blessing that Taleeb got to his destination without his GPS beeping. He knocked on Connie's door and she went to the window to see who it was. When she saw it was Taleeb, she came out onto the porch. Connie was 19 years old with a two-year-old son. She was a beautiful light skin Nubian woman. Her mother was white, and her father was Black. Taleeb was physically attracted to Connie, but she was not interested in Taleeb, and he couldn't understand why. Connie worked at the Village Mart where Taleeb met her. She had seen the rental sign in the window and the rest was history. Connie gave Taleeb the back rent money she owed. He asked her what happened to his truck that was in the back yard, and she said a tow truck came two months ago and towed it away.

Taleeb wanted to walk up to any police at random and blow their heads off. The detectives must have done a driver's license search on Taleeb and saw all the places that he ever lived, but how would they know he owned this place? Unless they did a property tax search and found out he owned it. "Who would want that raggedy truck?" thought Taleeb. He couldn't let the negative vibes ruin what he was trying to accomplish. Taleeb knocked on Bill's door who lived next to Connie, and no one answered. Taleeb was upset with his tenant Bill because he didn't answer the door. He told Bill he was coming over, but he was thankful he got the $1,200 dollars from Connie. She was three months behind on her rent and Taleeb didn't charge much because it was in a bad neighborhood, and it was a small one-bedroom duplex. Taleeb was shocked that she had the rent money.

Taleeb reported back to work-release at 5:00 p.m. He made some phone calls to find out where his truck was located. Luckily, the truck was at a place where he could take public transportation to get there. Sadly, Taleeb had to pay two hundred dollars to get it out of towing. Fortunately, the sheriff department didn't sell Taleeb's old truck, probably because it was old and dented up.

Later that night, Taleeb went to his room and the 400-pound

Wildebeest security guard was in there throwing stuff around. After Edda finished her search for contraband and whatever else she was looking for, Edda began cursing at him and his roommates. She said, "Get this place cleaned up you nasty MFs." Taleeb looked around the room and it was always clean until she messed it up. Nevertheless, they started making their beds and wiping surfaces that were already clean. Taleeb didn't know what Edda's problem was, but she told them that she had a place to stay and didn't have to live in this hell hole. Edda looked dusty and unkept. Her hair was uncombed, and her uniform was wrinkled. Taleeb told Edda, "I have a place to stay also, and this hell hole is temporary for me. You on the other hand, have to work in this hell hole for minimum wage to survive."

She told Taleeb, "If you say one more word, I will do everything in my power to get your ass kicked out of this program." I'll make it my special project to send you to jail."

Of course, Taleeb shut up because it wasn't worth the hassle.

Taleeb woke up Thursday morning on a full-blown mission. Not only did he have to pay all those legal fees, but his mortgage was also $1,200 a month for his house. He bought the duplex for 16,000 cash but he took out a loan and rehabbed it. He bought another new car that he didn't need. Taleeb saved money to buy more properties to rehab and rent out, but that money was almost gone. Taleeb's small room in the program was the same cost of his duplex.

Taleeb couldn't dwell on his problems, he had to execute a solution. Therefore, he put an ad in the classified section of the *Indianapolis Sun Newspaper*. He listed his house to rent out for $1,400 dollars a month. He didn't want to rent out his home, but he had to make a way out of impossible odds.

Another day had passed, and Taleeb still didn't have a job, but he had faith that a breakthrough was near. He walked up to Edda and told her that he had an interview at a towing company. She looked at him and said, "I don't give a F*** where you gotta go but don't come back here on time and see what happens." Taleeb thought, if hemorrhoids had name, it would be a dictionary picture of Edda irritating the shit out of somebody. He put the disgusting 3-D image out of his mind and focused on his truck. It took Taleeb three hours to get to the towing company because the bus had to pick up other people and drop them off at their destinations. After the long ride, he realized that he took driving for granted.

When Taleeb reached the towing company, the guy at the window told him where the truck was in the yard after Taleeb paid him $500 dollars. As Taleeb approach his vehicle, He couldn't believe his eyes. He had two flat tires, a busted headlight, and a busted taillight. He looked up to Heaven and asked God, "What have I done to deserve this kind drama?" Taleeb believed in Karma, what goes around comes around, but this situation was spinning out of control, he must be getting his father's Karma too.

Taleeb had to settle down because he could feel the heat going through his extremities and anger was taking control. He stopped a fork truck driver and asked him did they have any used tires for sale. The guy told Taleeb, "We don't sell tires, but I have 8 cans of Fix-a-Flat." "If the tires aren't severely damaged, the Fix-a-Flat could get you to the gas station down the street." "You can fill them up with air or replace them."

Thank you, how much do I owe you?"

"That'll be $20.00."

The 8 cans barely made Taleeb's wheels rise but the air didn't seep out of his tires and Taleeb felt he had a chance to make it to the gas station. His GPS didn't go off because the gas station was in route to the slave plantation. Taleeb thanked God, for reaching his destination. He filled his tires with air and made a quick stop at Auto Zone to get parts and tools to fix his front and back lights.

The next day, Taleeb walked up to Edda's desk humbly and let her know that he had a job interview at the library. She said, "Get the F*** out of my face." The smell of hot garbage eroded from her breath and Taleeb hurriedly did as he was told.

Taleeb went to the library and used their computer and logged onto the Indy.gov website. On that site, he was able to get the paperwork to change his name. Taleeb read the instructions and filled out the paperwork. He took it to the CCB and paid the proper fees. They stamped the paperwork and in less than a week the judge granted Taleeb a name change. His new name was Lance Battles. Taleeb changed his name because when he pulled up his police report at the CCB. His rap sheet was two pages long. Taleeb's background check made him look like he was a dangerous criminal, and nobody would hire him with a violent police record like his.

After Taleeb changed his name, he waited three days to let it marinate into the computer database. He later paid the fees to get a police record on Lance Battles and nothing showed up at the sheriff department, however it did show up at the police department. His social security number was tying the two names together, but Taleeb could act confused about the other name and tell potential employers that he was getting the other name removed off his record due to someone inappropriately using his name. Taleeb believed he could get a job if he got to the interview stage.

He was only going to use the name Lance Battles for employment purposes. And the way Taleeb was feeling about the system in the United States, he could use his new identity and start a better life in another country.

Later that day, Taleeb told the Cyclops that he was going to fill out an application at the Social Security Insurance office. He let the beast know he had to take care of business in two other places as well. She said her usual vile obscenities and Taleeb left to repair the lights on the truck. He was getting nervous because his money was running out.

While Taleeb was at the Social Security Office, he showed them the court order of his name change and they put Lance Battles on his new SSN card. Taleeb was hoping they would give him another SSN number, but they wouldn't. After he finished that ordeal, he went to the Marion County Public Health Department to put his new name on his birth certificate. Taleeb decided that if he had to do shaky deals with his credit, it would be in Taleeb's name. Under the name Lance Battles, the entity was going to be a perfect citizen and the way things were looking, the entity Taleeb was going to do a lot of illegal activities. Taleeb laid in bed all night thinking of scams. He decided ruining his good credit would solve his financial woes. Taleeb was going to buy television sets and other merchandise on credit from different stores and liquidate the items by selling them to people who needed it.

When Taleeb got dressed in the morning, he went to the job that his roommate was telling him about, Resort Shares Incorporated (RSI). As he approached the building in his truck, Taleeb was impressed with the modern style building. It had a sculpture of a huge hand holding the world in front of the building. The sculpture was silver, but the world wasn't a solid ball, it was an open circle with different countries around it.

Prior to coming to the company, Taleeb made a resume' at the library and hoped he didn't have to fill out an application at RSI. He went inside the building not focusing on anything else around him because he wanted to put all his attention on the matter at hand. Taleeb wore some round rimmed eyeglasses to look studious, but he didn't need eyewear. His aim was to overshadow the battle scars on his face with the nerdy boy image.

Taleeb didn't know why he was nervous because he was only going to drop off his resume and leave. There were ten people sitting, waiting to be interviewed and they were all women. Taleeb was disappointed to see applications laying on the table to be filled out. Nevertheless, he copied everything off his resume and put it on the application which was stupid considering it was the same information. Seconds later, a secretary came around the corner of the room and asked Taleeb and the other women for their applications and resumes. Taleeb handed her the documents as requested. She took the paperwork and disappeared around the corner again. He waited over two hours while everybody was being called. He didn't expect to be interviewed the same day. Taleeb was the last person to be called. A nice-looking tall slider White woman introduced herself as Angela Fitzgerald. Taleeb introduces himself as Lance Battles. She took Taleeb to a room with over forty computers and there were mostly ladies using them. Angela told Taleeb he had to pass a typing test to get the job. He was required to type 30 words a minute. Taleeb was computer savvy and typed often but he didn't know how fast he typed. Taleeb prayed in his mind.

The prayers worked because Taleeb passed the test and got the job the same day. Angela told him to sit in a chair next to her desk. Ten minutes later a representative named Cindy came out and introduced herself and showed him around. Cindy informed Taleeb that he had to go to a three-week paid training class. She explained to him that he would be selling vacations and insurance to their customers. Cindy said he would alternate from inbound to outbound calls daily. The job was based on commission and a minimum wage pay combined. Cindy told Taleeb that he would get base pay whether he sold anything or not, however she said if he didn't keep a certain quota per week his job would be in jeopardy.

Mostly all the employees at RSI were women of all nationalities. Taleeb felt like he hit the jackpot, he wanted to bow down to those beautiful goddesses and praise them. Taleeb would have worked there for free. There were about 200 hundred women who worked at RSI, and Taleeb hadn't been with a woman sexually in six weeks. His odds for him getting laid were high, he thought. Taleeb wanted a sophisticated woman that had her stuff together, but his situation was complicated. Therefore, he had to settle for mediocre.

There were so many women to choose from that Taleeb was confused. Every time he saw someone he liked, another sexy woman would glide into his view. The women came in all sizes and shapes. Taleeb had his eye on an ebony Nubian woman who walked like a Black Panther cat. Her name was Cierra. She was graceful and moved like a model on a runway. Cierra was so fine and elegant when she came near Taleeb, everything started moving in slow motion. When she turned and looked at Taleeb, he thought she could have been an angel.

Cierra wore a long dress that covered her body to her knees, but it clung to her like saran wrap. She was blessed with curves that made Taleeb wish he was the dress she wore. With each step she took, her rear end played the drums. Cierra looked athletic because her frame was stern. There was something seductive about Cierra and Taleeb had to have her.

Taleeb was wondering how he would measure up to a woman like Cierra. He ran 5 miles a day and did 100 pushups and 80 sit ups on a regular basis. Taleeb frequently visited the dentist because he wanted to keep his teeth white and straight. He wouldn't go anywhere unless he was well dressed. He wanted his appearance to be flawless. People often asked Taleeb was he someone famous, they would pause and look at him trying to figure out who he was. Taleeb hoped Cierra would focus on his appearance because he had nothing else to offer a woman of that caliber.

Taleeb's opinion about people and himself were changing after his incarceration. He made a note in his mind not to look at himself in the mirror unless he was shaving. He put his conceited attitude in check and began thinking about how he could help Black men in jail find jobs.

Five o'clock rolled around and Taleeb's shift ended. He was embarrassed about his truck and parked it as far away as possible from everyone else's vehicles. It was a 1978 Ford four door pickup truck with two big dents on both sides of it. The truck was the biggest vehicle on the lot. Although it was beat up and ugly, it was extremely durable and dependable. When Taleeb got back to work-release, he told them he had a job and where it was located.

The night was young, but Taleeb was tired and got in bed early, but sleep didn't come easy. Sex should have been the last thing on his mind considering his precarious situation, but it pecked at him like a rooster in a hen house. Taleeb dreamed about Cierra and her curves all night. He woke up in the morning with soiled underwear after having a wet dream.

While Taleeb was driving to work in the morning, he received six messages on his new cellphone concerning his fully furnished house for rent. He eventually talked to each potential tenant and chose a Black couple that appeared to be successful. Taleeb didn't have time to do background or credit checks on the potential new tenants because he couldn't find the time to do it and he needed the money quick. He did, however, make them fill out a rental application that he got from *Office Cart*. Taleeb also called their jobs to make sure they were employed.

Taleeb had serious issues navigating around the city because the prosecutor made a list of all the locations that were off-limits to him. The locations were confidential, but they were places Jasmine worked at or where her family members lived. It was a tough situation for Taleeb because he didn't know where Jasmine's kin folks lived but if he went near those areas his GPS would sound off. She also filed a restraining order against Taleeb because she told the authorities she feared for her life. Taleeb didn't remember Jasmine's last name, nor did he ever want to see her again. None of that mattered because the prosecutor made the case that Jasmine's life was in danger. The worst part of the court proceedings involving his case was no one ever asked him what happened. His entire case was predicated on what Jasmine said had happened and his input was invalid.

The only thing Richard told Taleeb was, he couldn't drive down 38th street or be near it. Which was almost impossible, because 38th street was a main artery in Indianapolis that extended to the farthest extremity of the city going east and west.

Three weeks later, Taleeb finished his training at RSI and was officially hired. Taleeb tried to blend in his unique environment like camouflage. The job was extremely easy because he was selling trips around the world to their own RSI customers. It wasn't like Taleeb had to find customers; RSI exchanged trips for their own clients. If one client had a condo resort in Florida and another person had a place in Cozumel Mexico, they could exchange with each other for a small fee. Also, the clients needed to keep their condo insurance up to date. Taleeb always talked to the clients about that insurance. He could see when it was due on his computer monitor. The first insurance policy he would try to sell was the 10-year coverage and most of the time that's what Taleeb sold. He very seldom mentioned the less expensive 3 and 5-year insurance policies unless the clients were adamant about other options.

RSI's clients wanted to go on vacations at the same time of year and they wanted to go to well-known places. The problem was the resorts were already occupied by clients who booked their vacations well in advance. Part of Taleeb's job was to get people to go somewhere that was not a popular tourist attraction. The solution to that dilemma was to make sure the clients' alternative trips were compatible with their preferred choice. To be successful in getting the client to switch was, everything had to be top of the line in quality. It had to be a five-star resort and a replica of their favorite spot. Taleeb was able to get the client to change their destination 99 percent of the time because he learned what the client wanted, down to the smallest detail which was easy to do because Taleeb was able to look up all the places on the computer they had been in the past.

Two months had passed, and Taleeb sold more trip exchanges and insurance than anyone had in the history of RSI. In one month, Taleeb made $10,000 on the job. The stars had finally aligned for Taleeb because he also rented out his house.

Taleeb asked his tenant Connie who lived in his duplex for help in exchange for not paying next month's rent. He needed her to get all his personal belongings out of his house in Geist before the new renters moved in. Taleeb also went to court to remove Bill, the tenant who lived next to Connie out of the duplex. Taleeb was glad Bill hadn't paid because Taleeb needed that side vacant in case, he had to move in it.

All hell was breaking loose with Taleeb's GPS throughout his tenure at RSI. The device was texting him to go outside to get a signal. The text pop up on his 9-inch box with a LED screen that Taleeb had to carry everywhere he went. The box communicated with his ankle bracelet. Taleeb had to go outside every hour and people were curious about the box he carried around; they were also annoyed about the frequent beeps it made. Soon Taleeb's strange activity caught the attention of his supervisor. Taleeb was reprimanded and given a warning about his breaks. They didn't know Taleeb was wearing an ankle bracelet that dictated his movements.

Taleeb had to tie up some lose ends financially because his job was in jeopardy. The system was working against him. Taleeb's tracking device recommended that he report downtown at once. He was angry because they were playing games with his livelihood. When

Taleeb reached his destination, his GPS overseer, Richard came out and asked Taleeb, "What is going on with your monitor?"

Taleeb told Richard, "The GPS keeps going off at work claiming it did not have a good signal. I have to stand outside 10 minutes every hour. Can you do anything to adjust the GPS because it is going to make me lose my job?"

Leroy told Taleeb, "We will see what happens," and dismissed Taleeb from his office. Taleeb didn't know what that statement meant but he had a bad feeling that jail was the game plan orchestrated by people who ran the CCB. Taleeb couldn't understand why the state of Indiana preferred he be incarcerated instead of pimping him for thousands of dollars a month. Unless he was worth more to them in jail.

Taleeb had to do another random drug drop in the same week. Most of the guys pass the drug test because a music store in Indianapolis sold natural products that could mask marijuana and other drugs so that the drug test could not detect the drugs. It usually took three weeks for cannabis to leave the body and it was convenient to use the music store's product because it did not remove cannabis but hid it. Some guys didn't pass the test because they were institutionalized and didn't care if they passed or not. One fellow name Dray told Taleeb that he used a fake penis that he bought from and adult store. The fake penis allowed Dray to put someone else's urine in it who was drug free. However, later that week Dray was arrested because the urine showed he was pregnant.

When Taleeb arrived at the drug testing site, there was a sign on the door saying that they had moved to another location, but they did not give him a phone number or address. The place was closed permanently, and no one had the decency to tell Taleeb. It was rude, and Taleeb called Richard to tell him the testing site was closed but Richard didn't answer the phone. Taleeb left a message and explained to Richard what happened.

The next day, Taleeb couldn't believe Edda was in a good mood. She joyfully told Taleeb that he had to go to court. Taleeb asked her why and she said, "I don't know but hopefully you're going back to the slammer." She chuckled and waddled away.

Taleeb had to call off from work to go to court. As usual, all the people in the court room were Black except for the judge, prosecutor, and public defender. The judge called Taleeb's name, and he walked up to a chair with a desk in front of it. Taleeb stood there and faced the Judge who was sitting 50 feet away from him. The judge sat on a throne that was elevated near the ceiling like he was God passing down judgment.

The judge told Taleeb that he had violated his probation by missing his drug test appointment. Taleeb told the Judge that the testing facility had gone out of business, and they hadn't left any information to where the new testing site was located. Taleeb's account of what happened fell on deaf ears. The Judge heard those excuses from half the people in his court room, and he didn't care.

Judge Warren was a short fat man with no conscious. He was a divorced alcoholic who learned how to hide his problems in a bottle. Warren was a seasoned judge who knew the rules of not emotionally attaching himself to any case. He was part of the secret society. The society controlled his paycheck, and he wasn't going to let anyone jeopardize that including the handsome fellow in front of him.

Warren wasn't racist like the rest of the committee members. He didn't hate black people at all, how could he hate people that made him a millionaire? Every Black person Warren saw was money in the bank. He couldn't believe how resilient black people were. Some of them worked at temp service jobs to pay their bills. He had more respect for a man trying to rob a bank then someone working for minimum wage. Warren couldn't imagine being in the shoes of a black man. He would rather die of a horrible disease than work for a temporary service. Warren felt sorry for the poor bastard begging for leniency. Warren gave Taleeb a warning.

The secret society, *Godsmen* decided to close all the drug testing sites throughout Indiana for two weeks. Everybody that was on probation were ordered to do their drug drops within the two weeks the testing sites were closed. By closing the sites, everyone on probation got violated. The propaganda behind *Godsmen's* scheme was to keep their quota of the Black people incarcerated. They purchased thousands of buildings and homes throughout Indiana under shell companies and assumed names. *Godsmen* brought their real estate in bulk through tax sales, surplus sales, and auctions. Their committee had low level board members in each entity that specialized in real estate. Money was coming in by the truck loads. Their main problem was they never had enough properties to accommodate the masses of Black people being incarcerated.

When Taleeb went to work, his supervisor called him into the office. Gino gave Taleeb his final warning for taking too many breaks. Gino reminded Taleeb that he could fire him without a cause because the state of Indiana was an At-Will hiring/firing state.

"However, I'm giving you the reason, right here." Taleeb wanted to tell Gino the truth about his situation, but he couldn't afford to get fired on the spot.

Taleeb began to pay all his bills in advance for six months. It was becoming impossible for him to stay out of jail. The odds were stacked against him. He told Cierra the truth about his situation. But he didn't tell her about the name change because that was his ticket out of the United States. Taleeb walked Cierra to his truck. He didn't care what she thought about it anymore because he was going to lose his job and was going to jail soon. He didn't expect her to wait on him while he was locked up because they had only known each other for a few months.

Taleeb was surprised when Cierra asked if they could sit in his truck and talk. They continued their conversation about Taleeb's shattered life. Cierra tried to comfort Taleeb by telling him that he was fortunate to have the money to get things in order. She wrapped her hands around his and told him she would wait for him when he got out. Taleeb marveled over her beautiful light brown eyes. He didn't know how Cierra would respond but he began kissing her. The bulge in his pants was uncomfortable. He needed relief and Cierra seemed to read his mind because she began caressing him. Taleeb wondered if he was dreaming because they were going to make love in his raggedy truck.

Taleeb was happy Cierra had on a dress. He looked around to see if anyone was watching. There were only two cars on the opposite side of the lot. Taleeb stood up on the passenger side of the door and pulled Cierra toward him.

When they connected, Taleeb wished that moment could last forever. Taleeb thought this had to be heaven because nothing in the world felt that good. Fifteen minutes later, Cierra announced her pleasure, and Taleeb followed soon after. He could barely stand, and his legs were shaking, He had no more strength. Taleeb thanked Cierra and told her he really needed that, and she said she really needed it too.

Taleeb had napkins in his truck and helped Cierra wipe off her inner thighs. Cierra kept laughing and fanning her face and chest with her hand. Cierra was hot and sweating but it was cool outside. Taleeb drove Cierra to her Lexus in the parking lot and told her he really liked her. Cierra explained to Taleeb that she had never done anything like that so soon. She said she really liked Taleeb also. They kissed and Taleeb said, "I can't wait to see you tomorrow" and Cierra said, "The feeling is mutual" and they departed in good moods.

When Taleeb got back to his room at work-release, he decided not to pay the seven hundred dollars for the room anymore because he wanted to make sure he had financial security when he got out of jail. Taleeb figured he would run out of money faster paying rent on a room and two mortgages at the same time. Therefore, he had to get his mind right to do six months in hell. Taleeb kept paying his court fees because he knew he would never be totally free unless he paid the fines off.

The next day when Taleeb got to work, he could feel it in his gut that his tenure with the company was ending that day. When Gino called him to the office, Taleeb felt awful. Gino told Taleeb to have a seat and for 5 minutes, Gino explained why Taleeb was being terminated. Taleeb didn't want to leave on bad terms and thanked Gino for the opportunity to work there. He told Gino that he was doing a good job as a manager and thanked him again. Gino felt bad after firing Taleeb. Everybody he parted ways with made excuses why they were ineffective at their job, but not this poor fellow. "He even complimented me", thought Gino. The man was extremely good at his job, but he couldn't allow Taleeb to abuse his breaks. Gino couldn't show favoritism for Taleeb, even though he was the top salesperson. He had already been counseled by his boss about giving certain employees special treatment. What bothered Gino was that he should have tried to understand Taleeb better and helped him with his problems. Gino didn't do anything for the man and now he lost a productive employee. As Taleeb walked out of the building, he said to himself, "All Richard had to do was to tweak the GPS monitor and I would still have my job." It didn't matter because Taleeb had it all under control. Three weeks later, two sheriffs showed up at work-release and took Taleeb to jail.

Two months had passed since he seen that abomination and he hated being in the facility more than he hated the woman that put him there. Taleeb skipped the preliminary process that newcomers had to go through entering the system. The one thing he did not skip was the perpetual flu shot.

Doc heard about Taleeb's reputation and was glad to hear that he was back. Doc wanted Taleeb to run his illegal operation because the word on D Block was Taleeb wasn't a snitch and he was a gladiator. Doc had big plans for Taleeb.

The inmates had different jobs such as janitors and cooks, but the most valued inmates were the trustees that were ground keepers. They were able to go outside the CCB and manicure the landscape. The ground men could get fresh air and feel the sun on their face. It was a sight to see, people from all walks of life hanging around downtown. The other perks for the landscaping job were they had access to drugs and cell phones that they brought into the facility. People who were associated with the trustees would drive their vehicles down the street near the CCB and throw distinct types of legal and illegal paraphernalia in areas where the inmates routinely worked outside. The guards in charge of the inmates knew what was going on but kept their mouth shut because they were getting paid by the dope dealers who were affiliates of the inmates. Over half the employees that worked for the CCB were on the take.

Doc was one of the inmates that worked as a ground keeper. He wanted Taleeb to run his business. Doc introduced himself to Taleeb and told him that he had what it took to operate a store. Doc said, "I'll make sure you have access to everything you need to be successful." Doc believed Taleeb would fight to protect the products and wouldn't sing like a bird if he got caught.

"What exactly would I be selling?"

"You my man, would be selling marijuana, cigarettes, homemade liquor, coffee, food, candy, and other supplies." Doc said, "Think of it like a mini mart. We have hair oil, toothpaste, deodorant, and such."

"How do I get compensated for operating the mini mart?"

Doc said, "Taleeb, if you run the store, you can have whatever you want in the store for free." Taleeb had to contemplate the offer because he didn't want to get caught selling drugs in jail. It would extend his jail time. Doc knew Taleeb was apprehensive about taking the position therefore he did not mention the other drugs the store sold. Doc didn't want Taleeb to quit once he found out about the other drugs, so he sweetened the deal. Doc said, "If you take the job, I'll give you this," Doc dangled a cellphone between his two fingers.

"Where is the store, can I do a walk through?"

"I'm glad you asked," said Doc. "Follow me my friend." Taleeb noticed that Doc always had two flunkies with him. Doc told them to put the merchandise in front of the new store owner's spot. "Ok boss," and the men disappeared. When Doc walked up to Taleeb's bunk, he said, "I present to you, the Mini-Mart."

"Hit it, Rico." An old temptation song started playing, For the Love of Money. Doc was in a fun mood and couldn't help chuckling. Doc's men came through the crowd struggling to carry a huge trunk with a heavy-duty pad lock on it. They put the trunk next to Taleeb's bed. Taleeb slept on the top bunk, but Doc told Rico to move to the top bunk. Doc explained the D block rule to Taleeb that all Alpha males take the bottom bunks. Doc gave Taleeb the key and said, "We will tally up tomorrow."

"How much do I sell this stuff for?"

"Rico will help you with the prices."

Taleeb was a health fanatic and had never smoked a cigarette before, but his nerves were bad and he needed one. He opened the trunk to look for cigarettes. "Where are the cigarettes?" asked Taleeb. Rico looked in the trunk and said, "We are out of cigarettes, but we got tobacco and rolling papers." Taleeb grabbed the paraphernalia and told Rico to roll it all up because they were going to sell some and smoke the rest. After Rico finished rolling up the tobacco, Taleeb said, "Let's go." They went to the restroom and started smoking. Taleeb coughed and hacked for five minutes. Rico tried patting him on the back but that only made things worse.

"Damn man, when was the last time you had a cig?" Taleeb didn't respond but he was determined to smoke.

"Take baby steps man," said Rico. Taleeb took a few more pulls off the cancer stick and inhaled the smoke more slowly. Taleeb's nerves had settled down, but the drawback was he liked it.

The deal breaker was the cellphone. Taleeb had access to Aaliyah and Cierra at his fingertips. He called them regularly and they were always elated to hear from him.

Taleeb started selling small bags of coffee for the same price as small bags of weed and tobacco. He liked having the store and wanted to own one when he got out of the slammer. He wanted to look as intimidating as possible to ward off any potential thieves who may have wanted to take his merchandise by force. Taleeb let his hair and beard grow longer. He kept his hair braided and his beard trimmed once a week by an inmate barber who was gay. Taleeb paid him with coffee or cigarettes, but the barber kept telling Taleeb he would do it for free. "No thanks," said Taleeb. Doc had his staff keep Taleeb's uniformed pressed daily by placing the uniforms individually under a flat mattress for a day. The uniforms looked like they had been taken to the cleaners. Doc wanted Taleeb to look like a professional businessperson. But for the first time in his life, Taleeb was unconcerned with how he looked. They were in jail and who cared? Doc knew what Taleeb was thinking because of his nonverbal expression, the 'I don't give a damn' look. Doc told Taleeb, "Don't let these bars take away your dignity man. I know what happened to you bro, but don't let that shit define you. How many men can make it on the outside of these walls and on the inside, man? You need to give yourself some credit. This is not the end; this is the beginning of a new life. You are rising above this mess and don't even realize it. Lose that attitude and make the best of your circumstances. You're not going to see better days unless you make it through this storm. Don't fall apart man, you got this. Trust me Taleeb, you are going to be a better man, but you have to be tested by The Creator. I know you're going to be back on top out there that's why I gave you my number and address, so we can help each other when we get out."

Taleeb needed that pep talk like he needed a cigarette. Doc was right, and Taleeb decided to lighten up and get into the groove. He started playing chess, checkers, and cards with the inmates. The games took his mind off his children, which was the root cause of his nervousness. He began to adapt, and the inmates treated Taleeb like he was family because he had all the goods. Nevertheless, Taleeb worried about everything, from how was he going to get a job when he got out or would Cierra leave him because he was broke. But his main concern was which inmate would snitch about the store.

Taleeb had one month left to serve before he was released, and he told Doc that he had to quit working at the store. Doc was sad because Taleeb was the best worker he ever had. But Doc understood Taleeb's situation and told him everything was all good. Time went a little faster in jail because Taleeb accepted his new reality.

Finally, Taleeb served his time and got out. Cierra was waiting for him by the front door. She drove him to her house for the first time and he was shocked to see the sign to her subdivision. It said homes starting at $500,000. When Cierra pulled up to her $700,000 home, Taleeb asked her "Is this your house?"

She said, "Yes, baby. Whose house did you think it was?" He wanted to ask her how she acquired the house, but he didn't want to seem intrusive.

The house was 8,000 square feet and Cierra didn't have any children. Taleeb wondered why one person needed a house that big. It had five bedrooms and five bathrooms and a finished basement with a mini theatre and bar. It had a fireplace in her bedroom, basement, and living room. It took a lot to impress Taleeb and he was in awe. He had a million questions to ask her about the house, but he had to keep his cool.

Cierra started taking off her clothes and Taleeb immediately snapped out of his trance, and he did the same. They couldn't wait to get to the bedroom and started having sex on the living room floor because Taleeb needed a lot of room to do every sex position that was ever created. He never went without sex for six months before and he had a heavy tension built up.

Cierra was so excited she prematurely let her love come down before Taleeb could get fully engaged inside her. Cierra moved her body gracefully on Taleeb to make sure he was satisfied also. When they finished with round one, Taleeb marveled over how beautiful Cierra was lying on the floor. But once wasn't enough and Taleeb and Cierra made love a few more times that night.

Soon after they were finally done, they took a nap in each other's arms. When Taleeb woke up, he felt like a million bucks. Cierra asked him, "Do you want to watch a movie?"

"Yes, I do, baby." Cierra found an action movie she thought he might like. Taleeb was enjoying the movie, but he didn't get to see much of it because Cierra talked through the entire movie. But Taleeb didn't mind because what she was saying was interesting and funny.

Cierra told Taleeb about her mother and father and how she was raised. Her child life amazed Taleeb because her mother and father didn't drink alcohol or do other drugs. Her father owned a gas station, and her mother was a lawyer. Cierra said her mother sacrificed her life to make sure she and her brother had plenty of love and encouragement. Cierra's brother got a baseball scholarship to Purdue University and Cierra had an academic scholarship at Howard University. Cierra earned a doctorate degree in Organizational Leadership and her brother went to the major league.

Taleeb had never known a family like Cierra's. Everybody he knew had an alcoholic mother or father. Both of Taleeb's parents were alcoholics. They didn't care if he went to school or not. His cousins on both sides of his family smoked weed, cigarettes, and everything else. Taleeb thought his family was normal but after Cierra told Taleeb about her sober family, he began to realize his family had serious issues. Taleeb wanted to keep his ghetto family away from Cierra's folks at all costs. Taleeb loved his parents dearly, but they used profanity often and it might offend Cierra's church-going kin folk.

Cierra took a week off from work to be with her new-found love. They had a wonderful week with each other. Cierra could not believe she fell in love with Taleeb so fast. She felt sorry for him because he lost his business and couldn't get his job back at RSI. He seemed to be in deep thought all the time. Taleeb appeared restless. Cierra prayed that he really loved her like she loved him. She tried not to get close to any man because she didn't want to get hurt again. She couldn't believe a sexual relationship could turn into love. Maybe she was infatuated with Taleeb, and it wasn't love at all, she thought.

Cierra thought about her husband who she divorced because he couldn't keep a job. Cierra met Bobby when she was a sophomore in college. He was taking classes to become a psychiatrist. Cierra liked Bobby because he was funny and could hold an enjoyable conversation. They got married when they both got out of college with bachelor's degrees. By the time Cierra got her master's degree, Bobby was fired from countless jobs. Bobby was a control freak and could not get along with people at his jobs or with Cierra. Bobby became upset and angry about his money situation and started to become mean and verbally abusive to Cierra. She tried to help Bobby by getting him odd jobs, but Bobby claimed those jobs degraded his manhood. Cierra could never figure out why Bobby wanted to become a psychiatrist because he could never resolve his own problems.

Cierra put up with the lazy bum for years. One day she got the courage and put Bobby out. Cierra took the new Mercedes she had brought him back to the dealership and leased an apartment for Bobby to stay in for one year. Bobby begged for Cierra to give him another chance, but she was adamant about not taking care of a grown man. Being married to Bobby was like having a child and she didn't want children at that stage in her life. Bobby stalked Cierra for years and still comes by her mother's house to this day. Cierra had relationships in her life, but she was sure that Taleeb was the only man she genuinely loved. She really liked the fact that Taleeb was wise beyond his years. He knew how the world worked from a literal perspective and he had street smarts. But in the back of her mind something was nagging her about Taleeb. Was he like Bobby in terms of getting and keeping a job?

The next day, Taleeb went home to his one-bedroom duplex. He had cleaned the place out after Bill left. Taleeb should have sued Bill for all the junk he left behind in the house. Taleeb had skills fixing up houses. He painted all the walls and put new carpet down. He installed new kitchen cabinets and remodeled the small basement. Taleeb could do everything to a house except for electrical work. He was excited because he ordered new furniture and he figured out how to get a new car. Taleeb knew Cierra didn't want his big ugly truck parked in front of her house. She appeared shallow to Taleeb because he believed she cared about what people thought of her. Cierra avoided introducing Taleeb to her family and friends because she didn't want them to ask him questions about his job and where he lived. Furthermore, she couldn't take the risk of them seeing her driving him around.

Doc had been released from Marion County and was glad to

get home to his wife who he'd been with since grade school. They had four kids that were grown and out of the house. Doc and his wife, Sherry, were empty nesters. Doc's real name was Farley Holland, but he got his nick name Doc because he was a nerd in school and always used big words that his peers couldn't comprehend, thus they began calling him Doc, short for 'doctor'.

Doc enjoyed reading the Webster dictionary and the Bible as a kid. He read both books numerous times. The Bible, however, left an indelible impression on him that he couldn't shake, and he began researching and studying its authenticity until he concluded the book had many flaws and contradictions. The Bible was close to a Steven King novel except the Bible was better than Mr. King's material. In the Bible, a mule and serpent could talk. A man walked on water and a woman had a baby without having sex. The woman who was called Mary was told by God's angel to name her son Emmanuel which meant "God is with us" but when her son was born Mary called him Jesus which meant Savior. Doc asked a well-known Christian pastor about Jesus and other confusing narratives concerning the book. Doc's confusion turned into bewilderment. The pastor John Adkins explained to Doc that God was Jesus wrapped in humanity. Jesus came to save the world of their sins. Pastor Adkins went on to explain to Doc that God represented a trinity, God, Jesus, and the Holy Ghost.

Doc couldn't sleep that night after Pastor Adkins answered all the questions he asked. He thought, it was physically impossible for God to impregnate a woman without having sex with her. Then she bore a son even though she was still a virgin. Doc tried to wrap his mind around the fact that God reincarnated himself into Jesus. Before Jesus dies, he prays to God and asked him why He forsook Jesus. But Jesus was praying to Himself because He was God. Therefore, He was talking to Himself. And if that wasn't mindboggling enough, at the very end of the bible in Revelations 22:16, Jesus says He is the offspring of David and The Bright Morning Star. Why is Satan also referred to as The Bright Morning Star? But John told Doc "all things were possible with God". Doc thought the Bible should have been rewritten to be believable. The most baffling thing about the Bible was God gave the life of His only son to save the world from sin. And Satan was the bad guy causing all the misfortunes to God's people. Doc asked Pastor John one final question that he couldn't answer. Why did God allow the Devil to live but killed His only son? Wouldn't that have solved the problems of the world? John grew tired of Doc's questions and told him to have faith and understanding will reveal itself.

Doc began to question all the books he read in school after reading the Bible and realized that every book he read were based off lies except for math, biology, and science. Fredrick Winslow, Sigmund Freud, Christopher Columbus and the litany of other European theories, philosophies, and discoveries were all debunked when Doc researched the theories. Doc's professor in college gave the class many assignments in his doctorates program to research everything they learned in their undergraduate programs, and all the students discovered none of what they learned was true.

Their professor was dying of cancer, and he wanted the class to know nothing was as it seemed. But why did Doc have to write countless theses and essays on those psychopaths and their discoveries? It hit him like a ton of bricks. He was being indoctrinated with systematic and deliberate brain washing. He was studying the European version of false facts but when their work was researched thoroughly, they either stole the knowledge from other non-Europeans or their discoveries were fabricated. In Docs mind, America was the greatest country in the world, but its foundation was based on fabrications.

Doc shared his knowledge with friends and was surprised that Taleeb was mostly aware of everything Doc spoke about. It felt good to be around someone who was equally informative about things. Taleeb's feedback on the Bible and the corruption in the system was similar to Doc's beliefs. It was exhilarating and unusual to talk to someone who was a free thinker and not constrained by the mainstream belief systems.

Doc was a 5' 10" medium built, brown-skinned man. His nickname may have planted the seed that began to bear fruit because 25 years ago, Farley (Doc) was presented with twenty scholarships from various colleges. Doc decided to change his doctorate degree program and go into the medical field since he had a Master's in biology. Doc accepted a scholarship at a local medical school called Indiana University-Purdue University because he couldn't imagine spending any length of time away from Sherry whom he married in his freshman year. Soon after Doc graduated from IUPUI, he got his Physician's Medical License and began working at Wishard Hospital as a heart surgeon. Life was wonderful for Doc and his family.

Things began to change for the worse when Doc's son, Dominique was arrested for loitering. Before he was detained, the police officer told Dominique to leave the area, but the boy refused to obey the unlawful command because Dominique told the officer that he lived in the area. Dominique continued his walk home and away from officer Greg Larson. Greg ran up to Dominique from behind and tackled him to the ground and arrested Dominque. Dominque was handcuffed and put in the back seat of Greg's police car.

Dominique was lectured thousands of times by his parents to follow all instructions given by police officers. "But I did nothing wrong," Dominique said to the officer. Larson smiled at Dominque and mocked his statement, "But I did nothing wrong!" Dominique spat at Larson, but the saliva got on the window because it was rolled up. Two other officers arrived at the scene and began chuckling at the spit rolling down the inside window. Larson asked them, "Did you see what this little black bastard done?" They were shaking their heads up and down.

"I'll show you who's boss, you little black spade." Larson

opened the back door, pulled out his gun and shot Dominque in the head. Fear replaced the smiles on the two police officers' faces. They couldn't believe Larson shot the kid in broad daylight while he was handcuffed. The two officers conversed with one another about what they should do about the situation. The officer driving the car yelled at Larson and said, "Keep our names out of the report or we are going to blow your head off like you did that kid," and they drove off in a hurry.

THE SYSTEM

Protests broke out all over Indiana because of the unjustified shooting. The mayor had a meeting with prominent Black pastors in Indianapolis to come up with a plan to stop the violent protest. The pastors gave a press conference and addressed the situation. Pastor Julian told the audience that they needed to stop tearing up their neighborhoods because it was counterproductive. "Please let the police do their investigation to find out what happened. Moving forward let's have peaceful demonstrations." Pastor Murphy gave the locations and dates where they were going to have peaceful marches. But a loud angry voice in the crowd yelled, "We don't want the police to do their own investigations, we want an independent investigation by the FBI." The pastors ignored the woman's comment and said, "That's all the time we have left. Thank you for coming out and supporting us." The two pastors walked off the stage.

One month later, the police department called the shooting a suicide which was impossible because the boy was handcuffed when he was shot. The question the news outlets were asking was how did Dominique have a gun to shoot himself if he was searched for weapons before he was handcuffed and placed in the back of the police car?

Steven Turner wanted to address the public because his department was getting negative press coverage and his officers were suddenly getting physically assaulted by citizens at a massive rate. Turner held a small press conference to convince Hoosiers that what happened to Dominque Holland was a justifiable killing.

Turner began reading the Teleprompter explaining the events that unfolded into the death of Dominique Holland. "My officer encountered a young man walking in a neighborhood where the residents in that area complained about Dominique's suspicious behavior. My officer was dispatched to the location where he encountered Mr. Holland. The officer asked the young man, why he was in the area. Dominique told the officer, none of his business. The officer asked Dominique for his Identification but Dominique told him that he did not have any ID. The officer told Dominique he was being detained until the officer could investigate if a crime was committed by Dominique. The officer searched Dominique for weapons but the officer stated that he did not find any weapons on Dominique's person. While the officer was standing outside writing his report, he heard a gunshot. The officer looked in the back seat of his cruiser and saw that Dominique shot himself in the head."

Turner then asked a reporter did she have any questions. Her name was Patricia Saunders, and she was handpicked by his office to ask simple and easy questions, but Patricia decided to go off script and ask the complicated questions. "Chief Turner, why did Greg Larson ask Dominique Holland for his Identification if he had not committed a crime." Turner became angry with Patricia because she was not supposed to mention the officer's name. She had put Greg's life in danger. Turner was not prepared for the question either and never considered Greg's actions to be inappropriate behavior. "No, Dominique had not committed a crime however the officer needed to assess the situation before letting Dominique go."

"Chief Turner, did you know that it is unlawful to detain an individual who has not committed a crime." Turner couldn't believe the question Patricia asked. Whose side is she on, he thought? "Well, Dominique wasn't necessarily detained, he was only being held for questioning."

"Then why was Dominique handcuffed and placed in the back

of your officer's vehicle?

"I'm not at liberty to answer that question right now."

"Why did officer Larson ask for Dominique's Identification if there was no criminal activity committed on behalf of Dominque?

"We had complaints from neighbors that Dominique's behavior was suspicious."

"Suspicious behavior should not have warranted officer Larson to ask Dominique for his Identification nor is suspicious behavior a crime, is it Chief Turner?" Before Patricia could ask another question, Turner pointed to another reporter, "What's your question", asked Turner?

"How did Dominique shoot himself in the head if his hands were cuffed behind his back?"

Turner was fully prepared for the question and said, "We are going to show you how Dominique killed himself." Turner motioned a man named Alex to demonstrate how such a suicide was possible. The officers on the stage moved out of the way so that the audience could get a full view of Alex. Alex asked the chief to handcuff his hands behind his back and Turner did so enthusiastically. Alex sat down in the chair and slowly maneuvered his arms behind him. Alex's arms were like rubber. His collarbones collapsed and miraculously Alex pulled his cuffed hands over his head. Once his hands were in front of his body, Alex reached into his high-top sneakers and pulled out a small pistol and aimed it at his head. The crowd was quiet and stunned but the fascination didn't last long. It became obvious to the crowd that Alex was a contortionist, and people began to boo and throw objects at the police chief and his carnival show. The police officers surrounded the podium and got into formation; they were holding long black shields with plexiglass at the top so they could look out of it. The police were in full riot gear, and they began to push the protesters back using the shields.

Meanwhile, Doc was at home. He had taken two months off from work. His wife and kids were together at his mother's house. Doc needed time to be alone. He cried so long and hard about Dominique until the wells in his eyes ran dry, but he sobbed anyway. The doorbell rang but he wasn't going to answer it, Doc was the only one home at the time. He looked out the upstairs window and saw a police car. "What the hell," Doc automatically went and got his wife's gun. Doc didn't believe in violence or guns, but he made an exception because he was dealing with demons in the police department.

A little voice in Doc's head told him to ignore the doorbell but he was curious, what did this devil want? There were only four reporters with their crew in the yard. It wasn't that many of them because young black boys were killed all the time by the police in Indianapolis. It was normalized and many people were unconcerned about it anymore. Black people were often hung in jail cells soon after they were arrested. The county coroner's autopsies most often concluded they were suicides.

What made Dominic's case different from all the other black men killed by law enforcement was he was killed while handcuffed in the back seat of a police cruiser. The bizarre explanation that the police gave got a lot of media attention. The reporters in Doc's mother's yard slowly dissipated the area because it was more action going on in the downtown protest. Doc opened the door, and it was only one policeman outside. I'll be damned, thought Doc, it was the cop that shot his son. Greg was supposed to be on leave of absence with pay for killing Dominique, but why did they let this bastard have the police car while he was off duty?

"What do you want," asked Doc. Greg gave his condolences and apologized for disturbing Doc. Greg politely asked Doc to drop the civil lawsuit he had against him.

"Mr. Holland, you already have a 10-million-dollar lawsuit against the police department there is no need to come after me."

Doc was infuriated and wanted to kill Greg where he stood. Doc knew Greg was going to get off on all charges because no police officer in the history of Indianapolis had ever been charged with killing an unarmed Black man.

"Get your ass of my property, you poor excuse of an officer, before I do to you what you did to my son."

Greg's peaceful disposition changed. "If that little asshole wouldn't have spit on me all this wouldn't be happening, you should have trained the boy better."

Doc pulled out his 22 caliber pistol in a split second and without hesitation, shot Greg in his head three times. Greg fell to the floor like a sack of potatoes with a look of total disbelief in his eyes. Doc had a look of bewilderment on his face because he couldn't believe he shot Greg.

"No! no! no!" Doc walked back and forth pacing the living room floor trying to think. He walked quickly to all the windows in the house to see if anyone was around who may have heard the shots. Luckily, there was only an old lady walking her dog about a half mile away. Doc patted Greg down and found his gun in a holster inside his rain jacket. Doc removed the gun and shot two bullets in the wall and then put the gun in Greg's hand. Doc wanted it to look like he was defending himself from the cop. Doc later called the ambulance and the police.

Doc spent 25 years in prison for second degree murder, even though he had the best lawyers in Indiana. Doc was lucky because he could have spent the rest of his life in prison without parole, but the jury was convinced it was self- defense. The all -white jury wasn't convinced that Doc had to shoot the officer three times to defend himself, therefore he was sentenced to two and a half decades in jail.

While Doc served his time, he devised a plan to kill everybody involved in both cases concerning him and his son, including the judges and lawyers. In fact, he wanted to make a bold statement to the powers that controlled the system. Doc needed smart people around him to pull it off. The main person he wanted on his team was Taleeb. It was a shame what they did to that young man and Doc knew he could persuade Taleeb and other convicted felons to join him because Doc had what it took to get a crew together and that was money.

Doc and his wife won a $6-million-dollar lawsuit against the police department over two decades ago. They didn't get the $10 million they asked for and their lawyer got more than a third of the proceeds. Two of Doc's kids had full scholarships to college and the youngest child was the only kid that did not go to a university. Doc's wife still had two million left, she spent more than half of the money. Doc had to think of what to say to his wife to get her to give him one million dollars to start his project.

Doc called Taleeb a month after he got out of jail. The phone rang five times and Doc was going to leave a message, but a deep voice finally said hello.

"What's up bruh?" said Doc.

Taleeb knew instantly who it was, "Hey Doc, what is going on?" Taleeb was ecstatic to hear from Doc. The two men talked on the phone for hours discussing what was going on in their lives. Taleeb told Doc about losing his house because of money issues. Taleeb soon realized how difficult it was to maintain a prestigious lifestyle once he got caught up in the system.

Doc asked, "Can you meet me at Fort Benjamin Harrison Park tomorrow? I want to talk to you about a business opportunity."

"Yeah man, of course." Doc gave Taleeb the time to meet him and the details of the location in the park where he would be.

Fort Benjamin Harrison was a beautiful forest with walking trails all around it. The beauty came with a $20 fee. Doc was going to give Taleeb the opportunity to make the money to take care of his debts. All Doc's advice was illegal and that is why he couldn't discuss it over the phone. Doc could kill two birds with one stone by meeting at the Fort. He needed the exercise, and he could conduct business at the same time. Doc needed something incriminating on Taleeb to get his cooperation and to keep him silent about what Doc was going to tell him. The plan involved a list of criminal acts that could get anyone involved the death penalty. But the walk in the park was not going to be about Doc's true goals. Doc was trying to groom Taleeb to do malicious crimes to get money into his pocket.

Fort Harrison Park was 1700 acres of pure beauty, Taleeb paid the fee to get in and followed the directions Doc gave him. Within 2 minutes, Taleeb saw Doc tying up his sneakers. Doc was wearing sweatpants and a long sleeve work out sweater. Taleeb wore an Addis work out outfit and he was ready to go on a long walk. The two men greeted each other, and Doc asked, "Are you ready?"

"Let's do it," said Taleeb. Doc began walking fast into the woods and Taleeb kept up with him, walking by his side.

"Damn, your pretty fast for an old man," Doc was 55 years old but in decent shape. He smiled at Taleeb and told him to keep up and Taleeb chuckled. Doc got straight to the point 10 minutes into the walk.

"You should burn the house down and collect the insurance money Taleeb."

"Burn down the house?" asked Taleeb

"Wouldn't law enforcement or the insurance company suspect me as the arsonist?"

"No, not if you make it look like an electrical accident."

"Naw man, I can't do any more jail time."

"You won't go to jail if you're not involved."

"What do you mean? How would I not be involved?"

"I know a guy who is an electrician that can make the fire look like faulty wiring. He charges $5,000."

"Damn Doc, I don't have that kind of money."

"Don't worry about it, I'll pay him for you."

"I don't know about this man, what if something goes wrong?"

"It won't, the guy has done this before, and everything went according to plan. You need the money, Taleeb."

"But what's in it for you?"

"Well, let's just say, I get a finder's fee from the electrician and 10 percent of what you net from the insurance company."

Taleeb wanted to net $50,000 from the ordeal, with that type of money he could make things happen and get back on his feet.

"Are you in?" said Doc

"Yes, I'm in."

After the long walk with Doc, Taleeb went back to Cierra's house. Taleeb was living with Cierra, but he kept his one-bedroom duplex on the side in case things didn't work out with their relationship. Cierra wanted to know every move Taleeb made. She wanted Taleeb to take her to work and pick her up on the weekdays. They were both embarrassed about him driving his truck around town and Cierra decided to let Taleeb use her car to take care of all his business needs. It was a degrading feeling for Taleeb. He was a helpless dependent. As soon as he picked Cierra up from work, she asked him, "Did you look for a job today?"

"Yes, I should be working with an insurance firm in a couple of weeks." Cierra gave him a list of companies who were hiring. She told Taleeb that her girlfriend's boyfriend had a felony record and got a job as a truck driver. "He makes good money too." Taleeb lied and told Cierra about the job interviews he had lined up. But Taleeb needed to focus on getting the tenants out of his house before it was burned down.

A week had passed, and it was time for Taleeb's routine visit to the barber shop. His barber, Rowmane was an ex-con who went to jail for 10 years for selling cocaine. Jail didn't persuade him to stop selling drugs after he got out. Row sold weed and cocaine his entire life as an adult. Taleeb asked Row why he didn't sell crack too. Row said crackheads were too worrisome and dangerous.

Row was into everything and didn't have to sell drugs, but he was greedy. He flipped houses, owned the barber shop, and rented out huge trash dumpsters with wheels that he made from scratch. Taleeb thought Row was the best businessman he had ever seen. Row was better than a common drug dealer, but it was a family business. Row's two older brothers were drug dealers, and they were Row's role models.

After cutting Taleeb's hair, Row said, "Follow me." They went to the back of the shop in Row's office. Row gave Taleeb a hundred-dollar bill.

"Why are you giving me this?"

"Look at it," said Row.

Taleeb looked at the money and was puzzled, "What am I looking for?"

"It's counterfeit," said Row.

"How did you get this?"

"I made it."

"How?" Row had a big elaborate printer in his office and walked over to it an took a hundred-dollar bill from his pocket and put it on the printer and hit the print button and a copy of a hundred-dollar bill came out, Row flipped the bill on the other side and copied the back side of it. He took the original bill and put it back in his pocket. Row took the printed copy over to the paper cutter and cut the bill out. Taleeb grabbed the bill and noticed the texture was off, it felt harder and not as flexible as real money, but the color was perfect. Row took a maker that checks money to see if it's real and swiped it across the fake bill and the mark turned black which meant it was fake. Row said, "You can ball the money up and alter the texture, but you can only give this money to street hustlers."

"Buy something from them that is inexpensive and give them the hundred dollars to get change in real money. If the vendor had a money maker to check the bill, just act like you didn't know it was fake."

Taleeb went from not personally knowing any criminals nor thinking of crimes to being inundated with illegal thoughts. Wow, what a difference six months in jail makes on a person's life. Nevertheless, Taleeb believed he could perfect the money, but his biggest obstacle was the paper to print the money on.

The tenants in his house were moving out at the end of the month and everything was going well, except for Cierra. She was arguing with him about everything. Cierra didn't believe Taleeb was trying hard enough to get a job. She said something that emasculated him. "I'm not taking care of no grown ass man." Taleeb played it cool and didn't respond because those words made the decision for him. The relationship was instantly over, but Cierra didn't know that. She was complaining about him using her car and staying gone too long. Cierra believed Taleeb had another woman on the side and nagged him every day about it.

Her friend Shondra made matters worse when she told Cierra that she saw Taleeb with another woman in Cierra's car. Cierra confided in Shondra and told her Taleeb had not found a job in two months. Everything the two women said about Taleeb was negative. Shondra said, "I don't care how good his stuff is, I'm not taking care of no grown-ass man, plus he's cheating on you too! Girl please." Shondra was envious of her good friend because Cierra graduated from an Ivy League School and people seemed to gravitate around her. She hated hearing Cierra talk about her sorority sisters every time they got together. In Shonda's mind, those hoes were nothing more than a cult.

Shondra secretly competed with Cierra. Shondra made an impressive wage working in the corporate world. She bought a house and car that was out of her price range. She worked all the overtime the job had available. The only way Shonda could support her lifestyle was to work every day including weekends. She lied about seeing Taleeb with another woman because she felt betrayed. She felt Cierra had enough friends without Taleeb sucking up the rest of her time. Before Cierra met Taleeb, the two ladies hung out more often, but nowadays their time together was scarce.

Taleeb called Doc and told him the house was vacant. Doc hung up the phone fast. Taleeb thought he should be paranoid like

Doc now that he had succumbed to a criminal type of lifestyle. He didn't want to break the law, but his criminal background record showed up under his new name as well as his old name. The names were attached to his social security number. He was baffled to why it didn't show up on his last job. Every job Taleeb applied for denied him employment based on his criminal record. His only recourse was to operate his own business, but he needed the insurance money to get him started.

The plan to burn down the house went awry. The so-called electrician Doc hired brought another person to help him do the job. Instead of making the arson look like an electrical failure, dumb and dumber tried to burn the house down using rubbing alcohol. They poured the alcohol on a throw rug in the kitchen and left the empty bottle next to the rug on the floor. After setting the fire 24 hours ago, the small rug continued to burn. Taleeb couldn't believe his eyes when he walked in the front door. The fire only caused damage to the rug. The house was smokey but when Taleeb opened the doors and windows the smoke vanished. The idiots took out the batteries in the smoke detectors and left the batteries on the floor. Taleeb was astonished at the level of stupidity that went into their work. It almost looked like a setup, thought Taleeb

Taleeb decided to take matters in own hands and burn the house down himself. He had to make it look like an accident. He decided to make it look like a crack head broke in the house. Taleeb played out the scenario in his mind. The crack fiend broke in the house and couldn't find anything to sell to the pawn shop. The only things in the house were a couch and chair. The addict made the best of the situation and got high in the house. When he ran out of drugs, the pipe fell in between the couch pillows, while he surveyed the floor looking for anything white that could have spilled out of the pipe. He didn't find anything and left the house looking for the dope man. Soon after he left, the blazing hot pipe caught the couch on fire and the rest was history. But how would that scenario play out in his affluent neighborhood? It was a hard sale, but wealthy people got hooked on crack too, thought Taleeb.

Taleeb started driving his beat-up truck all the time and never drove Cierra's vehicle again. She complained about his oversized truck in her driveway daily, but Taleeb didn't care. He was moving the rest of his clothes out of her house in two days, unbeknownst to Cierra. She argued with Taleeb the entire day and he heard absolutely nothing she said because he tuned her out. He was deep in his own thoughts and Cierra's words faded away before they passed his eardrums. Taleeb believed Cierra was bipolar because one minute she would be happy and the next minute she would talk negatively about his predicament.

Cierra knew Taleeb was ignoring her and it made her angry. But she knew what to say to get his attention. Cierra told Taleeb that it was his fault his daughter was in CPS and that he was a failure as a father. She told him he would never get his daughter back because he was a felon with no job.

GRUDGE

Taleeb almost lost muscular control, he visualized her throat being slit with a butcher knife. He had to hold it together because if he put his hands on her, prison would be waiting for him. Taleeb couldn't believe how someone so beautiful, and loving could also be so evil.

Taleeb didn't spend much time with Cierra at all after that comment. His side of the duplex was freshly painted and fully furnished. He moved all his belongings from Cierra's house. Taleeb's little one bedroom wasn't much to look at, but he cherished his peace of mind. Taleeb played some jazz and couldn't believe he could be happy moving back to the ghetto. His number one aim for the day was getting the paper consistency right for the counterfeit money.

The most surprising thing about the government money was they made sure no paper in America was the exact same weight as the United States bills. Taleeb worked on the project day and night for months trying to find a comparable substitute, but it was fruitless.

Guilt crept up in every cell of Cierra's brain until she broke down and cried. Her coworkers kept asking her if she was ok. She didn't blame Taleeb for not answering her calls. She was angry about his situation, but she knew her approach was cruel. Jealousy tugged at her heart when she thought of Taleeb spending time with another woman. Cierra was not performing her best at work because she thought about Taleeb every second. When Cierra got off work, she got in her car and drove home faster than usual. She was going to apologize to Taleeb and prayed he was home. He was aloof lately and always gone. Cierra's prayers were unanswered; when she got home everything Taleeb owned was gone. Cierra cried long and hard. She thought if there was ever a red line, she had crossed it.

Cierra had been listening to her other friend that she grew up with named Natalie who didn't like Taleeb because he wasn't the right man for Cierra. Natalie told Cierra, "He doesn't have anything to offer you. He is jobless and lies about everything. He claimed to have had three cars that the police took and a big, beautiful home up north, yeah right if he did, the money came from selling drugs." Natalie also believed he had another woman on the side because he was never home. "Where is he? He doesn't have a job, who was he spending his time with?" Natalie hated the fact that she was attracted to Taleeb in some strange way. Was it the sexy scar that ran down the side of his cheek and the other scar across his eyebrow. Maybe it was his curly hair that made her want to pull on it while they made love. Whatever the reason she hated Taleeb for causing her discomfort, especially when she had a husband at home. Natalie would have preferred marrying another man she loved dearly, but instead settled for Harald whom she met at a night club.

Everything Natalie told Cierra made since, but she still wanted Taleeb back. She didn't know where to look for him. She didn't ask enough questions about his life because she didn't believe much of what he said. Cierra believed what her friends said about Taleeb and now her man was gone. She sobbed in her bedroom after Natalie left and thought of ways to find Taleeb.

Giant Steps was located on the northeast side of Indianapolis in a distressed Nubian neighborhood with countless cases of kids taken from their parents. Some of the cases were legitimate reasons for children to be taken away from their parents, however most of the kids that were taken by the system were without merit. The system didn't work in the best interest of the children most of the time. Parents who were falsely accused of child abuse by jealous friends or neighbors had to sell their souls to Lucifer to get their child back no matter how successful they were financially. On the other hand, parents that were poor drug addicts with no food in the house would get their children back without jumping through all the necessary hoops. Taleeb signed in and went through the usual procedures to see his daughter. As soon as Aaliyah saw Taleeb, she did her usual yelling, "Daddy, Daddy". She ran up to Taleeb and hugged him as if he was going off to war. Taleeb was glad her skin had cleared up and she looked clean. The social worker Carla told Taleeb that Aaliyah's caretaker Elizabeth cleaned up the house and got rid of the puppies. What Carla didn't tell Taleeb was that Elizabeth's boyfriend was living in the house which was prohibited because he was a convicted felon. CPS had rules of conduct that temporary foster parents had to uphold. CPS was more powerful than the police because they could take children from parents if they believed the children were in a dangerous situation. CPS made it clear to Elizabeth that if she didn't take better care of the children in her custody, they would take her biological children away from her because she would be considered an unfit parent.

Aaliyah looked better since CPS spoke to Elizabeth. Taleeb missed his child, and he couldn't believe how strong their bond had grown for one another. He would do anything to get her back, but he had to make sure he didn't end up in jail trying to make enough money to support them.

A week after Taleeb's visit with Aaliyah, he was reading an advertisement magazine at the barber shop, Taleeb highlighted the address of a cleaning franchise he was interested in buying. But the color on the marker seemed to fade. Taleeb asked Row, "Do you have your money marker handy?"

"It's in my office" Row disappeared to the back of the building. Two minutes later he reemerged with the marker and gave it to Taleeb.

"What do you need the marker for?"

"I want to see something."

"What, did somebody give you some counterfeit money?" chuckled Row.

Taleeb didn't respond because he was concentrating on what happened when he stroked the magazine with the money marker, the ink vanished. Finally! thought Taleeb, he finally found what type of paper to use for his fake money. He couldn't tell Row about his discovery because Taleeb wanted to be the only person in town to make counterfeit money that could pass the same test of real money.

The first thing Taleeb had to do before investing any more time in making fake money was to burn down the house. Taleeb bought two crack pipes, screens, and grain alcohol that drug users used to light the torch. The Arabs that owned the Marathon gas station near his duplex had everything drug users needed to get high with, including needles. They even sold single cigarettes called Lucys.

Taleeb drove to Geist dressed in all black and parked his truck a mile away from the house. It was one o'clock in the morning and he hoped his nosy neighbors were asleep. Taleeb had a backpack with grain alcohol, pipes, and tools to make it look like a break in. He walked through the wooded trail near his place. He was exposed when he got to the lake in the back of his house. If anyone saw him, he would have to abort the mission and act like he was just having a midnight stroll because he couldn't sleep. No one was in the area. Taleeb decided not to use the hammer or screwdriver to break into the house because of the noise. He had to be as quiet as possible because everybody had dogs. Taleeb wrapped his elbow with his jacket and tried to bust one of the side windows next to his front door, but it didn't work because the glass was too thick, therefore he wrapped the jacket around the hammer and busted out the window. The houses in his neighborhood were far apart and hopefully nobody would hear the noise. He reached his gloved hand in the window and unlocked the door. He didn't take too much furniture out of the house because he didn't want it to look staged. Taleeb put the two crack pipes on the couch and poured the grain alcohol all over the couch. He took a hanger and broke it off six inches long and rapped cotton around the tip of the hanger. Taleeb dipped the tip into the flammable liquid and before he lit it, he grabbed the 40-ounce beer bottle with gas in it. He poured gas on the couch and threw the rest on the walls. Lastly, he lit the tip of cotton and dropped it on the couch. The flames erupted with such force it shocked Taleeb. He quickly ran out of the house and walked briskly to his truck. After driving 40 miles from the scene of the crime, Taleeb poured the rest of the gas out of the bottle. He threw the empty bottle in the trash can at a gas station near his duplex. Taleeb was a nervous wreck when he got home; he worried about everything, did someone see him? Did anyone get hurt? His biggest concern was the police knocking on his door.

The sun came out too early, and Taleeb didn't get much sleep. His head hurt something awful. Taleeb had to go look at the house and see what kind of condition it was in. When he pulled up to the house, he was saddened by its appearance. The fire did a lot of damage which made Taleeb happy, but at the same time he was sad about destroying the home he had built from the ground up. He remembered all the upgrades he added to the house to make it fabulous and now he would remember the burnt image instead.

A firefighter was going through the ruble and Taleeb asked, "Do you know what caused the fire?"

The Fireman asked, "Is this your house?"

"Yes, it is."

The man said, "It appears that someone broke into the house and was doing drugs." The Fireman went on to say, "I believe the fire may have been an accident. This matter is under investigation."

Taleeb acted shocked, and said "What is the world coming to?" The man figured the question was rhetorical and didn't reply and kept on doing his job.

Before Taleeb drove away from the site, he noticed a GQ magazine wedged in the back seat in his truck. He didn't remember putting it there but when he pulled it from the seat 5 photos of Taleeb fell out of the pages. The photos were images of him entering and exiting his house the night he set fire to it. Taleeb looked like he seen a ghost. His hands began to tremble like a 90-year-old man. He wondered who was blackmailing him? Someone also wrote on one of the pages in the magazine with a marker, 'See You Soon'. Taleeb was frightened beyond words and began to suspect everybody he met in the last six months. Although panic gripped his thought process, he overpowered the dreadful feeling. There was a way out of this hell whole if the magazine paper was the solution to his counterfeit money problem. Taleeb went to the office supply store and bought a money marker to check for phony bills.

Anxiety and excitement caused Taleeb to smoke a cigarette. He was going to quit the nasty habit because he was smoking cigarettes even when he didn't want one. The smoke was hurting his chest and he didn't like the way the smell lingered on everything it touched. Taleeb frantically opened the magazine and took one of the markers and stroked a line in one of the pages and the black line turned brown and slowly faded away. A big smile appeared on Taleeb's face, but he had to solve two more problems with the counterfeit. The paper was glossy and slick, and the texture was wrong. But those were small problems that Taleeb knew he could solve if the blackmailer didn't ruin his life first.

Cierra wanted to know where Taleeb lived, she missed him so much, it hurt her deep inside. She was ashamed of herself for not giving Taleeb the chance to prove what he said about his past success. Cierra's last relationship before she met Taleeb was based on lies and

Cierra automatically thought Taleeb was the same.

Cierra had a friend named Kevin that worked in the human resources department at RSI. Kevin looked up Taleeb's address on his computer and gave it to Cierra. Kevin told Cierra, "I could get fired for giving out this information and please don't do anything stupid that would get both of us in trouble."

"I won't Kevin and thank you." She kissed him on the cheek and went to the Geist address and was impressed with the area. Cierra really felt like an idiot for not believing Taleeb and then her heart sank when she saw the house was badly burned. The uninhabitable structure had to be the address on the paper because she looked at the neighbors' addresses next to the burnt home. Cierra looked up to the sky with tears in her eyes and asked, "What have I done? Please don't let Taleeb be hurt God, please God." She began sobbing.

She tried hard to remember a conversation she had with Taleeb about a duplex he owned. She recalled the duplex being near the same block her cousin lived on. Cierra sped off to Vermont street. As she got closer to the poorly developed area, the homes descended into cracker jack boxes. She went from dream homes to a *Nightmare on Elm Street*.

Cierra's heart almost leaped out of her chest went she saw Taleeb's raggedy truck. She hopped out of the car and ran to the side of the duplex that the Truck was parked in front of. She rang the doorbell and knocked on the door rapidly.

Who in the hell is at the door? thought Taleeb, if it's not the police somebody's got an ass kicking coming. "Hold on damn it." Taleeb had to hide the bills he printed and other counterfeit paraphernalia. He looked out the window and was surprised to see Cierra. When Taleeb opened the door to let her in, Cierra ran up to Taleeb and hugged him hard. Cierra kept saying she was sorry. Cierra didn't care if Taleeb had another woman over or not. "I said some horrible things to you, and I didn't mean any of it. I made the biggest mistake of my life, and I am so sorry, please forgive me Taleeb."

Taleeb felt sorry for Cierra, she looked sad and miserable. He hugged her back, but the love he had for Cierra dissolved away like Alka-Seltzer in water. Nevertheless, he had sex with her anyway and Cierra left his house early in the morning feeling happy and relieved.

It was back to business for Taleeb, he had ordered the nonglossy magazine paper from Norfolk, a paper company based in Illinois. He couldn't find anyone who sold that type of paper locally. Taleeb had to buy the paper in bulk, and it came on a large roll weighing 200 pounds.

The paper was delivered to *United Parcel Service* (UPS) far away from Jasmine's job. It came on a Wednesday. Taleeb didn't think of getting any help putting the paper on his truck. He busted his ass lifting the awkward spool, but he got it on his vehicle. The spool had a hard cardboard core in the middle, and it was wrapped with professional looking cover paper so it wouldn't get damaged. Red letters tattered the product with the name Norfolk advertised everywhere on the covering. The spool was designed to be put on a paper machine in a warehouse setting, but Taleeb didn't have or need such machinery.

Taleeb had a top-of-the-line printer that he spent three weeks shopping for. It was exceedingly difficult to get the right printer because the green ink was not the exact color of money. Taleeb was a perfectionist, and everything had to be precise.

He took a box cutter from his pocket and cut the 36-inch-long cardboard covering and it slid off the paper with ease. The paper looked like it could get the job done but he had to use a paper cutter to cut the paper to fit his copier. Taleeb only needed enough paper to experiment with. Once the paper was cut, he used a heavy book to flatten the paper because it curled from being on the spool.

The next day, the paper was flatter, and Taleeb put a hundred-dollar bill on the printer's scanner, and he placed the paper on the printer scanner. The printer scanned the bill and printed it. The printed copy looked identical to the original bill. Taleeb took the money marker and put a line through the fake bill, and it turned light brown and almost faded away. The texture and weight of the paper were carbon copies of the real thing. "Bingo! "I'm rich! I'm rich!"

Taleeb learned how to print on the back of the bills to legitimize his efforts. He only printed $100 bills and only three bills could fit on each sheet of paper. It took Taleeb two weeks to print a million dollars. He spent hundreds of dollars on ink and paper to get the job done. Later that day, he checked his mailbox. One of the letters was from his insurance company. Taleeb rapidly opened the letter, and it was a check for $200,000. It was less than he expected, but the insurance company estimated how much it would cost to repair the house back to its original form. Everything was going great, but Taleeb had a nagging feeling that someone was watching and following him.

Doc had his men follow Taleeb. Doc knew he was wrong for blackmailing Taleeb, but he needed Taleeb to be his number one lead man to execute the operation. Doc had gotten a diagram of the sewer system downtown near Chase Bank. Doc was going to rob the bank, but the robbery was going to be a diversion because Doc's real intent was to kidnap the judge who tried the case involving his son.

Jasmine lost her supervisor job with UPS because she stopped going to work. Jasmine's life was spiraling out of control. The crux of the problem was that she wouldn't take her medications. Jasmine didn't like the way the meds made her feel and that's why she left Mia at her mother's house and none of Jasmine's family members heard from her again.

Every month when Jasmine got her restitution check from the court, she was reminded about how she destroyed Taleeb's life. She had been following him every day since he got out of jail. Jasmine believed in some strange way that she was responsible for Taleeb's house burning down. She felt bad for Taleeb until she found out he was screwing another woman.

Jasmine thought, "I'll be damn, that ho is leaving his broke down duplex early in the morning. Jasmine wanted to hit the hussy with her car, but now was not the time. Jasmine tried diligently to talk to Taleeb, but he hated her. And if she couldn't have him, nobody would. Jasmine wanted Taleeb back in jail for the rest of his life and she planned to carry out just that!

CPS told Taleeb he could get Aaliyah back in two months, if he could prove he was financially stable and had gainful employment. Taleeb had to get a job but first he wanted to increase his finances. Taleeb had six dope boys interested in buying the counterfeit money he made, and he put the $200,000 insurance check in his bank account.

Taleeb wanted to celebrate his good fortunes, but he didn't have a significant other to rejoice with. He saw a few cute women in the parking lot of a church called the North Star. Taleeb observed the activities from his window. The church was across the street from where he lived. Taleeb thought if he could get a religious lady, she wouldn't be so crazy. Would I be going to church for all the wrong reasons, he thought? Nevertheless, on a Sunday morning Taleeb went to church. The parking lot was full as he strode across the street in his new suit. As he entered the building, Taleeb realized that he shouldn't date anyone for a while because his life was complicated.

The women ushers looked at him seductively as he walked near them, Taleeb sat in the back pew and noticed the man sitting in front of him was working on a project on his computer. Every time an usher walked past the man, he tried to hide what he was doing because being on his computer was inappropriate in church.

After the church service was over, Taleeb approached the man and introduced himself. The man said his name was Fred.

Taleeb said, "Fred you look like you were working on something mighty important."

Fred said he was selling his business. He had made brochures and accounting documents for anyone who was interested in the restaurant business. The documents contained figures pertaining to the investment in the company, analysis of customer flow and profit and losses. "I apologized for conducting business in church, but I'm always busy. I must utilize my time wherever I can to get things done." Fred began explaining to Taleeb all the stuff he oversaw at church. "I am the youth minister, the choir director, and the marriage counselor."

As the two men exited the building talking, Taleeb asked Fred, "Can I have a look at the brochure?"

"Yes of course." Fred handed Taleeb various brochures, pamphlets, and other documents. Taleeb was impressed with the professionalism that went into the documents. One of the brochures had a picture of the inside and outside of the restaurant called the *Fishhook*, it was located at 46th and Arlington. The place was about 1400 square feet. It was a fine-looking restaurant with four big screen TVs in each corner of the facility. The ambience was consistent with the name of the place. It had a boat steering wheel on the front of the wall and various sea creatures. Taleeb was skeptical about owning a restaurant because he had no experience with the food industry, and he knew it would be arduous work. However, there was a positive aspect that outweighed the downside. He could launder his ill-gotten funds through the business and CPS would be satisfied with his employment.

"I'm interested in the restaurant," said Taleeb.

"That's good news. Can you meet me at *Stacker Barrel* for breakfast this weekend?"

"Yes, I can do that, Fred"

"When we go over the details and if you're still interested, I will introduce you to the staff. They will train you on how to operate the business." Fred gave Taleeb the time and date to meet him.

Taleeb said, "I'll see you Saturday morning" and they parted ways.

Cierra was on her way to work feeling sad because Taleeb didn't act as if he loved her anymore. She wasn't sure if Taleeb even liked her. They used to talk to each other, laugh and play board games. He didn't call her anymore and when he spoke to her, she had to initiate the conversation. Tears found their way in the wells of her eyes and slid down her cheeks glistening as they went their way. Cierra was waiting for the day when Taleeb would tell her, it's not you, it's me and move on.

Taleeb went to his barber, Row, to get his hair trimmed and to discuss when he was going to sell the money to Row's connections. Row was amazed with Taleeb's counterfeit money and wanted to know how Taleeb made it. Taleeb told Row everything about the money except the main ingredient, the paper. Row was upset with Taleeb because Row knew Taleeb was leaving something out of the details. Row tried everything he could to get the money right but to no avail. He believed that Taleeb should be more forthcoming since he gave Taleeb the idea. Row's brothers wanted to buy the money, but they didn't want Taleeb to sell it to anyone else. Row always talked about his brothers in a respectful way, but Taleeb never met them before. Row arranged a meeting with his brothers and Taleeb at the barbershop. Row said he was going to close his shop on the day of the meeting. The two men agreed on the date. Taleeb left Row's shop thinking; I can sell my money to whoever the hell I want to sell it to.

Saturday morning rolled around so fast that it caught Taleeb off guard. He had to hurry and get ready. Taleeb grabbed his laptop computer, notebook paper, leather folder and put the contents in his briefcase and dashed out the door. Taleeb hated to be late for anything, so he drove like a race car driver to get to *Stacker Barrel* on time. He got there 10 minutes early and was surprised to see Fred already there. Fred was sitting up front by the fireplace and waved Taleeb over to his table. Taleeb was hungry and the *Stacker Barrel* was one of his favorite food joints. Fred and Taleeb shook hands and ordered their food. Taleeb got his favorite, the Auntie Herschel Special. It came with fried catfish, scrambled eggs, grits, a biscuit, and a potato casserole. Fred didn't eat much, he got two eggs over easy, bacon and toast. They both ordered coffee.

"How's things been going?" asked Fred.

"It's been good, what about yourself?"

"It's been ok. A man once told me Okay was good," said Taleeb.

Fred laughed showing his perfect white false teeth. Fred was cleanly shaven and had no hair on his head. He wore thin gold rimmed round glasses. He was a quiet speaking man and sounded highly intelligent. Fred was about 6 foot tall and thinly built. The lights in the place beamed off Fred's head making his bald head glow. Fred was dressed in a Gucci jogging suit and tennis shoes.

Fred laid out all the documents pertaining to the business on the table. Fred showed Taleeb the photo of the restaurant and narrated when he opened it. Fred explained where he got the authentic artifacts hanging on the walls of the establishment. Fred told Taleeb to get a bank account in the same strip mall where the restaurant was located because it would be easier to make frequent deposits and get change and other money transactions with the bank being in the proximity. Fred was talking to Taleeb as if he already purchased the restaurant.

After Fred finished telling Taleeb about the business, the food came, and they began eating their meals.

Taleeb asked, "How much?"

Fred said $40,000. Taleeb thought the price was too high, but he knew he would make the money back dealing with Row and his brother's. "

Why are you selling the restaurant if it was turning a decent profit."

Fred said, "I just got my bounty hunter's license and with the rest of my ventures taking up all my time, I'm too busy to keep up with it anymore."

That was enough info for Taleeb, and he agreed to buy the business. Fred said, "I'll introduce you to the manager and she will show you how to work the cash register and how to prep the food."

"You must keep a $1000 in change in the safe and I'll show you where it is located. I'll leave you a list of venders I deal with and their phone numbers." Fred gave Taleeb a ton of information and they talked for hours. Fred noticed that women were staring at Taleeb. Fred thought Taleeb was a nice-looking man but there was something about Taleeb that frightened him. Taleeb reminded Fred of a UFC fighter. Fred made a note to himself, not to leave his gun in the car the next time they met. Both men left *Stacker Barrel* in good spirits.

Taleeb couldn't wait to get home to print another million dollars. As soon as he walked in the door, Taleeb changed the ink cartridges before it got low because the green would start getting too light. He always put the faded bills in the shredder. Taleeb often burned the shredded bills in a barrel in the back yard.

Paranoia got the best of Taleeb and he put steel bars on his windows and added decorative steel storm doors to the front and back doors. He installed multiple locks and latches on them for extra support. Taleeb always kept his basement and bedroom locked when he wasn't home. Moreover, he put an ADT alarm system in the house. Taleeb installed cameras on the front porch and back entry.

Before Taleeb left the house, he separated the million dollars and put the bills in five different trash bags. Taleeb didn't want all the money in one bag in case something went wrong. Taleeb wanted to make sure everybody came out a winner when the deal was done. Taleeb believed things would work out because he wasn't greedy, the money wasn't real, and he could always print more.

When Taleeb got to Rows shop, he noticed three vehicles parked in front - Row's Cadillac, a Hummer, and a Rolls Royce. Taleeb was ashamed to park his truck near the vehicles. Taleeb took one of the bags with him and left the rest under the front and back seats. He called Row to let him know he was there before he walked up to the glass door.

Row came to the door and asked, "What's up?"

Taleeb said, "You," and Row escorted Taleeb to his large office in the back of the shop. Row didn't look like his brothers. Row was 5 "9" with long locks and at the top of his head, he was going bald. Row was a smooth gentle being with camel skin. His brothers looked like they ate their young and Taleeb didn't trust them. Row introduced them by their nicknames, one brother's name was Dog and the other one's name was Pouchie. Row introduced Taleeb as a good friend, and they all bumped fists and sat down.

Taleeb got straight to the point and pulled out a thousand dollars in one-hundred-dollar bills and spread it across the coffee table in front of them. One thing they didn't know was Taleeb put three real hundred dollars in with the bills. Row's brothers didn't want to marvel over the money because they figured Taleeb would go up on the price if they showed excitement. Therefore, they all agreed the money was just ok but needed work. Taleeb took the money marker and put a line across the money, and it disappeared. The men look unimpressed with Taleeb's theatrics. They were bored and on the verge of putting Taleeb out of the shop for wasting their time. Dog was about 5 "11" and a well-dressed man with a tattoo of a crown on his neck. His hair was cut short with waves. Dog had muscular build like he had been to prison. Men in prison that lifted weights looked more sculptured than men that weren't locked up. The average person couldn't tell but anyone that's been to jail knew the difference.

Dog said the money looked fake. The older brother Pouchie chimed in and said the money didn't feel right. Row was on his brothers' side and said, I tried to tell Taleeb about that. Taleeb smiled at them and said, "Some of the $100 bills are real." Row was surprised along with his brothers. They began holding the money up to the light and flipping it on its back, they rubbed and folded the money. Taleeb knew they were lying about the appearance of fake money because they were taking too long to find the real money. All three men worked together as a team to find the real money from the fake. They disagreed with each other about which bills were real. Finally, Row got them to agree on four hundred-dollar bills. Taleeb had the real money marked because he could barely tell the real money from the fake money. To Taleeb, the fake money looked more authentic than the real money.

Taleeb said, "You're right, Row, except for this fourth bill." They seemed upset with Taleeb. Pouchie had a short Afro and wore a lot of gold jewelry. Taleeb thought it was ironic that his grandmother's dog was named Pouchie. Pouchie was a crazy Doberman Pincher that was blind because it stayed in the basement with no lights for years. Taleeb only saw the dog once, but he heard the dog bark 24/7. The dog ran around the basement like it was exercising. Taleeb couldn't believe that the tall slender man looked exactly like his grandmother's dog. He was a nice looking fellow with a menacing disposition. He had an athletic build with a touch of prison aura around him. Pouchie said, "Man, you act like you are the one that started this shit. My brother put you on to this money-making business. Now you want to charge a brotha, we should just take the money."

Row said, "Hold up, nobody is taking shit around here." Row's brothers must have respected him because they calmed down.

Row said, "Everybody sit y'all's ass down!" Taleeb couldn't believe Row could get that angry. He must have misread Row's soft smooth demeanor, but his brothers knew something Taleeb didn't because they obeyed without protest.

Row said, "Taleeb what do you want for the money?" Taleeb was afraid because it was three against one. Taleeb thought that all the prayers in the world couldn't save him from these jokers kicking his ass. Taleeb was going to charge them a $100,000 for a million but that price dropped dramatically considering his situation. Taleeb knew the only one he had to convince was Row. Taleeb believed Row controlled these thugs which was surprising because they were older, and they bought Row into the drug game.

Taleeb listened to his instincts and said, "Row, I'm hurting man, I'm in debt up to my ears. You know how it is when you first get out of jail. I lost everything; you see what I'm driving Row."

Row smiled, shaking his head.

"I need your help Row; I'm trying to get my daughter back from CPS, but they said I have to have a job and I have to move because my duplex only has one bedroom. They said my daughter must have her own bedroom."

Row had three daughters around the same age by different

women, but Row was a good father to them. The two men talked about their children every time Taleeb got his haircut. Lastly, Taleeb said, "I'm trying to buy a business that cost $40,000 and that's my ticket out of this mess. I'll work with you guys in terms of selling this counterfeit after this deal. I'll make it up to you guys."

Before Taleeb continued, Row put his finger up to his own lips. And Taleeb quit talking. Row made the decision for his brothers. He told Taleeb to get the rest of the money and Taleeb went out to his truck shaking uncontrollably. Taleeb tried to calm down, but he couldn't. He didn't have a gun, but he was going to buy one after this deal. After Taleeb bought the bags in, Row and his brothers counted and examined the bills. They could see Taleeb shaking, and they realized that Taleeb was smarter than he looked. Rows brothers wanted break into his house and kill Taleeb, but Row told them, not yet. Row gave Taleeb the $40 grand in a bag and Taleeb thanked him. Row said, "we will talk," and Taleeb left.

Taleeb didn't want to count the money or check it in front of Row. He waited until he got home to count and check the money. Taleeb had to make sure no one was following him home. He was going to get out of the counterfeit business and sell it to Row because he felt death was near. Taleeb hoped the restaurant would pan out; therefore, he would make a strong effort to be a successful business owner. The restaurant was honest work, and he didn't have to keep looking over his shoulder for danger.

Meanwhile, Jasmine followed Cierra to work one day after Cierra left from visiting Taleeb. Jasmine waited in the parking lot by Cierra's car until she got off from work. Then Jasmine followed Cierra home. Jasmine only weighed 110 pounds and her long hair was thinning. Her face sank inward, and she quit bathing. She hadn't drunk any water for days, that's why she was able to wait in the car for eight hours without urinating. Jasmine had hair fibers from a brush Taleeb used to style his hair. She was going to leave a few fibers by Cierra's body when she killed her. Jasmine didn't want to shoot Cierra. She wanted to feel the knife entering Cierra's body multiple times. Jasmine wanted to see the look in Cierra's eyes when she stabbed her in the chest. She wanted to hear Cierra plead and beg for her life while she jabbed her to death with the knife.

The doorbell rang and Taleeb thought it was Cierra popping up over his house again without calling. Taleeb believed that Cierra was trying to catch him cheating because he asked her on numerous occasions to call him before she came over, but she never followed those instructions. Taleeb looked at the camera monitor by the side of the door and it was Doc with two other dudes he didn't know. Taleeb was pissed, why in the hell are people just coming over my house unannounced. Taleeb kept his place immaculate, and he made sure nobody knew what he was doing, that's why he didn't leave mail and any other stuff laying around the house. Taleeb unlocked the locks and latch and opened the door. He forgot to turn the alarm off, and it started peeping. Taleeb touched the keypad with his code, and it stopped. Doc could tell Taleeb was angry by lines that danced on his forehead. Doc started talking fast because Taleeb had a reputation of being a brawler.

Doc said, "Hey man I'm sorry for the intrusion but I got excited about my plan, and I wanted to share it with you."

Taleeb butted into Doc's conversation and said, "Who in the hell are these thugs?"

"Oh! my bad, this is my man G, and this is LT."

Taleeb thought this can't be happening, now I'm meeting acronyms. They said what's up and wanted to bump fist, but Taleeb just stared at them.

"Why did you bring them to my house Doc?"

G started moving toward Taleeb, "Take one more step and I'm going to crack your skull wide open."

LT was getting ready to pull out his gun and Doc put his hand on LT's arm and said, "Everybody calm down."

Doc continued, "Hey man, these guys are my bodyguards, I'm into a lot of illegal activities, they go wherever I go."

Taleeb thought Doc was institutionalized because in jail he always had a crew of guys hanging around him. The first time Taleeb ever saw Doc by himself was when they went walking at Fort Harrison. Taleeb thought Doc needed constant comradery.

Doc told LT to get the floor plans, diagrams and his pointer stick out of his SUV. Taleeb was puzzled and figured this thing is going to be complicated. Nevertheless, Taleeb was curious and interested. LT came back with so much stuff he had to kick on the door because his hands were full. G went to the door to help him bring the items in. Taleeb told them they could use the kitchen table and coffee table if they needed to. They began setting up the boards, diagrams and placing stick men at distinct locations on the displays. They used paper cars and buses that were stuck on the board and diagrams. Taleeb realized that they had been practicing this orientation because it was organized, and they moved in unison knowing where all the pieces went.

Taleeb started getting nervous because there was a picture of a bank and an engineered layout of tubes going everywhere. But ten tubes were highlighted in blue leading to the bank underground and there were a few tubes highlighted in orange. Taleeb guessed they were getaway tubes. The getaway tubes lead to high traffic areas and the top of the tube had lids. Taleeb started sweating, he didn't want to rob a bank.

Taleeb asked "Is it hot in here?" Everybody said, "No." Oh my God! Not only are these idiots going to rob a bank. They're going to rob a gun store and a pawn shop too. Why the heck was Doc showing me this garbage? Doc didn't add the kidnapping to the portfolio because he wouldn't be able to convince Taleeb to help him if he knew of that detail.

The illustration was extremely detailed and graphic. It looked like so much was going on that it got confusing. Doc stood up with his pointer and began explaining it all to Taleeb. Doc also explained why the illustrations looked confusing. He was creating a diversion in the chaos. Doc told Taleeb he had worked on the project for 20 years and Taleeb believed him.

After Doc finished his presentation, Taleeb stood up and said, "Doc I must admit that this scheme looks like it can work. I'm truly impressed but I can't get involved with something like this. I'm trying to get my child back and you know this man, so if you guys don't mind, I have to take care of some business. I'm sorry, Doc, but I wish you the best and if anyone could pull it off it's you."

Doc ordered his men to get all the stuff and take it to the SUV. Doc smiled at Taleeb, dropped an envelope on the floor, and left. Taleeb was scared to pick the envelope up, but he did and opened it. There were pictures of Taleeb in separate locations by his house the night it burned down.

Taleeb got emotional because he would have died for Doc. He couldn't trust anyone anymore. He was going to break ties with everybody including Cierra and become a loner. Taleeb felt pressure closing in on him. His goal was to get Aaliyah back, make as much money as possible and get the hell out of Indianapolis within a year or sooner.

COUNTERFEIT

It was his first day at work and Taleeb didn't know what to expect but he knew how to dress down. He wore old jeans, a shirt and gym shoes. Taleeb came ready to work hard. Fred had on another designer sweat suit with a gun sticking out of the holster. Fred didn't look like he was going to do anything strenuous.

"Hey Fred," Taleeb put a check for $40 grand on the counter in front of him. After they signed the paperwork, Fred asked, "Are you ready for this?"

"Yes sir." Fred put the check in his wallet and showed Taleeb to the kitchen and introduced him to the staff. "Hey everybody this is the new owner, Taleeb Anderson."

"Hey Taleeb," echoed the employees. There was a girl named Denise that went by the name Dee. She was the supervisor that worked the cash register and helped in back when she wasn't busy. Dee was a pretty 23-year-old who told Taleeb that she also worked at Long John Silvers and was the supervisor there. Mark was a tall and heavyset person around 27 years old. He was a stupid looking guy who wanted to be called Big Daddy, but nobody called him that. And there was Kathie that went by the name Cat. She was a plain looking woman in her 50's but didn't want to tell her age.

Fred showed Taleeb the safe and the $1,000 change that was kept in a money pouch with a zipper. Taleeb tried to compensate Fred for the money he left in the pouch, but Fred said don't worry about it. Fred told Dee to train Taleeb and then he left. People were waiting at the door to get in. The restaurant opened at 11:00 a.m. and the Fishhook didn't serve breakfast. The restaurant specialized in seafood, but they sold chicken as well because the people in the Hood kept asking Fred to sell it.

The strip mall was next to Arthington High School and the teachers and staff members began ordering their food by phone. Before they opened the restaurant, it was already busy placing orders. Dee finally let the customers in and Taleeb was shocked by how many people came into the Fishhook. Taleeb didn't know if he was happy the business was doing well because he worked harder than he ever worked in his life. The restaurant closed at 7:30 p.m. on weekdays and 10:30 p.m. on Fridays and Saturdays. It was closed on Sundays.

When Taleeb got off from work, he rushed home and took a hot bath. While he was soaking in the tub, the doorbell rang. Taleeb was tired and in a bad mood. Taleeb looked on the monitor and saw two white men in suits at the door, He automatically knew they were detectives. Why were the police at his door? The money was well hidden in a concrete brick block in the wall behind the furnace in the basement. Why are they coming over this late at night? Taleeb believed they were at his door because he had burned down his house. He was nervous but he had to let them in because they probably knew he was home. Taleeb put on his pants and shirt. He went to the door and asked, "Who is it?" Only one man answered and said, "Detectives Martinez and Malone." Taleeb opened the door and asked, "How may I help you? Martinez asked to come in and Taleeb waved them in like an usher. Taleeb told them they could have a seat, but they walked around the house like they owned it. "My, my, my," said Malone a shifty eyed blonde guy with a military haircut. "What have we here? All these locks and bolts, who are you trying to keep out, a Buffalo?"

Taleeb wanted to say your mama but instead he said, "What's

this all about?" Martinez was a thick necked stubby fellow who combed the back of his hair forward to hide his bold spot, asked,

"Do you know a Cierra Humphrey?"

Taleeb's heart fluctuated, "Yes, I do, what's going on?"

It was Malone's turn to speak, they were a tag team.

"She was murdered four days ago at her house." Taleeb shed tears instantly and Martinez asked, "Where were you on October 3rd?"

Taleeb asked, "What happened? Why would someone do that?"

Malone had a menacing grin on his face and said, "Someone stabbed her multiple times in a rage, and she bled to death. Again Mr. Good Looking, where was your black ass at Saturday night," asked Malone.

Taleeb told them everything he did that day and gave Martinez a copy of the VCR that showed Taleeb coming and going to and from his house for the month of October. Malone said to his partner "Let's go."

As they were leaving, Malone turned back and said, "If there is one thing out of place with your story, we are going to come back and skin your black ass alive. Have a good night."

"Why are you doing this to me, Taleeb cried out to the empty space in his room?" Taleeb had bad days in the past, but this was a nightmarish year. Taleeb made a vow to the empty space; "I will rise above this because I am a survivor and a conqueror." The anger swelled up in his soul and Taleeb said, "This too shall pass. I am a winner, this will not defeat me." He went to sleep uttering a two-hour mantra, "I am a warrior that can't be defeated. These events are dust in the wind."

Taleeb woke up with tears in his eyes. He dreamed of something, but he couldn't remember what it was about. He went to the liquor store early in the morning and got a six pack of beer and a half pint of cognac. He began drinking alcohol and smoked a joint on his way to work. He worked for two hours and left. Taleeb enjoyed the food at his restaurant and ate there twice a day. He learned everything about the business. The restaurant didn't bring in much cash until the weekend, Nevertheless, at the end of the week, he broke even. After Taleeb paid all the bills and workers, he barely had enough to pay himself.

Something had to give, Taleeb needed to get more money out of the restaurant. Therefore, he decided to open on Sundays. All meals came with sodas and two pieces of bread. He had to stock those items too often. He made two changes to the menu. Taleeb gave customer's one piece of bread instead of two and he stopped giving out free sodas with every meal.

Taleeb always considered himself a solutionist and not a complainer until Row pulled up to the restaurants' front door and parked. Taleeb thought, "I'm only here two hours a day and out of two hours I have to see this punk." Taleeb liked Row and considered him a friend but all that changed when he met Rows brothers. Suddenly, Row was dangerous to Taleeb.

Row walked in and said, "Look at our new restaurant. What's up Taleeb. Nice place we got here; I like it."

Taleeb said, "Row, you got to move your car; you are blocking the entrance."

"I'm not going to be here long. Sit with me, we need to talk."

Taleeb sat at the table with Row. Dee came over to the table,

"May I take your order sir." Before Taleeb could say no, Row asked Dee, "What should I get?" Dee was smiling and batting her eyes at Row. "I like the Jumbo Shrimp Basket. It comes with hush puppies, fries and coleslaw."

"Okay baby, I'll take that with a Pepsi."

"We don't have Pepsi, would a Coke be ok?"

"Yes ma'am." Dee walked away, switching her butt as she walked back to the kitchen. Row turned to see if Dee had a nice butt and was satisfied with the results.

Row asked Taleeb, "Are you hitting that?"

"Nope."

"I think I might have to tap that ass," said Row.

Taleeb didn't believe Row was interested in Dee because Row had a fiancée whom he loved and an ex-wife that had three kids with him. The ex-wanted Row back and so did three other women. Row couldn't get any more women in his lineup if he tried.

Row never moved his car. Dee brought out the food and bumped Row with her hip and bounced away. Taleeb never saw Dee act like that. She was always professional. Row said, "Man I promise this is the best shrimp I ever tasted."

Taleeb was agitated and asked, "What's going on Row?" Row seemed to be enjoying his meal. He didn't say anything else until he was finished.

"Taleeb you really need to relax, you seem uptight man. But anyway, I need two million ASAP. You told me you were going to make it up to my brothers and I because you needed the money for our restaurant."

Row acted like he was part owner of the restaurant, but Taleeb mellowed out because the alcohol was kicking in. Taleeb said, "Row I'm going to give you the deal of a lifetime. I'm going to give you the two million dollars and show you how I make it. I'm even giving you the printer and everything else you need for $100,000."

Row said, "Man you're robbing me."

Taleeb played into Rows big ego and said, "Row that's nothing to you, you are probably riding around with more than that in your car. Row, you will get that back in a month. I know you're going to Chi - Town to exchange the money for drugs."

The streets talked, thought Row, because he didn't remember mentioning Chicago to Taleeb. Row figured what the hell, he was going to get the restaurant too eventually.

Row said, "Okay let's go."

"Where?"

"To my car to give you the money." Row left Dee a fifty-dollar tip and Taleeb prayed it wasn't counterfeit. Taleeb told Dee he would be back, and she smiled like she hit the lottery. Row told Taleeb to bring a trash bag. Row opened his trunk with four briefcases inside it. Row counted out the money and put it in the bag and gave it to Taleeb. Taleeb could not believe Row was doing this in the front of the restaurant with large glass windows surrounding it. People in that area would kill someone for $20. The entire neighborhood would get riddled with bullets for a $100,000. Row was oblivious to what he was doing but Taleeb was horrified. Taleeb took the bag from Row and put it on the front seat of his truck and drove the correct speed limit all the way home. Taleeb didn't want to get pulled over by the cops for any reason. When Taleeb got home, he analyzed the money to make sure it was legit and then put it in his hiding place.

Taleeb began putting two thousand dollars in his bank account every day. Soon after, he purchased a used Ford Explorer and put a security deposit down on an upscale two-bedroom condo with a bonus room in Fisher's Indiana. It had two full bathrooms and a 2-car garage. Taleeb believed he had to impress the people at CPS to get his daughter and he wanted to look successful. He bought new furniture for every room in the condo, and it was to be delivered on his move in date.

Taleeb filled out an address change form at the post office to have his mail sent to a Post Office mailbox address. He bought it because he didn't want anybody to know about his new place. Taleeb also made the address change to the duplex because he would only be there to print and hide money. He didn't want the mail at the duplex to overflow. Taleeb didn't take anything out of the house when he moved, and he left his old truck in the backyard. He installed lights that automatically came on in the inside and outside of the house. The lights on the inside came on at 8:30 p.m. and the lights on outside came on at 9:30 p.m.

It was a beautiful day outside, but Taleeb hadn't noticed. He had arrived at *Giant Steps* to see his daughter, but his mind was somewhere else. He didn't see his friend that worked there and that was a good thing because he wasn't in the mood to talk to her. When Aaliyah saw Taleeb, she said "Hey Daddy," ran up to him and they hugged. Afterwards, they sat down and talked for an hour. Taleeb told Aaliyah about the restaurant and the new condo. The mediator was in the room and wrote down everything that was said. Aaliyah was a very loquacious girl and took over the conversation. She talked excessively and unfortunately Taleeb was not listening because he had too much on his mind. "Who would want to kill Cierra?" he thought. Aaliyah tried to talk about all her issues in an hour. After their visit was over, they both said, "I love you" and Taleeb continued his quest to get his child back.

His next destination was the Child Custody Department.

Taleeb got there in 15 minutes. He waited two hours to see his caseworker. Finally, Algina called his name, and he raised his hand like he did during attendance in third grade and said, "Here." Apparently, she didn't have an office because Algina came over to the bench where Taleeb was sitting. She asked, "What do you have for me, Mr. Anderson?" with her head in the air like she owned the world. Taleeb stood up and she became a dwarf looking up at him. "Hello, Miss Stuart. Here is the paperwork to my restaurant with the profit and loss statement. And this is the lease to my condominium." She took the paperwork and looked through it. She said, "This should do it for you, Mr. Anderson, we will be talking to you in two weeks. It would have been sooner but I'm going on a vacation. Taleeb didn't want to ask her where she was going because he didn't care. He said, "Thank you for your time," and left.

Everything was in motion for getting his life in order and the phone rang. Damn! It was Doc.

Taleeb asked, "What's up?", in a dry and cold voice which became his usual greeting with Doc.

"Hey man I'm sorry about the confrontation we had at the house, but I really need to talk to you, but not over the phone."

"Meet me at the Fishhook restaurant off 46th and Arlington at 5:00 p.m.," said Taleeb. "Okay I'll be there." Taleeb didn't trust Doc, that's why he decided to conduct business with him around a lot of people.

Taleeb was sitting at his favorite table away from the windows facing the front door. The table was near the exit door. Taleeb liked the exit door because it was the third door to his business. The door opened into a hallway that allowed him access to another way out near the front of the building. People mistakenly thought the door belonged to another business. Doc came in the restaurant without his muscle men, but Taleeb knew they were in Doc's car, but he couldn't see them because of the tinted windows. Doc always wore a suit, and this time was no different. Dee came over to Taleeb's table. Dee looked at Taleeb and asked, "May I take your order baby; I mean boss," she began to giggle. Taleeb ordered Baked Salmon and Greens. Dee turned to Doc and asked, "What will you be having sir?"

"I'll try the Whiting and Fries." Both orders came with Coleslaw.

Dee used to like men that looked like Tony, the heavy-set cook. Dee was chubby in high school, but it slowly went away as she got older. Nevertheless, Dee felt she was still on the heavy side. Her high school sweetheart was overweight, and they were together for eight years and she broke up with him because he loved the streets more than her. She had a six-year-old son with him, and her mama helped her raise her son. Dee didn't like men that looked like Taleeb because they would probably cheat on her, and she was not having it. Dee's mom sat her down and told her to get with a man that had his stuff together, leave those broke men alone. Get someone that can help you.

Taleeb was not paying any attention to Dee even though she wore a short dress that clung to her round buttocks and showed off her thick athletic thighs. Doc said, "Your waitress got it going on, she seems to like you." Taleeb didn't know what had gotten into Dee lately. He thought of her as a sweet innocent shy girl.

Taleeb said, "No I don't think so, she is just a very nice person."

Doc let Taleeb live in his fantasy world and said, "Taleeb all I need you to do is pick up the money and drop it off at different locations away from the robberies. I know I messed up our relationship, but I trust you Taleeb, you're not a snitch and that is a rarity these days. I want the best for you man. The money can help you and your daughter have a new life. Taleeb, if you do this, I'll give you $150,000 now and 20 percent of the loot when we finish the job."

"Can I think on this some more Doc?"

"Yeah, I'll give you three days."

Dee came with their orders and overheard $150,000. Dee also saw the money transaction with Taleeb and the man that gave her the $50.00 tip. She didn't know what Taleeb was involved in but her attraction for him bloomed like a wildflower. She was beginning to think Taleeb was a drug dealer on the side and she wasn't going to get with a drug dealer. But the way Taleeb ignored her subconsciously turned her on. She made decent money in tips on the weekdays and was able to save money. She knew it had to be the dress because the men were flirting with her all day. Everybody was looking at her except the main person she wore the dress for. She needed to get some more advice from her mother to get Taleeb's attention. She quit her second job at Long John Silver because Dee was making more money in tips on the weekend than her gross weekly at Long John's.

Doc really wanted to make things right with Taleeb and he didn't care about the money as much as he did about the mission. The money he was going to give Taleeb was for forgiveness and to get Taleeb on board. Taleeb walked Doc to his car and sure enough his two thugs were in the front seat. Doc got in the back seat and rolled down the window and handed Taleeb two long tubular containers with floor plans inside. Taleeb took the items and put them in his SUV. Dee saw the exchange take place in the window. She said to herself, "Taleeb may not be a drug dealer, but he was definitely a hustler."

Cat came out of the kitchen and started cleaning the tables and saw Dee looking out the window, Cat went over to the window and Taleeb put something in his truck. Cat said, "Girl you look so pretty in that outfit, where did you get them shoes? That dress is beautiful. Why are you coming to work in that outfit girl?"

"Cat, these are old clothes I had in the closet."

Cat gave Dee a big smile and asked her, "Do you like Taleeb?" Dee looked down at the floor not knowing if she should tell the truth or not. Cat was tickled and couldn't believe Dee was acting like she was a love-struck child. Dee didn't have to answer the question because the long pause was the answer.

Dee snapped out of it and said, "I don't do pretty boys, Cat," and walked away embarrassed. Cat couldn't keep the smile off her face and thought it was hilarious the way Dee avoided eye contact with her.

Taleeb came back in the restaurant and told Dee, "When you close the store, have Tony walk you to the car after you lock up. I'm leaving, I'll see you tomorrow, have a great day."

Dee said "Okay." She was happy he told her to have Tony walk her to her car. Taleeb cares about me, thought Dee. She asked, "Why don't you walk me to my car?", just loud enough for Taleeb to hear as he left.

After they closed the restaurant, Dee went over her mother's house and said, "Mama the dress got me a lot of tip money, but Taleeb didn't even notice me." Dee's son ran over to Dee, and she picked him up and kissed him all over his face, and he loved it. She put him down and he ran off to play with his toys.

"What am I to going to do mama?"

"Take it slow Dee, Timbuktu wasn't built in a day." This was something new to April because she never had to coach Dee on how to get a man.

"Mama, Taleeb thinks of me as a child."

"You do look like a teenager baby."

"Mama, you're not helping me."

"Okay, let me meet this man and I'll tell you what to do." Dee told her mom to be ready tomorrow. She was going to find out when Taleeb was coming to work. As soon as Taleeb walked in the door, Dee was going to call her mom and tell her he's here and hang up. April only lived 8 minutes away.

"I really like Taleeb mom because he doesn't flirt with any of the women that come in the place."

"Maybe he's gay, said April."

"Wow!" Dee never thought about that.

One of the talking head detectives called Taleeb and told him to come in for questioning at 9:30 a.m. Taleeb wasn't too worried about going there because they would have arrested him already if they thought he killed Cierra. Taleeb still had to drink a half pint of Hennessy to calm his nerves before he went in and then he took a piece of peppermint candy to mask the smell on his breath.

Taleeb went to the officer's desk by the front door and told him, "I am here to see M&M, the Siamese twins."

Before the officer could pick up the phone Malone snuck up behind Taleeb and patted him on the shoulder and it scared Taleeb. Taleeb's reflexes made him raise his arm out into a punching posture. He was able to stop the punch from connecting to Malone's jaw.

"Slow down big fella before I have that arm amputated," said Malone.

"Let's go, Rambo." Taleeb followed Malone into the interrogation room. Taleeb wasn't surprised to see Martinez siting at a table. He said, "Your alibi checked out. Lucky for you because I was going to make a chair out of your skin."

Malone laughed and said, "How long did you know Cierra? When and where did you meet?" They were the same questions they had already asked him at his house. "Did she have any enemies that you know of?"

Suddenly Taleeb instantly thought about Jasmine. "Taleeb said, "There is a possibility that the girl who filed a battery case on me could be a suspect. Her name is Jasmine, and she is crazy enough to do something like that. I saw her smack her daughter hard for no reason and her daughter didn't even cry. When Jasmine came over my house the day, I was arrested. She was naked in the dead of winter. She only had a coat on."

"And you had a problem with that?" laughed Malone.

"No, it wasn't that, but after we had sex, she got aggressive and started fighting me saying I saw what they did, and you didn't help me. I had to smack her to get her to snap out of it, and she grabbed a blanket and ran out the door."

"Why are you telling us this Taleeb?"

"Because she could have followed me over Cierra's house. I believe she was capable of doing something like that in my opinion."

The talking heads looked at each other and said, "Okay, you can leave. We will talk to you soon."

Taleeb wasn't a snitch, but that B tried to destroy his life.

Row called and wanted the merchandise and Taleeb delivered it at Row's shop after making $10 million dollars. Taleeb burned the paper to make the money in the barrel in his backyard. Taleeb gave

Row everything he needed to be successful, and Taleeb showed Row how to work the equipment. Taleeb didn't tell Row about the paper and where he got it, and Row didn't ask. Row was happy as a fat kid in a candy store.

Row said, "I like your restaurant, have you thought about selling it?"

Taleeb was thinking about a lot of things and selling the restaurant wasn't off limits. Taleeb was thinking about leaving town with his daughter and never coming back.

"Yes, I thought about it."

"How much would you sell it to me for, old friend."

Taleeb said, "Sixty thousand because I changed the way we did business at the restaurant, and it will profit an extra thirty thousand dollars at the end of the year because I open on Sundays now."

Row said, "I'll give you what you paid for it." Taleeb didn't give a damn because he was getting the hell out of Indianapolis.

"Okay" said Taleeb, "We will talk about it in a few weeks, and I'll have the paperwork ready for by then."

"Later, said Taleeb" and he left.

The furniture was being delivered to Taleeb's condo, and he couldn't wait to get there. It was nice to be in a beautiful place again, Taleeb decided not to smoke weed in the place but drinking alcohol was on the menu. Women didn't enter his mind which never happened since Taleeb was 11 years old. He sipped on his expensive wine and took a hot bath and fell asleep in the tub for two hours. Life was good at that moment, but drama was always near.

CPS came over to Taleeb's house at 10:00 a.m. and he was up

and ready. Taleeb heard three hard knocks on the door, it sounded like the police. Taleeb opened the door, and a rude white lady came into house, "Are you Taleeb Anderson?"

"Yes, I am." The lady started taking pictures of the condo. She opened the refrigerator and took pictures of the contents inside. She acted like she was a close relative of the family.

"May I ask you your name, your highness?"

The lady chuckled and said, "My name is Barbara."

"It's nice to meet you Barbara."

"Likewise." She went from room to room looking in the closets and moving things around and putting things back the way they were. After Barbara was done, she gave Taleeb her business card and said, "You have a delightful place," and left.

Time seemed to be moving faster than normal. Taleeb owned the restaurant for four months already and it was doubling what it was making when he bought it. Opening *The Fishhook* on Sunday's was a profitable idea because Sundays brought in more revenue than Monday through Thursday combined. The people didn't notice or complain about their meals not automatically coming with sodas, nor only having one slice of bread. Minor changes like that saved Taleeb time and money because he didn't have to frequent his vendors for the merchandise.

Taleeb was busy stocking the place and when he finished, Dee called him out of the kitchen.

"What's up Dee?"

"Taleeb, I want to introduce you to my mom, April."

"I'm pleased to meet you."

"Thank you, Dee talks about how nice the restaurant is, and I wanted to experience it for myself."

"Well, I hope you like it, and don't worry about paying for it, I'll take care of your bill."

April was flattered and said, "Thank you."

Taleeb gave Dee his usual instructions and left for the day.

April said, "Dee, he is too old for you, let me have him."

They laughed and April said, "You didn't tell me he was that fine."

"Mama, I said he was handsome."

"You didn't describe the man right. The version you gave me was tall, handsome and thin. He looks like he plays football in the NFL."

Cat came out of the kitchen and went over to Dee and her mom's table. Dee introduced Cat to her mom. Cat knew they were talking about Taleeb, and she wanted to get into the conversation. But they changed the conversation because Dee thought it was unprofessional for a supervisor to be talking to the staff about her boss. Cat got the message and told Dee that she would oversee everything while Dee talked to her mom.

April said, "I'm taking you to my hairstylist because those ponytails make you look younger than you are." April didn't want older men being attracted to her daughter, that's why she didn't inform Dee on how to dress to get a man. Dee's usual dress code was tennis shoes and baggy clothes. Lately, April gave Dee pointers on what to wear and how to act at the restaurant to get more tips. April liked Taleeb's persona and he appeared to be successful, therefore she was going to help Dee lure Taleeb into a relationship with her only child.

"If you're going to get a man like Taleeb, you need to upgrade your image. After we get our hair done, were going to get manicures and pedicures on a regular basis." April believed Dee had what it took to get Taleeb but if he was only interested in men, it would be an impossible endeavor.

CHAOS

The day finally came for the heist, Doc already gave Taleeb the money for the job months ago. Taleeb studied the graph's illustrations and was confident the plan would work but he didn't want to do it. Taleeb was being blackmailed by the man he considered a father figure. Taleeb had to be inside a tunnel connected to the downtown sewer system. His job was to ride an electric scooter and pick up the stolen goods from Doc's men at different checkpoints. When Doc bought the scooter, he modified it to collapse so that it would fit inside the manhole to be retrieved by Taleeb. Doc engineered the scooter to run off a battery power pack to reduce the noise in the tunnel and allow Taleeb to get to his routes faster.

Doc's men posed as construction workers and built a canopy around the utility access hole near the bank downtown. They lowered the getaway scooter down the hole where Taleeb was waiting to retrieve it. Taleeb was relieved to see the scooter being lowered down to him because he was exhausted from jogging to that checkpoint. Soon after he unclasped the scooter, they lowered a mini caboose down to him that attached to the scooter. There were three sections, that Taleeb connected to Scooter and each compartment could expand and retract. It was flexible enough to maneuver around turns. The caboose was designed to carry a lot of money and merchandise. Taleeb was instructed not to go faster than 15 miles per hour because the contraption would become unstable. Prior to Taleeb's arrival on the scene, Doc's men bore a large opening that connected the sewer system to the escape tunnel.

Taleeb did a trial run with the scooter and its components on an empty business parking lot and Doc was satisfied with the results. They also practiced dropping off the various supplies in tunnels of the sewer system. They wore bands around their heads with a light on the front of it. Taleeb hated being in the tunnels because rats were running around making squeaking sounds. Plus, it was filthy and smelled like feces. Taleeb was scared and didn't trust Doc's guys, but Doc insisted that his men were solid. Doc gave Taleeb a Glock pistol with an extended clip and a bulletproof vest, just to be on the safe side.

The day of the robbery, rush hour was beginning to formulate around 4:30 p.m. that Friday and all hell broke loose. There were a couple of broken-down school buses in the main arteries near downtown. The news stations were reporting about the traffic jams downtown and gave viewers alternative routes to their destination. Reports of a bank robbery hit the airwaves, but the police were unable to get to the location because of the clogged streets. The news was inundated with the mess going on downtown. Other cities began reporting what was happening in Indianapolis when the robberies of a gun store and jewelry store were added to the chaos. It became international news when an Indiana judge got kidnapped all in one day. Helicopters were flying around all over downtown. People stood outside their vehicles looking at the traffic in the sky and talking to other people stuck in the traffic jam.

Underneath the city, Taleeb followed the blueprint and drove the scooter to his first location. Five men were running toward him with army duffle bags. Two of them had been shot. One man was shot in the leg and the other guy was shot in the lower stomach where the bullet proof vest didn't reach. The vest should have protected him, but nothing in life was guaranteed.

"What happened" asked, Taleeb?

"We had a shootout with some security guards and the police," said the man holding his stomach.

"Did anyone else get hurt beside you two?"

"Yeah, we had to unload on they ass, a police officer and a guard were shot."

"Are they dead?"

The robber that was limping said, "What you need to do is get to your next location, or Doc will tell us to kill your ass."

The men began putting the stolen money from the duffle bags in their money belts. What the men couldn't get in their belts was left in the duffle bags that they had thrown on the ground. The man with the limp saw Taleeb's expression and said, "Doc told us to do it this way."

But Taleeb didn't believe him. "We will meet up with you tonight," and they went on their way.

Taleeb didn't think the man shot in the leg was going to make it because blood was leaking from his wound like the bullet hit an artery. The tunnel broke off in multiple directions and the men were supposed to split up and go to their designated locations. Taleeb was horrified with the information the robbers gave him. Taleeb knew if he was caught, he would spend the rest of his life behind bars.

Taleeb started sweating profusely like he had a fever; his underwear and T-shirt were drenched. He put the duffle bags into the compartments of the caboose. Doc told Taleeb nobody would get hurt but he only said that to get Taleeb onboard with the plan. The problem with the plan was Doc trusted his men, but they were stealing from him.

Something was telling Taleeb that Doc wasn't straightforward about the heist. Taleeb drove to the second location where the guns were going to be delivered but nobody showed up. He waited for ten minutes and couldn't wait any longer. Doc told Taleeb that he had to be at each location on time with no exceptions. Nevertheless, Taleeb was 8 minutes late at the last pick up. Taleeb squinted his eyes to see the men coming toward him who did the jewelry heist. Taleeb yelled out to the men, "Let's go! let's go!" because they were off schedule. The men began jogging away from Taleeb as he slowly approached them with the scooter. Taleeb decided not to pursue the men because they were armed and dangerous. He didn't want them to take his duffle bags and kill him.

A fascinating idea came to Taleeb, but he had to execute it fast. Taleeb was going to switch his counterfeit money with the bank heist money. Luckily for Taleeb, his duplex was only five minutes away from downtown. He looked at the blueprint and pulled out his compass to make sure he was headed in the right direction.

When Taleeb got to the area on the blueprint where the sewer manhole opening was located near his house, he prayed the coordinates were correct. Luck was on his side. Taleeb pushed up the heavy steel lid and looked around and saw that he was under a parked truck. He could see under the vehicle and couldn't believe he was in the middle of the street. Taleeb was thrilled to see he was near his duplex, but cars were parked everywhere as far as he could see. He went back down the steel ladder built in the sewer system. Taleeb disconnected the scooter from the caboose and folded it. He strapped the two duffle bags around his shoulders and climbed back up the ladder with his scooter. Taleeb pushed the two duffle bags and the collapsed scooter out of the hole first and then he slid from under a truck with the goods. He walked through the crowded street and people were looking at him like he was crazy.

Taleeb didn't walk straight to his house because he knew he

looked suspicious. Taleeb took a mini detour. When Taleeb finally got to his duplex, he hurriedly went to the basement. He went to his hiding place and switched the money. Taleeb didn't want to go back to the sewer system because there were too many witnesses around. Therefore, he rode the scooter on the sidewalks and maneuvered around traffic on his way to drop off the money in an abandoned warehouse that Doc owned.

The warehouse was a small building found in the downtown area not that far from Taleeb's home. Traffic was at a standstill because the police cut off twelve streets, entries and exits to the highways. Taleeb couldn't tolerate smelling himself. He stunk from body odor and the stench from the sewer.

When Taleeb got to his destination, four men were waiting by the sewer where Taleeb was supposed to appear from. However, the men saw Taleeb coming toward them on the scooter and they pulled out their guns on him. "Why are you coming from that way instead of the tunnel like you were told to do?" asked Eric.

Taleeb responded quickly and told them. "Your boys were shooting everywhere in the tunnel; I climbed out of it because it was unsafe. They tried to rob me."

"And you only got two bags of money?"

"Yes, they kept the rest of the money."

"Your guys that were supposed to deliver the guns didn't show up. I waited for as long as I could for them, but Doc told me to be on time with the deliveries. I was late getting to the third spot because I waited on them too long. When I got to the jewelry checkpoint, the men that had the jewelry ran in different sections of the sewer when they saw me. I could see them from a distance, and I called out to them, but they started running. One of them shot at me, so I took an alternative route."

The men lowered their guns, grabbed the duffle bags, and went into the warehouse. They knew not to kill Taleeb because Doc spoke highly of him. They didn't believe the men shot at Taleeb because Doc threatened his men's life before the robberies. Doc said he would kill anyone who harmed Taleeb's physical wellbeing.

The men put the money on a long plastic table with fold out legs and began counting it. They joked and laughed about how bad Taleeb smelled. Taleeb asked, "Can I go now? Doc said he would hook me up tomorrow." Eric made a phone call and more than likely he was talking to Doc, thought Taleeb. Before Taleeb could get out the door, Eric said, "Hold up," and he told Doc what happened verbatim. After Eric was finished talking to his boss, he said, "Yeah man, you can go. Get your nasty ass out of here," and they all laughed. He waved Taleeb away like he was swatting a fly from his face.

Taleeb was thankful he was still alive and decided to take out a life insurance policy on himself when he got home from the scooter ride. He would set it up that each child would receive $300,000 upon his death. Taleeb hadn't noticed the congested streets and honking horns because he was in deep thought about his mortality.

When Taleeb got home, he ran up the steps on the porch with his scooter and turned on the news. He went to the pantry and got a pint of rum and drank half of it in three quick gulps. The strong taste made him grimace. Channel 9 news reported about a judge that was kidnapped at the time of the robberies. He took his clothes off and put them in a plastic bag along with his shoes. Taleeb made sure the bag was tied tight so the funk wouldn't leak out. He was going to burn them in the morning to get rid of the evidence. Taleeb was lightheaded and wanted to watch the rest of the news, but he was nauseated by his smell. He took a shower and then ran hot bath water. He put Epsom salt and bubble bath in the water.

The news reported that a security guard and a police officer were shot and killed during the bank robbery. They mentioned that the two bank robbers were wounded in the assault and had escaped. Taleeb drank the rest of the liquor and became woozy. He sat in the tub in disbelief. The news reporters were excited and saddened by the events that unfolded. They went on to say that three men were killed trying to rob Ron's Guns store.

They interviewed Ron and he said, "Everybody that worked for him carried loaded guns and they were trained to shoot their weapons every day." Ron tried to end the interview saying, "I can't believe anyone could be that stupid. Now you know what happens when you try to rob me."

Helen who was covering the story, asked Ron "How were the perpetrators shot and killed if they were wearing bulletproof vests?"

"My staff uses Teflon bullets that glided right through their bulletproof vests." Helen asked other questions, but Ron declined to answer them and walked away.

Plagued with drama that seemed endless, the news droned on. They talked about the jewelry store that was robbed by two gunmen that got away with a million dollars in cash and merchandise. Nobody was injured in the altercation. Taleeb got out of the tub, dried it off and turned off the TV. He went to bed and slept for 12 hours.

It was noon when Taleeb woke up, and he had to be in juvenile court by 1:00 p.m. He took a bath last night and didn't have time to wash up that morning. He brushed his teeth and rinsed his face off. Taleeb put on a suit, fixed his hair, and rushed out the door.

Thank God, Taleeb got there on time. They called his case as he walked in the door. Miss Stuart, the rude lady that came over his house, motioned Taleeb to sit at the end of a rectangular table. She sat on the opposite side of Taleeb near the prosecutor. Damn, it never dawned on Taleeb to bring an attorney. Taleeb thought he was only going to sign papers. The judge asked Taleeb, "Are you Taleeb Anderson?"

"Yes."

The judge began reciting Taleeb's accomplishments and when she was done, the prosecutor reminded the judge that Taleeb was a convicted felon. The judge responded, "Taleeb served his time, paid all his court fees, and received a good recommendation from CPS. Therefore, he has a right to have custody restored to him by this court." After the judge hit the gavel, Miss Stuart told Taleeb to come with her and they went to the second floor on an elevator. When they walked through the double doors on the second floor, Aaliyah yelled out "Daddy! Daddy!" and they hugged. Taleeb thanked Miss Stuart and she said, "I hope we don't have to meet again under these circumstances."

"We won't," said Taleeb.

She smiled and said, "Aaliyah is all yours," and gave him the paperwork from court.

Surprised and bewildered, Taleeb didn't expect to be taking Aaliyah home on the same day. He was genuinely happy about the results in court, but his life and freedom were on the verge of being taken. And now Aaliyah's life was in his hands. Taleeb never drank or smoked in front of Aaliyah, but he needed a drink in the worst kind of way. He went to a liquor store with a big front window so that he could see Aaliyah while he got a pint of cognac. He was paranoid and didn't want anything to happen to her. When Taleeb got back to the car, Aaliyah continued to talk about everything under the sun and Taleeb heard nothing. Taleeb told Aaliyah, "We are going shopping at the mall to buy you some new clothes."

Aaliyah was thrilled and said, "Let's go."

While they went to different stores in the mall, Taleeb told her to pick out something in Forever 18.

"I have to go to the bathroom." He was going to drink the rest of his liquor. Before he left, Taleeb told the cashier in the store to keep an eye on Aaliyah while he went to the restroom. The cashier looked at Aaliyah and thought her dad needed to relax and quit babying the pre-teen.

When they finished shopping, they went home. Aaliyah told Taleeb how nice the apartment looked and asked him which bedroom was hers as she looked around. Taleeb pointed her in the right direction, and she took her clothes to her room and put them in their place. Then Aaliyah got in bed and went to sleep as soon as her head hit the pillow.

The next day, Taleeb talked himself out of depression, he didn't have time to pity himself, he couldn't wait for things to happen, he had to make them happen. He made breakfast for Aaliyah and then called the grade school in their area to get her enrolled. They gave him a separate location to bring the necessary paperwork to get her enrolled into the school. Taleeb had to change his schedule and life around his daughter. He had to leave her at home by herself for the first time. Taleeb was only going to be gone for three hours. He told Aaliyah to hold down the fort until he got back.

When Taleeb got to work, his staff was discussing the robberies that happened yesterday. He loathed the fact that a police officer was killed. There were going to be grave consequences for murdering a cop. Taleeb saw a new face in the kitchen. He went in there to ask Dee why was the woman in the kitchen? The woman looked familiar, but Taleeb couldn't recognize her. Cat elbowed Dee in her side and Dee looked up and smiled at Taleeb. Was that Dee, thought Taleeb? Her hair was dyed with blonde streaks. It was longer from the perm. She blinked her long lashes and gazed into Taleeb's eyes. He never saw Dee with lipstick and makeup on before. He thought of her like a little kid that made him want to pinch her on the cheeks. Cat told Dee, "Well, I think you accomplished what you wanted."

Tony saw them looking at each other and said to Taleeb, "Lil Dee looking good ain't she boss?"

Dee walked toward Taleeb and gave him a hug, pressing her body close to him. She looked up and whispered in his ear. "I was so worried about you, I missed you so much."

Taleeb was tired and needed the hug. He had to hold back the tears while he held Dee in his arms. Dee could feel his need, "It's going to be ok."

Tony and Cat looked at them smiling. Tony told Cat, "He's going to tap that ass ain't he Cat," she popped him with a towel and said, "You need to tap them dishes, that's why you don't have a woman because you're vulgar and don't have any class."

Dee could see the hurt in Taleeb's eyes as she backed away, "I'm here for you Taleeb whatever you need, I'll give it to you." Taleeb looked down on the floor and said, "Thank you Dee."

Cat couldn't help the jealousy building up inside her. She called the previous owner Fred and told him about everything that was going wrong in the business. Cat told Fred that Taleeb was open on Sundays and Taleeb stopped giving soda pops with the meals. Fred was upset because he was a religious man and didn't want the store opened on Sundays. He sold the business to Taleeb, but he had contingencies attached to the sale that Taleeb was unaware of.

When Dee got off from work, she went directly over to her mom's house. As April opened the door, Dee grabbed her hand and said, "Mama, it worked like a charm."

April said, "This qualifies for a celebration."

"Mom, he was looking at me like he didn't know who I was."

"I told you girl. Men like women that care about their looks."

"Mama, he hugged me like he really needed me, and I think he's sad."

"Wow, y'all were hugging?"

"Yes, I hugged him when he came into work because I missed him."

"I don't know if that was a good idea, Dee. He isn't sad girl; he is in love."

"Are you serious mama? Don't play with me mama."

April held Dee's hands and said, "You are a beautiful young woman, Dee, and if you want that man, you will get him, trust me. Have I ever steered you wrong?"

"No, Mama, I really want him. Please help me."

REVENGE

Dread washed over Taleeb when he answered the phone, and it was Doc. Taleeb hated Doc and wanted to get as far away from him as possible. "Taleeb, I didn't want to call you on the phone, but you wouldn't answer the door. I wanted to talk to you about our project but not at your restaurant. Can you meet me at the warehouse?"

"I'm busy right now Doc."

"My men haven't seen you in days, what's up with you, are you alright?"

"No, I'm not alright." Taleeb knew not to say anything incriminating on the phone. "What do you want Doc?"

"What do I want? I got your money for cutting my grass."

"You can keep it," Taleeb hung up the phone.

Meanwhile the kidnapped judge was locked in a room and handcuffed to a steel chair bolted to the floor. He was tired and hadn't eaten in days. Judge Carlisle began to reflect on all the Black people he conspired against and the lives he ruined. He cried and asked God for forgiveness, even though Carlisle didn't believe in God, but he didn't want to take any chances. He believed if there was a heaven, his chances would be slim of getting into the pearly gates.

The room Carlisle was in was set up like a courtroom. It felt awkward for him to be on the other side of the king's throne as he called it.

"All rise for the honorable Farley Holland," said Raymond who was the bailiff.

Carlisle was insulted and refused to stand up for a self-proclaimed judge, but that name sounded familiar. It would be difficult to rise with the tight cuff around his wrist anyway. Doc came in the room with a colorful African robe on.

Doc said, "The penalty for you not standing up and respecting my court room is the loss of a finger."

"Bailiff go get the bolt cutters."

Carlisle jumped up, "I'm sorry; I didn't know the penalty. I wasn't thinking because I'm tired and hungry."

Doc said, "Ignorance of the law is not an excuse to disrespect me."

Raymond returned with the bolt cutters and Doc said, "Carlisle hold out the finger you want cut off."

"No! no! no! please let's talk about this Mr. Holland."

"Did my ears deceive me?" Doc looked at Raymond and he nodded his head from side to side. Raymond was afraid of what Doc was going to do next. "Go get the axe in the other room next to fire extinguisher and cut off the right hand of this corrupt conspirator."

Carlisle couldn't believe what he was hearing, this must be a dream, he thought. But realization sank in when the bailiff arrived with, the axe. Doc had plenty of goons who were incarcerated for macabre acts of violence and would have enjoyed watching a judge suffer, but

Raymond wasn't that type of person and Doc knew it. Doc was becoming more cynical and wanted Raymond to prove his loyalty. Raymond needed the money that Doc paid his crew, and he feared Doc especially after he killed the men that betrayed him.

Carlisle's eyes were open wide, he was looking at the axe and felt weak. Raymond told Carlisle to put his hand on the table. Carlisle put his shaking hand on the table without protest and closed his eyes. The blade came down on Carlisle's wrist with a lot of force because Raymond didn't want to repeat chopping on it. Blood squirted out onto Raymond's clothes and Carlisle passed out in the chair. Raymond almost fainted next to him. Doc told Raymond to tie a rope around Carlisle's upper wrist to stop the bleeding. "Get the medicine box over there on the shelf and some rags." "Clean the wound with peroxide and put him back in his cage." Doc gave Raymond other chores to do to keep Carlisle alive for his next court date.

If only Taleeb had someone to help him with Aaliyah, he could think straight. His sister Venus moved to Georgia two years ago and the rest of Taleeb's immediate family followed her. Venus worked as an administrator at Georgia Tech University and owned a business selling spices from all over the world. She visited Taleeb once a month and did more than enough for Aaliyah, but he needed help with Aaliyah now. Taleeb started thinking of all the people that could help him with his child and Dee came to mind.

While Taleeb was on his way to the restaurant, he listened to the news on the radio. They said a woman by the name of Jasmine Crawford, who was fired from the Post Office stabbed Cierra Humphrey ten times over a man they were involved with. Taleeb was happy and sad at the same time. He cared deeply about Cierra and felt bad about her demise, but he was happy he wasn't going to jail for a murder he didn't commit. The news sounded like he lived in Iraq with all the killings in the city. Taleeb didn't want to hear any more bad news and turned off the station and started listening to his jazz CD.

As soon as Taleeb got to work, Fred called him on the phone. "I don't like the way you're running the business."

"What are you talking about?"

"I heard that you're not selling sodas that go with the meals and you're open on Sundays." Fred told Taleeb he knew everything that was going on in the store.

Taleeb got upset and said, "What the hell are you going to do about it?"

Fred told Taleeb, "I still own the lease on the building, and I can get you kicked out of the store because you're not on the lease."

Taleeb told Fred he was going to get back with him in four days and hung up. Taleeb wanted to fire all his employees except for Dee because he believed one of them was in direct contact with Fred. It had to be Tony or Cat and he thought Tony was a complete idiot and didn't care about anything. Taleeb figured it was Cat.

Taleeb told Dee, "I'm going to call you about something important later today. Take care of things while I'm gone, I'll see you soon."

Dee smiled and said, "I'll take care of things while you're away." Dee daydreamed all that day about Taleeb asking her to be his lady.

Taleeb got Aaliyah in school, but she got kicked off the school bus on her first day. Taleeb had to pick her up from school, but he had to see her principal first. The principal was a short well-dressed Black man that had on a big bow tie. He looked like a disciple in the Nation of Islam. His name was Antonio Mason, and he was a very likable person. Mr. Mason told Taleeb that the bus driver told a group of kids on the back of the bus to quiet down. Aaliyah told the driver it wasn't her and to shut the hell up."

Mr. Mason explained the event in front of Aaliyah and Taleeb. Aaliyah said, "The driver was looking at me in the mirror when he said it and I wasn't talking." Taleeb told her it didn't matter, and she was in the wrong. Aaliyah had her bottom lip poked out and her hands were folded across her chest. Taleeb told Mr. Mason it wouldn't happen again and the two left his office.

Taleeb was going to scold Aaliyah when they got into the car, but he had a more pressing issue to talk to her about. Taleeb asked Aaliyah, "Do you want to meet a friend of mine?"

Aaliyah said, "I don't care daddy," trying to look angry, but she was curious and asked him "Who is she?"

Taleeb explained the details to Aaliyah and tried to end the conversation by saying, she is going to look after you when I'm not home.

"I'm too old for a babysitter." Aaliyah began to bombard Taleeb with questions that were ignored because he was playing out scenarios in his mind about leaving the United States with a felony on his record.

"Do not call him, said April, let him call you." Dee was getting anxious; her mind was all over the place. The phone rang and she answered it in the middle of the first ring. April was trying to tell Dee to let it ring a few times, but Dee was too frantic.

"Hello," Dee hated the way her voice sounded. She was too excited and couldn't help panting.

"Hey Dee, how are you?" April wanted her to put the phone on speaker. "I'm fine Taleeb how are you?"

"I'm well. I wanted to ask you, could you help me with my daughter, I'll pay you?"

Dee was holding the phone tight and said, "You don't have to…." April jumped in front of Dee's face shaking her head no. "

How can I help her?"

"Can you watch her when she gets out of school?"

"Of course, what days and how long?"

"On weekdays from 3:00 p.m. to 8:00 p.m."

Dee asked, "What about the restaurant?"

"I want you to train someone to do your job and you can check on the restaurant whenever you can. You will be doing my job. Taking money to the bank ordering the food for the restaurant and picking it up. Have Tony stock the place. I'll pay you $1,500 a week."

Dee thought she may not have heard him correctly. "How much did you say?"

"One Thousand Five Hundred Dollars, and you can bring your son with you to watch Aaliyah because my daughter loves kids."

Dee couldn't speak and her mother stood by Dee with her hand on her chest, eyes wide and mouth opened.

"Hello! Dee, are you there?"

Dee snapped out of it, "Yes, I'm here. I'd love to help you with everything Taleeb and I'll do whatever you want me to." April got in front of her face shaking her head no and frowning. "When do I start?"

"Tomorrow."

When the conversation was over, she hung up the phone. April said, "Ok was good enough that's all you had to say, not, I'll do whatever you want me to."

"Wow, mama I'm so happy!" Dee yelled, "I'm getting ready to get paid" and they started screaming and laughing.

Everything was going bad, but Taleeb was going to create art out of madness. He was going to have Dee train Cat on how to close the restaurant. Since Cat already knew how to do most of the job, Dee could train her in a few hours and then check on her every now and then. Taleeb didn't trust Cat and knew she would steal money from the register, but Taleeb didn't care. Taleeb had over five million dollars and the store became a business front. Taleeb wanted Cat to trust him and mislead Fred about the goings on around the place. Taleeb didn't buy a new car or anything that would bring attention to himself. He was going to sell the business to Row for whatever Row wanted to buy it for. He knew that Fred was a bounty hunter and had police connections. Taleeb was going to play the two against each other and hoped the outcome would be fatal.

Taleeb paid a lawyer to put some of his money in a Switzerland bank account in a business name they created. His bank account and all his money transactions were under the name Lance Battles. Taleeb made transfers electronically from his PNC bank account to his Swiss account. Taleeb was getting his affairs in order as quickly as he could. Every day, he completed major tasks.

Taleeb called his friend, Blake who had connections in Panama. They went to the same college a decade ago. The two talked to each other every other month. Taleeb called Blake on a disposable cell phone that he wanted to put a generous sum of cash money in the bank. He wanted to put it in a Panama bank because Panama was known for having corrupt banking policies and practices. Taleeb looked up banks in Panama that were caught in scandals and bribery.

He was skeptical about using his Switzerland connection for the task because they were more sophisticated, and he didn't have any connections there. His dealing with them was as legal as possible.

Panama had more poverty which made people susceptible to criminal activity. Blake told Taleeb about a bank that wasn't on Taleeb's list. Taleeb told Blake that he would give him six figures if he could make it happen. Blake thought Taleeb turned into a drug dealer because Taleeb was talking in codes and calling Blake using different phone numbers. Taleeb also wrote him a letter, telling Blake to be discreet on the phone when he called. Blake respected Taleeb and loved him like family. They were frat brothers in college and had a lot of fun with the ladies in school. They were both tall and didn't look alike but people always got them confused because they were always together. They stayed in contact with each other although they went to different universities in other states when they pursued graduate degrees.

Blake wanted to help Taleeb because he knew Taleeb was smart and detailed oriented and could get away with anything if he put his mind into it. Blake was doing well for himself, but he could always use more money. Blake befriended a powerful executive named Adrian at the Banco Nacional de Panamá. The owner of the bank trusted Adrian with all the sensitive information concerning the bank.

Adrian and Blake had a lot in common. They both spoke multiple languages which was common in Panama, and they liked to party with beautiful women. At one of their rendezvous, Blake had spoken to Adrian about an investor in the United States who wanted to put a large amount of cash money in his bank.

"This is not America, Blake," said Adrian. "It's not illegal to put a large amount of cash money in the bank."

"How much is it?"

"I don't know because my contact doesn't want to disclose the amount."

"Well, whatever the amount is we will accept it because we're in the business of making money but there may be a fee if it's over a certain amount."

"That's fine, I think he will expect to pay a fee."

Taleeb thought Doc's plan using chaos in the city was brilliant because the police and FBI were baffled about Doc's true intentions. However, the FBI was slowly unraveling the case. Taleeb was creating chaos of his own. He knew it was a matter of time before Doc found out the money was counterfeit. The money could have a flaw that Taleeb hadn't thought of. What happens to the money if it got wet, would the ink wash off? Thankfully, Doc and his men were not spending the money because Doc wanted to wait till things calmed down.

Taleeb began mailing yellow envelopes with $5,000 inside to Black business owners throughout Indianapolis. He also paid young boys hanging around underdeveloped neighborhoods to deliver packages of money to the residents' mailboxes with a thousand dollars inside.

Taleeb opened bank accounts in Ohio, Chicago, and Kentucky to offset any alerts that could be triggered from repetitious money deposits entering the banking system in Indianapolis. He put two thousand dollars in those accounts on a regular basis. It required too much driving and Taleeb was gone from home most of the time.

Taleeb decided to ask Dee if she and her son could move in with him and he would pay her more money to take care of his affairs. It would only be a short stay before they would have to move because Aaliyah would have to share her room with Dee's son, Jeremy. Dee would have paid Taleeb to move in with him, but she listened to her mom and was grateful for Taleeb's offerings.

She never met a man that didn't want to have sex with her on the first date, but Taleeb was different. She knew in her heart Taleeb wasn't a homosexual because of the way he looked at her. Dee could tell Taleeb was trying to be a gentleman and she was thankful he was patient. Dee didn't want Taleeb to be her lover, friend, or man. She wanted to marry him and have at least one more child. Taleeb was buying her flowers and taking the family out to dinner at expensive restaurants. Jeremy and April also loved Taleeb and Dee wanted to talk to him about their relationship because she didn't want her heart broken.

The bank robber that got shot in the gut hid a bag of money in the tunnel in case he was caught trying to escape. He went back into the tunnel days later to retrieve it. When he got to the site, he looked around for visible threats before he opened the bag. The bag made a loud pop sound and red dye exploded everywhere. The man was perplexed because he and his accomplice opened bags of money two days ago and nothing happened. He thought, out of all the bags, I get the only bag that explodes. Three minutes later, he was shot in the head by one of Doc's men.

People in the downtown area called the sanitation department about the smokey red dye coming out of the gutters. Plumbers from the health department went into the sewer system and discovered a dead man with a bag of money covered in red dye.

The FBI was notified and Simona Giovanni, who oversaw the investigation, met her team at the site. None of the agents wanted to go in the sewer system, including her. Therefore, she ordered Lincoln into the sewer to video and take pictures of the crime scene. Andy and Glen volunteered because they knew Simona was going to make them go into the shit show. They usually dusted for fingerprints and helped her narrate the events that took place. Simona gave her crew masks and gloves. She thought long and hard about going into the tunnel herself and finally said, "What the fuck!" and went in. Simona had to get a firsthand observation of what took place. Two more brave souls followed Simona down the hatch hoping their valor wouldn't go unnoticed. The smell was awful and seemed to take on a life form of its own. The stench was an abomination to inhale and it wanted to be remembered for a lifetime.

"Simona over here!" called Andy who was standing over a heavyset dead Black man. It was obvious the man died from a gunshot to the head, and he was shot in the abdomen.

Simona asked, "Lincoln did you take pictures of this?"

"Yeah" hollered Lincoln.

"Help me turn him over," said Simona.

"Hold on Simona, Andy and I will help you." When they turned the body on its side to examine the midsection injury, Simona said, "The bullet was probably a .45 ACP judging from the damage to the tissue and size of entry and exit wounds.

Glen said, "Yeah the gun that housed that bullet was the Sig-Sauer P 227 pistol. This wound came from the policeman or the security guard at the bank," said Andy. "The gunshot wound to the head was from another weapon.

"He was probably killed by his own people," said Simona.

"He must have been shot right here because that's the bullet shell over there," Andy pointing to shell on the ground.

"Over here," yelled Bella the young agent who was on the west side of the tunnel. The group followed her voice and was surprised to see another dead body lying on the ground. "It's obvious this man died from a bullet wound to the thigh," said Bella.

"The weapon used in the altercation was consistent with his partner's," said Glen.

"The bullet hit the perpetrator's femoral artery and he bled to death," said Simona.

Andy said, "The guy tied a belt above the wound to stop the bleeding, but he had already lost too much blood." Simona believed that he had preexisting health issues that aided in his death. She saw an old cut on his neck that hadn't healed properly. Simona believed he was diabetic. An image of a pictogram formulated in Simona's mind and the kidnapping began working its way into the puzzle. She was under tremendous pressure from her superiors who wanted answers that she didn't have.

The mayor was up for reelection, and he needed the case resolved quickly. His Republican opponent ran a negative campaign ad against him after the kidnapping and robberies, saying the mayor was soft on crime.

The governor was a good friend of the judge who was kidnapped and vowed that the criminals would be hunted down like dogs. Furthermore, he promised that the men responsible would be brought to justice in body bags. The media went into a frenzy and couldn't believe the statement the governor made.

The INPD was going rogue and began doing their own investigation and that was why Simona had to step in and put the department on notice. She explained to chief Turner that the FBI was taking over the case and he was furious.

"We have dead police officer out there, and the savages responsible are going pay in blood and there is nothing the FBI can say or do to change that!"

"I understand you're angry, Mr. Turner but I'm on your side. We need to work together to find the individuals responsible for this atrocity. Can we have a meeting with your men tomorrow? I want to give them a few details we have about the case. Hopefully the meeting will build trust between the two departments," said Simona.

"I don't know how well the meeting will be received by my men, but I'll have some free time at 10:00 a.m. tomorrow."

"Thank you, Mr. Turner, I'll see you tomorrow."

Later that night, Simona practiced what she was going to say to Turner's men. After she felt confident her words could inspire the INPD to work with the FBI, she set her work aside and made a few cocktails. Soon after, she fell asleep on the couch and slept like a baby.

When Simona woke up the next morning, she took a shower and headed to work. She was anxious about the meeting and drank six cups of coffee before it started. The caffeine played a significant role in her jitters. She thought about drinking decaffeinated coffee for weeks but thinking about a caffeine-free expresso seemed redundant.

Chief Turner introduced Simona to his department and said, "I'll let you take it from here." Time to get the show on the road she thought.

"Hello everyone, I won't take up too much of your time. I'll make this as brief as possible." Simona gave them bits and pieces of information she knew they didn't have. She had to be careful about what she divulged because it could be leaked to the press. But she always had an angle if those small details were revealed. Simona began wrapping the meeting up and said, "This case is far from over, but I promise you that the perpetrators will be caught. If we work as a team, we will catch these monsters quicker. Are there any questions?"

No one asked questions, "That's odd," she thought. Simona

hoped the speech went well but apparently not, judging by the glaring stares she received.

"Okay then thank you for your time."

After Simona's speech was over, Turner told his men, "Re-canvas the areas where the businesses were robbed and follow up with the witnesses. Go door to door in every neighborhood these transgressions took place. Requestion the witnesses, find new witnesses. Bring me back something we can burn these bastards with."

Under normal conditions, the FBI would have taken over the case entirely and made the local police stand down. But this case was different, it had a lot of moving parts and Simona needed all hands-on deck. She included the police for other reasons as well. They wanted retribution for their fallen fraternity brothers and Simona knew that anger would have them working double time to get answers.

Problems were mounting, not one soul in any Black neighborhood spoke to the police. Only one white man whose truck was stuck in traffic gave an account of what happened. He gave a vague description of the man that exited the sewer system and the location of the individual.

Black people considered the criminals to be heroes. The kidnappers and robbers were celebrities according to the Black newspapers. People were talking about the men being freedom fighters and how they gave back to their communities. Simona couldn't stop reading the articles and wondered why someone would steal money and give it to the poor. The world didn't work that way, it had to be a bigger picture that she couldn't grasp but she was determined to find out. This was the worst-case Simona ever had, every day it was more shocking news. Counterfeit money was showing up in 31 states and spreading rapidly. Ninety percent of the money was concentrated in Indiana. Simona had a hunch that Indiana was where it originated from. Simona wondered if the money that Robin Hood gave out was counterfeit?

The plot thickened when someone mailed a man's hand to the governor's home. A DNA test was done on the hand to see if it belonged to the judge. The FBI did a saliva swab on Carlisle's son to see if the DNA matched the hand samples. It was confirmed that the hand was not Carlisle's. Little did the press know, Carlisle's son was illegally adopted in Russia's brothel house. The woman that bore the son was made a prostitute because her family was in debt to the Russian mob.

The case was more taxing than Simona could have imagined and, for the first time in her career, she thought long and hard about retiring. She was sixty-one years old and wanted to travel around the world. Simona enjoyed working for the FBI, but she let the job suck the life out of her. Part of it was her fault for not taking enough vacations and working longer hours than necessary. She decided this was her last case.

Tensions were flaring between law enforcement and the Black community. The INPD was angry because Black people were supporting the criminals that left an officer dead. Black people in Indianapolis didn't trust the police. It all came to a head when the police followed up on Tom's interview. The same witness that was stuck in traffic on the day of the controversy. Detectives mapped out where Tom said a Black man rolled from under his truck with two large duffle bags. The sketch artist tried to help law enforcement but was unable to do his job because Tom said didn't see the front of man's face, it was a side view and covered in dirt. All Tom knew was the man was tall and muscular built. Tom felt like his was being interrogated, he couldn't see the man's eyes or nose. The detectives in the room were angry with him because he didn't give them enough to ID the faceless man. Tom didn't know the man's nationality, nor did he see the house the man went into, but the truth was getting him punished.

Therefore, Tom began to tell them what they wanted to hear.

Tom said, "I do remember the man's hands, they were those of a Black man. And if you take me to the street where I saw him, I'll show you the house he went into."

After Tom showed them the house, at 3:00 a.m. the next day a SWAT team went to the house and rammed the door open and shot a 9-year-old boy 37 times and beat his 85-year-old great-grandmother to death.

It was a public relations nightmare; Simona witnessed the most cowardly act of violence that she had ever seen. She tried to understand the level of hate that went into the brutal murders and concluded that she was not dealing with human beings. Those creatures that killed the innocent boy and his great-grandmother were soulless monsters. This was done intentionally, to send a message to the Black community, thought Simona. She tried everything in her power to charge those responsible for murder, but qualified immunity protected them from any wrongdoing. It was enough to make her vomit, knowing that police had a license to kill innocent people without any repercussions.

Shots rang out 24/7 in Indianapolis and bullets riddled police vehicles. Fire departments in different counties' windows were shot out. Twenty-five officers were shot at while driving down the street. People called the police baby-killers, serial killers, and the slave patrols. The INPD was losing millions of dollars fixing police vehicles with bullet holes, flat tires, and shattered windows. Chief Turner was to blame for all this mess, thought Simona. She advised him and his department that they were only going to assist the FBI but under no circumstance where they allowed to make an arrest.

Governor Jennings was glad he didn't live in Indiana, but he claimed the state as his residency to win the election. Jennings was a Democrat that turned Republican. He ran a campaign that was based on the war against crime and drugs. Jennings didn't care about either political party, but he loved the power that the governorship gave him. He believed that both political parties were the same. Money controlled their behavior and who ever had the most cash dictated both parties' decision making. Jennings hated the Hoosier state and the occupants that lived there. The core of his constituents was poor white trash. Jennings played the race bating game to keep himself in office, but he didn't have anything against black people. With the black uprising formulating, Jennings went on a secret vacation in fear for his life.

Simona and mayor Peterson met at his office to come up with a solution on how to stop the violence. Simona said, "You should do a press conference and fire chief Turner and the eight members on the SWAT team that killed the boy and his great-grandmother."

"That's a good idea that I have already contemplated," said Peterson.

"I'm going to do more than that," he told her.

"I'm also going to get rid of every cop that has disciplinary actions against them for excessive force and being involved in multiple shootings."

Simona said, "The longer you wait on this, sir, more innocent people will die."

What the mayor said was a step forward in the right direction, however, Peterson was afraid of the police because they had a reputation for killing people in high places. Moreover, the mayor and the governor belonged to the *Indoctrination of Black Men* society. Their organization was also considered a spying agency that often-used lethal force to get what it wanted. He would need to contact the organization to get their approval.

The *Indoctrination of Black Men* used the INPD to kill protesters in 31 states. The INPD were the most dangerous plague in Indiana, and they were the leading cause of death amongst Black men in Indianapolis.

Simona was considered a Black woman, but her boss was the only one in the department that knew she was biracial. She doubted her staff would care about her nationality because they were a multicultural bunch, but her ethnicity was none of their business. Simona's mother was Black, and her father was Italian.

Simona didn't have any kids and didn't want any. She had been in a seven-year relationship with Dexter, but her real man was the FBI. Her boyfriend often complained to Simona about not spending enough time with him. She felt guilty but she explained to Dexter in the beginning of their relationship that she was a busy woman. She told him how hard it was to oversee a team of agents in the FBI. She hoped he understood but it was clear he wanted something she couldn't give him. Simona often apologized to Dexter for working long hours. She was afraid that he would leave her because he wanted to get married and have kids.

Simona thought she was being groomed for the Director's position at the agency and worked long hours to be noticed as an industrious leader. But as time moved forward, Simona was passed over for the position. She was outraged that they gave the job to a man who had half of her qualifications and now the idiot was her boss.

She gave up everything for the job. Simona did the job better than any man that worked in her department. But after dealing with the drama in Indiana, it was time for a change. The police were out of control and the people in the city treated her like she was a police officer. Black people in the Hoosier state hated all law enforcement, and the politicians too. Simona didn't blame them because the leadership in the city failed them miserably.

The case was moving as slow as molasses oozing down a tree because none of Indiana's citizens wanted to help except for a few white bystanders. The missing pieces of the puzzle were out there, and Simona hoped one of the perpetrated would slip up and help bring the investigation to a close. Simona's staff were overworked and stretched thin.

The gun stores sold more guns in Indiana in four months than all the surrounding states combined. It felt like a revolution was coming and she wanted to get out of town before it happened.

Judge Carlisle had a habit of stretching his fingers and then making a fist to evaluate how bad his arthritis was, and it got worse when it rained. He felt pain in the fingers that were missing. He couldn't see his digits, but they ached, nonetheless. The black spades put cocaine on his wrist with the detached hand to stop the pain. The wound was numb and felt cold at the tip. Carlisle was fed three meals a day and received plenty of water.

The so-called bailiff came and got Carlisle for his court hearing. Carlisle sat in the same chair he was in a month ago. The bailiff said, "All rise," and Carlisle stood up quick. Doc asked Carlisle, "Do you remember a case about a Black teenager who was shot in the head by a police officer, while the boy was handcuffed? It happened 20 years ago," said Doc.

Carlisle's intuition was right, he knew Doc was angry about a court decision he resided over, but he didn't remember Doc. He remembered the case because it was unusual, and people protested for months.

"Yes, I remember that case," said Carlisle.

"Why did you personally seal the police officer's criminal record in that case." "The police officer was a serial killer, yet you told my lame ass attorney that any information about the police officer was inadmissible in court."

"The prosecutor didn't have to do anything because you personally protected the police officer that killed my son."

"How did you know that?" asked Carlisle.

"Don't worry about how I got the information. I know other things about you that will make an average person's skin crawl. I advise you not to lie to me because you're under oath and next time you give me static, I won't be so nice." Carlisle sang like a bird. He told Doc everything that he asked Carlisle.

"Sir, I belong to a secret society that ordered me to seal the records of the officer. I was instructed to hide evidence and falsify documents in the case."

Carlisle continued to rattle off information. "The policeman that shot your son planted a gun on him to make it look like suicide. It's common practice for officers to carry an extra gun with the serial numbers filed off. They plant the guns on unarmed Black men who are fatally shot by officers."

"What's the name of this society and how did they make you their lap dog?"

"They're called *Indoctrination of Black Men*, but they are white millionaires with unlimited power. The power they have is given to them by a more powerful organization, but I don't know the name of the group, but I heard they were billionaires. Some of them were presidents of the United States. It's a syndicate that's been around for centuries. They toppled governments around the world and installed leaders to do their bidding. Their main objective is to help the European population grow and stay in power. They know that the European's genes are recessive to people of color. Black people's genes are dominant over all the other races. They believe Black people are a threat to our survival, especially the Black male, and that is why they formed the society."

Doc was disgusted and told the bailiff to put Carlisle in his room. Doc wanted to hear more about the gang Carlisle claimed to be a part of therefore his life was spared for now.

"It was a piece of cake," thought Row. He couldn't believe Taleeb sold him the restaurant for three thousand dollars. His brothers wanted to kill Taleeb because he was a witness that could tie them to the counterfeit money, if the law got involved. They didn't want any loose ends. But they changed their minds after Taleeb sold their brother the restaurant for peanuts. Row believed Taleeb feared his brothers and that's why he let it go so cheap.

Row made a lot of changes when he got the Fishhook from Taleeb. He fired Tony because he caught Tony stealing boxes of frozen fish. Tony thought he was slick by wheeling the trash can outside to the dumpster, but Row was suspicious because the trash was only a third full. Row told Tony to pull the trash bag out of the trash can and when Tony did, five boxes of frozen fish were left in the trash container.

Row told Tony, "You're fired and don't worry about your belongings because they're mine now."

Row also fired Cat for stealing money from the cash register. Her drawer was always short. It was a shame how they were doing poor Taleeb. "He was a complete imbecile," thought Row.

Things were going wonderfully for Dee. She was enjoying life. Dee didn't have to work at the restaurant anymore, even though Row begged her to stay. Dee was worried about having nothing to do all day but quickly found out she had to work just as hard. She had to keep the house clean, take care of the kids, and run errands for Taleeb.

Dee had been with Taleeb for nine months. They never had sex and she was ready to consummate their relationship. She loved Taleeb and he proved his love for her because of the things he did and said to her and Jeremy. Taleeb was ten years older than Dee, but she didn't care. He was stable and very affectionate. When they kissed, it was magic. Dee asked her mom to watch Jeremy and Aaliyah because Dee wanted to give Taleeb a birthday present, he would never forget. April wanted to know what Dee was going to get Taleeb for his birthday and Dee giggled and said, "He's getting, me." Dee didn't have time to give her mother all the details because she had a lot of errands to run. She went to the lingerie store and got a naughty red and black see-through negligee. After she made her daily bank deposits, Dee went to her favorite clothing store and brought red high heel stilettos to go with her hooker outfit. She got her hair, eyebrows, and lashes done after her manicure and pedicure. People complimented Dee everywhere she went but her only concern was how she looked to Taleeb.

When Taleeb got home from taking care of his finances, he went into the condo, and it was spectacular. Balloons made of hearts were floating in the air and candle flames danced around on their wicks throughout the place. Taleeb was suddenly in a good mood; he took off his jacket and yelled,

"Hey baby where are you!!!?"

"Hold on sugar," said Dee.

Taleeb yelled, "Where are the kids?"

Dee yelled back, "Over mom's!"

There was salmon, greens and sweet potatoes on the stove and Taleeb began eating the food while it was still in the pots. The table was decorated with a beautiful runner and specially made napkin holders. The food was still warm, and Taleeb made their plates. Dee came into the kitchen with a cake in her hands and yelled, "Happy birthday, baby!"

Taleeb couldn't believe his eyes. Dee had on a sexy lingerie outfit and high heels. Taleeb had seen hundreds of nice-looking women that were built like brick houses. But Dee was built like a stallion. She looked marvelous and mischievous.

Dee asked seductively, "Do you like it?"

"I love it, you look fantastic." Taleeb forgot about the food and cake and kissed Dee passionately. She grabbed his hand and took him to the bedroom. He took off his clothes and they made intense love and Dee had the first orgasm in her life. She had only been with one man since high school, her baby's daddy, who obviously wasn't good in bed. She loved Taleeb with all her heart and wanted to get married. She waited patiently for him to ask her.

Taleeb had never been in love before but he loved Dee. She could cook and clean a house, which was unusual for a young lady. She was always in a good mood and happy to see him. Taleeb missed his family when he was away and couldn't wait to get home and see Dee and the kids when he got home. Jeremy called Taleeb daddy and Aaliyah called Dee mama. Taleeb treated Jeremy like his biological son.

Jeremy's father was a nuisance because he wanted to get back with Dee. When Jeremy's father got out of jail, he called Dee. Patrick didn't want to talk to his son, Patrick wanted to talk to Dee. She told Patrick she was in a relationship. Patrick overheard Jeremy call Taleeb daddy and Patrick asked Dee, "Can I speak to Taleeb?"

"Why do you want to speak to my man?"

"Because my son is calling that bum, daddy, and I'm his daddy."

Dee said, "Patrick, Taleeb has done more for Jeremy in a year than you have done for him in his entire life. I allowed Jeremy to call Taleeb daddy because he spends time with Jeremy, something you never done."

"Is there a problem?" said Taleeb.

"I'm sorry, baby. Jeremy's dad is on the phone. He overheard Jeremy call you daddy and he's upset. He wants to talk to you."

"I'll talk to him," but Dee was apprehensive about giving Taleeb the phone.

"It'll be ok," said Taleeb and Dee gave him the phone. Taleeb's deep baritone voice vibrated through the receiver saying, "What's going on?"

"You know what going on, why are you letting my son call you daddy, punk."

"Your son calls me daddy because he loves and respects me. I would appreciate it if you respected me as well. Oh, and by the way my brotha, watch your tone."

Patrick couldn't believe Taleeb had spoken to him that way and Patrick told Taleeb "I will beat the shit out of you as soon as I find out where Dee lives." Patrick was released from Pendleton Correctional Institution where they put prisoners with mental disorders. Patrick was sure that Taleeb would be terrified of him once he found out where Patrick did his jail time. Patrick believed Taleeb would end his relationship with Dee especially if Taleeb saw the pictures, he sent her of his oversized weightlifting body. Taleeb kissed Dee and gave her the phone back.

Dee hung up the phone and asked Taleeb, "What did he say?"

"Nothing," said Taleeb.

Dee looked at him puzzled and smiled. They continued their day like nothing had happened.

One of Doc's men got locked up for putting a down payment on a new car using counterfeit money. Doc posted his bail and the bail bondsman told Doc that the money Doc was using to post bail was counterfeit. The bondsman knew Doc on a personal level otherwise he would have reported Doc to the authorities. Doc was dumbfounded because he used the money from the bank robbery. Somebody must have switched out the money, but who? Doc was going to find who made the switch after he tortured his flunky who was recently incarcerated for answers.

When Row pulled up to his restaurant early in the morning, five police were present along with Fred, the original owner. Row thought someone broke into the place, or maybe they were there because of the counterfeit money. Row was doing so many unlawful things; he gave up on trying to figure out which law he broke.

As Row approached the building, Fred walked up to him and said, "It's over, Row."

The two men met each other at the restaurant a month ago. Row asked, "What are you talking about?"

A police officer told Row he couldn't enter the building.

"What do you mean I can't enter the building? I own the business." Fred informed Row that he wasn't on the lease.

Fred said, "You're banned from the premises."

"What about my belongings inside?"

The police officer said, "Sir you may not enter the building and if you don't leave the premises, you will be arrested."

Row asked Fred, "Do you know who I am?"

"I've heard of you," Fred lied.

Row got into his car and said, "I'll see you soon, Fredrick."

Fred wrote down Row's license plate number and paid one of his comrades on the police force to do a background check on Row. Fred wanted to know what he was dealing with and how he could use that information against Row.

Fred had a complex business hustle. It was almost impossible to prove he committed a crime. Fred made millions from his scandalous dealings and his crimes never put him in jail because the remedy for his actions were civil matters. Fred had sold his restaurant five other times before he sold it to Taleeb. Once the new owners took over the business, Fred took his business back using the lease scam. He also had a pool hall that he sold 15 times using the same tactic.

Fred always sold his businesses to church people because they trusted him as an honest and well-established individual. When Fred wasn't playing the piano, he would sit near the back of the church and open his laptop with displays of the business he wanted to sell. He was searching for a sucka in the house of the Lord. If no one took the bait, Fred would approach a person that was new to the church and pitch the business to them. Fred would only invest his time with people that looked prosperous. He often followed people he didn't know outside to the parking lot to see what kind of vehicle they drove. If they drove a raggedy vehicle, he wouldn't deal with them anymore.

Fred played the piano for two churches. Dozens of church members and both pastors knew about Fred's hustle, but they never warned the new members about him. Large profits and packed pews were the main reasons everyone overlooked the lives Fred ruined.

It wasn't challenging anymore for Fred. Nevertheless, stealing money from church folks was safer, at least in Fred's mind. He was facing 3 lawsuits for his devious business dealings. But he wasn't the slightest bit worried because his wife, Sylvia was one of the best attorneys in the state of Indiana. She specialized in real estate civil suits and the judges knew her well. Nevertheless, they were suspicious of her repetitious cases involving Fred whom they later found out was her husband, which was a conflict of interest that they overlooked.

Sylvia was a depressed woman whose mouth drooped in each corner. She always looked sad and it amazed Fred how somebody that unhappy could win all their cases. She hated what Fred was doing to people but she was afraid of him. Sylvia told herself she was going to leave him after their four kids were grown. She grew up without a father and Sylvia didn't want her kids to grow up the way she did. When the kids reached adulthood, Fred was reading Silvia's mind. He threatened Sylvia with his police connections and told her if she ever tried to leave him, he would kill her and get away with it. Despite the circumstances, Sylvia had to get away from the demon that possessed her soul.

Fred had a 15-year-old girl pregnant in church and a two-month-old baby by another teenager. Fred loved them both. He took care of their parents' needs financially so they wouldn't cause him any legal ramifications. One day while in church, Fred motioned his underaged mistress to give their crying baby boy to his wife, while he played the piano. The newborn stopped crying as soon as Sylvia wrapped her thin arms around the boy. Soon after, she began rocking him to sleep.

Fred learned his devious ways from his father who was a minister. Fred made a good living off gullible people. He had been scamming people his whole life. Fred wore the latest fashion in clothes, he had a big, beautiful house and plenty of money. He was always aware of his surroundings because he scammed a lot of people. Fred was worried because Taleeb sold the business before he could pull the scam on him. That had never happened to Fred before, and Taleeb sold it to the biggest dope dealer in Indianapolis. Fred didn't find out that Row beat a murder case until after his criminal record was ran. Fred was angry at himself because he got too busy and didn't take care of business fast enough.

The day was a perfect time to surprise Dee. Taleeb gave her the day off and asked her to wait for him at home. She wished Taleeb would just tell her what was going on because the anticipation was overwhelming. When Taleeb got home from taking care of business, he yelled, "Hey baby!" He could hear her doing something in the laundry room. As soon as she came near him, she said "Hey baby!" Taleeb got down on one knee with her engagement ring and asked Dee to marry him…. and before he could finish, she jumped up and down and said, "Yes! The ring is beautiful!" He put the ring on her finger and she kissed him all over his face, with tears in her eyes. He said, "Would you mind going to Barcelona, Spain for a vacation?" Dee held her hands to her mouth, "Oh my God! Are you crazy? Of course, I will go to Spain, Taleeb!"

"Beautiful," said Taleeb. "When we leave, pack light because I'm going to buy us new clothes when we get there."

"Okay, baby. I will. Mama can watch the kids while we are gone. Oh wow, I can't wait to tell mama we're going to Barcelona, Spain!"

Undercover surveillances were conducted by different agencies. They were watching Taleeb's duplex. White men in black suits where in an all-Black neighborhood believing they were undercover. They would have been less conspicuous if they wore yellow neon outfits with cops written on them. The men from the various agencies were curious about each other and began researching for information on one another. Doc's men were parked near the front of Taleeb's duplex. The white men thought Doc's people were friends of Taleeb and they became more interested in the men.

Row's brothers pulled up and parked five cars away from the house. The white men in the two cars were paranoid because too many peculiar cars were showing up at the same location. They couldn't understand why Taleeb's friends were waiting outside his home for hours. It seemed like they were on a stakeout. Doc's men informed him about the detectives waiting on Taleeb to get home. Doc's posse left the scene but planned to come back later that night. Row's brothers left to use the bathroom and to get something to eat. They came back one hour later only to find detectives walking around Taleeb's house. They must have gotten tired of waiting and boldly did their jobs while the other men watched in surprise. The men walking around the house were wearing badges and the other parties watching from a distance slowly drove away. Doc's men were supposed to break into Taleeb's house and find information about his whereabouts. Doc wanted to know if he had anything to do with the counterfeit money and find him before the cops did. The question on everybody's mind was what happened to Taleeb.

The FBI had a skeleton crew working on the bank heist because the case was getting cold. Simona believed that the robberies were a diversion and the person who orchestrated the chaos had a vendetta against Judge Carlisle. She had her staff look up all Carlisle's court cases to see who might want to kill him. The judge was an evil man. The Black people that came before him always got the maximum sentences and the children were always charged as adults. His court room was typically filled with African Americans who made up 9% of Indiana's population.

Carlisle had enemies all around the world and that made it difficult to pin down who would have kidnapped him. There was one case the judge made a horrible decision on that caught Simona's attention. It involved a boy that shot himself in the head while handcuffed in a police car. In that case, Carlisle withheld critical information involving the police officer Greg Larson. Greg had a history of using excessive force against Black people that could have influenced the outcome of the trial. Larson's record was sealed, but Simona was able to see the sealed criminal history. She was appalled at what she saw. Larson had a history of killing Black men and five women. The man was a psychopath and needed to be removed from the force. The boy who was murdered was the son of a prominent doctor who coincidentally shot and killed Larson. Larson had the audacity to visit Doctor Robert Holland while the officer was on a paid leave of absence from his job. Larson got what he deserved. Simona had no more suspects, but she wanted to give it her last hurrah. Why not check out the only person that was smart enough to pull off a perfect crime? She thought to herself, was this doctor capable of doing something that heinous? Nevertheless, Simona had two agents watching the doctor's house.

It took Simona a year to understand what was happening with her case because of the riots and the silent treatment her agents were getting from the public. Vigilantes were taking out their frustrations on law enforcement and killed officers known to have been violent toward Black people. Mobs of people on the streets were praising the bank robbers. They wore shirts and jackets that read Black Robber Hoods. The masses were comparing the bad guys to Robin Hood. Thank God I'm retiring in two months thought Simona, but her goal was to solve the case before that glorious day.

Taleeb had to go to Spain prematurely without his family because the villa that he wanted had multiple offers on it. Taleeb traveled under his new name, Lance Battles. Blake wanted Taleeb to seal the deal and not take any chances on letting the property slip away. He had an inside source on all the offers made on the estate. Blake urged Taleeb to sign the documents on the same day of his arrival because the seller took Taleeb's higher bid on the property.

Taleeb didn't mind going to Spain earlier than he anticipated even though he was coming back in a few weeks. He wanted to make his visit productive and decided to put furniture in the house so that it would be livable before his family got there. Taleeb barely got to the airport on time, he jogged to the ticket terminal and checked in. After he went through the rigmarole of getting on the plane, he ordered a couple of stiff drinks. It was a nine-and-a-half-hour plane flight to Barcelona from Florida. Taleeb was thankful to have a friend like Blake. Blake wanted the best for Taleeb that's why he didn't want him buying any property on the internet because scammers in Spain preyed on Americans buying real estate on their turf. Blake spent months driving in expensive areas looking for properties for sale and collaborating with realtors who weren't scam artists.

Blake's hard work paid off because he saw a beautiful Villa for sale while taking one of his girlfriend's home. The house was extravagant, and Blake knew Taleeb would like it. Blake mailed Taleeb pictures of the real estate in every angle. He wanted to get Taleeb in a thriving area where the value of homes increased on a regular basis. Blake's only concern was the price. It was over a million dollars, which was at market value. Blake knew Taleeb was well off, but he didn't know if Taleeb wanted to draw attention to himself by living lavishly. Taleeb was very secretive and seemed to be eluding the authorities by using a different name to open bank accounts and to buy property. Blake didn't care what Taleeb was doing, he was glad his dear friend was moving in his neck of the woods.

When Taleeb got to the airport in Barcelona, Blake was standing where the passengers exited the unloading area. "Hey, Taleeb over here," said Blake. They did their special handshake that lasted for a minute and then they hugged. The men were excited to see each other, and both had a lot to talk about. Blake received the two million dollars that Taleeb mailed to him over the course of a year, but he couldn't put it into the bank unless Taleeb was there to sign the papers in his business name.

Blake took Taleeb to a fancy restaurant on the outskirts of town. Taleeb was impressed with the ambience of the restaurant and the culture in Spain. The restaurant was busy, which was a perfect sign that the food was good. It was a seafood restaurant with more seafood choices than Taleeb ever saw. They had swordfish, octopus, squid, and other fish Taleeb never heard of. Taleeb wanted to try something different and ordered the Fugu served with quinoa and broccoli.

Blake asked, "Are you crazy? That fish is deadlier than cyanide." Taleeb laughed at the expression on Blake's face, "I want to try it man."

The restaurant had two bars, one upstairs and one downstairs. They stayed downstairs because upstairs was a romantic setting usually for couples. The two men talked about their school days when they were in the fraternity and all the girls they shared. They were having a wonderful time, but Taleeb needed to get down to business. After they finished their meals, they went to Blakes's house to get the money and put it in the bank.

Blake's bachelor pad was nicely decorated. He had paintings of people with no eyes or mouths. But Taleeb could tell that the figures in the painting were happy because of their body language. The kids were playing, and the adults were holding hands. The paintings were full of colors, and they were done by a well-known local artist. The artwork matched the Aztec decoration of Blake's furniture. Blake lived in a high rise with a beautiful view of the landscape. It had a balcony overlooking the beach and the city.

"Damn," said Taleeb, "Did going to college do all of this?"

"Most of it," said Blake. Blake did well for himself, and Taleeb was proud of him.

Blake told Taleeb, "The bank is going to charge you twenty thousand dollars to put that much cash in a business name."

"Also, can I get my fees for the bank hook-up and the villa?" Taleeb gave him a hundred thousand dollars from one of the luggage bags that Blake brought out of his bedroom. Taleeb trusted Blake but he was worried about the money. Two million dollars could change a friend into an enemy quick. Taleeb was thankful Blake was a loyal friend. When Taleeb gave the money to Blake, all Blake could say was "I love you like a brother," he hugged Taleeb tight to show his appreciation.

Blake said, "I'm going to open a nightclub with this money. I 'm going to have live bands playing jazz to entertain my customers. Do you want to go into business with me Taleeb? There are millions of beautiful women here and the club would be packed with them."

"I'm getting married, Blake and loose women can get me in a lot of trouble. The last thing I need in the world is trouble." Blake couldn't believe his ears. "You were always a player. man; how could you give all that up for one woman?"

"It's called love, my dear good fellow. I plan to marry her here in Barcelona."

"Really, I know a nice spot for a wedding, I'll show you where the big ballers do their thang after we take care of business."

"Sounds like a plan my man," said Taleeb.

"Let's go," said Blake who was coming out of the bedroom with a rolling Gucci suitcase bag. He gave the other carrying bag to Taleeb. They put the luggage into Blake's BMW. Taleeb wished that Blake would have put the money in something more inconspicuous. Nevertheless, what was done was done, thought Taleeb.

The bank was only 20 minutes away from Blake's home. Before they went inside the bank, they had to get the luggage that attracted too much attention. Blake told Taleeb to have a seat and pointed to a large fancy chair. Blake went to a large office made of windows. Mateo looked up from his computer and smiled. He motioned Blake to come inside his office. The two men talked about the transaction that was going to take place. This wasn't their first discussion about the matter, but today it was happening. When they finished the conversation, Blake immediately left out of the room. He held up his hand and waved Taleeb to come toward him. I guess I'm the bellhop thought Taleeb as he took the luggage into the museum looking office.

Taleeb had already informed Mateo about the transaction on the phone while he was in Indianapolis. "Before we began," said Mateo, "I want to re-negotiate our fee." Mateo was only supposed to charge Taleeb $20,000 but now he wanted $50,000 before he would complete the transaction. Taleeb didn't care about the fee increase but he acted like he was insulted because he figured that if he acted nonchalantly the fee would increase even higher.

Taleeb said, "I thought we agreed on the price, what's going on?"

Mateo knew Taleeb couldn't put that much cash money in a bank anywhere without raising eyebrows.

Mateo said, "Taleeb, you bought $1,900,000 dollars in cash to our bank. We are not asking you any questions about how you came about this money, but it looks suspicious however we are overlooking the possibility of criminal activity. But because you are a good friend of Blake, we are willing to accept the money."

"Blake told us that you own various businesses that are successful. He said you are an honest man who will invest in this bank by getting loans for your future business endeavors. We will loan you whatever you need so you won't have to touch your own money, if you like. We are at your service and the $50,000 will consummate our deal.

Can we do business with you Taleeb?" Taleeb acted reluctantly and said, "Sure we can," and they shook hands. Taleeb filled out the paperwork to open the bank account.

When the documents were signed, Blake said, "Let's go and get the money." The two men got the luggage and followed Mateo through a long corridor which led to a prodigious steel door. Before Mateo could enter the room, he had to do an eye scan. Once inside the steel and brick room, Mateo entered a code to turn off the alarm lasers. The room was already set up to count money. There was a table and chairs in the middle of the room with four counting machines.

Mateo said, "I am showing you this restricted area because I wanted you to see how secure your money is at my bank." Mateo bragged about his security system for an hour as he showed them the thickness of the steal and how it was burglar proof. Taleeb was impressed but he wouldn't put all his money in Mateo's bank, Taleeb wanted his money spread out in different locations because he was paranoid.

After the introduction was over, Mateo called for his accountants. Minutes later four accounts came into the room and greeted everyone. Mateo gave them instructions and the accountants sat at the tables.

"There should be $1,850,000 in those bags, if that count is different let me know ASAP," Mateo told his staff. There were cameras all around the room with little red lights on them which made Taleeb feel that the money was in safe hands.

While the money was being counted, Mateo told Taleeb and Blake to come with him. They went back to Mateo's office and celebrated with a few drinks. While the men talked about money ventures, Mateo received a phone call. After the call was over, Mateo said I have some good news. The money was added up correctly and was entered into the database. Mateo walked Taleeb over to a female teller's booth and gave her the information about Taleeb's account. She typed the information into her computer and looked up from time to time showing Taleeb her beautiful smile. She then printed documents and a receipt for Taleeb. Before they left the bank, Blake decided to put his $100,000 in Mateo's bank as well.

Their next stop was the villa. It sat on two acres of land. Blake drove faster now that he didn't have the money in the car. He couldn't wait to see the expression on Taleeb's face when he saw the place. As they got closer to the destination, Taleeb said, "Blake I hope this is it man," and they pulled up to the luxurious house. It had a swimming pool and a horse stable. The estate was near the beach by the Mediterranean Sea. The outside view was spectacular, the inside was glamorous. Taleeb liked the marble floors, and each room had its own unique graving around the border on the walls. The home was impressive, and Taleeb hugged and thanked Blake. Taleeb hurriedly signed the rest of the paperwork to consummate the deal. Prior to Taleeb's arrival in Barcelona, Blake had to forge Taleeb's signature under the name Lance Battles on the documents to stop the bidding process on the estate. Now that Taleeb signed the original paperwork, Blake would take the corrected documents to his uncle who was a real estate lawyer.

Taleeb asked Blake, "Can you take me to some furniture stores?" He wanted to buy the beds and couches before Dee got there. She could make changes and add to the list of things to get for the house when Taleeb bought her back with him. Later that day, Blake took Taleeb to an expensive furniture store and Taleeb ordered the necessities for his new house. The store gave Taleeb the days they would deliver the merchandise, however Taleeb was leaving in a couple of days.

"Blake, can you let the movers inside the crib on the delivery dates?" "You know I can do that for you man."

The men went to bars, restaurants, and other popular places in Barcelona. Taleeb loved the atmosphere in Spain and hoped Dee would like as well. As the day faded away, Taleeb was worn out from going to all the places he visited. Blake wanted Taleeb to like the country and went out of his way to show Taleeb an enjoyable time. They had a bond and were elated to be in each other's company.

Two days had passed, and it was time for Blake to drop Taleeb off at the airport. The men said their goodbyes and Taleeb waited for his flight to arrive. An hour later, Taleeb got on the plane and played chess on his computer to pass the time away. The passenger next to him asked, "Did you like your stay in Barcelona?"

"Yes, I really enjoyed the scenery, and I can't wait to come back." Taleeb asked the man who had a British accent the same question? The man said, "I didn't get to see much because I was in a meeting most of the time. And after the daily meetings, I stayed in my room the rest of the time writing a speech for his boss who is the president of a pharmaceutical company. From what little I saw, it looked pleasant." The two talked about their professions, and it made the nine-and-a-half-hour flight pass quickly.

When Taleeb got off the plane, he expected to see Dee and the kids. His heart sank when they weren't there to greet him. He called Dee and her voice mail came on. Taleeb left her a message saying he was worried sick about her and the kids. Taleeb talked to Dee everyday while he was in Spain. He called April to find out if Dee was over there. He tried to ask April calmly about Dee's whereabouts. He didn't want her to worry like he was doing.

April said, "I haven't seen her." April became concerned because Taleeb's voice had a quiver to it.

"Is everything ok Taleeb? Where would she be?" April asked.

Taleeb cut the conversation short and said, "I got to go."

Taleeb drove home like he was in the Indy 500 race. When he got to the condo and opened the door, the alarm went off because he failed to deactivate it. There was a letter on the kitchen table with blood on it. Taleeb picked it up with shaking hands. He opened it quickly and there were pictures of Dee and the kids huddled together sitting on the floor. The fear on their faces made him feel sick. The letter said, "You know where to come and bring my money.

Taleeb would have given Doc anything he asked for including his life to free his family. He knew they were in a room inside the warehouse because of the background in the pictures. Taleeb did a lot of unpleasant things in his life but killing someone was the ultimate abomination. He believed that murder would harm his soul, but Taleeb was ready to kill Doc and his crew. He didn't like carrying his gun because the holster was uncomfortable. Taleeb kept the gun Doc gave him for protection in the tunnels.

Taleeb used to carry a gun inside his pants waist band near his front pocket but after a year had passed, it began to irritate that area. He then began wearing it inside his pants near the crease of his butt and six months later his rear end got sore. The gun was called a Beretta. It had an infrared light on it, but he never used the beam when he practiced shooting it because the point of entry of the bullets were off by an inch. He usually hit his mark without the assistance of the red beam. Taleeb decided to leave the Glock that Doc gave him at home to protect his house. He hid the gun by the furnace near the money. His reason for hiding it there was in case someone held him at gunpoint demanding the money. He would lead them to the location and hopefully shoot them before they killed him. He kept the Baretta in his vehicle. The only time Taleeb shot the guns was once a month at the firing range.

Taleeb didn't know how many people were on Doc's payroll. Maybe I should get a deadlier weapon than a handgun, he thought. I need a machine gun that can fire a thousand rounds in a minute and with accuracy. Taleeb planned to keep the machine gun strapped tight on his back shoulder. He wanted to let the bullets be his voice. He wanted his words to be felt.

The one person that could put Taleeb in contact with high body count weapons was his first cousin Benny. Benny was taller than Taleeb and his voice was deeper. Benny knew a lot of people and he still had the friends he grew up with in grade school. Five of his school friends were serving long jail sentences while others were being released from jail. Because Benny was a well-known DJ, he was able to increase his circle of companions. He was an honest person that enjoyed being in the company of others. Benny's main job was at General Motors where he worked for 35 years. In Benny's past, he abused drugs, and his drugs of choice was crack and alcohol. Benny turned his life around when he found Christianity. Benny had been drug free for 10 years. At 55 years old, Benny could now say, he was genuinely happy.

Everything that Taleeb ever needed help with, he called his cousin Benny who always came through.

"Hey cuz, how's life treating you?" said Taleeb.

Benny said, "Everything is cool, how are you doing?"

"I'm good. Hey man can we meet somewhere, I need to talk to you about something." Benny was curious because Taleeb was a straightforward dude, but he seemed to have a secret that couldn't be expressed over the phone. It must be important thought Benny, "Yeah, I'll be over mom's house cutting the grass. Come on over, I'll be there for a few hours."

"Ok, I'm on my way," said Taleeb.

Benny's mother Gladys was Taleeb's aunt and she lived in a large two-story duplex building. The property was her parent's home and when they died, they left it to their three children. Taleeb's dad was one of those children. Gladys and her brother Edward had a sister that died of cancer. Gladys and Edward fought over the house for years. Edward wanted to sell the house and split the money. However, Gladys wanted to keep the house in the family for anyone who needed a place to stay. Their relation became more toxic when Edward's name was missing on the Will. Edward was furious with Gladys and claimed that she altered the document. Gladys asserted that their mother took Edward off the Will because he never helped take care of her, nor did he spend any time with either parent when they were sick. The two siblings avoided each other's presence for the rest of their lives.

Everybody knew Gladys was a much more responsible candidate to take care of the property than her siblings. Gladys was a humanitarian. She would let anyone who fell on tough times live in the house and she would feed them for free. The family owned the estate for the past eighty years. Benny's mom also acquired the land next to the house in a tax sale. Gladys used the annexed land for parking and social gatherings.

The neighborhood was old and the people who lived in it had been there for generations. Everybody knew each other and Taleeb waved and spoke to the neighbors as he drove by. The area was going through gentrification and three white people had moved on Gladys' block. Realtors and investors were offering Black people triple the amount of money for their homes then market value. None of the Black people on Gladys' Street sold their properties because of sentimental reasons. The few houses that were acquired by outsiders had been abandoned for years.

Taleeb didn't care how valuable the properties were, he didn't like the area. It reminded him of challenging times. On Taleeb's father's side of the family, they despised him because he didn't look like Edward, and he was treated like an outcast. Taleeb had light skin and was the clone of his mother. Edward was a handsome brown skin man. Taleeb's brother and sister looked like Edward and they were treated like royalty. The gentrified neighborhood took Taleeb back to those dreadful times where danger lurked around every corner and poverty was omnipresent.

The lawnmower roared as Taleeb pulled up in the alley entrance to the backyard which was encased with a 10-foot fence. The huge gate was open, and Taleeb pulled up to the other cars in the graveled part of the yard. Benny was a perfectionist and wouldn't talk to Taleeb until he was finished cutting grass. Two of Benny's friends were there sitting outside in chairs smoking weed and drinking beer. Both men were drunks and they lived less than a block away in homes their parents left them. Taleeb grabbed a chair and joined the conversation and waited for Benny to finish. Taleeb knew the men well and they were harmless. They were talking about the number of people who wear glasses nowadays compared to when they were young. It was a discussion that Taleeb didn't comment on because he had murder on his mind. Darryl offered Taleeb a cold beer even though he didn't like Taleeb. Darryl tolerated Taleeb because of Benny.

Darryl was a simple man who didn't work because he was on disability. He didn't like Taleeb because he was uppity. Darryl cherished his neighborhood and everything around it and Taleeb was a part of it. But according to Darryl, Taleeb carried himself like he was the prince of Wales. Darryl could think of a hundred things he didn't like about Taleeb. There was something about Taleeb that made Darryl's upper lip turn up in disgust. Benny's brother Delray came out of the house and took over the conversation. Delray was the tallest person in the family, and he lived with his mother Gladys his whole life. Delray was supposed to take medicine for paranoid schizophrenia, but he didn't like the way it made him feel and it made him sleep too much. Delray was a lunatic and an attention whore. He didn't drink alcohol, but he smoked two packs of cigarettes a day. Delray was a comedian in his own mind. He laughed at his own jokes and went from topic to topic like a madman. Delray was also a genius. He disassembled a stereo system, a computer and television. Delray reassembled the devices inside a mannequin. It was a homemade robot that played music from its chest and had an operating TV as its face. Weeks later, Delray beat the robot unrecognizable with a baseball bat. He said the government took over its mainframe and was gathering information about him.

Delray hated and loved Taleeb at the same time. The hate often outweighed the love which made Taleeb his enemy unbeknownst to Taleeb. Delray called the police on Taleeb on several occasions and told them he was a drug dealer. Delray wanted Taleeb to go back to jail so he could keep his third eye on him. Delray remembered he set Taleeb up to be robbed but things went terribly wrong. While Taleeb was on the streets selling CDs and DVDs to Delray's crooks, they attempted to rob him. Taleeb was holding a plastic case full of music and movies. He also had a gun pointed in the men's direction, but they couldn't see the gun because the plastic container's side handles hid Taleeb's hands. Taleeb felt the aura of bad intention in the air and told the man directly in front of him. I have a gun pointed at you. If you are not interested in what I'm selling keep it moving or die. The men hurriedly backed away, got in a car, and drove away.

Delray blamed everybody he knew for the problems going on in his life. But Taleeb occupied a third of the space in his brain. Delray's paranoia led him to believe that Taleeb was the reason he couldn't keep a job. The voices in his head told him that Taleeb was calling Delray's temporary job lying on him. Taleeb never knew Delray was crazy because they grew up together and there wasn't a such thing as normal back then. The two of them always wanted to spend the night with each other when they were young, but they fought all the time.

As they grew older, Delray told Taleeb that he was God. Delray said he had the power to change the weather and create storms at his command. Taleeb was thirty years old at the time. It didn't dawn on

Taleeb that Delray was crazy until Delray repeated those same utterings his entire life. Taleeb realized that Delray was serious and believed what he was saying.

Delray asked Taleeb, "Did you hear that?"

Taleeb said, "Hear what?"

"Every time someone dies, I can hear their soul leaving their body."

On that day, Taleeb and told Delray he needed to get on disability because the things he was saying were not normal. Everybody that knew Delray would vouch for his unstable mental state. Taleeb said, "Man you need to go down to SSI, and I promise they will not deny you your money." Delray was mentally ill but not stupid. He took Taleeb's advice and with the aid of his mother, Delray got a Social Security check for the rest of his life. It wasn't much money left after child support took out their cut for Delray's four children.

Benny was the only person in the yard that absolutely loved Taleeb and cared about his wellbeing. The mower went silent, and Benny yelled, "Taleeb!" Benny went to the enclosed front porch away from his company. Taleeb followed his cousin. The dog wanted to come out and Benny opened the door and Chaos walked over to Taleeb for a pat on the head. Chaos was a brown and white pit bull that bit the face off a teenage boy. Chaos wasn't euthanized for biting the young man because the boy was on house arrest and wasn't supposed to be in that area. The incident was never reported which was a shame because the boy received 36 stiches across his face. The boy thought Chaos remembered him as he cracked open the door to kiss the dog.

Another incident that occurred with Chaos was when he broke his leash in the backyard and jumped over the side of the fence which was much shorter than the back part and killed Betty's German

Shepard. It wasn't much of a fight because Betty's dog was 12 years old. Glady's had to take out a loan to pay Betty $4,000 for the death of her dog. The money was not enough to repair their 40-year friendship, but Betty remained cordial with Gladys. That is why Chaos had to be chained up or locked on the porch. Chaos's head was as big as his body. He had light brown eyes and muscles that flexed with each stride. Taleeb was slightly afraid of the dog after he saw the face of the boy that was bitten in a photo.

"What do you want to talk about cuz," asked Benny?

"Do you know where I can get a sawed-off shotgun and a machine gun."

"Dang cuz, who got you all riled up?"

"It's a business proposition I have to take care of."

"Listen Taleeb, if you're in any kind of trouble, I got your back."

"Thanks, cuz, but I have it under control."

Benny said, "you know T-Bone got a gun collection and he has some of everythang." T-Bone lived nearby, he was as big as a bear and meaner than a junkyard dog. Nevertheless, Benny bought out the Teddy Bear in T-Bone. Taleeb wanted Benny to be the intermediary and talk T-Bone into selling the weapons. T-Bone was apprehensive about parting ways with his guns. He could have sold thousands of guns, but he fell in love with all of them. He was becoming more of a gun collector than a salesperson.

T-Bone was sitting at home eating a super large pizza with everything on it. He sweated profusely on a regular basis. The phone rang and it was his old friend Benny. He hadn't heard from Benny in a while. He couldn't believe his ears, Benny was asking him about high powered guns.

T-Bone said, "I may not have the exact weapon you're looking for, but I can get close to it."

Benny said, "I'm bringing Taleeb with me."

T-Bone didn't care if Taleeb came because he had his shit together and didn't have to worry about him trying to steal his merchandise. He knew Taleeb was a lady's man, but he never did anything to make T-Bone mistrust him.

RUNNING OUT OF TIME

There was a special knock that Benny used to let T-Bone know it was him. T-Bone opened the door, and his massive size covered the opening doorway from top to bottom. Sweat was pouring down his face.

"Come on in, does anyone want a beer?"

Both men declined.

"I guess y'all want to get straight to the point. Come on." They followed T-Bone to the basement and Taleeb couldn't believe his eyes. Benny already saw some of the arsenal in T-Bone's collection, but T-Bone kept getting more weapons. T-Bone had all his merchandise locked in cases. The cases had red velvet backgrounds with the name of the weapons engraved on gold-plated labels. Every inch of the wall was occupied with a weapon. T-Bone unlocked a steel door with illegal weapons of all kinds. Gun accessories were on hangers and laying on the tables. Taleeb could tell T-Bone adored his arsenal because of the time it must have taken to get such weapons. T-Bone had a favorite room with antique guns mounted on the black walls. The decorations and designs surrounding the items made them stand out like jewels.

Taleeb was overwhelmed with all the choices. T-Bone sounded like an encyclopedia, and proudly narrated the functions of each weapon that Taleeb observed. Taleeb and Benny were impressed with T-Bone's knowledge about the weapons. T-Bone told them when the weapons were made, how they were used and their accuracy rate.

Taleeb didn't see an AR 17 machine gun that white boys used to shoot up schools, but he was surprised to see the M-16. The M-16 was a military machine gun that Taleeb trained on and received an expert medal that he wore on his uniform back then. Taleeb decided not to get the shot gun because it was too bulky. The M-16 and his Beretta would get the job done. T-Bone knew Taleeb wanted the M-16 because he was thoroughly checking it out.

T-Bone told Taleeb, "You can't afford the M-16."

Taleeb asked him, "Do you want to sell it?"

"Yeah for $40,000," said T-Bone hoping to deter Taleeb's interest in the weapon. Taleeb didn't expect to pay that much for weapons but there wasn't a price limit for getting his family back. Doc and his men were going to die even if Taleeb got his family back safely. Retribution had to be paid - in blood.

Taleeb didn't have time to negotiate the terms. He wanted the long bullet proof vest that looked like a trench coat, and the gun holster for his Baretta.

T-Bone said, "You're at $48,000!"

Taleeb said, "I need to go to my truck."

As T-Bone let Taleeb out of the house, he asked Benny, "Damn man, is he driving around with that kind of cash on him?"

Benny said, "I don't think so."

Taleeb came back with the money in a grocery bag. It was obvious that Taleeb was going to kill someone, and T-Bone respected him for that.

"Hey man if you need some help, I could bring Genocide," said T-Bone.

T- Bone went into a locked closet and pulled out an M-60 machine gun. The Weapon looked like it could cut down buildings and it had a tracer bullet every twenty rounds. The tracer contained a small explosive allowing the gunner to zero in on the target. The weapon was heavy but someone like T-Bone could manage the weight.

Taleeb said, "I'll pay you twenty grand to go with me, but you may have to kill someone."

T-Bone needed a little excitement in his life, and he said, "I would have done it for free, but I'll take the cash."

T-Bone and Benny kept asking Taleeb, who was his beef with and why, but Taleeb said, "I'll explain everything after this is over." Taleeb knew he couldn't mention his family was kidnapped because Benny would have tried to take over the mission and Taleeb didn't want him to get hurt.

T-Bone was thrilled to use his weapons on live targets. The thought of killing human targets called for a celebration, he pulled out his best weed to get the party started. T-Bone knew Benny didn't want to partake in the festivities, but he was taken aback that Taleeb didn't want to smoke or drink. Taleeb saw the surprised look on T-Bones face and said, "I need to be in my right mind, or we could end up dead."

Benny tried to talk Taleeb out of it, but Taleeb was adamant about his decision. Benny felt bad for taking Taleeb over T-Bone's house. He knew Taleeb wanted to hurt someone, but Taleeb bought enough weapons to commit mass murder.

"I can walk home," said Benny "y'all go ahead and do whatever y'all gone do."

"Are you ready T-Bone," asked Taleeb?

"Yeah, I just need to get my night vision binoculars that allows me to see in the dark, the walkie-talkies and some extra bullets for our guns."

"What's the plan," asked T-Bone? He looked like a fat kid whose parents were taking him to a food fest. Taleeb began to explain the details to T-Bone.

"When we get to our location, I need you to get on top of the building next to the warehouse I'll be conducting business in. Don't shoot any females or children."

"Wow man, you don't have to worry about that. I do have standards" T-Bone said offensively.

Nighttime slowly overpowered the sun, and darkness ruled. T-Bone sat in the back seat of Taleeb's Ford Explorer because he needed extra elbow room. The vehicle leaned heavily on the side T-Bone sat on. Taleeb explained the rules of engagement to T-Bone while they watched the warehouse from a distance. It was a two-story building with the lower-level windows bricked in.

While Taleeb and T-Bone were talking, the FBI pulled up on the side of his SUV and arrested the two men. They confiscated everything in the vehicle and towed it. The FBI took the men to the station and put them in two different interrogation rooms. A medium height Italian looking woman came into Taleeb's room and sat in front of him with a stack of papers. She was pretty for an older woman, but her looks didn't take away the fear Taleeb was feeling. He was fidgety and didn't have time for the questions and answers.

Simona sat down across the table from Taleeb and asked him what his involvement with Doc. Taleeb was shocked that she asked him about Doc, he thought she was going to interrogate him about the weapons and the money. She would probably get around to that later, thought Taleeb.

"I met Doc in jail, and we became friends. It's as simple as that."

"So why does he have your family in his warehouse?"

Taleeb got angry and said, "If you knew he was holding my family hostage why are we sitting here doing nothing?"

"Taleeb, why does he have your family locked in his warehouse?"

Taleeb told her an altered version of the truth. He mixed lies into the facts. Taleeb couldn't tell her everything because he would incriminate himself. "I owe him money for the restaurant that he purchased from me, but I sold it to someone else before he could take possession of it. I didn't give him his money back because I used it to make other investments."

Simona started asking him hundreds of questions about the bank robberies and the kidnapping of a judge. Taleeb kept saying, "I don't know anything about it, nor was I involved in it. The only information I have pertaining to your questions is from the news."

Simona asked him, "Where did you get the illegal weapons we found in your vehicle?"

"A friend of mine, named Row gave them to me when I told him my wife and kids were kidnapped."

"You know that's a 20-year sentence if convicted." Taleeb looked Simona in her eyes and said, "I need to save my family and that's why I have the weapons."

"Where did you get the money to buy the weapons?"

"From selling my business to Row."

Simona knew she was onto something big, but she couldn't put all the pieces together yet. But Taleeb was the key. She had one detective following Doc and two others follow his men. Simona was making a career ending decision. Simona should have arrested everybody in the building for kidnapping, but she wanted more. If something happened to the family, she could lose her job and her pension. On the other hand, she could win it all and retire as a heroine.

Simona asked Taleeb, "What do you know about the counterfeit money floating around town?"

Taleeb knew Simona was trying to solve the mystery. Doc made everything confusing on purpose and the only way for anyone to understand it was to question somebody involved in the ordeal. Taleeb didn't believe in snitching, but he needed to control the narrative.

Taleeb gave Simona some bait and said, "Word on the street is that Doc and his people were spending substantial amounts of money in the strip clubs. A stripper I know said Doc is known as Robin for the Hood. I'm not aware of any counterfeit money but they are spending a hefty amount of cash."

Simona was surprised and excited. She could hold the people accountable for the robberies and counterfeit with one single blow. This could be the breakthrough she needed.

Simona fell into the trap that Taleeb set. She told Taleeb if he wore a wire and got Doc to talk about his involvement with the counterfeit money or the bank robberies, she would drop the weapons charges against him and clear his criminal record. Taleeb asked her, "Can you drop T-Bone's charges as well?"

Simona said, "I will modify T-Bone's charges but if you try to back out of the deal or can't get Doc to admit to any criminal activity on a recording, you and T-Bone are going to prison for a long time."

"Okay, it's a deal. Can you also release my vehicle from the towing place?"

Simona made a call to the police vehicle evidence parking area. Simona's team seized the evidence in the vehicle and dusted for fingerprints, they left the keys in the ashtray as instructed. Thirty minutes later, Simona told Taleeb his SUV was in the parking lot across the street from where they were sitting.

As a precaution, Simona planned to get a warrant to search T-Bone and Taleeb's houses. She wasn't worried about Taleeb coming to her office the next day because she was going to have him followed. She also believed he wouldn't abandon his family and go on the run because she had a good judgement of character. Simona was secretly rooting for Taleeb to get his family back unharmed. Hopefully, this case was coming to an end.

Dee and the kids were in a small room with paint peeling off the walls. The room looked as if it was used as an office in the 1940's. It had a desk with an old typewriter and a rotary telephone on it. The kids didn't know what the items were. Dee had seen a rotary phone at the Goodwill when she was a child. Her mother didn't buy the phone because it was outdated but she showed Dee how the phone worked but Dee couldn't remember.

They were perplexed by the missing buttons on the phone. Dee couldn't remember how to make a call. Dee picked up the receiver and put it next to her ear and heard a noise in her ear. Then she heard a voice in her ear and a person said, "If you would like to make a call, please hang up and dial the number." She tried to tell the person on the other end she was in danger, but the phone kept making a loud busy sound. Jeremy put his finger in one of the ten holes and turned it clockwise, and the clear spindle allowed him to move it to the end of its destination. He took his finger out of the hole and the rotary moved counterclockwise automatically. Dee could hear clicks in the receiver part of the phone every time Jeremy put his finger in the hole and repeated sending it to its ending point.

One of Doc's men called him and told him to come quick. "You got to see this Doc it is hilarious." Doc came into the camera room to watch the young folks try to use the phone and the two men laughed until tears came out their eyes. Doc really needed the laugh, but he didn't want to take a chance on the kids figuring it out. To be on the safe side, he told his worker to take the phone out of the room because it still worked.

The room was void of windows and somebody installed a toilet in a tiny back room when the warehouse was built. Dee and the kids used the sink to wash their faces and hands with an old bar of soap that was left behind years ago. A man opened the door to the room an came in with a ladies stocking cap over his face. It smashed the features in his face until he looked deformed. They backed as far away as possible from the door entry. The man dropped three bags of food and water on the concrete floor. He took the rotary phone and left without saying a word.

Dee and the kids ate the cheeseburgers and fries like they were starving. Jeremy drank the water too fast and started coughing. The kids kept asking her, where was Taleeb? The kids were worrisome, and Dee had to tell them something to calm them down. Dee told them to be brave until Taleeb came to save them. He will be here soon.

Dee was worried about Taleeb, but she wondered if their relationship was worth saving. She was sleeping on the floor and heard a voice yell out in agony from time to time. Dee knew Taleeb was into something illegitimate because of the constant bank deposits she made on his behalf. She respected his education and all his accomplishments but something he did went terribly wrong. And now this family lay here on a concrete floor waiting to die.

With all the drama coming at Taleeb from every angle, he was still able to execute a plan A and plan B. Pressure was mounting. Simona wanted something from Taleeb that was almost impossible to get. Doc lost what little credibility he had in Taleeb because he was supposed to be at the warehouse yesterday. Doc wouldn't trust having and opened conversation with Taleeb without checking for a wire.

Doc wanted his money from the bank robbery, but he couldn't tell Simona that because he didn't want her to know he was involved. Doc couldn't be 100 percent sure that Taleeb betrayed him, it could have been one of his boys. If by some miracle he was able to record their conversation, Simona would think he was the counterfeiter. Taleeb needed to control what was said but how could that be done? he wondered. That's where plan A would come into play, Taleeb had to draw Row into this fiasco. Row had been calling Taleeb and threatening his life because Row felt he had been conned. Fred was shot in the chest a month after the incident and lay in the hospital in critical condition. Row and his brothers vandalized the place, and it closed down.

Simona was in good spirits and released T-Bone as well. She told Taleeb, "Come back tomorrow at 3:00 p.m."

"Tell Doc you will meet him at the warehouse at 4:30 pm. You and Shack are not to leave town under any circumstances."

"Understood," said Taleeb on his way out the door. Taleeb dropped T-Bone off at home. Later that day, he called Row who answered the phone saying, "Well, well, well, if it ain't my boy Taleeb. You got some explaining to do, and while you're explaining you better to have my money."

"Hey Row, I didn't know the business was structured that way."

"Shut your jaws Taleeb and bring my money ASAP."

"Okay meet me 1501 Capital Street at my building." "It's an old warehouse." "I'll be there at 4:30 p.m. tomorrow and don't bring your punk ass brothers." Taleeb hung up the phone. He wanted to get Row upset so he would come ready to kill. Row was looking at his phone in disbelief. Taleeb was going to die tomorrow, Row thought to himself.

His brothers were laughing when Row told them what Taleeb said on the phone. They wanted to kill Taleeb before the phone conversation anyway, now they wanted to brutalize him before they ended his life. Taleeb was the only person who could link them to the counterfeit money, and they wanted him out of the picture. They went to the warehouse that night to see how they were going to get into the place. The warehouse looked secured with brick windows on the first floor and the windows on the second floor were sprayed with white paint. Typically, Row would delegate assignments to his people but this time, he wanted to get dirty. Row wanted to personally beat Taleeb's face into a pulp. Row showed Taleeb how to make the money and he had the audacity to charge Row for money that wasn't real. Taleeb had gotten too overconfident, and Row wanted to see him beg for his life.

Row's goons made sure the building was empty and checked for alarms before they picked the lock of the maintenance door to get inside the 3-story building next to the warehouse. They used the back stairwell to go to the top of the building. Once they got to the third floor, Row went to a large window and could see the top of Taleeb's so-called building. He took pictures of the warehouse. He saw two cars parked by the warehouse and figured they belonged to Taleeb's friends who were going to die with him. Row thought, getting on top of the warehouse would be complicated but he knew a cat burglar that could do it with ease.

Row needed to know what and who was inside the place. He called Snookie, the cat burglar and gave him the details of his assignment. Snookie also sold brand new merchandise with receipts that came with the stolen goods. Snookie accomplished that feat by going into a Walmart or other stores with his crackhead wife. They would get a large TV that was already in the store and put it on a store cart like they were going to buy it. The two drug addicts would wheel the item around the store like they were shopping and then go to the return desk. Snookie would tell the cashier that they were returning the television because they got the wrong brand. He would explain to the cashier that they only wanted to exchange the TV. Because the box wasn't opened nor tampered with, the cashier would let them exchange the TV without a receipt. Soon after Snookie returned to that cashier's desk with another TV the transaction was finished. The two thieves left the store with the merchandise and a receipt. They had rules so they wouldn't get caught, never go back to the same store for a few months and never tell anyone how the hustle worked.

Snookie's specialty however was breaking into cars and houses. He was sneaky and quiet and often broke into people's houses while they were sleeping. Snookie got excited when he answered the phone, and it was Row. Thankfully, Row wanted him to do something that needed his professional skills, like scaling a wall and breaking into a building. Snookie was always dressed in black and ever-ready to use his God-given talent. Snookie told Row, he was on his way.

The two FBI agents who were watching the warehouse were unconcerned about their surroundings. Nothing special was supposed to happen until tomorrow. Four men went in and out of the building, but nothing was unusual about their actions. The agents talked about sports and made bets on who was going to win the basketball game between the Chicago Bulls and the Lakers. Meanwhile, Row could see the two men in the car with his binoculars, but it didn't matter because the men were unaware of their surroundings.

Row showed Snookie the landscape and the best way to approach the building without being detected. Snookie appreciated Row's advice, but he didn't need it. Snookie was the best burglar in the world, so he thought. He got the rope with the three prong hooks that he made. Snookie went between the two buildings and threw the rope up on the roof, but it didn't hook onto anything, and it came back down. He threw it up again and the spiked prongs hooked onto part of the pole that encased the air conditioner. Snookie was 5'11 and only weighed 110 pounds. He smelled like liquor, but he moved like a crack head on a mission. He scaled the wall effortlessly and was on the roof in 3 minutes.

Snookie believed he was created to slip behind doors and blend in with the shadows. He slithered to the door and picked the lock like a surgeon operating on a delicate procedure. Snookie entered the warehouse and tiptoed down the steel stairs. Snookie resembled a ninja training for combat. He suddenly stopped because he heard men talking in the distance. What were they saying? Snookie slowed his breathing and concentrated. The men were saying, they were going to kill him anyway and put his body in a concrete slab in the basement. Wait a minute, Snookie heard another man moaning in agony. Snookie gilded back up the steps in a hurry. He went out the door and took his rope and attached it to the edge of the building so he could unhook it easier when he got to the ground.

Row and his brothers were waiting by Snookie's stolen car. Snookie told them men were inside waiting to kill Row and his brothers. Snookie said, he heard a man moaning in agony. One of Row's brothers paid Snookie with crack, but Snookie needed money too. Row also gave Snookie $200 in counterfeit because Snookie was dependable and efficient.

Simona was up all night looking at the board full of pictures. She moved a few pictures around to different areas on the board according to their importance. Judge Carlisle's picture was at the top and Doc's picture was next to his. A large circle was made on some of the image's, written notes were above the pictures. A map drawing of downtown Indianapolis was in the center and a blueprint of the underground sewer system was beneath it. Lines and arrows pointed in various directions. Simona figured out most of the plot, but she didn't know who all the players were. She fell asleep in her chair and dreamt that she was conducting a bank transaction on the day they got robbed. As she walked out the door, a bomb went off in the bank. The blast from the explosion threw her across the street from the bank. Bodies and glass were all around Simona and she drifted away in a summer breeze.

Tired and hungry, Simona woke up with a stiff neck and didn't remember her dream. Simona's arms were folded with her head in the middle. Her body was sore from sleeping that way at her desk. She got up and took a hot shower and didn't want to get out of the water. It felt so good. After she got out of the shower and dried off, Simona got dressed and cooked a couple of eggs over easy, toast, and two slices of bacon. Simona washed the meal down with black coffee.

Simona left the hotel that the FBI had paid for and walked to her rental car. She opened the trunk and put the large chart that she was working on into it. Simona got to work 30 minutes early to make sure everything would go according to plan.

Simona believed Taleeb when he said Doc would search him for a wire. Therefore, she had her tech guy to work his magic. Mohammad graduated at the top of his class and had 36 patents on electronic devices that he created by the time he was 25 years old. The FBI hired him while he was still in college. Mohammad didn't need the money the FBI was paying him because he was rich from his inventions. Mohammad wanted to contribute to making the world a safer place and has worked for the FBI for five years. For this case, Muhammad created a wireless recorder that worked using the analog system with a frequency of 400 MHz Mohammad used a camera the size of a button to infiltrate the rest of the buttons on Taleeb's shirt that he was going to wear. A mini audio device was streamlined into the collar of the shirt. The shirt was flashy with a name brand all over it to distract anyone closely observing the collar or buttons.

Taleeb got to the police department an hour before Simona. He didn't get any sleep because he was worried sick. As he waited in the parking lot, he saw Simona enter the building and followed her inside. Simona went to make a cup of coffee and was surprised to see Taleeb coming in the waiting area.

"Hello Taleeb, come with me."

"Good morning, Simona."

She asked Taleeb, "Do you want some coffee?"

"Yes please."

"Cream and sugar?" she asked.

"Two sugars and a spoon full of cream." They drank coffee and discussed ways to get Doc to say something incriminating without Doc becoming suspicious.

Taleeb asked Simona, "Can I take my gun with me?"

"No Taleeb, you know I can't let you do that. Doc's men will likely search you and take it from you anyway."

"Exactly, and he will find out I'm wearing a wire."

Simona said, "Come with me, I want to show you something."

She took Taleeb to the debriefing room where Mohammad was working on the shirt. Simona introduced Mohammed to Taleeb.

Simona told Mohammed, "Show Taleeb what you're working on." Mohammed began explaining how everything worked, "This button on your shirt is not just any ordinary button," said Mohammed who was wearing bifocals. "It's a camera and we placed it at the top of the shirt so we can get a clear view of everything inside the warehouse. Make sure you don't block it's view with hand gestures. The collar of the shirt is a recorder, and this watch you are going to wear operates the button and collar. Touch the 12 o'clock hand to start the recordings, the 6 o'clock hand turns on the camera. We will be in our mobile unit that will be a few blocks away from the warehouse receiving the transmission."

"One question?" asked Taleeb. "How do I stop the recording?" Before Mohammed could answer, Simona said, "You can't stop the recording under no circumstance, do you understand that?"

"Yes, I was only asking to protect the department from possible illegal procedures that may occur during the rescue."

"Don't worry about that Taleeb." Taleeb was relieved that he didn't have to wear the traditional wire, but he wanted to stop the recording if Doc implicated him in the robberies. Simona explained to Taleeb, "If anything goes wrong, we have the place surrounded, our objective is to get your family out of the warehouse safely." Simona hoped that would make Taleeb feel better, but it didn't.

After Taleeb received his instructions, a convoy of law enforcement agents went to the warehouse in separate vehicles. The agents followed Taleeb from a hundred yards away. Taleeb's hands were sweating which was odd because his hands never sweated before. He was feeling uneasy about the situation; there were too many things that could go wrong. Taleeb didn't want his fiancé or kids getting hurt. Taleeb drove slower than he normally did. He was thinking about plan B, escaping to Barcelona with his family.

Simona got word that other men were in the area and could be a threat to the operation. Simona couldn't afford getting into a shootout outside the building which would alert Doc's men inside.

Furthermore, the unknown men were in motion before Simona's crew could set up.

Row and his crew were already at the warehouse scanning the area. He didn't see anything out of the ordinary. Row paid Snookie to help his men get on the roof. From there, all Snookie had to do was unlock the maintenance door. Snookie put large knots in the rope to help Row's 10 goons climb up after him. Once on top of the roof, Snookie told the men what to expect and showed them an alternate route to get inside the building through the vent. One of the men, who must have been their leader ordered two men to go through the vents and the other men went through the door.

A quick decision had to be made and Simona sent Taleeb into a death trap. She felt bad for sending him to the warehouse, but her career was more important than Taleeb and his family. She was ashamed of the way she felt, nevertheless, Simona was going to do her best to get them out safely if that was remotely possible. After Row's men entered the warehouse, Simona's snipers were finally on the rooftops of the adjacent buildings to the warehouse. She told them to look for anyone who was watching the situation with binoculars.

Row heard someone running up the stairwell. He noticed a few vehicles outside that looked out of place, but Row had 10 armed men inside the warehouse and his two crazy brothers were with him on the third floor of the building next to the warehouse. The footsteps got closer to their proximity, and they drew their weapons.

Shooting erupted inside the warehouse, it sounded like the war in Iraq. Dee and the kids held each other tight; they were terrified. Bullets that hit steel objects ricocheted off the metal and found their way through flesh. Taleeb was in shock and couldn't think straight. What the hell was going on? he thought. Men came running down the stairs shooting. Taleeb ducked under a table and came face to face with a man laying on floor slowly dying in front of him. Taleeb took the man's gun from his side leg holster. The guy never had a chance to remove it. Taleeb recognized six of Doc's men who were firing back at Row's men. Taleeb started the recording and yelled into his watch, "I need assistance, there are men firing at each other in here."

The SWAT team was determining what type of fire power the men were using before they went into the building. The team new machine guns were being used but the shotgun sounding off was intimidating. The SWAT team was not following orders to go inside the warehouse as soon as the gun fire erupted because they were scared. Their targets were usually unarmed Black families unaware of the circumstances surrounding them. It was easy to bust down doors of people that were terrified of them. The SWAT team waited until the firing almost came to a stop, and then they caved in the warehouse door with a military truck that had an elongated steel pole protruding in the front of it. Half the brick wall encompassing the door began to crack and part of the wall fell to the ground like dominos. SWAT entered the building blasting their weapons at everything moving. They didn't care who died as long as their team went home to their families at the end of the day. Simona showed the team pictures of Taleeb and his family before their arrival. They had been instructed not to shoot the individuals in the pictures. The commander of the SWAT team was also told not to shoot Doc. Simona needed him alive to confirm her suspicion that he was the mastermind behind the chaos that went down in Indianapolis.

With the smoke in the air and bullets holes in the walls, Joel told his men to kill anybody that presented a threat including the people in the pictures. The men that were shooting at each other began to shoot at SWAT. They knew SWAT was going to kill all of them if they didn't stick together. Row's men began communicating with Doc's. Four men from SWAT were dead and three were seriously injured. Half of Doc's men were dead, and Row only had two men left alive but collectively they still outnumbered SWAT.

Through the noise of the gun fire, Taleeb heard a woman's voice loudly scolding someone to get back away from the door. Taleeb yelled in the direction he heard the voice.

"Dee, is that you?"

"Yes, please help us," yelled Dee.

The SWAT team realized Taleeb was the man in the picture. Part of their mission was to keep him alive. One of Doc's men fired at Taleeb while he was moving cautiously to the door. SWAT mortally wounded the man who fired at Taleeb.

Someone else hollered from another room, the voice was from an older man who sounded tired. Taleeb wasn't concerned about the person in the other room. His priority was saving his family.

The shooting was coming to an end because there were only a few people alive that were firing their weapons at each other. Taleeb told Dee through the door to stand as far away from the door as possible. Dee took the kids to the tiny bathroom. Taleeb shot the door lock, but he still couldn't get the door open. He shot the lock two more times until the door opened. Dee and the kids came running to him and Taleeb gave them hugs and kisses. The man in the other room hollered for help again and Taleeb told his family to follow him. Taleeb went to the door where he heard the man's voice and shot the door lock. The man in the room had a foul odor and was malnourished. Taleeb put the man's arm around his shoulders and helped the man stand up. He told his family, "Let's go." Taleeb was surprised that no one was trying to stop him from getting to the front door. Taleeb was looking around making sure everybody was safe. The shooting stopped and the men inside the warehouse were dead or seriously injured.

Taleeb slowly opened the warehouse door and the INPD and FBI had their guns pointing at them. Taleeb's family slowly emerged into view. Simona yelled to her people, "Stand down! Stand down!

Don't shoot, Lower your weapons!"

Ambulances from every county arrived on the scene. Taleeb walked the judge to an ambulance and the paramedics got out of their vehicle and helped the injured individual. A news anchor lady from Channel 6 News asked Taleeb, "What happened in their sir? Can you tell us your name and how you participated in this atrocity?" Taleeb didn't answer any of her questions. Other reporters began asking his family questions from afar and they remained silent.

Simona walked in front of Taleeb to kept reporters away. She told the crowd of people that she was going to give them details of the events that unfolded. Simona told the reporters to meet her at the FBI Media Center at 10:30 a.m. tomorrow. Simona gave reporters the address of the forum and other pertinent information.

Simona ushered Taleeb and his family to her car and asked was anyone hurt. The family was fine, and nobody was injured. Simona took them to Taleeb's vehicle and told him she was going to pick him up at his home at 7:00 a.m. the next day.

Everybody was hungry and tired, and Taleeb ordered pizza while he was driving home. The kids went to sleep in the SUV and Dee held Taleeb's right hand all the way home. The pizza was delivered by the time they got to the condo. When they got home, Dee wanted to take a bath and the kids discussed who was going to get in the shower first. The condo only had two bathrooms with showers in them. Taleeb said I'll wait to take my shower last. But when the food arrived, they all agreed to eat first. The family talked about the ordeal they went through at the warehouse.

Dee asked Taleeb, "What did you do to cause us to be kidnapped?"

Taleeb wanted to be truthful with Dee, but the truth never served him well. Furthermore, the less Dee knew the better. He told

Dee part of the truth because if she knew everything, Dee could be an accomplice to the crimes he committed.

Tomorrow morning faded yesterday away. Taleeb woke up tired, but he got a goodnight's sleep. Dee kept hugging Taleeb tight making it harder for him to get out of bed.

Taleeb said, "I have to go, baby."

"Do you want me to make some coffee?" she asked.

"Yes, thank you." Before Taleeb could get out of bed, Dee got on top of him, and they had early morning sex.

Taleeb took a hot shower and it felt so good that he didn't want to get out. But he didn't have that much time left because of the love making with Dee. After Taleeb got out of the shower, Dee had breakfast and coffee waiting for him. Taleeb took a couple of bites out of his food and was on his way to the door before Dee stopped him to give him his lunch with coffee and a kiss.

Traffic was congested at that time of morning going near downtown. Taleeb hated driving slowly, but what could he do? His mind was all over the place, he had to relax but the coffee wasn't helping. When he got to his destination, he got out of the car with his lunch and entered the FBI building. Two agents were near the door, and they stopped Taleeb. He said he had a meeting with Simona. One of the agents let Simona know her contact person had arrived. Simona told the agent to bring Taleeb to the interrogation room. Taleeb was surprised to be in the room. He should be in a welcoming setting considering he saved Judge Carlisle's life.

Ten minutes passed and Simona entered the room.

"Hey Taleeb, how are you?"

"Not good, what's up?"

"Hey, don't worry, I just want to ask you some questions and this room was the only one available."

Taleeb thought, "She must think I'm a complete idiot, so let me act like one."

Simona said, "Taleeb we are going to talk to your fiancée and kids about their kidnapping and what they remembered about the men involved. We know they have been through a lot, but we need as much information as we can get."

"I need to talk to them tomorrow, can we meet at your house in the morning?"

"Yes, that's fine. Furthermore, you are a witness and a potential suspect in the events that unfolded this week."

Taleeb tried to act appalled by the comment, and asked "How so?"

"The 3 men that we interviewed told us you made the counterfeit money. We caught them on the top floor of the building next to the warehouse. We arrested them for illegal possession of firearms. We suspect that they had participated in the warehouse debacle. We also got a search warrant on their businesses and homes. We found the fake money in all those locations. The men are brothers and they all told us the same story that you made the money and sold it to them, and you are the one that told them to meet you at the warehouse. What's going on Taleeb?"

"I want to talk to my lawyer," said Taleeb.

"If you did nothing wrong, why do you need a lawyer?"

"Because I don't trust you. Am I under arrest?"

"No, Taleeb, you're not under arrest but we need answers."

"All I can tell you about the three individuals is that Row is the ringleader of his two brothers. He is an acquaintance that I met at his barbershop, and he became my barber. I sold Row a restaurant that I owned."

Simona said, "Row must be the nickname for Rowmaine?"

"Correct," said Taleeb.

"Where is the rest of the counterfeit money Taleeb?"

"I have no idea what you are talking about."

"Why did you tell them to meet you at the warehouse at the same time we were there?"

"I didn't tell them to meet me there, they were following me."

"Why were they following you?"

"Because when I sold Row the business, things went sideways. The former owner ran a scam on all of us and Row wanted his money back."

"Is that when you told them to meet you at the warehouse?"

"No, I was trying to avoid them because they are dangerous."

"Sounds like you set them up Taleeb."

"Like I said, I want a lawyer."

"Okay, Taleeb calm down, we have more pressing matters to take care of. For now, Taleeb, you are a hero. You are on the front page of newspapers across the country. You are an overnight celebrity and people want to hear from you. I have a press conference in an hour, and I would like for you to be there."

"I have no problem speaking at the press conference."

Simona said, "Meet me back here in an hour."

"Sounds like a plan," said Taleeb.

The lunch that Dee made for Taleeb was tasty. Since he didn't have enough time to eat his breakfast, an early lunch would suffice. But sadly, break was over, and Taleeb went back to Simona's office. She was on the computer and talking on the phone. She motioned Taleeb to sit down. When Simona got off the phone, she put all her attention into Taleeb. She gave Taleeb a five page print out of what he was going to say. While he was reading it, Simona was giving him instructions on how to respond to the reporter's questions. She gave Taleeb too much information at once because of her time restraints. Taleeb absorbed everything Simona said but what she didn't know was he was going to freelance most of what came out of his mouth. And what he didn't know was Simona intended to arrest him as soon as she got enough evidence against him.

Simona had to change the venue from the FBI media room to a space in the Convention Center downtown because too many important people wanted to attend the event. Simona's team informed the press of the change. The space at the Convention Center was set up to hold 300 people. It was the perfect place to give a few speeches and take questions from reporters. People wanted answers and law enforcement wanted to hold the criminals involved accountable.

Simona felt like she had conquered the world until one of her agents pulled her to the side and told her the three men that were arrested yesterday, were dead.

"How did they die? Or should I say who killed them?"

"One of the brothers was hung in his cell, the cops are saying he committed suicide. Brother number 2 was shot in the head by an officer who said his partner was attacked by the subject and a struggle ensued and the gun invertedly went off. Lastly, the oldest brother was savagely beaten and was suffocated to death by a prisoner."

Just like that, her world crumbled. Simona asked the agent if the press knew about the incident. He said he didn't know. She didn't want to be asked about the deaths without being prepared. Simona called the chief of police to get more details, but the voice machine came on and she left a message. Twenty minutes before the press conference, Chief Turner called her back. He gave her the information she requested but none of it made sense. Simona didn't have time to dig deeper into the conversation. A full FBI investigation was brewing in Simona's mind. Now she clearly understood why the protesters were angry and they would get closure if it were up to her.

Lights, cameras and action, the conference meeting started. There were more people than they expected but the technicians and security handling crowd control were able to adjust rapidly to the situation. Simona began her speech by thanking the reporters and other people in the audience for being there. Reporters were asking her questions, but Simona told the audience to hold their questions until she was done.

"Let's start with the good news, as you may already know, we found Judge Carlisle yesterday, alive. He was in critical condition yesterday, but he is doing better today. His kidnappers were killed in a shootout with SWAT. The leader of the kidnappers, Farley Holland had history with Carlisle. Twenty years ago, Mr. Holland's son died while in custody of the police. Mr. Holland blamed the judge for not filing criminal charges against the officer. Also, we have a lead on the perpetrators who have plagued the great state of Indiana with counterfeit money, and we are building a solid case against the individuals involved. Now are there any questions?"

The room erupted with noise, cameras clicking, and everyone was trying to speak to Simona at the same time. She picked a reporter in the middle of the conference room. The lady began to speak, and Simona stopped her and said, "Could you state your name and what organization you are with?"

The lady said, "My name is Stacy Cantrell, and I am the anchor for BNC news. It's a Black News network that streams on the internet." The news anchor said, "What do you know about the Black men that were arrested yesterday?" My second question is how were they killed in jail under your supervision? What do you have to say, Ms. Giovanni about these strange coincidences?"

The crowd grew loud and angry. Damn, why did the first question have to be about a topic she prayed nobody would ask. How did this woman know about confidential information that wasn't a day old? Somebody had to leak the story, but who would benefit?

Simona was deep in thought when the news anchor asked, "Ma'am are you okay?"

Simona snapped out of it and apologized. Simona answered the questions and said, "The men were brothers with extensive criminal records. They were witnesses in a high-profile case and we are investigation their deaths."

Simona decided not to give any more information about the matter. She said again, "The case is under investigation and that's all we have on it right now."

The same news anchor asked her last question and it stunned Simona. "Why is it that every time a Black man is murdered by law enforcement, you people disclose information about their criminal record? Are their murders justified because they had records?"

Half the crowd was yelling, "Amen!" and, "Tell it like it is,

Queen!"

"Look people, I know you are upset but let me make it clear, we are going to find the underlying cause of this situation." This time Simona pointed to someone else in the audience and the man said his name and the news station he worked for.

"What was Taleeb's role in the ordeal? Did he know the kidnappers?"

Simona stepped aside and motioned Taleeb to come up to the mic and speak. Taleeb was under duress because Simona told him earlier that she had a lead on the perpetrators that plagued the city with counterfeit money. Taleeb was beginning to think Simona was investigating him. But he was relieved when the reporter asked about the three men that died in police custody. Taleeb believed it was Row and his brothers. Without them, Simona wouldn't have a solid case against him.

Taleeb went to the podium and announced his name, he told the crowded room that his family was also kidnapped by Farley Holland, AKA, Doc. "I owed Doc some money and he kidnapped my family for ransom. I didn't know who Judge Carlisle was but after I saved my wife and kids, I heard a man asking for help behind a closed door. I was able to get the door open and saw a frail man sitting in a chair. I helped him up and the rest is history."

"Are you going to get the $500,000 reward that Judge Carlisle's family put up for him?" asked the reporter. "

If any money is awarded to me, I would like to ask the Carlisle family to donate my $500,000 to the Holy Family Shelter, Dayspring Food Center, and Freedom Mission Ministries for battered women. I want to tell the good folk of Indianapolis that I feel your pain, I too have been a victim of police brutality. I too have been incarcerated and served time based off hearsay. Everything I worked hard for was taken away from me by this corrupt system. This city was built on the backs of poor Black people. When you walk in any courtroom in Indianapolis all you see is Black people except for the judges, lawyers, and prosecutors. We financed the state of Indiana with our court fees, traffic fees, bail bonds, jail fees, work-release fees, and GPS tracking fees."

People were cheering loudly, and Simona's agents took the microphone from Taleeb. Simona was angry because Taleeb didn't stick to the script. Her colleagues warned her not to put Taleeb on the stage, but she wanted to lift people's spirits in Indianapolis because there was too much bad press for over a year. Whatever she thought, it wasn't a good idea. But the show had to go on, she called on different reporters and answered questions until her conference was over.

Simona was so angry at Taleeb she was trembling. She walked up to him and said, "What kind of stunt was that?"

"What do you mean," asked Taleeb, who was on the verge of smiling but he could see that Simona was upset.

She started poking her index finger into his chest, "You know what I'm talking about, buster."

Taleeb remembered his grandmother using that terminology when she was angry at somebody. Taleeb was holding back a chuckle and hoped he wouldn't break out laughing.

"Do you think this is a game? I told you what to say, we went over this, what is your problem?"

"Are you trying to start another riot? Have you lost your mind? I want to arrest you for inciting a riot and I believe you have something to do with the counterfeit money."

Taleeb got serious because Simona pushed him backward and

threatened him.

"I asked you a question. What kind of shenanigan did you pull out there?"

"I know you're angry Simona but…"

"You're damn straight I'm angry Taleeb, you ruined my career."

"Simona you're exaggerating, how…."

"Don't tell me I'm exaggerating. I went against my better judgment and trusted you." There is way too much tension between Black people and the police, Taleeb. You don't understand what's going on, you may have caused the destruction of this city."

"Hear me out Simona, you are a heroine. You obviously had a hunch to stakeout the warehouse and was successful in solving a kidnapping case. I'm on your side Simona, I also want to heal the city. We want the same thing; we are just going about it in different ways."

"Get the hell out of my face and you better not leave town."

Three minutes later, Simona's boss Stanley called and asked her about the case. Simona knew he was making small talk and she was agitated. Stan knew everything that was going on because he had spies everywhere.

"What's really on your mind Stan?"

"Take it easy Simon, I'm genuinely concerned about you. I know how hard you have been working on the case and we are happy with your results. Your retirement is today, have you forgotten?"

Simona had a lot on her mind and couldn't believe she had forgotten about a major milestone in her life. "Who does that?" she thought.

"It's that time Simona. We have someone else to take over from here."

She couldn't believe what Stan was saying. "After all the sweat and tears I put into this job, you're going to give my case to somebody else?"

Stan didn't have the heart to tell Simona she had made some bad decisions. He believed Simona was getting soft. She used to be heartless, and he liked her that way. What was she thinking? Letting a convicted criminal who was a suspect in a criminal investigation talk in a media setting about an ongoing case. As far as Stan was concerned, Simona was lucky to retire without being reprimanded.

"It would be in your best interest to retire today, Simona."

"Who is going to replace me?"

"Tyler Cravits will take over and can you fill him in on the details of the investigation."

She hung up on Stan. She hated Tyler with every fiber of her being. Simona got into her car cursing on her way home. She drank a bottle of wine and went to bed early to put an end to the ratchet day.

Things were progressing well for Taleeb, but what he didn't know was law enforcement wanted him dead. They were conspiring against him because Taleeb became the voice for civil rights leaders, the homeless and women advocacy groups. He was an overnight sensation therefore he was an enemy of the state of Indiana. The police department had a problem with murdering Taleeb too quickly because they were still trying to cover up the three murders they committed yesterday. There were too many loose ends because the rogue police that killed Row and his brothers were overconfident and didn't cover their tracks well. The murders weren't planned out because they believed nobody would care about the black hoodlums. They killed thousands of Black men, women and children and nothing was done about it. They always got paid time off when they murdered someone. The cops that killed Row and his brothers worked seven months out of the year, but they got paid for 12 months. Their all-white communities gave them free food and liquor in every establishment they frequented. They got raises based on the number of kills they had. It was a beautiful lifestyle, and they loved their jobs. But this time things were different. Something didn't feel right. The atmosphere changed dramatically, and they had to switch up their statements to make it believable.

Their first mistake was killing the three men on the same day. They should have staged the murders further apart, but they had to do it fast because the three officers planned a trip together with their families.

The inmates the cops set up in prison to take the rap for killing Row's brothers were reneging on the deal. The problem with Row's murder was they hanged him in the cell to make it look like suicide, but his body was severely mutilated. The cops used his body as a punching bag to let out frustration for their fallen comrades at the warehouse. The last brother they killed was seen on one of the camera's that actually worked and if that wasn't bad enough a prisoner and a deputy witness the murder.

The three officers were in Las Vegas partying like rock stars while chief Turner was trying to clean up their mess. The men created their own gang called the Dark Blue and they were the most feared cops in the precinct. They terrorized underprivileged neighborhoods and robbed the dope boys. But this time they may have gone too far, they were out of control and the chief had to figure out what to do with them.

All eyes were on the police department and news channels began reporting mysterious deaths involving white officers killing unarmed Black men. The powerful organization governing Indiana called the *Indoctrination of Black Men*, paid those same channels millions of dollars to change the narrative about police officers using excessive force. The recent version of the news would depict cops as a necessary force to save Indianapolis from thugs and criminals taking over the city. Immediately after the money was paid to broadcasters, images of Black protesters vandalizing stores bombarded the air waves. Rush Dumbrough and other far right conservatives dominated the radio stations. Their white constituents believed that Black people were attacking the police and deserved to be shot and killed. The focus was taken away from the bad cops and the racial divide. The narrative in the news stations changed back to the war on drugs and crime. It was a major slap in the face for Black people.

Taleeb was thrilled to be home and everybody in the house wanted his attention. He realized that he had been taking life for granted. Taleeb appreciated what he had but he didn't cherish it. He never knew his purpose in life but seeing his family happy manifested a joy deep in his soul. Taleeb wanted this day to last forever but unfortunately it wouldn't because he spoke negatively about the police and unified his people. The ultimate sin was committed, and Taleeb had to pay with his life. The clock was ticking, and he had little time to make a move to Barcelona with his family.

Reporters interviewed Judge Carlisle's family and they thanked Taleeb for his bravery and philanthropic work. They donated a half million dollars to the charities Taleeb listed at the news conference earlier that week. After the interview was over, traffic began to accumulate onto Taleeb's condominium complex. Media outlets were standing around Taleeb's condo trying to get a comment or pictures of him. "How did they find out where I lived?," thought Taleeb. His neighbors complained to the Homeowners Association because they couldn't move their vehicles due to being blocked in by the large groups of media folks and they were being harassed by reporters concerning Taleeb. The HOA knew Taleeb was moving in two weeks, but things were getting out of hand, and told him to move before the due date or they would take legal action against him.

Appalled and disgusted by her boss' suggestion, Simona didn't want to retire. Her curiosity was getting the best of her and being extremely nosy helped her solve more cases than any of her peers. She knew that Doc planned the robberies, and she was going to prove it, even if they took her off the investigation. Because of her, not only did they find counterfeit money in Row's shop, but they also confiscated all the machinery and devices Row used to make it.

The mystery was where did Taleeb fit into the scenario? Was he the missing link? She was so close to answering those questions until the dumbest police officers imaginable murdered her witnesses. Stan took her off the investigation because it was practically over. The FBI didn't need the manpower to follow Taleeb around when the men responsible for making the counterfeit money were dead. The kidnappers were dead, and the FBI was ready to wrap up the investigation and move on to other issues in the world. Simona wanted to stay on the job to bring Taleeb to justice. Being on the inside of the FBI walls was better than being on the outside if she was going to solve the case that her colleagues considered solved.

Simona was angry at Taleeb, but he was doing something noble. She had to admit that she wouldn't give that type of money to charity. She thought it would be in her best interest to help Taleeb stay alive. His chances of surviving were slim because someone enormously powerful was protecting the police. They were acting like they had full immunity to the laws that governed Indiana. They were doing a horrible job of covering up evidence, but it didn't matter because the police were never convicted of a crime, they were involved in. It was clear the police were corrupt, and it appeared that nobody could do anything about it. Sadly, Taleeb was going to be their next victim. Simona wanted to protect Taleeb, but she was still going to send him to jail if he committed a crime.

SECRET SOCIETY

The *Indoctrination of Black Men* took orders from the Godsmen. Nobody ever met the Godsmen nor talked to them but when they wanted something important done, the president of the United States would deliver the message. The Godsmen were the invisible power structure that governed the world. The Godsmen held a meeting in an elaborate underground bunker concerning the protest, riots and the notorious police gang known as Dark Blue. They very seldom held meetings because they were a secret society and wanted to remain anonymous. However, things were going wrong in Indianapolis, and it had to be dealt with right away. Reporters were asking questions about judge Carlisle tampering with evidence in a 20-year-old case involving Doc's son. Questions were also being asked about Dark Blue being on vacation in Las Vegas pending their murder investigation. Who gave reporters this information? How did they know about the officers' gang name? Those were fundamental questions they would discuss if time allowed.

Their underground bunker was two miles long. The architect and the men that built the paradise underground were executed 700 hundred years ago by the secret society because the builders were witnesses to the structure beneath the earth in Georgia. It was like a museum inside. The walls were covered with pictures and drawings of experiments done on Black people dating back a four centuries until present day. In the beginning of the illustrations, there was a nacked Black man who was described as a human. Hu was from the root word hue meaning shade or color. A man of color was a human. The pictures on the walls began to evolve and the human being was clothed in fine linens and wearing a gold crown decked in distinct types of jewels. He had jewelry on his neck and arms. He was worshipped as a God and there were people bowing down to him. Slowly the pictures took on an unfamiliar perspective. Four African pygmies' heads were stuffed and mounted on the wall. White scientists were studying the human's brain by cutting off the heads of millions of Black people. The images of the heads were used on post stamps and was the most selling stamp ever. Therefore, hunters in Africa began beheading the pygmies, making them nearly extinct. The heads were sold for hundreds of dollars to Europeans countries. The heads were believed to ward off evil spirits and were also used as souvenirs.

Another artist painted a depiction of the Biotech Pharmaceutical company. Their gruesome experiments hung on the wall. In the painting were images of Black people getting vaccinations and taking medicines made by Biotech Pharmaceutical. The side effects of those vaccinations and medicines were a grisly scene.

There were hundreds of sad and disturbing illustrations, but the last pictures were showing the genocide of Black people. On the display were black and white photos of thousands of bombings of Black neighborhoods and towns that spanned over hundreds of years. After the destruction of those towns, Europeans buried the evidence deep underground. Soon after, white people made beautiful lakes above the dead bodies with million-dollar homes around them. Under 40 manmade lakes in America, black towns lay underneath them. The monsters that destroyed those successful Black towns were photographed by each lake.

The members representing the counsel consisted of 33 men. They belonged to the most powerful group in the world called the Godsmen, like their forefathers before them. They ruled the *Indoctrination of Black Men*. The 33 men wore masks passed down to them through many generations before them. Each man had on a different mask. The masks were formally worn by the Egyptians who the *Godsmen's* ancestors worshipped as Gods. Those worshippers destroyed their mortal Black Gods and took the knowledge they learned from them and ruled the world until present day.

The masked man with the snake protruding from the top of it was a descendent from the Rakefuller family. He was angry to be at the meeting because he was supposed to be spending the day molesting Asian children that he bought in Cambodia. Why did this meeting have to take place when they had unlimited resources at their disposal to have places like Indianapolis obliterated? He didn't know why they had to wear masks; their identities were supposed to be unknown to each other, but the men were Billionaires who paid a lot of money to find out the identities of each member in the room.

Before anyone could speak at the meeting, the speaker had to hold up a small sign with an Egyptian symbol on it which meant to speak. While the meeting was in session, the snake let his anger be known to the other members. "Why are we here discussing a city that we plagued with heroin and crack decades ago? We paid off their pastors to be non- political, these people have no unity. One man who is a nobody cannot bring these people together, let's just pay him to shut his mouth or kill him."

The man with bulls' horns sticking out of his head harness was the oldest member in the group. He was a descendent of the Rethschild family who called the meeting. He was a doctor that was bored experimenting with the severed genitals of the pre-teen Black boys trying to cure the impotency problem with older men. He ordered his bodyguards to scatter the remains of the boy's bodies throughout Atlanta to make it look like a serial-killer had done it.

In his spare time, he surgically switched boys' penises to different boy's body. But for the operation to be successful, the boy's blood type had to be compatible. After 15 years of research, he solved the erectile disfunction problem in older men.

The doctor needed a break from his work and do something more adventurous, that's why he set up the meeting. He wanted to be back in the bunker that his ancestors built. He hadn't been inside there for 30 years, and he missed the place. He needed a reason to be in the bunker because he wanted to break up the monotony in his life.

The 75-year-old trillionaire responded to the snake. "The *Indoctrination* tried to pay the man called Taleeb, but he wasn't interested in our offer. If we kill him, he will become a martyr and unite the most powerful people in the world. We know their history and we must continue to stop their progress in more subtle ways."

The Snake said, "We can inject him with heart attack serum. It served its purpose on the other Black leaders."

The old man was against those measures because he wanted to know what made Taleeb tick. Taleeb held his interest, and the old man didn't want him killed yet.

"Let's put killing Taleeb on the back burner for now."

A third man spoke up. He was wearing a gold crown and a mask with scorpions on each side of it. He was heir to the throne of England and owner of the largest corporation in the world known as the United States of America. The men in the room were his biggest investors but money didn't matter to him because he had unlimited capital and power. Nevertheless, his investors were worried about their number one consumer who were Black people.

He said, "Black people are a major monetary part of the corporation because of their spending power. They are still in slavery, but they don't know it because we repackaged and rebranded it. We mass incarcerate them and abduct millions of Black people every day and sell them into human trafficking. We allow them to put a church on every corner in their communities to keep the people on their knees praying instead of fighting their masters. Through our challenging work and service, we kept Black people mentally and physically incapacitated. But after all the obstacles and trickery that we imposed upon Black people. They are still rising to a higher state of being. Something began to change spiritually with the natives. They are waking from their slumber."

The elitists had to solve the problem because their money makers were out of control. Police had been killing Black men and women for centuries. But because of social media and videos of police shooting them, it became a problem.

The Godsmen's enjoyed the profits they made off black misery, but they had to keep their population at a certain level. Fifty years ago, the group began to eradicate Black people in European countries. The Godsmen's scientific research revealed that if European and Nubians coexisted in harmony, the black gene would dominate the recessive white gene eradicating Caucasians by default. Therefore, their forefathers set in motion a plan to systematically erase Black people's existence. They were successful with exterminated them in Argentina and they were going to use the same play book in other counties, but the money they were making off Black people prolonged their efforts.

"Why don't we give them money," asked the feminine male voice. The voice was from a Russian oligarch who was an heir to the Gotenberg family. The family's origin was in Prussia during medieval times. Their rise to power came when they got into the banking industry and laundered money for the richest people in the world. The female voice wore a mask that had nothing to do with Egyptian face attire. The mask was made of a thin white rubber and clung to his face like a suction cup. The mask was of a woman but the voice emanating from it was from a man. The man loved paying Black men to have sex with him, but he supported the Godsmen's decision to exterminate Black people slowly.

"We can give them reparations or give the African American

people in general a stimulus check." "It would ease everyone's anxiety and people would be too busy spending their precious dollars on worthless things to make them happy, said the soft feminine voice." "It would make them think America cares about them."

For once the unisex had a point, "How much should we give the people?" asked some of the men simultaneously?

"$2,000 or 3,000 dollars, I suppose that would solve the problem. Please keep in mind that this may only be a temporary fix, until we convince people that the police department will be held accountable for shooting unarmed men. People will be more receptive to hearing about comprehensive police reform rhetoric with more money in their pockets. Once we sell them on the police propaganda, we will create loopholes whereby nothing will change. We can also pass laws in republican ran states to make it illegal to have videos of any activities involving police officers."

The men in the room were astonished by the rubber face's conclusion. He had a respectable insidious plan. The 33 men voted in favor of the underhanded idea.

"Finally, the last topic to discuss is Dark Blue."

"Do they live or die?"

"Let them live, they are our brothers," said the man with the bird mask. He raised his symbol fast before leather face came up with another idea. The Birdman was from the Bloodberg family and chair of the Electoral College. He decided who was going to be the president of the United States with the approval of the men in the room.

"We should retire those officers immediately and give them a hefty pension."

Some of the men in the room wanted the officers dead but

they didn't want to get bogged down in a long debate, therefore everyone turned their pyramid signs to the symbol side that meant agreement. The men in the room were relieved because they solved the problem in one day. Usually issues of that magnitude could take days to debate and solve.

Things should have been going well for Taleeb. He was on all the talk shows and people viewed him as a hero. His life appeared wonderful but there was a dark side to his sudden fame. Taleeb was getting threatening phone calls. The police pulled him over and gave him traffic tickets on numerous occasions for no reason. Aaliyah was stealing from stores and acting out. He had to take Aaliyah to a psychiatrist to find out what was wrong with her. Furthermore, Taleeb was being followed by the FBI, CIA, and other types of agents. He was always paranoid and on edge. He had already overstayed his welcome in the United States. In a few days, he was going to take his family and secretly slip away to Spain.

Friction was bubbling up in the FBI agency, Simona didn't retire as planned and she was sticking her nose in places it didn't belong. She was demoted to a desk job making less money. Stan knew she liked working in the field, but he wanted her to quit because she was good at figuring out puzzles. Some things were meant to be left alone. People in high places wanted the case closed. Stan chalked it up as a win and celebrated with the entire department. Simona didn't partake in the festivities and left work early.

Simona couldn't get the case off her mind. It was an open wound that wouldn't heal. Who murdered her witnesses? Simona knew it had to be the police. She had three contacts in high places in the bureau that would help her get information on the perpetrators, but her peers were warned that helping Simona would lead to disciplinary actions including termination.

Simona was hot on Taleeb's trail but getting the dirty cops off the streets was more important. She was doing something in her field that was unprofessional. She was taking her work personally. But she couldn't help it, three young men were brutally murdered. Simona reflected on her childhood. She remembered the police severely beating her father. There were no actions taken against the officers and that was why Simona got into law enforcement. She wanted to prevent senseless killings of unarmed Black men by the hands of police officers, and she learned that it was an uphill battle that she couldn't win.

The Dark Blue were having the time of their lives in Vegas. Danny was the oldest of his crew and the leader. He was an Irishman and most of his friends called him Danny Boy. Danny never wanted to be a cop even though his father and grandfather were policemen. Danny was a stereotypical boy growing up in Queens, New York. The men in his family were alcoholics. His father was a racist and abusive to his wife. Danny's mother was a soft-spoken woman with long beautiful red hair. She was a meek woman and very thin. She loved Danny and her other three children more than life itself. But she died at 34 years of age. Danny's father continued to raise the kids in the worst way. Oscar took Danny hunting when he turned eleven. Becoming a man came with challenges and killing a deer would induct Danny into manhood.

Today was that day. Danny and his father were in camouflage clothing, and the deer didn't see them. Oscar looked at Danny to make sure he saw the animal. Danny saw the deer through the scope of the rifle and aimed it at the deer's heart just like his daddy showed him. But there was something majestic about the animal that made Danny hesitant to shoot it. The deer was beautiful and peaceful. Danny's mind began to wonder. Was killing the deer wrong? Why kill something so wonderfully made? Something spooked the deer, and the creature sprang out of his sight. Danny was relieved that the deer got away, but his father was angry. He called Danny a faggot and a disgrace to the family name. Danny was hurt and tried for years to get his father's respect, but he was invisible to his dad until Danny became a police officer.

Jack was the second addition to the crew. He was a skinny misfit kid in his school, and everybody picked on him. He grew up in a poor neighborhood on the south side of Indiana. His parents were hillbillies and were proud of it. They became members of the Ku Klux Klan in the town church. Their pastor was the Grandmaster Klansmen, and he was Jack's mentor. In Jack's mind, nothing existed outside their small community and the world evolved around pastor Nicholas.

Being an outcast and spending all his time killing small animals, Jack had the propensity to become a serial killer. However, he made a detour and joined the police force to kill people legally. From there, he met Danny who took Jack under his wing. Jack was a strange person, but Danny knew he would be easy to control. Jack was elated to have a friend like Danny. Jack was Danny's errand boy that did everything Danny told him to do without question.

Scott was the third member of Dark Blue. His fame began when he was a college quarterback for Indiana University. He was severely injured in a game and had two surgeries on his knee and back. It was a miracle that Scott was able to walk again. Scott listened to his doctor who recommended that he give up the game of football or become crippled. Jack walked with a slight limp but that didn't keep from passing the police academy.

Scott always had questionable friends and that was the reason he was drawn to Danny. The two worked together as partners in the highest crime area in Indianapolis. Scott wasn't raised to be racist, and he had nothing against black people, but he had no problem assisting Danny in using excessive force on the black people they arrested.

The trio had a bond that appeared unbreakable, but Scott was having trouble sleeping at night, his conscience was taking a toll on him. Scott and Danny killed a Black man a year ago and Scott kept reliving the murder in his dreams. The dreams were weird. The murdered man was always pointing at something in the distance, but Scott could never make out what it was, but it was getting less obscure each time he dreamed the same dream. Scott didn't want to know what it was the Black man was trying to show him because he was afraid. Scott was falling apart at the seams and Danny hoped the vacation would cheer him up. Nevertheless, Scott's marriage was eroding away ever so quickly.

Danny needed to worry about his own wife. He was on his third marriage, and he had to make it work this time. Danny didn't want to be a 40-year-old failure because it would mean he was the problem. What Danny believed about marriage didn't exist anymore. He believed that women should be seen and not heard, and it was a man's world. Danny's wife Gloria complained about him being verbally abusive and being drunk all the time. She was secretly seeing a lawyer who was helping her divorce Danny and get what little money he had.

They all pretended to have an enjoyable time, Scott's wife was going to move in with her mother, she couldn't deal with Scotts endless nightmares. She tried to talk to him about it, but Scott wouldn't discuss it with her. She knew he had secrets probably about his job. She hated Danny because of the way he treated Gloria, and she believed Danny was the cause of Scott's trauma. She also didn't like Jack very much either because he looked like he had dead people in his basement, and he smelled like mildew. He was Danny's flunky and didn't have anything going for himself.

Jack only married Sheila to appear normal but deep down inside he was a raging lunatic and didn't like women at all. Everything about him was an illusion, he had acted like he was a typical loving white man, but he was a predator, and the residents of Indiana were his prey. Sheila was oblivious to what he was doing. Jack was out all times of the night, but she didn't ask him too many questions about his whereabouts as long as he came home once in a while. Sheila was overweight and had low self-esteem about her appearance. She would never leave Jack under any circumstance even though they never had sex.

The vacationers didn't know they were being watched by a man with shark eyes. The man went by many names but this year, he was Oliver. He was hired by *Godsmen* to track the three men.

The police were killing too many Black men a day. The Godsmen's gave white officers $200,000 to kill a Black boy or man and $80,000 to kill Black females. They already paid Dark Blue $600,000 for their recent killings. The Godsmen's ordered Dark Blue to stop killing people for one year until things turned back to normal. If Dark Blue didn't follow those instructions, Oliver would dispose of them. Dark Blue thought they were invincible because they had the most powerful organization in the world backing them. Nevertheless, the three men were going to be executed if they made one wrong move on their vacation.

Taleeb had taken flight lessons at the Indianapolis Regional mini airport where he befriended the 80-year-old Black pilot who trained him. David fought in the Vietnam war where he flew the Bell OH-58 Kiowa. The helicopter was commonly used for observation purposes. On a few occasions he had to use the guns and rocket pods on the chopper in a reconnaissance mission that he was assigned to. David learned to fly airplanes when he finished his six-year tour in the army. But now he was getting too old to keep flying. He was losing his hearing and his vision was terrible. David liked Taleeb and treated him like his own son, that's why he began showing Taleeb how to fly the small aircraft.

Before meeting Taleeb, David saw him on the news. He

believed Taleeb was in danger and that's why he decided to help Taleeb in any way he could. David was going to fly Taleeb and his family to Florida. David had an old friend who was ready to fly Taleeb anywhere he wanted to go from Florida. Taleeb didn't give David the details of his destination until they got to the tropical city. Dee packed light as Taleeb instructed her to do. Taleeb put a couple outfits to wear in his suitcase.

THE GETAWAY

Before Taleeb and the family met up with David, Taleeb had to lose the people that were following him. Taleeb paid Sandra, the restaurant owner of Southern Kitchen to block off the alley leading to her restaurant. Two of her employees blocked both ends of the alley with their vehicles. They used their emergency blinkers to make it look like they had car troubles. Sandra had her van parked at the rear door of the restaurant. As soon as Taleeb and his family entered the establishment, Gloria walked them to the back door, and they hurriedly got into her vehicle, and they pulled off at a reasonable speed not to draw attention to themselves. One of Gloria's employees moved his car from the north end of the alley and the van with Southern Kitchen truck exited the alley.

The posse outside the establishment was focused on the front of the building but a few undesirables were watching the back exit. They saw a truck leaving the alley, but they didn't know who the occupants were inside because a big dumpster obscured their vision. It wasn't anything to worry about because the truck was only making a delivery.

After waiting for 30 minutes outside, an FBI agent went inside the restaurant to keep a close eye on Taleeb. A few other men that didn't look like they belonged to the area entered the restaurant after the agent. The men from different agencies were asking the restaurant employees if they had seen the man in the picture they were holding. Taleeb was a living legend to his people, and nobody talked to the authorities.

Before they got to the airport, Taleeb switched vehicles and he and his family took a cab the rest of the way. Taleeb knew the men watching him would figure out how he and his family got out of the building unnoticed. However, they were going to be looking for a truck with Southern Kitchen decals on it and that would buy him time to leave without complications.

Dee had to use the bathroom. They stopped at a Subway restaurant for Dee to relieve herself and get food at the same time. Taleeb asked the cab driver if he wanted anything to eat and he said yes. As Taleeb approached the men's bathroom, he noticed an expressionless man with peculiar looking eyes. The whites in his eyes were missing, his entire eye sockets were black. The man tried to look uninterested with Taleeb, but Taleeb felt bad energy radiating from shark eyes. One of the men in Godsmen's circle was going against their leader. He ordered *Indoctrination of Black Men* to put a hit out on Taleeb and they paid Oliver to do the job.

Oliver planned to shoot Taleeb in the back if he was using the urinal. If he was taking a dump, he would have to wait until Taleeb opened the door to shoot him in the heart. Black people were easy to kill, thought Oliver, and Taleeb would be no different. Oliver didn't care how fit Taleeb appeared to be because Oliver was a CIA agent trained in martial arts. He also was a skilled marksman who claimed he could shoot the wings off a Mosquito.

When Oliver opened the door, he hoped to see Taleeb using the urinal with his back turned because it would be a quicker and easier kill for him. But things always had to be complicated. Taleeb was taking a dump. Oliver was annoyed because there was another man in the bathroom defecating next to Taleeb's stall. Oliver didn't want the other man to witness him kill Taleeb because Oliver would have to kill him too.

Taleeb was afraid because he knew the man with holes for eyes came into the bathroom. Taleeb was listening intently and could hear the man shuffling around. The man was doing everything, but he wasn't urinating. Taleeb had been shot and stabbed ten years ago, three drug addicts robbed him at gun point. The robbery left Taleeb with a gift to detect danger and his radar was going off in the restroom. Taleeb didn't have a gun because he couldn't get on the plane with a weapon.

Dee's son came into the bathroom and urinated. The boy said, "Daddy are you alright?"

"Yes, son I'm fine I'll be out in a minute."

"Ok I'll tell mom you will be out soon." Jeremy washed his hands and left. Taleeb made sure to be a positive role model for the boy. But Taleeb couldn't think of that right now because his life was in danger.

Oliver hated kids and wanted to kill the boy out of pure hatred. He decided to kill Taleeb slowly because his annoyance reached an all-time high. Oliver was going to take his time and watch the life float out of Taleeb's body. The man in the other bathroom stall finally flushed the toilet leaving an awful smell. He should have flushed the toilet three more times earlier as a courtesy flush and that would have cut down on the foul stench in the air, thought Oliver. Taleeb weaponized his belt by taking it off and wrapping the tip of it around his hand. He let the heavy thick buckle hang two feet away from his fist. The rest of the belt was wrapped in his fist.

When the man opened the door to his stall, Oliver hid his gun. Taleeb came out of his stall immediately after to use the man for cover. Oliver saw the man come out of the stall but looked away from Taleeb coming out of his stall. Oliver tried to be incognito and if he played his cards right, he could enjoy himself. The man that made the foul smell in the bathroom walked out the restroom without washing his hands.

Oliver was shocked and disgusted. Before Oliver could pull out his gun, Taleeb smacked him in the face with the belt buckle breaking three bones around his eye and shattering his cheek bone. Oliver didn't know what hit him. He was dizzy and pure instincts made him kick at the tall object in front of him. Taleeb tightened up his stomach making it hard as Oliver's leg connected to Taleeb's abs. Taleeb caught Oliver's leg and held onto it as he kicked Oliver's other leg and fractured it. Oliver yelled out in pain as he fell to the floor. He tried to grab his gun again, but Taleeb smacked his hand with the belt buckle breaking two of Oliver's knuckles. Oliver never conceded a fight in his life but every move he made ended in excruciating pain.

Taleeb took Oliver's gun and said, "If I ever see you again, I'll kill you." Taleeb would have killed Oliver if witnesses and cameras weren't around. The street code that Taleeb lived by was never let a man live that pulls a gun on you. Taleeb smacked Oliver in the mouth with the buckle knocking out five of his teeth. Oliver lay there unconscious, and Taleeb hurriedly left the bathroom.

Taleeb saw his family eating at a table with the cab driver when he walked out of the bathroom. "It's about time," yelled Aaliyah, "Did you get it all out daddy?" laughed Aaliyah.

"Let's go, said Taleeb." We only have 15 minutes to get there. Everybody hastily grabbed their food and they left.

Dee held Taleeb's hand on their way to the airport. She could feel his hands trembling. Dee became afraid because she knew something bad had happened. A buildup of perspiration appeared on Taleeb's forehead, and it was cool in the cab. Dee asked Taleeb if everything was alright, and he said yes but she didn't believe him. They were getting hate mail and threatening phone calls. Dee believed something happened at the subway because Taleeb was acting strange ever since they left.

The cab driver was constantly looking in his mirrors and Taleeb looked out the back window and saw a black Camaro advancing on them rapidly. Taleeb told everybody to make sure their seat belts were fastened.

"Hey man, you need to pick up speed," said Taleeb.

"I'm already going ten miles over the speed limit," said the driver.

Taleeb said, "The car behind us may want to kill everybody in here." Their driver sped up, but the Camaro was already on the side of them.

Taleeb said, "Everybody get your heads down."

The man on the driver's side of the Camaro pulled out his gun but the highway only had one lane in each direction and an 18-wheeler blew its horn. The Camaro slowed down and got in the back of the cab.

The Camaro slammed into the back of the cab and Jeremy began crying, "Maaama, I'm scared!" Aaliyah was crying and praying.

The cab driver's eyes were wide as silver dollars and Taleeb looked back at the man on the passenger's side of the Camaro. He was aiming a gun at the back window of the cab. Taleeb pulled out the gun he took from the weirdo at the subway. Taleeb shot out the back window of the cab with six bullets striking the front window of the Camaro. The Camaro weaved out of control into oncoming traffic and collided head on with a flatbed truck. The Camaro flipped in the air and came back to the ground on fire. The flatbed truck tipped over on the side of the highway. The two vehicles that crashed caused other vehicles to crash into each other because they were following too close. Everybody in the cab looked out the back window and were horrified at what they saw.

The cab driver was slowing to a stop to help the people in the accident and Taleeb told him, "Don't worry about it. Keep driving and I'll give you $500 extra dollars," but the driver said, "It's not about the money, it's about saving lives."

Taleeb told him, "You need to worry about your life."

The cab driver's bladder got weak, and he kept driving. Dee was afraid of Taleeb and gently pulled her hand away from him.

Taleeb apologized and said, "Hey guys, I'm sorry about all this but the men in the car were trying to kill us and we need to get to the airport on time because our lives are in danger."

Hundreds of calls bombarded the police department about a pile up on highway 600. The FBI was investigating the crash because two men were shot, and one man was savagely beaten at Subway. The video at Subway showed Taleeb buying food for his family. The FBI were trying to figure out if Taleeb was the perpetrator of the horrendous events that transpired. It was suspicious that the dead men in the Camaro and the man that was beaten in Subway's had no identification. Oddly enough, the Subway man left the hospital without the doctor's approval.

The FBI put out a $100,000 reward for anyone who had information about Taleeb's whereabouts. The news reported that Taleeb shot and killed the two men on highway 600. The news lied about the reason the men were shot. The media claimed the highway incident was caused by road rage.

Black people were skeptical about what was reported on the news. They believed that the police wanted Taleeb dead because he spoke out against them. Simona was angry about the "Wanted" pictures the FBI submitted to the police. She took a three week leave of absence to find Taleeb before the police did. If Taleeb shot the men, it had to be for a good reason, she thought.

Simona was at home listening to the police radio, drinking coffee. She was apprehensive about believing anything that came on the news in Indianapolis. The system was broken, and the city was the pillar of everything that was wrong with the judicial system. A friend that worked in Simona's department helped her with the computer surveillance of the area Taleeb was in during the altercations. After 30 minutes of surveying the area, Simona noticed that a small airport was in the vicinity of the accident. She had a hunch that Taleeb could be at the airport trying to get out of the city. She finished her coffee and told Tim the computer Tech, good job and left out the door.

Oliver's ego was crushed, he couldn't believe a Black man had beat him in a fight. He made a vow to kill Taleeb and that was his only mission, but he had to heal. Oliver stayed off the grid and stopped answering his phone. The bureau sent agents out to find Oliver, but he knew where to hide and how to blend in with the scenery. Oliver was in bad shape and all he could think about was different ways to kill Taleeb.

Other people wanted to kill Taleeb as well, including the police. Law enforcement was told to stand down until they got confirmation from the top to execute Taleeb, but a deep seeded hatred fueled the fire that burned in their hearts. Feeling pressure from the Fraternal Order of Police, Turner took the money from the Police Charity Fund and paid Dark Blue $300,000 to kill Taleeb. Dark Blue had orders to hang Taleeb's dead body in a Black neighborhood to break the spirit of the uprising.

David had the plane ready for Taleeb and his family who came in looking like they saw a ghost. He knew traffic was blocked up because he could see the bad accident from a distance. Trucks were turned over and something was on fire. It was the worst accident he ever saw. It was a miracle that Taleeb got through the traffic jam.

David said, "Did ya'll see what happened back there?"

Taleeb said, "Yeah some idiot tried to go around a truck and hit another car going in the opposite direction."

"Wow, that's sad, I hope nobody got killed," said David.

In David's mind, Taleeb was a civil rights leader. He respected anyone willing to give up their life for a cause and David was going to do whatever it took to help Taleeb.

The flight to Florida would have been quiet and tense but David tried to lighten the mood by talking about the weather and the olden days. Taleeb didn't hear anything David said because he was in another world. Taleeb regretted shooting in the car. He tried to tell himself that he didn't mean to kill anyone but as he reflected on the incident, he had no other choice.

Taleeb was arguing with himself in his mind. His better half was telling him there were other alternatives he could have taken. His mind began to play out better scenarios he could have taken to change the events that occurred. The survivalist side of himself was more deliberate and instinctual. He told himself that stopping the threat was the only choice that could have been taken considering the situation. His family's lives were at stake and it was his job to protect them.

He felt ashamed because they seemed afraid of him. Or was it his imagination? What could he do or say to build their trust in him? Taleeb had taken his family through a lot, and they didn't deserve it. The positive vibration of his soul was relentless and began nagging him about the consequences of defiling his spirit by taking a life. Taleeb had to silence his mind with a mantra saying, I made the right choice in protecting my family. Taleeb said that over and over in his mind to drown out the alternative choices.

Dee was lost in her own thoughts; she could hear David drone on about something, but she didn't know what he was talking about. She really loved Taleeb, but she was afraid of him and respected him at the same time. She never saw that side of Taleeb before. Had he killed anyone before this? Taleeb acted like a character in a James Bond movie. His actions looked professional. She was wondering if she knew Taleeb at all. There was too much drama surrounding him and it made her uneasy. Were they on the run from the law for the rest of their lives? Who were the men trying to kill them? Questions were mounting and she needed to have a long talk with Taleeb.

Jeremy thought Taleeb was amazing. The boy wanted to be just like Taleeb when he grew up. Jeremy started shaving his hairless face and did five pushups a day. He walked confidently like Taleeb with his back straight and his chin slightly lifted in the air. The boy felt safe around Taleeb because nobody could beat his dad. Taleeb would kill anyone who tried to hurt them, and Taleeb was Jeremy's hero.

Aaliyah was shocked that her father shot at the car, she thought he was soft. Aaliyah tried to downplay her father's success because she believed he was a weak pushover. She didn't respect Taleeb until now, he had proven himself on two major occasions. She had to give her dad credit for keeping them alive, but he was the reason they were in all this mess in the first place. Aaliyah had the same dualities playing out in her mind as her dad.

After David finished talking about the good old days to distracted listeners, he told them they had to change planes when they got to the small airport in Florida. David explained to them his plane didn't have the capacity to make long trips, but his acquaintance had one that could fly half a day non-stop.

Taleeb was paranoid and had already put David's life at risk. When they got to Florida, Taleeb finally told David where he wanted to go. The less he knew the better, it also protected Taleeb as well because he was a fugitive. David made sure his friend would be ready to make a long trip before they got there. Two hours passed and David showed up with the prettiest plane Taleeb had ever seen. It was two toned with the top half burgundy and the bottom half was periwinkle. It was shining like it had been professionally waxed. David introduced Bernard to Taleeb and his family. Bernard was a middle-aged Jewish man who wanted to be paid before they took off. Taleeb gave him a hundred a fifty thousand dollars out of the briefcase. Bernard counted it to make sure the figure was correct. He usually didn't charge that much but Taleeb was a fugitive and harboring such a person was a serious felony.

The plane was lovely inside, it had leather sets and a bar. It was equipped with TV's and a small lounge area. Everybody was mesmerized except for David and the owner of course. Taleeb asked if he could get a drink and David went to the bar and told him what was on the menu. Hennessy wasn't mentioned which was Taleeb's favorite, but he asked for brandy and a coke.

Dee held Taleeb's hand and said, "Baby do you think you should be drinking? It might not be a good idea considering our situation." Dee wanted Taleeb in his right mind because people were trying to kill them.

"Aw baby, I'll just have one drink how does that sound?"

"Well, I guess it'll be okay but only one baby, ok?" "Ok sweetie."

"On second thought, hold the coke and give it to me straight," said Taleeb. He needed the drink to calm his nerves. Taleeb was worried about everything simultaneously. "

Don't stress yourself," said David, "I got everything under control. I know what you're going through, I was in a similar situation fifty years ago when I was in Vietnam." David began telling a story about his helicopter being attacked with gunfire 20 miles from Saigon. The story was fascinating, but it was only partially similar to Taleeb's situation. Taleeb listened to David tell the story anyway.

David filled Bernard in on the location they were going to traveling. Bernard punched the coordinates on the plane's panel. He then began flipping switches and told his passengers to buckle up. The plane glided off into the sunset. After a few bumps and shakes, Bernard put the plane on autopilot.

Dee couldn't believe that all the excitement made her horny. What was that all about she thought. She needed Taleeb to take care of it at once because it was getting out of control. Dee looked at Taleeb and waited for him to look back and when he did, she raised her index finger up and flexed it back and forth. Taleeb thought he was in trouble. Dee stood up and went to the bathroom and Taleeb followed. The area was small, but it was doable. Dee pulled off her shirt showing her lovely contour and Taleeb went to work kissing and liking everything that was exposed. Dee wanted have sex with Taleeb without the kids knowing but she let out a moan and put her hands over her mouth. Dee wanted to skip the foreplay because she needed a climax quickly. She stood up and rapidly pulled down her panties and Taleeb unzipped his pants, and she could see he was excited. Dee told Taleeb to sit on the toilet and she mounted him. She tried to do it quietly, but bumping and smacking sounds were emanating from the bathroom. Dee couldn't hold it anymore and let out some oohs! and ahhs! before she got what she needed. Taleeb followed suit and was relieved of all his stress.

It was obvious to the passengers that the two were having sex, and it put them in an awkward situation. David didn't know why he was embarrassed; he did nothing wrong, nevertheless he didn't want to make eye contact with the children.

"That's disgusting" said Aaliyah.

Jeremy said, "What's disgusting?" trying not to laugh.

Aaliyah popped him upside his head and said, "You are

disgusting."

Dee and Taleeb came out of the bathroom looking like they went to a fitness center. They were hoping no one heard them. David was busy reading something which was odd because he was always talking about something or other. The kids were smiling at them.

"What's going on guys," asked Taleeb?

"That's what we want to know," said Aaliyah laughing out loud and Jeremy chimed in with giggles.

"Oh, damn", thought Dee, "they heard us." She looked at Taleeb and smiled and Taleeb smacked her on the butt, "That's gross," said Aaliyah.

Time went fast and everyone tried to enjoy themselves despite the dangerous situation they were in. David tried to lighten the mood and made some strange looking hors d' oeuvres and they teased him for making the funny tasting edibles, but he loved the attention.

The plane landed smoothly in Girona-Costa Brava Airport, an hour away from Taleeb's estate. Everyone said their goodbyes, David and Taleeb promised to keep in touch. Blake was waiting in his usual spot happy to see Taleeb and the feeling was mutual for Taleeb. Taleeb introduced everyone to each other.

"So, this is the beautiful family my best friend was telling me about."

"Hello pleased to meet you," said Dee.

"Likewise."

"Okay, guys let me show you our beautiful country. Taleeb can you help me put the suitcases in the trunk," said Blake.

While they were driving, Dee was amazed by all the architectural work that went into the homes and surrounding buildings. The people obviously liked bright colors, she thought, because every color God created was in their clothes. She wondered if matching colors mattered. Whatever the case, the colors were beautiful.

Blake made sure the lawn care service kept the yard manicured. He told the chief to have a home cooked meal for five people because Blake planned to eat with them. Taleeb was excited and hoped Dee and the kids would like the villa.

By the time Simona got to the small airport in Indiana, she drank a canister of coffee and was geeked up. She went to the ticket desk and showed her badge. Simona produced a picture of Taleeb from her pocket and asked the young lady at the counter if she saw the man in the photo. The girl remembered Taleeb and his family because they acted nervous. The girl gave Simona the details of her encounters with the family and where they were going.

Unbelievable, thought Simona, Taleeb wasn't supposed to leave town because he was under investigation. She had to remind herself that the investigation was over. He must have been plaining on leaving Indiana before the killings. Why was he going to Florida, did he have a relative there?

Simona was able to sweet talk the aviator manager to let a pilot fly her to Florida to catch the fugitive she was after. Simona was one day behind Taleeb, and she needed to catch him before the wrong people did. Taleeb wouldn't last a week alive with the psychopaths that wanted him dead.

When Simona got to the tiny airport in Florida, she realized someone was tracking her. The perpetrator was a woman sitting in a chair who was using a small mirror to put on lipstick. Simona thought,

"I must be paranoid", but their eyes connected a couple of times and Simona's suspicion heightened. Simona tried to figure out why someone would be following her. Could it be her agency? She was frightened and thought of ways to secretly slip away from the woman without her knowing.

Simona was observing the airport but couldn't find anywhere to hide or slip away from the woman. She called a cab to take her to get a car rental. She wanted to save money and drive herself around. The cab driver pulled up to the curb and Simona got in hastily.

"Where to?" asked the driver.

"Budget Car Rental."

The cab sped off to the destination. Simona didn't know where the car rental place was, but they were driving for 45 minutes.

Simona said, "We should have been there by now," even though she didn't know where the car rental was located. Simona's anger turned to fear when she saw the vast wooded area and heard the doors lock.

"Who are you? Are you with the agency?"

"Now, now, Ms. Simon, who I am is irrelevant and yes, I am with the agency. They told me to bring you in to find out what you know about Taleeb. They believe you're holding out on pertinent information and that's not good. The agency wants to talk to you."

"Why didn't they just call me!?"

"Calm down Ms. Simon they will explain everything when we get there."

"Call me Simona, idiot."

The agent erupted with laughter and said, "We will be there soon Simon."

If Simona had a gun, she would have shot his ear off, but she was restricted from bringing a firearm on the plane. The agent was very unprofessional, and she was going to report him at once. The ride was long and irritating and when they finally reach their destination, Simona said, "hurry up and unlock this door asshole." The doors unlocked and as Simona exited the vehicle, she saw Tyler standing in the doorway of the cabin.

Before this encounter, Tyler was shocked when he got Simona's position. He believed she was far better at the job than he would ever be, but she was supposed to be retired. Furthermore, she was aiding and abetting a criminal. Stan must have received the authorization to promote him from the powerful people his dad worked for. Although Tyler was the lead FBI agent in the field, he was severely unqualified for the job.

"Well, well, well Tyler said sarcastically, who do we have here?"

"Who in the hell do you think it is asshole?"

"Now is that any way to talk to your superior agent Giovani?"

Simona walked inside the open door and said, "Why am I here Tyler and where is Stan?"

"Stan is not here, and he won't be coming any time soon. He wanted me to detain you and get information about Taleeb's whereabouts. We know you are meeting up with him somewhere in alligator land. It's a violation of the code of conduct to commingle with a fugitive and a dereliction of duty to continue working on a case that is closed."

Simona didn't care what Tyler was talking about, "What is this place?" asked Simona? This site looks unauthorized by our agency. And the unprofessional slime ball that picked me up couldn't work for the FBI. He is an idiot that wouldn't tell me his name, for Christ's sake."

"The quicker you tell us what we what to know, the faster you can be on your way," said Tyler. "If you can please take a seat at that table, we can get this over with."

Simona sat in the chair at the table and said, "What do you what to know, Tyler?"

"Where is Taleeb Anderson?"

"I don't know where he is, but I believe he is here in Florida. If you guys knew how to do your jobs you would have followed me until I met up with Taleeb. Why would you interrupt your surveillance on me prematurely," asked Simona?

"Because we are under time restraints, and you were trying to send us on wild goose chase." "You were aware that you were being followed and we couldn't afford losing you."

"How did you know Taleeb was in Florida?" asked Tyler.

"Because I am an FBI agent that knows how to do my job. You have a log cabin here in Florida already, now that is impressive," said Simona.

"A client of mind allowed us to use this cabin."

"Who is the client?"

"That's none of your business and I'm the one asking the questions."

"Let me guess who the client is," said Simona. "I heard

whispers from the upper echelon in our agency that the *Indoctrination of Black Men* controlled all of Indiana's institutions." Simona was fishing for answers. The other agent, Jerry parked the car and took the Taxi sign off it. He came into the cabin at the tail end of the conversation and looked at Tyler in shock. Tyler changed his surprised, caught off guard look to a nonchalant attitude. Never did Simona imagine that the cabin belonged to the organization, nor did she believe that Tyler or the slime ball guarding the door had any involvement with the group but that all changed with her fishing expedition.

Tyler said, "I've never heard of that outfit and Black men aren't in charge of anything around here."

It was too late for the men to make light of her statement; Simona already had her answer. Her next actions had to be smooth and calculated because she knew camaras were mounted all around the cabin watching her every move. The two blundering Neanderthals had in their earpieces listening for instructions on what to do with her.

Simona chose her words carefully and said, "I don't know where Taleeb is, but I do know he has family here in Florida. The last time we spoke, Taleeb said he needed a vacation after the ordeal with the warehouse debacle. He said his cousin offered him and his family to stay in a mother-in-law section of his house near Miami Beach."

"Does this cousin have a name?" said the homo erectus guarding the door.

"I have a name but I'm not going to give it to you. Nevertheless, I will collaborate with you guys and help you catch Taleeb. He had something to do with the counterfeit money floating around Indiana. Taleeb was giving lots of money to Black businesses and poor people in the city. Was he part of the bank robbery?" Simona asked rhetorically. "I know the case is closed, but my informants told me that Taleeb was the money man. Once I find Taleeb and get answers to those questions, he's all yours."

Tyler got a message from Stan in his earpiece telling him to search Simona's belongings. Stan told Jerry to keep Simona distracted while Tyler placed a tracer inside her small handbag. Ten minutes later, Stan told them to let her go but he wanted her followed.

"Okay Simona you can go now, Jerry can drive you to your desired location."

"I appreciate your concern, but I don't trust the disrespectful bastard."

"Watch your mouth before I put a muzzle in it, said Jerry"

"I like to see you try moron."

Jerry walked over to Simona and Tyler grabbed him by the arm.

"Relax Jerry, we need to get this lady on her way."

"Let's go Simona, I'll take you to the car rental service," said Tyler. "Jerry, watch the monitors until I get back. If something comes up on the radar call me ASAP." Jerry looked at Tyler with discuss without responding.

On the way to the car rental service, Simona made small talk. She wanted to keep the conversation away from Taleeb's whereabouts because she didn't know where he was, she talked about how Tyler got into the FBI. Simona already knew the answer, but she listened to the lies he told. She wanted to know why he partnered up with that disrespectful guard dog. Simona didn't care what his response was because they were little pawns on a big chess board.

Taleeb was doing all the right things to stay undetected by law enforcement. He had a passport with his new name Lance Battles. An acquaintance Taleeb befriended in lockup helped him get his wife and kids new names on their passports. If anyone in Spain happened to ask them where they were from, they would say California. They had to lie about their total existence. The safest way to stay undetected was to stay to themselves.

Now that his family was safe in another country, Taleeb had to get the FBI to stop looking for him. He had to go back to the states and fake his death. It would be risky, and he needed help to pull it off. Taleeb made all the necessary calls to put the plan into action.

Taleeb didn't want to leave Dee and the kids, nor did he ever want to return to the states. The thought of faking his death left Taleeb with a dreadful feeling in his gut. The sad part of it was his family in Georgia had to believe he was dead.

Six months had passed, and things had settled down in Indianapolis. The media moved on to other news. The local authorities pacified Black people hoping that would stop the violence; therefore Channel 25 hired its first Black male Meteorologist and the other channels followed suit by hiring their first Black female anchor or sports analyst.

The crisis in Indianapolis had no effect on the racism running rampant in Atlanta. It was time for Taleeb to make a quick appearance to Georgia. After he finished his mission in the ATL, Taleeb vowed to never return to the states again. Although things were moving forward in a positive way, the FBI had Taleeb on the top 10 most wanted list. There were other agencies that took Taleeb off their radar and stopped searching for him, nevertheless he wanted to make sure he was off everybody's radar.

Blake introduced Taleeb to a world renown plastic surgeon who removed the scars on his face. After the scars were no longer visible, Taleeb shaved his head bald. He also shaved all the hire on his face. Dee and the kids didn't like his new look. They teased him about the nerdy round eyeglasses he wore and complained about him looking like a different person.

Taleeb was trying hard to look different, he even lost 20 pounds to make sure he was unidentifiable. Blake was stunned by Taleeb's fresh look.

"Man, I'm not used to seeing you without hair on your face. You look plain," said Blake who didn't like the way Taleeb looked either.

"Trust me Taleeb, your own mother wouldn't recognize you bro."

Blake frequented the ATL regularly because his girlfriend lived there. He knew more people in Atlanta than Taleeb. Blake introduced Taleeb to a friend who owned a funeral home in Georgia. The funeral home was passed down to Junior from his father. Blake gave Junior pictures of Taleeb months ago and a physical description of him as well. Thankfully for Taleeb, there was an abundance of Black homeless men in Atlanta that were the same height and weight as Taleeb. Unfortunately, one of them was going to take Taleeb's place in the casket.

Junior had an acquaintance that worked in a shelter who kept an eye out for a homeless man that was Taleeb's height and skin tone. Five days later, Quincy notified Junior about a man that showed up in the shelter fitting Taleeb's description. Quincy said the man was Taleeb's height, but he was terminally ill with cancer. Soon after the phone call, Junior went to the shelter to see the man. Wow, Junior thought, he had a lot of work to do to make this poor fellow look like a GQ model dying of cancer. Quincy introduced Junior to Larry.

"Hello," said Junior, "I'm here to help you live more comfortably during your final days." "I work for a non-for-profit organization called Hope. At Hope, we will provide all your needs. We provide shelter, medicine, and the best food in Georgia."

Larry asked. "Where do I sign up for such a program?"

"Come with me and I'll personally set you up in the program."

Junior schooled Larry on their way to Living Waters Hospice Center for people that were dying within a year. Junior gave Larry Taleeb's wallet with Taleeb's birth certificate, social security card and other ID's.

Junior told Larry, "For my people to help you, tell them your name is Taleeb Anderson. I want them to think you are my brother so they will give you the best treatment possible. I will visit you every day to make sure they are taking care of you to my standards." Junior gave Larry a new phone and said, call me on this phone if you have any questions or concerns."

Larry started crying and asked, "Why are you helping me Sir?"

Junior said, "That's why humans were put on earth, to help each other."

When they arrived at the Living Water's Hospice Center, Junior introduced himself to the caretaker and told her about his dying brother.

She said, "Normally the hospital where Taleeb was diagnosed with cancer would summit him there."

Junior said, "I had a private nurse that was helping me take care of him at home, but she moved out of town. I don't have time to find another nurse and I'm too busy to take care of him myself."

Junior gave the woman $500.00 and said, "My brother doesn't have insurance or anything, but I will be donating money to this establishment on a regular basis through my non-for-profit organization. I will be giving you $500.00 cash every other day if you promise to take exceptional care of my brother."

The woman wasn't supposed to take tips or any other monetary gifts, but she wasn't going to turn down the money regardless of the policies. Afterwards, Junior and the women exchanged numbers.

Keisha grabbed a wheelchair and asked Taleeb to have a seat. She then told Junior that Taleeb would be in room 256. She waved bye to Junior, and he left with a feeling of accomplishment.

Junior called Blake and informed him of the details, but Blake informed Junior that he didn't want damaged goods. Junior explained to Blake that because Larry was in a hospice facility, they didn't have to call 911 or an ambulance when he died.

"There wouldn't be any police investigation because everybody in the facility was going to die. One of the perks of using Living Waters is they will contact me first as Larry's closet relative. When they contact me, I'll make the funeral arrangements. From that point, I'll make miracles happen."

Blake was impressed with Junior's intellect.

"Wow man, what made you think of such an insidious idea?"

"Hey man I didn't think of the idea until I saw Larry. But don't worry about anything because I receive hospice bodies all the time in my profession, and I know how to put closure to this situation."

Blake needed Larry to die quickly because when the hospice facility put Taleeb's name into the database the authorities would eventually show up there. Blake relayed all his concerns to Junior on a throw away phone. They talked to one another using black slang and codes to confuse possible listeners. At the end of the conversation

Junior said, "I'll take care of it," and hung up.

Blake was helping Taleeb with all his affairs because he loved him like a brother. He wanted Taleeb to spend as much time as he could with Dee and the kids before they left, but in between time Blake was going to try and talk Taleeb out of going back to the States.

Junior called Keisha and asked her out to lunch and she accepted because she knew money was involved. They met at a coffee shop and Keisha realized that Junior was somebody famous because people were exceptionally nice to him and addressing him on a first name basis.

"What's happening Junior," said multiple customers in the cafe.

Keisha told Junior, "You do more than philanthropy work because everyone seems to know you."

"I own Jacobs Funeral Home on Peach Tree Street."

Keisha said, "I've been there a few times, it's a really nice place. Are you married?" asked Keisha smiling?

"No, I'm not married." It was thousands of gay men in Atlanta but she thought it would be inappropriate to ask Junior if he was gay. So, she asked him if he liked women.

Junior chuckled and said, "I love women! Is there any way I can prove it?" asked Junior smiling.

"Yes, I need proof, Junior," laughed Keisha.

The waitress came by overhearing the conversation and thought to herself, "Get a room already."

"What can I get this nice-looking couple?"

Keisha got coffee and a bagel and Junior ordered iced tea with a lemon.

The two were attracted to each other and Junior wanted to prove to Keisha he wasn't gay - tonight if she was willing. But first they had to discuss the business at hand.

"Keisha my brother made me promise to euthanize him when the pain got unbearable, and that time has come. I don't want to see him like that, can you help me?"

Keisha said, "I think you're handsome and I like you Junior, but I can't do anything that would compromise my job."

"Would $30,000 change your mind?"

"Of course, it would Junior, when will I get the money?"

"As soon as it's done."

"I will need half up front."

"Okay," said Junior, "Can you do it by tomorrow."

"Tomorrow! Junior that takes time and planning…." While she was talking about why she couldn't do it tomorrow, Junior said, would $40,000 get it done tomorrow?" Keisha hated herself for being greedy, but she needed the money to buy a new car.

"Yes Junior, $40,000 would get it done tomorrow."

"Meet me at the Hyatt Regency on 4000 Summit Boulevard tonight at 8:00 PM and I'll give you $20, 000 dollars."

"What else are you going to give me mister?"

"Whatever else you need, I got it," said Junior.

"Is that right, then I'll see you tonight Junior?"

After they parted ways, Keisha tried to convince herself what she was doing was the right thing. Junior's brother was suffering and putting him out of his misery was a blessing. She wanted to help other patients in her care die because they were horribly ill. It was an honor to give Junior's brother peace, she told herself.

Time flies when you're busy, thought Keisha, it was time to get off from work already. She was in a rush to get home and change clothes. Keisha didn't want a one-night stand with Junior, she wanted a relationship. She had been celibate for eight months because she was picky, and she liked men with money. She broke up with her last boyfriend because she found out he was on the down low which made her have trust issues and low self-esteem. Keisha wasn't serious about Junior proving he wasn't gay but if he said the right words and touched her in the right spots, she was going to have sex with him.

Junior didn't have a steady girlfriend, nor did he have any kids because he was way too busy with the Funeral Home. He really thought Keisha was cute and he liked her plump curvy body. He asked himself was that the reason he picked the Hyatt Regency to meet her. He told himself it was only going to be a business meeting and nothing else. But Junior didn't believe he could accomplish that if she started flirting with him.

It was busy at the Hyatt Regency and Junior was surprised to see Keisha there on time. She was sitting in the lounge area with her legs crossed. Keisha had on a black dress with fringes on the end of it. Junior knew he could not resist sex when he saw those big, beautiful legs. When she saw Junior by the service desk to get a room, she went over to meet him. The fringes of her dress were dancing to the movement of her butt that look like it was playing the congas.

Junior turned around, after he got the room and was

memorized by the rhythm moving towards him.

"Hello Mr. Good Looking," said Keisha as she reached out and held Junior's hand.

"Hey Keisha, that dress was made for you and your looking good."

Well, thought Keisha, he is getting some tonight.

They took the elevator to the ninth floor and Junior opened the door to the room with the card the desk clerk gave him. The room was nice. It had a mini refrigerator with alcoholic beverages in it.

Junior asked Keisha, "Do you want anything to drink?"

"I'll have a wine cooler." Junior grabbed her a cooler and a beer for himself.

He put the briefcase on the bed and opened it.

Keisha asked, "Can I count it?"

"Yeah, go ahead." She never saw that much money at one time before. She grabbed a stack of hundreds and smelled them. The scent of cash money was exhilarating, and it got Keisha excited.

Junior grabbed Keisha from behind and hugged her. She could feel his hard-on pressing up against her butt and she liked the way it felt. Keisha pushed her butt back and wiggled it on him. She asked Junior to unzip the back of her dress. Not only did he unzip her dress, but he also pulled it off her shoulders. She bent over and pushed the money to the side of the bed. Keisha turned around and they started tongue kissing. Her big breasts were begging for attention, thought Junior. He lightly back her up to the bed and gave her breast the attention they needed. They took off their clothes and had sex with the lights on.

At 5:00 a.m., they were awakened by Junior's alarm clock on his phone. The two were no strangers to starting their day early. Keisha had to be at work at 6:30 a.m. and Junior usually arrived at work around 7:00 a.m.

While getting ready for work Junior said, "I think I want you to be my woman."

Keisha responded with, "Oh you're so sweet Junior and I want you to be my man."

"Then it's official," said Junior.

"It most certainly is," said Keisha as she walked next to Junior and kissed him on the lips. Keisha was skeptical about Junior's quick commitment and believed he was only trying to use her, but she decided to play along and get paid while doing it.

"Why does your brother have a different last name than you?"

"We have different fathers." Junior changed the subject and said, "Keep the brief case and call me later with the details on my brother."

"Okay, Junior. I'll call you on my lunch break."

"Okay, I'll be waiting." They kissed and went their separate ways.

While at work, Keisha's full focus was on getting fentanyl and morphine out of the locked case. She was going to make a concoction that would ease the patient's pain forever. It took a couple of hours for nurse Cratchet to go to lunch; she usually took it at 11:00 a.m. but this time she was taking it at 1:00 p.m. It was exceptionally busy today and Cratchet left her keys by the phone at the front desk. It was the perfect opportunity for Keisha to get the medicine out of the case.

Keisha could have just used the fentanyl or the morphine to get the job done but the right dose of her mixture would give Mr. Anderson a nice high before he died. Keisha was able to get what she needed. She mixed the drugs and put it into a syringe. Keisha went to Taleeb's room while he was sleeping and slid the needle into his IV bag. He moaned with ecstasy and made his journey to the afterlife. Keisha eased out of the room and put the keys back where she found them.

Five minutes later room 256 emergency light came on accompanied with a loud peeping sound. Staff members went to the room to find Taleeb unresponsive with no pulse. Nobody lost any sleep over Taleeb's death because he hadn't been a patient that long. Someone died once a week at the facility and the staff was trained not to get personally involved with the patients.

Keisha didn't call Junior during her lunch break, and she was unable to answer his phone calls because it was a hectic day at her job, however she called him immediately when she got off from work. Junior answered the phone in the middle of its ring.

"Hey Keisha, is everything all right?"

"It's done," said Keisha.

"You'll have to pick up the body by tomorrow morning."

"I'll see you at, let's say 8:00 a.m. tomorrow, said Keisha." Junior thanked her and hung up the phone.

Junior called Blake and said, "The Eagle had Landed," and hung up. Blake relayed the message to Taleeb. Most of Taleeb's stress was squelched but he was upset that Blake had to convince everyone that he was dead.

Taleeb asked Blake, "Do you think Junior can make the dead

man look like me?"

"Yes, I do. Junior is the master in his field, and he can make it happen."

"Okay, make the call," said Taleeb.

Blake called Junior and gave him the details of what Taleeb wanted. For the money Junior was being paid, he could make Larry look like Elvis Presley.

People in Atlanta praised Junior for the spectacular work he could do on cadavers. Junior's customers always told him that the bodies he worked on looked better dead than they ever did alive. Junior's reputation preceded itself, he was well known, and considered the best at his craft. Many Black people complained about his prices and that's why Junior catered to people that had lots of money.

At daybreak, Junior was at the hospice center, signing papers and collecting the body. Usually, he would have had his employees help him, but this situation was confidential. Time was of the essence. When Junior got to his destination, he had to drain the body of its blood and then fill it with embalming fluid before rigor mortis crept inside the corpse making it stiff. After that, Junior went to work on the body with the passion of an artist. He had to make an incision from the back of the hair line to the front. He then tore open the back part of the skin. He pushed the skin forward to gain access to the cheek bones. Junior used an adhesive clay and molded it on the cheek bones to make them more pronounced. He chiseled the area around the forehead and Junior completely altered the bone structure of the nose and face area. When he was finished, Junior pulled the skin back to its place of origin and stitched the back of the head. He used a great deal of makeup to give the face a lighter hue. Junior finalized his work and made two fake scars going across his left eyebrow and right cheek.

The next day Junior called Blake after working all night and said, "I finished the masterpiece." Blake couldn't believe that Junior altered a human body in one day. It was impossible. Junior told Blake he would send him pictures, but Blake wanted to see the body for himself. "Of course," said Junior. Blake let Taleeb know about the phone call with Junior. But Blake didn't expect Taleeb to go to Atlanta with him and he couldn't talk Taleeb out of it.

Taleeb wanted Blake to tell his family in Atlanta that he died of cancer. He couldn't let anyone know where he was because their life would be in danger and the authorities were looking for him. "Blake please give this letter to my mother." "It's in my handwriting telling her why it is in her best interest to let you handle the funeral arrangements."

BACK TO THE STATES

The two men left for Georgia midday and got there in 13 hours. They ate lunch at Cava. It was a Mediterranean cuisine joint in Atlanta. The food was better down south than in Indianapolis thought Taleeb. He gave Blake the money to finance the trip and all their transactions were going on Blakes credit card. Taleeb didn't want to use his new legal name for trivial matters because of his heightened sense of paranoia.

When they were done eating, they went to Jacob's Funeral Home. Taleeb had never seen a funeral home where the body could be seen from outside. A person could see the body in the drive-though. It was amazing. The outside of the funeral home was impressive but inside of the establishment look like a Black Roman Catholic Church. It had marble floors and black artifacts in every room.

Blake and Taleeb's heads were up in the air looking at masonry work done on the ceilings. The secretary asked the men in wonderland, "May I help you?"

"Yes, we are here to meet Junior," said Blake.

The secretary at the front desk dialed his extension. "Junior, your visitors are here." Junior came out of his office to meet his guests.

"Hey Blake, I'm glad you came," said Junior. "I'm glad to see you as well my friend" and the men hugged.

"Wow, man you look tiered as hell," said Blake. "Of course,

I'm tired, I've been up for 36 hours."

Blake said, "I'm sorry about the inconvenience man. Oh, by the way, this is my best friend I was telling you about on the phone."

"Pleased to meet you Taleeb."

"Likewise," the two men bumped fists.

"Man, you look completely different from your picture," said Junior.

Taleeb took that as a compliment considering the circumstances.

"Follow me," said Junior.

They went to the cooler where Junior kept the bodies. Junior walked them over to Taleeb's avatar. Taleeb had the strange feeling that he was looking at his own dead body. It was a weird feeling. Taleeb must have stared at the body too long because Blake said, "Are you alright man?"

"Yeah, I'm fine, I just had a moment of nostalgia."

"Junior, you do excellent work. Thank you, man, I appreciate you."

"It's no problem, this project gave me a chance to work outside the box."

Blake gave Junior the rest of the money for his service.

Taleeb asked, "Junior, can we do the funeral Saturday?"

Junior said, "Man, for the money you paid me, we can do the funeral today, Mardi Gras style for a week." "Okay cool," said Taleeb.

"Blake, let my family know the date and time of the funeral."

"Junior as soon as the service is over, cremate the body."

Blake, make sure my mother abides by the letter I gave you."

"The body must be cremated. There is not going to be a burial but make them think they are going to the burial site, meanwhile Junior will burn the body while everyone waits for further instructions."

Taleeb couldn't rid himself of the sickening feeling that he was betraying his people but it was the only way to keep them out of danger. He wanted to see if his enemies would show up at the funeral. He believed the FBI would be there and he hoped Simona would show up too. Taleeb needed to find out how he could watch the funeral without being there.

He asked Junior, "Can you install cameras and record the people at the funeral?"

Junior said, "For the right price, I can add microphones with the cameras throughout the place.

"Cool, then make it happen, Junior." said Taleeb.

A warning alert flashed across Simona's screen indicating that their top ten most wanted perpetrator was in Atlanta, Georgia. It was Taleeb Anderson. Why would he be in Atlanta? He should have been out of the country, thought Simona. Maybe he got tired of being on the run and wanted to see his family one more time before he went to jail. How was he able to elude us this long and suddenly show up on the radar? Simona had hundreds of questions swirling around in her mind. She was elated that Taleeb was still alive and Simona wanted to keep it that way.

Simona got up from her desk and went to Stan's office. Tyler and Stan were having a conversation about nothing, she thought.

"Hey Stan, can I talk to you for a minute."

Tyler was annoyed because she didn't knock, she just barged in the office like she was in charge.

"How can I be of service to you Simona?" Stan said sarcastically.

"Let me go to Atlanta and bring Taleeb to Justice," said Simona.

"I don't think you have to worry about that Simona. The alert came from Living Waters Hospice Center," said Stan. "We called the center, but they wouldn't release any information over the phone."

"Stan, please let me check it out, I promise I will deliver results favorable to us."

"Really," said Tyler, "how pathetic is this that you're begging for assignments. You're a disgrace to the agency."

"You lame piece of trash, the only reason you are here is because your daddy works for the *Indoctrination of Black Men*. You haven't solved one important case since you been with the FBI, you prick." The two men were caught off guard and were shocked that Simona knew information that could get them all killed.

Stan wanted to ask Simona how and where she got the information but if he asked that, he would be confirming that her allegations had merit. Tyler was going to call her a dead woman, but Stan said everybody dial it down before we say things we'll regret.

"Simona, I assigned you to a desk job. You're the Operations Manager and you're doing a very good job. We don't have anyone to replace you at your current position. I want you here at your desk where you belong," said Stan. Tyler was smiling at Simona condescendingly.

"Stan, if you let me go in the field on this last assignment, I promise I'll retire the same day I bring Taleeb Anderson back to you in cuffs."

Stan had to think about what Simona said for a moment. He wanted Simona out of the agency as quickly as possible. It was obvious she was medaling around in top secret files because she mentioned the *Indoctrination of Black Men.* Using that name loosely around the office was a death sentence. He could kill two birds with one stone by making Tyler work with her. Stan didn't like Tyler as much as Simona thought he did. Tyler was a privileged asshole and had everything given to him on a silver platter including the job. The house speaker of the Republican Party promoted Tyler to the position and there was nothing Stan could do about it because he already tried.

"Okay Simona, I'm going to let you back in the field for your final job. Don't make me regret it."

"Stan why are you letting this cunt back in the field? She's a complete failure," said Tyler.

Simona was going to saying something back to Tyler but was caught off guard when Stan said, "Oh, by the way, Tyler, you and Simona will be working together on this."

They both began arguing with each other and at Stan.

Stan said out loud, "I don't want to hear it guys. Find a way to overcome your fascination with each other and get over it." Stan was enjoying the disbelief on the faces. He tried hard not to laugh, and he could fill the corners of lips slowly turning upward into a smile.

Stan said, "Okay, guys you heard me. I need my office back, I have things to take care of. Let me be frank. Get out of my office, the both of you!"

Tyler's ego was flying low. He thought, how could Stan have me working with a has-been. I'm her boss not her equal. Tyler told himself that all he had to do was bide his time because soon he would be Stan's boss.

After Simona got over the shock, she got angry. Why would Stan have her work with someone that had ties to a group of people that could overthrow the government? She knew Stan wanted her out of the agency but at what cost, her life?

Simona broke the silence and said, "Tyler, let's start by taking a flight to Georgia. Hopefully, we can gather enough information from Living Waters Hospice Center to find Mr. Anderson."

Tyler didn't appreciate his subordinate telling him where they were going to start and what they would gain by visiting a location. He was the shot caller not her. Nevertheless, she was right, but it was obvious what they had to do, thought Tyler. He didn't need the commentary.

Blake knew something was on Taleeb's mind because he was quiet and that was unusual. Taleeb was always talking about a business venture or diverse ways to make money.

They were eating at Pappadeaux's restaurant and Blake said, "What's up, man? You haven't been saying much lately."

"I'm worried about Junior; he knows too much."

"Taleeb, you don't have to worry about Junior, he is into The Black Panther movement, and he is anti-law enforcement. The police in Atlanta kill more Black men than in Indianapolis. The Black people in Georgia call you a freedom fighter and the Black Robin Hood. They believe the two men you killed near the airport were federal agents. We are enamored by your philanthropy. You bought Black people together all over the world. I'm not just saying that because you are my best friend. I'm saying it because it's true. The New York Times claim's that you started a revolution. The Republican Press calls you the anti-Christ. Man, you are famous! You are the most powerful Black man in America."

"I don't know about all that," said Taleeb. "I just want this over with so I can get back to Dee and the kids. It's a damn shame that mama and pops think I'm dead, though."

"Yeah man, I understand, but your sister took it harder than your parents. Your brother didn't seem fazed by your passing, but he always wanted to be hard core."

"Yeah, the thug of the year," said Taleeb.

"Hey man when I told your people about what happened to you, it felt like you really died. I damn near cried watching them get emotional man. The guilt weighed heavy on me brother. I feel awful about putting your people though that man."

"I really appreciated it, you saved my life," said Taleeb.

Blake dropped Taleeb off at the Hilton Hotel under Blakes name. Blake didn't want to be with his girlfriend who lived in the ATL. He wanted something new. He got two rooms because he was going to party all night and planned to bring company back with him. Blake asked Taleeb to go out with him, but Taleeb declined the invitation.

As soon as Taleeb got into his room, he called Dee on a burner phone, and she answered on a throw away phone that he gave her. She was excited to hear Taleeb's voice and wanted him to come home. Taleeb asked Dee, "How did your day go?" She told him about the fun she was having playing with the kids in their beautiful home. He asked to speak to the kids and Dee put them on speaker phone. When Taleeb finished conversing with them, the two adults talked about what they were going to do to each other sexually when he got home.

After they said their goodbyes, there was a knock on the door and Taleeb said, "Who is it?" the voice said, "Room service."

"Blake ordered your food."

Taleeb was happy Blake ordered his food because he was hungry. He opened the door, and the man pushed the cart of food inside the room. When the man looked up at Taleeb, he couldn't believe who it was. Shark eyes were wearing glasses staring at him emotionlessly. Taleeb began throwing punches at the man's face, but the shark blocked every punch gracefully. It scared Taleeb, because his opponent was using a combination of blocks that threw Taleeb slightly off balance. Out of nowhere the shark jumped up in the air and kicked Taleeb in the chin. Taleeb fell backwards on the glass table shattering it. Taleeb quickly got back on his feet because the shark had a vendetta that came with a death sentence. Taleeb was disoriented and he knew another blow to his head would cost him his life. Taleeb had to make sure to block all kicks, but the shark faked a kick and hit Taleeb in the face with lighting speed, knocking Taleeb's head back.

Oliver was enjoying himself; he could see the fear in Taleeb's eyes. Oliver wanted to play with his prey before he carved the skin off Taleeb's carcass. Oliver decided to do a spin kick on Taleeb and in the middle of his turn, Oliver felt a crushing blow to the back of his head. It knocked him forward. He felt blood streaming down his neck. As he finished the spin, Oliver saw that Taleeb tore a light fixture off the side of the wall and hit him with it. The fear he saw in Taleeb's eyes was replaced by rage.

Blood ran down from Taleeb's nose and only one of them was getting out of the hotel room alive. Taleeb held on to what was left of the broken fixture. Taleeb wanted to hit shark eyes again in the head, but he had to use caution because the man was fast. Oliver would never do a karate move again where he didn't have a complete visual on the subject, not even for a split second. Oliver decided not to use the fancy moves he practiced for six months. Playing games were over, he wanted to end the fight with one or two quick blows that he was an expert at administering.

Taleeb had to make it to the pillow on the bed. He didn't want to telegraph where he was trying to go. The shark was aggressive; therefore, Taleeb decided to retreat and back slowly away. It was a strategy he never had to use. When the shark advances forward, Taleeb through the rest of the broken piece of the light fixture at the shark. The shark ducked and Taleeb ran and dived onto the bed. He reached under the pillow and grabbed the loaded gun. When Taleeb rolled over, the shark was on top of him. The gun went off while the shark was strangling Taleeb. He had to shoot the shark three more times to get the mad man to loosen his grip. Taleeb pushed the body off him and gasped for air. The silencer on the gun muffled the noise on the weapon.

"Damn, damn, damn!" Taleeb said out loud. "How can I fix this!!?!!" Taleeb checked the shark's pockets for Identification, and he didn't have any. This guy was working for somebody shady, possibly the police. Taleeb hoped no one heard all the commotion that was made during the altercation.

Someone was opening the door and Taleeb was standing behind it waiting to kill another person. Blake stumbled inside holding the hand of a dancer from the strip club. He wanted Taleeb to see what he was missing before he went to his room. They were drunk and laughing at some jokes Blake was telling. But the fun ended abruptly, when Blake saw the gun, he gave Taleeb pointing at his head. Taleeb's hostile behavior made Blake sober up quickly because he knew something had gone terribly wrong.

Taleeb took the gun away from Blake's face and Blake said, "What happened man?!!!!," Blake looked around the room and it looked like a UFC fight took place in there. Taleeb looked at the stripper and was surprised that she wasn't scared. Blake saw Taleeb looking at her and introduced them to each other. Her name was Candice and Taleeb automatically didn't trust her. Why wasn't she afraid, thought Taleeb, she must be undercover. Blake and his companion saw the dead body lying on the floor and Blake freaked out, but Candice was unfazed. Candice saw Taleeb looking at her and pretended to be frightened. Taleeb didn't believe Candice was intoxicated or high off marijuana.

There was another knock at the door, Taleeb didn't want to be near the door in fear of being shot. "Who is it," said Taleeb? "Its security," said the male voice on the other side of the door. Blake had a difficult time pushing the dead body under the bed. When the body was hidden, Blake went to the door and looked out the peek hole. Sweat dripped down his brow as he opened the door.

"How may I help you sir?" said Blake.

"I'm sorry to bother you Mr. Bocelli but we got a complaint about loud noises coming from your room." Candice took off her dress and went to the door in her lingerie and the two security guards at the door eyes got big as they stared at the beautiful woman. Their eyes changed direction and they looked at the wires hanging from the wall where the light fixture used to be. Candice said, "I'm sorry about the noise and the broken fixture, but I was doing some acrobats and got carried away. We will pay for all the damages. Blake, do you a have tip money for these handsome fellows for wasting their time coming to our room," asked Candice?

"No ma'am, you're not wasting our time at all." Blake gave the men a hundred dollars apiece and said, "Sorry fellas for the noise."

"No problem Mr. Bocelli."

Taleeb came out of the bathroom and couldn't believe Candice was wearing lingerie. She was built up like an hourglass, but Candice was an 8 and Dee was a 10. It didn't matter how pretty a woman was because Taleeb was committed to one woman anyway.

Taleeb had to wrap his mind around the matter at hand, Candice was clever, and he was happy about the way she managed the situation. But why wasn't she scared of Taleeb and Blake for having a dead man in the room. Something seemed off, not only was she calm about the situation, but she also made herself an accomplice to murder.

"Blake said what happened Taleeb!!!?"

"Man, the dude under the bed, knocked on the door and said he was room service. He said you ordered me something to eat so I let him in. When I looked at him, I remembered who he was because his eyes look like a Shark's. I had an altercation with the dude six months ago in the bathroom. The man tried to kill me, but I whooped his ass. He tried to kill me again and this time the dude almost succeeded. The guy knew Karate man, he was beating the shit out of me, but I was able to get to the gun you left me under the pillow. I checked his pockets, but he has no ID or a wallet. I think he's an FBI or CIA agent."

Before Blake could ask Taleeb another question, Taleeb asked him, "Where did you met Candice?"

Blake said, "At Magic City, it's a strip joint not too far from here."

"How long have you worked there?" Taleeb asked Candice. "Two years and why all the questions" asked Candice?

"Because normally a woman would be terrified of a dead man lying on the floor in a hotel room with men she doesn't know."

Candice jumped off the bed and said, "Oh my God please don't hurt me!! I won't tell anyone what you did! Just please let me go!" Taleeb and Blake looked at her horrified and Candice began laughing at them.

"First of all, you two don't look or act like killers and I work with murderers. For example, Blake is wearing a suit with a shirt and tie. He has cuff links on his shirt sleeves. And you Mr. Taleeb are wearing a real Rolex watch with a $30,000 diamond ring on. Both of you guys sound like y'all went to boarding schools as children and graduated from Harvard University."

"Let me give you a little background on me. I did a private party a couple of months ago for one of the regulars at Magic City. Things were going well until the party was over and he put all his friends out the house. I made a lot of money at his venue that night and he wanted to have sex with me to show my appreciation. I told him, I don't get down like that and he got abusive. He slapped me around and started tearing off the outfit I was wearing. But before he could rape me, my bodyguard kicked the door down and beat the man to death. I tried to stop Rex, but he kept hitting the man until he was dead. Guess what?" Rex is outside the hotel waiting for my return. He followed me here to make sure I'm safe. All I have to do is dial his number and say no, that means I'm in danger. If I don't call in 30 minutes, he will show up at this door. If I want to have sex, I'll call him and tell him to go on about his business. I pay Rex good money to protect me."

Blake said, "Would you call Rex and tell him to go on about his business?"

"No, Blake, we won't be having sex tonight because you have a dead body in your room! But I would like to see you again. Blake and I have a friend for you Taleeb."

"No, thank you, Candice, I appreciate the offer but I'm getting married soon."

"Oh congratulations, I hope you boys don't end up in jail before that happens."

"Me too," said Taleeb. "Do you want me to get Rex to help you guys dispose of the body?" "Yes, I would appreciate that," said Blake.

"Don't thank me, it's going to cost you big time."

Taleeb felt better about Candice because she became an accessory to the crime. She would have to keep her mouth shut if she wanted to stay out of jail. Candice was all in.

"It's going to cost you $25,000," said Candice.

"You drive a hard bargain," said Blake. "But how are we going to get the body out of the building?"

"We can put the body under the food cart, nobody would see it because the sheet will hide it," said Taleeb.

"Yeah, but management might stop us from rolling the cart outside," said Blake.

"Candice called Rex and without saying a word she hung up the phone."

Candice said, "You guys can leave now, Rex and I will take it from here."

"But how are you going to get the body out of here," said Taleeb?

"Don't worry about that right now. As soon as we put the body in my car, have my money ready."

Taleeb put on his hoodie and the nerdy bifocal glasses to disguise himself. Blake grabbed the suitcases and said, "Let's go partner."

They took the back stairwell down to the first floor and proceeded to leave building, however before they got out the front door, a large Black man entered the hotel. As impossible as it sounds, the man resembled a T-Rex dinosaur. His head was huge, and his thighs were too big for the pants he was wearing. The pants legs were 6 inches too short, showing his dingy white socks. Taleeb and Blake looked at each other and said at the same time, "Rex."

The two men waited in a rental SUV, looking at the front entrance of the hotel. As they waited, Taleeb thought about something Candice said and she was right. Blake and Taleeb looked too preppie. They stood out from the ordinary, but their purpose was to blend in and not be conspicuous. They were obviously not meeting that objective. Taleeb talked about it with Blake, and he agreed to buy some casual clothes. Taleeb took off the Rolex and diamond ring and said "Blake, let's go shopping tomorrow."

"Cool," said Blake.

Rex pulled the body from under the bed and Candice cleaned the blood off his face. She used a wash rag with soap to clean the blood off the dead man's shirt and the back of his head and neck. Rex cleaned up the room and put everything that was broken into the two waste baskets. Candice placed her hand over the dead man's eyelids to close the scary looking stare. She poured alcohol on his shirt to make it smell like the man had been drinking. Candice dug in her purse and took out her sunglasses and put them on the man. She pushed his mouth upward into a smile, but it was more like a smirk because rigor mortis hadn't fully set in yet. Rex picked up the body without any effort and

Candice put the dead man's arm around Rex's thick neck. Candice got on the other side of the body and held its cold hard hands. They left the room and got on the elevator and luckily no one was in it. But when they got off the elevator there were four people in the public area including one of the security guards she talked to earlier. He waved at her as he approached them. Candice began talking to the dead body, I told you about drinking like this Mark. I'm not inviting you to anymore after parties.

The security guard said, "Hey pretty lady, you must have put too much on him" and he started laughing.

"It didn't take much," said Candice and they both started laughing.

"Okay ma'am, you have a good night" and he winked at Rex.

"You too," said Candice.

Before Taleeb finished his paranoid conversation with Blake, he saw Beauty and the Beast exiting the building.

"There they are," said Taleeb.

"Okay, I'm going to follow them to their car," said Blake.

The awkward couple put the body in the back seat of the Benz and propped it up to the side. The dead man slouched in the rear of the vehicle looking like he was sleep. Blake pulled up to their car and got out of his rental and popped the trunk. Ordinarily Candice and Rex would rob a person riding around with that kind of cash, but Taleeb looked paranoid and dangerous. Any wrong move the couple made would have ended in blood shed. Taleeb pulled out his pistol and was ready to use it. Blake was prepared to spend a large amount of Taleeb's money in Atlanta because they had an overwhelming amount of business to take care of. Blake counted out the $25,000 and put it into a plastic Wal-Mart bag. Candice rolled down her window and Blake gave her the money. She told Blake that her and Rex cleaned up the room and would give the hotel $5,000 in damages for the broken items. Taleeb heard the conversation and was shocked.

Blake said, "Thank you very much, I think we should stay in touch" and Candice gave him two business cards and pulled off. Candice wanted to gain their trust because she needed to be around anyone with that kind of money to spare. They didn't flinch or try to negotiate the price. She needed more friends like that.

"Wow, did you hear that, Taleeb?"

"Yeah man, that's stellar, we need to keep her on the rolodex."

"Here's her card," Taleeb took the card and put it in his wallet.

"Follow them," said Taleeb. "We need to make sure they correctly dispose of the body." Blake followed the couple from a safe distance because he didn't want the duo to know they were being tailed.

The Benz pulled into an abandoned apartment complex in a hostile neighborhood. There were bums, drunks, and drug attics in the area. The Mercedes stood out in the hood like a white pearl on top of a black silk scarf. The vehicle finally came to a stop.

Taleeb said, "Drive over there off the road were those trees and bushes are."

"Stay here, I'm going to see what's happening." "Hold on Taleeb, I should go with you." "No, Blake someone might steal the car."

"Okay man, be careful." Taleeb got out of the car and jogged near the Benz hoping not to be seen by Candice. Syringes and liquor bottles were everywhere on the ground. He saw Rex carrying the body up two flights of stairs, seconds later, a fire erupted from the third floor of the apartment building.

Taleeb was satisfied with how the couple operated and hoped he didn't need their services anymore. He ran back to the rental where Blake waited impatiently.

"Do you see that!!!?" asked Taleeb, the question was rhetorical, but Blake answered, "Yeah man! How could anyone miss it?"

As they drove away, Taleeb said, "Man I think they're professionals."

"Blake said, it looks like they know what they are doing, that's for sure." Everything about the current events worried Taleeb, but the deadly duo bothered him the most.

The day of the funeral came like a thief in the night, quick and silent. It brought with it soft sounds of crying and sniffles. All Taleeb's friends that he played sports with were there, from high school and college. It was nice to see so many people come to his funeral considering most of them lived in different states. Taleeb's family sat in the front row with tears in their eyes and it made Taleeb cry as he watched the service from a secret room inside the funeral home. He felt like he literally died. The room Taleeb was hiding in was installed behind a fake wall where various caskets were displayed for sale. That area was closed off during the funeral.

Taleeb couldn't believe what he was seeing on the video monitor, it was Simona. She was a very pretty women, thought Taleeb. She came with a man who looked like he worked with the FBI. Taleeb figured she might come. Simona reminded Taleeb of the actress Sophia Loren. Simona had a sophisticated aura that made her stand out in a crowd. She appeared sad as she walked in front of the casket. It looked like she could have been crying prior to coming inside the funeral home. The other agent followed her back to her seat at the end of room.

Tyler told Simona, "We need to get figure prints from that body."

"Really Tyler, how do you propose we do that?"

"I don't know yet but I'm working on it."

"Do you doubt Taleeb is dead?" said Simona.

"It's protocol Simona, you know better than anybody how this works."

Simona already knew to check for prints, but she was surprised that Tyler was smart enough to know the inner workings of the FBI. He was an inexperienced prick. She planned to slip away from Tyler when the opportunity presented itself. Simona decided the best time to get away from him would be around 2:00 a.m. in the morning. She hoped he would be asleep by then and he wouldn't know she was missing.

Simona didn't trust Tyler and if the fingerprints didn't match, she knew Tyler would try to kill Taleeb if he ever caught him. Simona believed the body was Taleeb's because of the cuts on the face and the length of the body. However, the man in the casket didn't look exactly like Taleeb but he died of cancer and that could have affected his appearance. Simona hoped the body in the casket wasn't Taleeb's because she liked Taleeb as a person. Simona had a dilemma; was she going to bring him to justice or help him escape the dreadful consequences if the prints didn't match?

Junior's sister Marva did the eulogy. As she addressed the crowd of people, Marva spoke about Taleeb's accomplishments, and it was impressive. Marva ended the eulogy by saying that Taleeb's was philanthropist who donated much of his time and money to the poor and disenfranchised. He was a leader of the Black community and will be remembered as our hero.

After the service was over, Blake reminded everyone that the repass was going to be at the Silver Center in two hours. Everyone was leaving except for Tyler and Simona. Thirty minutes later, Junior came to get the casket. The two FBI agents were confused. Tyler said, "I'm going to tell the man that we are the FBI, and we need to confiscate the body."

"Tyler, have you lost your mind?"

"We can get sued!" said Simona.

"We are a government entity Simona; the taxpayers are going to pay for the lawsuit anyway." Simona realized that she underestimated Tyler's intellect.

The two agents kept their eyes on the door Junior went in. They tried to be patient, but the man had been in the room for an hour. Tyler knocked on the door, no one responded, Tyler knocked on the door again and a nice-looking bold man opened the door and said, "Yes, may I help you?"

"Hello sir, my name is Tyler, and this is my assistant Simona. We are with the FBI. What is your name sir?"

"My name is Junior."

"Okay, Junior we need to confiscate the body because the person in the casket was a fugitive, and we need to confirm his identity."

Junior said, "Tyler don't you need to get authorization from the family to do that?"

"No, Junior we don't." Tyler radioed in for backup. Simona pulled Tyler to the side and whispered, "Is that necessary Tyler?"

He ignored her. "Junior, I would advise you to leave this room, or you will be arrested." "Okay it's all yours," Junior said with a smile.

"Simona, go with Junior to make sure he doesn't leave the premises."

"Am I under arrest Tyler?"

"No, Junior we just need your help to complete our investigation."

Taleeb had left the funeral home through the escape door that led out to the side of the building where Blake was waiting. While they were driving away, they saw police cars coming to the funeral home. "Man, that was cutting it close," said Blake. "Too close," said Taleeb.

Tyler checked out the large room to see if anything was awry. He saw the large incinerator and asked himself, "why is the casket in this room?" "He shouted the F-bombs as he walked over to the casket. When opened the beautiful cherry wood casket, it was empty. Tyler went over to the incinerator, and it was still hot. "Oh my God, what the hell is going on?" Tyler was angry and tired of playing nice. He walked out of the room looking for the dizzy dame and the spade that thinks he's Houdini.

While Junior and Simona talked about the funeral, Tyler approached them with an attitude. "What the hell is going on Junior?"

Simona didn't like his tone, "Calm down Tyler, what happened?" asked Simona.

"Shut up Simona, I don't want to hear crap out of you."

"Well, you stiff back prick, you're going to hear it anyway. First of all, check your tone when you're talking to me. Secondly, tell me to shut up one more time and I'm going to blow your foot off."

Tyler settled down and Junior looked at Simona with admiration and a touch of fear.

"Junior what happened to Taleeb's body? It's not in the casket!" said Tyler. "

What's going on Junior?" said Simona. "

Hey guys there is nothing going on, the body was cremated."

"But why, said Tyler?" "Because Taleeb wanted to be cremated."

"Why was he in the coffin if he was going to be cremated?"

"We thought he was going to be buried," said Simona.

"I'm sorry," said Junior, "The family rented the casket from the funeral because it's much cheaper to rent."

Tyler would've punched Junior in his smug mouth, but Simona would have made a scene.

The police arrived as well as two detectives. They searched the funeral home without a search warrant. Junior didn't care because they weren't going to find anything other than legitimate documents pertaining to Taleeb's death. It was part of a well-executed plan.

The repass that Blake orchestrated had gotten out of control because too many people came out to support Taleeb's family. People were bringing too much food and flowers. The event was supposed to be held inside the Silver Center, but the crowd spewed outside as well. Blake asked supporters to help him add tables and chairs outside the building to accommodate the people. He never imagined so many people would show up. Blake started asking people how did they know Taleeb? One man said he didn't know Taleeb personally, but he heard about the feds illegally searching Jacob's Funeral Home on the radio station. They said the feds were confirming Black Jesus was dead. Blake had been stroking Taleeb's ego by telling him, he was the most powerful Black man in America but now Blake truly believed it.

After the repass was over, people volunteered to help clean up. It made Blake feel proud that so many people cared about what was going on in their community. Everything went well and Blake couldn't wait to get back to the motel to pick up Taleeb. Blake asked Junior to drop him off at a bar. Taleeb gave Blake instructions on how to outmaneuver anyone that might be following him. Blake went out the back door of the bar to the alley where a rental car was waiting.

Blake cautiously drove the car to the Maverick Motel because he didn't want to get a ticket or anything to slow him down from getting out of Atlanta. When he got to the motel, Taleeb had everything packed. Blake was tired and needed to rest; therefore, Taleeb drove to Florida while Blake slept. Taleeb was paranoid and wanted to take precautions. He decided not to take the Atlanta airport but fly out from Daytona Beach International Airport to Spain.

Taleeb kept staring in the rearview mirror looking to see if anyone was following him. It was a long drive and Taleeb pondered the question, how did shark eyes find him. Did anyone else know his alias name Lance Battles besides the few people in his inner circle? Did the FBI believe he was dead? There were hundreds of questions running through his mind until a police car turned on its lights behind him. Taleeb slowed down and pulled over to the side of the road, but the police kept going. It frightened Taleeb to his core and he couldn't stop his hands from shaking. But he calmed down by telling himself, I am Lance Battles, and nobody is looking for me.

Back at the FBI headquarters, Stan notified Simona and Tyler that the Taleeb Anderson's case was officially closed. The documents they retrieved from Jacob's funeral home were more proof that Taleeb was dead. Stan thanked them for completing the mission and working as a team. The last statement was a sarcastic joke, but Simona didn't care because she was retiring as the words came out of Stans mouth.

Simona had the intuitive wit that Taleeb was still alive somewhere. He was smart and the FBI didn't have any DNA to prove Taleeb was dead. Now that she was retired, Simona could spend a small part of her time figuring out how he could've pulled it off.

After the long tedious plane ride, Taleeb finally made it home to his family. He enjoyed having Dee back in his arms. From the patio sofa, they watched the waves from the Mediterranean Sea rush up against the shoreline and retrack again on a continues cycle. They listened to the melody of the soft wind play a symphony with the birds and waves. Taleeb looked into Dees eyes and said, I will love you until eternity. And they made love under the beautiful orange moonlight.

Craig A. Banks

ABOUT THE AUTHOR

Craig Banks is a native of Indianapolis, Indiana who received his undergraduate degree in liberal arts from the University of Indianapolis and his Master's degree in business management from Indiana Wesleyan University. Before Craig Banks retired from the trucking industry, he was an entrepreneur in various platforms of business. In Mr. Banks' lifetime, he owned three Pager/Cellular phone stores, a cleaning franchise company, a seafood restaurant and two computer repair stores.

Mr. Banks is married to his wife, Deborah and has three children, Sharell, Christopher, and Akila.

Craig A. Banks